May 4, 2014

dearest Mady & Mery,

enjoy the adventure!

with my thanks,

Ariana Brg

Son of Earth and Sky

Ariana Borg

Cover design by Nicole Solis

Copyright © 2014 Ariana Borg

All rights reserved.

ISBN: 1495411192
ISBN-13: 978-1495411199

*to Matt, co-conspirator, fan and critic,
thank you for always believing and giving me time to write.
to Josh, my son, Weapons Master and Fight Coordinator,
and to Mariana, our lovable little cherub.*

The Nephilim were on the earth in those days, and also afterward, when the sons of God came in to the daughters of man and they bore children to them. These were the mighty men who were of old, the men of renown.
- Genesis 6:4

Contents

1.	Nightmares and Night-Sweats	1
2.	A Sulfurous Encounter	8
3.	Aloysius and Vitalis	16
4.	The Enemy Revealed	22
5.	Making Friends with Puttis	30
6.	The Burning Ones	44
7.	A Piercing Rescue	55
8.	Pets and Peers	61
9.	Test of Twenty	70
10.	The Gothic Sword	82
11.	T377SF	96
12.	Nocking with Patience	107
13.	Elementary Guardianship	122
14.	Blade Versus Sticks	132
15.	The Hand Of God	144
16.	Interrogation	154
17.	A Secret Shared	167
18.	Protectors of Men	176
19.	Nighttime Visit	183
20.	Halo Attack	191
21.	Paper Trail	203
22.	The Puzzling Palindrome	215
23.	An Unlikely Savior	222
24.	Introduction to Aeronautics	234
25.	The Elite	248
26.	Jasmines and Seraphic Butterflies	258
27.	A Golden Necklace	268
28.	Prefect and Pebbles	275
29.	Dark Gifts	290
30.	Curare	299
31.	A Fight for Truth	310
32.	Versus	317
33.	Beyond the Wall	333
34.	Angelical Law	349
35.	Honoring a Hero	362

1
Nightmares And Night-Sweats

David carefully plunked a sad assortment of coins on the counter of 7-Eleven, clutching two donuts in one hand with his small slurpee sweating beside the register. He looked longingly at the rack of revolving hotdogs, trying to avert his eyes from how delicious they looked. But hotdogs were pricier and the two-for-a-dollar donuts would do the trick in filling up his raging stomach. Dang it! He was always hungry. The slurpee was a treat he could barely pay for, but he needed the sugar rush to carry him through the day.

"How you doing today, Oscar?" David smiled at the man behind the register, somewhat comforted by the familiar face. It was six in the morning and David was at his usual gas station getting whatever breakfast he could afford, and Oscar was always the one at the counter.

"Dig deep, kid." Oscar smiled back, waiting patiently as David emptied out his pockets, hoping defeatedly that more money would appear. That was the great thing about Oscar. He was such a nice guy about all the coin excavation.

"All there!" David said with relief, counting out the coins and pocketing the dime leftover. He really needed a job today.

As though reading his mind, Oscar said, "Hope you get work today, David." His face turned serious, looking out the store window. "But there's a bunch of you waiting, so better be quick on your feet."

Then he added, "And pray the weather holds 'coz those clouds look ready to burst."

"Thanks again, Oscar." David replied, mentally snorting with the thought of praying for good weather. *Prayer*. Yeah right, as if that would help.

With his slurpee and donuts in hand, he walked out the store and ambled towards the lounging crowd of men. They were all waiting for a job, some gulping down cheap coffee, others having a cigarette for breakfast. Some nodded to David as he approached. They've gotten familiar with each other.

"Eh, Dahveed!" said Rodrigo, a mexican dude who had worked alongside David on several jobs: painting a picket fence, installing decorative lights, unloading furniture, and one time, some roof work. Rodrigo helped David survive that job because David's only knowledge of roof work was to climb on top one. Well, he lived and learned.

"Hey Roger." David greeted back, using the name that Rodrigo insisted he be called. Made him feel very american, he had told David with a wink. It was no secret that Rodrigo was an illegal.

"Donuts and slurpee again, Dahveed?" Rodrigo shook his head at him. "Dat's gonna put a hole in jour brain."

David took a big bite from his donut in cheeky defiance and protested. "Hey, unlike you, I don't have a wife who'll cook for me."

Rodrigo's objection was immediate. "I don't got a wife!" he mustered school-boy innocence, while David slyly quipped at him. "I bet you do in Mexico."

Rodrigo guffawed, his laughter an admission of truth. He was only in his early twenties but he had a family to support. "What can I do?" he shrugged, "the chica loved me so much, you know?"

"And I bet her papa's shotgun convinced you even more." was

David's audacious comeback.

Rodrigo laughed good-naturedly, sprouting off funny stories while David quickly gulped down his unhealthy breakfast. He didn't want to be caught eating when work drove in.

His life at the moment was about making it through the day, working for food, and existing under the radar of authorities so he wouldn't get carted back to foster care.

It was Day 285 of his self-imposed exile.

The reason? His last foster parents.

At fifteen and orphaned since birth, David had gone through so many that he hardly remembered all of them clearly. Sometimes he was lucky enough to land really kind and attentive ones, like the fat couple with the fat kid whose house smelled like stale chips. All their windows and blinds were closed day or night as though the sun would burn them to bits, but David knew this wasn't the case because they did go out, in the daytime, in the sun. They just preferred their house to be dark, dank and infused with the stagnant air of limp cornchips.

But they were generous and the wife was an unbelievable cook. David even gained weight under their diligent care.

Other times his luck turned sour, handed to foster parents so mean that it was unimaginable how their meanness escaped the radar of Child Protective Services. Like Nasty guy and his nervous wife. Short, thin with a well-meaning face, he cleaned-up very well and only did foster care for the money. Most of the time he packed foster kids in his house like overcrowded crayons and handed out more insults than he did food. He sucked the happiness out of every soul he met – black-hole of despair that he was – and thrived in assuring all the kids that they had no bright future to look forward to except for a worthless job and a life way below the poverty line. He really was fortunate that he hadn't been hacked in his sleep yet by an angry kid. As for nervous wife, all she did was squeak her yesses and do his bidding as fast as she could.

But his last foster parents..........

How can David even explain them?

Mr. and Mrs. Rick and Kathleen Littlefield. He was a teacher, she was a full-time housewife or as she labeled it – *homemaker*. She was also really really pregnant, as if little Littlefield was going to pop out any second.

Mrs. Littlefield was extremely pretty. Large hazel eyes with green highlights, a gorgeous smile that was so warm and welcoming, it made David want to be adopted by them. She was just so nice and encouraging, listening to David jabber on and on about his life so far and school and previously unspoken dreams now confessed to her priest-like ears. She took him seriously and for the first time, David felt he was treated and acknowledged as an adult. It became his favorite part of the day, sharing his thoughts with Mrs. Kathleen Littlefield, in their cozy kitchen alongside soda and chips (she was super cool!) and a traditional plate of cookies. And when it was dinnertime and Mr. Littlefield came home, they truly felt like a family; eating their dinner together and talking about their day, the three of them cleaning up afterwards. David would do his homework and Mr. Littlefield – call me Dad or Rick – would sit in front of the TV with Kathleen and they would just sit and talk, laugh easily, or quietly read.

Under their sincerity and offered love, David opened-up more and really did his best in school to make them proud. Rick tutored him and kindly but firmly stressed the importance of an education. Kathleen mothered and nurtured him, and soon a change came over David. He felt more confident, he expressed his ideas more, his customary slouch straightened to a posture of self-assurance, and he actually began to believe that he could make something of himself in the future. That he had a future. And it could be a good one. He *might* even be part of a family soon.

And then the night-sweats began. The groggy but disturbing dreams that he couldn't remember. Suddenly Mr. and Mrs. Littlefield gave him the creeps. Whenever they were with him or near him or coming towards him, all the hairs on his body stood on end like panic prongs sending clangs of alarm to his brain.

Leave! *Leave!* His mind said and he didn't know why.

He started getting nauseous around them as though he couldn't stand the smell of them. Then his mood became affected and David found himself sullen and listless and depressed for no apparent reason.

The Littlefields continued to be good and kind, and the kinder they were, the more afraid of them David got.

And then he began remembering the dreams. His stuporous and heavy lids opening at three in the morning and *she* would be there. Mrs. Kathleen Littlefield, crouched at the foot of the bed, hands planted on the mattress, feet on tiptoes close to her hands, pregnant belly sinister and enormous. She crouched in absolute stillness but looked ready to spring on him any second. Her long hair was unbound and cascaded all around her, sometimes obscuring her face. Whether he could see her face or not, David knew she was looking at him, malevolently, maliciously, hungrily.

And her eyes glowed a sick yellow.

David thought he was going insane and maybe he was. The morning after such nightmares, his room always smelled like burnt matches and rotten eggs, and the stench lingered for days. Once, he made a comment about the smell to Mrs. Littlefield but she only smiled with a touch of confusion. "I'm pregnant David and my nose is very sensitive especially to bad odors. I really am sure that your room doesn't smell like rotten eggs."

Other times it was Mr. Littlefield at the foot of his bed. Not crouched on the mattress but just standing there looking at him. He looked different too, like a dark shroud with blurred outlines. The stench would be stronger and yellow vapor hanged in the air. He seemed to be watching and waiting for something, but what?

David tried to wake up during these nighttime attacks but couldn't. He became more sluggish and the sleep deprivation left him exhausted. He lost weight and what scared David most was how slow and dim-witted he became. He couldn't absorb his lessons, just couldn't understand what his teachers were saying. They were speaking Venutian and expected him to know it. His reflexes dulled and his brain felt like a shriveled and dried raisin. He moved like he was sedated and underwater at the same time. The school noticed and began asking concerned questions.

What could David say? That his foster parents stayed at the foot of his bed night after night to stare at him? That their eyes glowed in the dark?

It was insidious and all the more frightening how they were normal and incredibly nice in the daytime. Mrs. Littlefield remained attentive and cheerful while Mr. Littlefield proceeded to act like a father to David.

The torturous nightmares lasted for a month until David could take it no more.

Taking his chance while Rick was at work and Kathleen at the grocery, David filled his backpack with the essentials he could think of and left the Littlefield's creepily hearty house. He kept looking behind him the entire time, certain they would follow him and drag him back to their version of hell. Even now, 285 days later, he was still looking behind him.

2 † A Sulfurous Encounter

Today was a bad day.

David loitered at the gas station the entire morning, he and Rodrigo trying to keep each other's morale up, but since it was miserable and wet, there were no jobs to be had. They waited and waited, some, fumbling in their pockets for coins and munching a little something from 7-Eleven, but otherwise, no takers today. Their hopeful faces beamed at every SUV and pick-up truck that drove in, but eventually dimmed by noon time.

Rodrigo took out a small towel from his pocket and mopped his face with it. It was already October but the Texas heat prevailed. Even the rain couldn't dial down the humidity.

David got up and stretched, "Maybe tomorrow, huh, Roger?"

Ever optimistic, Rodrigo gave him a thumbs up. "Tomorrow is our day." Then, punching David lightly on the shoulder, he said, "I gotta go now, Dahveed. Maybe I make my cousin give me a job today." And with that plan, Rodrigo was off.

What a bust! David thought, shouldering his scruffy backpack – it housed everything he owned – and lowered his head against the beginning drizzle. Too soon, the gentle droplets amped-up to pelting rain and had David jogging towards the nearest soup kitchen, already sopping wet.

Looked like another day of living off the kindness of strangers. Or begging.

Or stealing.

David shook his head, not allowing himself to worry, obliterating panic.

Sure, he only had a dime left in his pocket, but he had survived on his own for almost a year now, what was one more day?

The clouds grew darker by the minute and the Dallas skyline forked and sizzled with lightning. David knew he'd better get indoors soon if he didn't want a blasting hello.

He was four blocks away from the soup kitchen but David didn't mind the distance, when it wasn't raining. He only had 3 sets of clothes and now that he was soaked anyway, he didn't bother throwing on his plastic poncho with the hood. Might as well enjoy the bath.

Hunched from the rain and rapidly turning a corner, David bumped into an oncoming person, his head snapping up, ready to apologize.

His first view was of a hugely pregnant belly.

"Hello David." Mrs. Kathleen Littlefield smiled warmly, eyes glittering.

David automatically recoiled from her, sickened and frightened by her presence.

No! No! No!

They had found him!

She continued to smile at him, her eyes full of concern.

How could she still be pregnant? David wondered. Either this was their second child or that freak of nature was potty-trained in her belly by now, learning his ABC's as well. And where was Mr. Littlefield?

David turned this way and that, eyes frantically scanning for Rick, realizing belatedly that he had walked into an occupied alley.

He had been upset by the zero-job morning and got distracted by the rain that he walked blindly into this alley without checking for safety. It was one of his shortcuts, but he always checked to make sure no one was around. What was the matter with him? How could he be so stupid!

What was he going to do?

"Running won't help, you know." Mrs. Littlefield said softly.

"We'll still get you." She tried to hold his hand but David backed away.

"Where's Rick?" he asked suspiciously.

She sighed. "We told you to call him Dad. We've been so worried about you." Her face implored kindly, "David, why are you making your own life difficult? You can come home with us........have a permanent place to stay, your very own room........no more running away." she paused for her most tempting offer. "And you don't have to work just to put food in you. Picture it David, hot and delicious meals three times a day, and snacks too. No more hard labor for food."

David closed his eyes at her words, for a second very much tempted to just give in, a picture so clear in his mind of what she was offering: a home, food, to just be a kid with no worries.

Mrs. Littlefield's face was gentle and sincere, but her eyes flashed jaundiced yellow, ruining her saintly appeal. "Please come home, David."

David shook his head at her, her outline blurring in the rain. Vapor was rising from Kathleen Littlefield and there was that smell again – rotten eggs and burnt things. He was never going back to them!

They had been in the rain for some time now, but only David was drenched. Mrs. Littlefield appeared impenetrable and quite dry, the rain bubbling and evaporating from her skin on contact.

"What are you?" David whispered in horror.

"The opposite of you." was her reply, remaining calm and now amused by David's fright. "You just don't know it yet." she looked at him hungrily. "But we could make you just like us."

"Stay away from me." David warned her, ready to bolt but looking around again for Mr. Littlefield. He was here. He was nearby.

Mrs. Littlefield gazed upwards with a beatific smile and David followed the direction of her vision.

A thing was swooping towards them, coming at David in a rush. It was something dark............with expansive wings thumping against the wind. And the pouring rain didn't help at all, making visibility difficult. David couldn't make out what it was.

Beside him, Mrs. Littlefield happily called out towards the thing, her voice changing with added layers to it, as though a thousand beings spoke through her. "Rick!"

Every muscle in David's body tensed, recognizing that something was incredibly wrong. There was evil in the air.

Run! His mind screamed.

David tried to, but suddenly, something was holding his midsection, locking him in place. David looked down to see what was preventing his escape and he yelped in horror.

It was the baby!

Mrs. Littlefield's bulging stomach had stretched further and two baby arms with claw-like hands protruded from it. The tiny hands were strong, latching onto David to keep him from running. In front of him, Kathleen Littlefield was cackling in delight over David's reaction.

David didn't want to touch *it*, repulsion coursing through him, but there was no other way. He grabbed the protruding baby arms and yanked it away from his body. Mrs. Littlefield shrieked in response and slapped David hard in the face.

She was unnaturally strong and David found himself sprawled on the wet ground, reeling from her slap. His head felt smashed and he knew his cheek was fractured, but at least he was free from her grasp.

Somehow David got up and sprinted away from Mrs. Littlefield and whatever freak was inside her womb. The other end of the alley drew closer and he couldn't help the bloom of hope in his chest. If he could get to where other people were.........

A dark shroud landed in front of him, barring his escape.

David stumbled in shock, his legs almost collapsing under him. The thing in front of him.........it was Rick! From his nightmares.

David knew he had to escape but he was also staring in hypnotized horror at the being standing in his way. He knew it was Rick.

But it wasn't human.

It towered over David, tall and hulking. Its skin was a leathery and mottled gray with hideous protrusions. Huge and bony wings snapped menacingly behind its back. Most repulsive of all was its demonic face – glowing yellow eyes burning with malice, slits for a nose and blackened snarling lips exposing fangs dripping with yellow slime.

The thing grabbed David by the throat, lifting him clear off his feet as he dangled and fought to breathe. Already, David's peripheral vision was dimming but he refused to give in to it. He was not going to black out. He mustn't! Not if he wanted to survive this.

"You will come with us." grotesque Rick said, his voice so inhuman that it was an attack to the senses. David's feet tried to push onto something, anything, but Rick dangled him away from any surface. David's attempts to kick at Rick were irrelevant and puny and his efforts to claw away the grip on his throat produced no result. The thing was an immovable force.

"There now," a multi-layered voice whispered near him. "loosen your grip." Mrs. Littlefield commanded. "We don't want the boy dead, but simply subdued." She remained her cheerful self, still sinisterly pregnant and now with a dizzying vapor of yellow cloud hanging around her. She looked deep into David's bulging eyes, smirking at how he struggled for air. "Are you going to be reasonable now, David? Are you going to come with us?" she waited for his reply.

David stared defiantly at her, straining and pushing against the vise around his throat. "Never!" he choked out.

Grotesque Rick dropped David forcefully to the ground, plastering him on the concrete as he lay coughing and clutching his throat. He sucked in lungfuls of breaths, gasping for as much oxygen as he could to get his brain going again. As David spluttered in the rain, dainty feet approached him.

"You will come home with us." Mrs. Littlefield said calmly. "Conscious or unconscious. What will it be David?"

David pushed off from the slushy pavement and stood up on wobbling legs. He looked at his foster parents with all the hatred he could muster. "I pick choice number three." he rasped. "You go back to hell and take that freak baby with you." then turning rapidly on unsteady feet, David ran.

It was futile.

He heard them close in on him right away and immediately, he was pummeled by kicks and blows. "Unconscious then." Kathleen Littlefield announced with glee in her terrible voice.

David connected a hard punch to Mr. Littlefield and the thing staggered backwards in surprise. David also shoved Mrs. Littlefield a couple of times, pushing her away so that she herself stumbled to the ground.

The second time David did so, Kathleen Littlefield stood up so fast it was a blur and then she was facing him, heaving and huffing in anger. She was changing before David's very eyes, her body rippling and writhing, her eyes burning red, her hair bursting into flames.

And then she attacked.

David fell to his knees, crumbling under their assault, unable to fight back any longer. He saw the flash of their venomous eyes and his head spun from their repellant breath of toxic fumes.

Mr. And Mrs. Littlefield were winning and David was so scared of why they wanted him or what they wanted to do with him or that he would wake up and be like them that for the first time in his life his mind cried out, *Help Me! Oh God help me!.........somebody please.........please help me!............*

And then silence.

Absolute silence.

For one second, the world paused. Even the rain halted mid-drop.

Then, there was a sudden brilliance, blinding David.

A shock of white light and energy pushed him to the floor.

The world and all its sound came thundering back and David heard the beating of enormous wings and the explosive sounds of fighting. Someone was holding him down, or trying to cover him. David wanted to see what was going on but his eyes were blurry with sweat, blood and tears. Someone was also blocking his view, protecting him from further harm.

David attempted to get up. To fight again. To survive. But his body refused to cooperate and all he could accomplish was the agony of lancing pain from his many broken bones. And now he could hardly breathe, as though someone had turned off his lungs. His body was giving in to his injuries, unable to hang-on to consciousness any longer.

"David. David!" someone was calling him, urging him awake, but David's head hung limply, his gaze unfocused, eyes rolling to the back of his head.

I'm going to hit that floor hard was David's last thought as he blacked-out.

But before he could smack his head on the cold cement, someone caught him.

3
Aloysius and Vitalis

David smelled fresh linen.

He hadn't smelled linen this fresh for nearly a year now. He also felt a fluffy pillow under his head and a firm bed under his body.

This is it, he thought. *I'm dead. Nice warm bed, really soft sheets, I must be dead.*

But he didn't feel dead and his body was too sore to be dead.

Fear immediately slashed his heart as he arrived at another conclusion. Had the Littlefields won? Was he back to their creepily perfect house?

A gentle humming sound greeted his now very alert ears and cautiously, David opened his eyes.

There were windows everywhere. Huge windows that was lightening from a dark tint to transparent, hence the machinated humming sound. The dazzling rays of the sun now filtered through the glass and David squinted against the sudden shift of darkness to light. The humming stopped and he gazed in awe at the view before him. Even at an awkward angle from his bed, the panorama layed-out beyond the windows stupified David to absolute stillness.

He was surrounded by snow. And mountains. And snow-covered mountains.

Whatever building he was in, it was the only man-made

structure on this land, because as far as his eyes could see, there was nothing outside the window but endless snow and the craggy peaks of mountains.

Wherever he was, it was in the middle of nowhere.

"Ah, I see you've decided to stay with us after all." a cheerful voice greeted him. Too cheerful. David was mad at himself for not hearing the person approaching. "For a moment there I wasn't sure if you were going upstairs or just staying here with the rest of us."

David tried to sit up but the room tilted nauseatingly with his effort. He slowly turned his head towards the source of the voice. "Huh?"

"Oh, I've only confused you. Sorry about that."

David's eyes widened at the little girl standing next to his bed. She had ruler-straight blond hair and a small pixie face. She was wearing white scrubs and looked officially medical. Mini-medical.

"Are you eight?" David couldn't help asking, his voice thick and scratchy like he hadn't vocalized in years.

"I'm ten!" she snapped at him, "and yes, I'm a little short for my age but I can perform many duties now."

"Who....who are you? And where am I?" David stared hard at her. "Are you with the Littlefields?"

"Who?" was her puzzled reply, much to David's relief. "As for where you are, you're in the Infirmary, of course. You've been out of it for four days now....I thought you wouldn't make it." she finished the sentence with wide baby blue eyes.

You've got to be kidding me, David thought. He wasn't capable of keeping up with this little girl's confusing wide-eyedness at the moment. Gritting his teeth in forced patience and politeness, David said, "Thanks for the vote of confidence, but um...how did I get here? And where is *here*? And don't answer Infirmary, okay?"

She pinkened at his words. "Sorry about that. Welcome to the Monastery of Messengers-"

"Monastery! I'm in a Monastery?!"

She rolled her baby blue eyes at him. " Well, if you would only let me finish.........yes, you are. As I was saying, welcome to the Monastery of Messengers-"

David was gaping at her in disbelief.

"- I am Elizabeth, your Healer. You may call me Liz."

"I may?" David couldn't help the sarcasm. He was confused, achy, and he had an eight year old little girl to contend with.

"Ten!" she snapped at him again.

"Can you read minds?" David wondered.

"No." she huffed at him. "But I knew what you were thinking."

This was too much to wake up to.

"Liz, please." David clasped his hands together, imploring. "A grown up. Let me talk to a grown up."

"But I'm a -"

"Please!"

Liz narrowed her eyes at him. "Oh very well. If you insist." She paused, uncertain, "Do you?"

"Yes!!!"

"No need to get mean." she said in a hurt little voice, then she flounced out of the room, her blond hair swinging with every step.

David collapsed back on the bed, fervently hoping that Liz was coming back with someone who had answers. Someone not in any way connected with the Littlefields.

What had happened in that alley? How did he get here? And where were his evil foster parents?

He flicked his blanket aside and made a quick inventory of his limbs. All arms and legs present. All fingers and toes. His body seemed intact and fully functioning. Just a little soreness here and there, which was a miracle really. Weren't his bones broken from the Littlefield's attack? David swore he had countless broken bones from that encounter, but looking at himself now, he seemed fine. How long was he out?

In a short while he heard footsteps coming towards him as two men approached. Despite the fact that they were absolute strangers and David's first impulse was to get up and run, the kindness in their eyes and their welcoming smiles calmed him down – a little bit. That had been the Littlefields signature move too – kindness and welcoming smiles. So it was smarter to be on guard.

The older of the two was a tall, middle-aged man with sandy brown hair sprinkled with white. He had a gentle but capable face. Like Liz, he was wearing white hospital scrubs indicating that he worked in the Infirmary. Honestly though, he looked more carpenter than doctor.

The younger gentleman was also tall with sharp, intelligent eyes and very pale, almost white hair, cut cleanly and styled very neatly. He appeared androgynous and there was something almost robotic about him, as if he wasn't real. He looked about twenty years old. He was wearing a crisp black suit that fitted him most meticulously but seemed a weird choice for the climate and location. The suit was like essential armor for him though and David couldn't picture him wearing anything else.

"David Christopher Cross." said the young man gravely. "We have been waiting for you. Thank heaven you called upon us and that we came to your rescue just in time."

David's brain jumbled at his words. "What-"

The man held up his hand to stop David from interrupting.

"We will answer all your questions David. But first, let me proceed with the necessary introductions. I am Aloysius Anderson, the Abbot of the Monastery, and this is Doctor Thomas Vitalis, our Head of Infirmary."

"You're the Abbot?" asked David in surprise. He couldn't help himself "That means the director or something like that, right?"

Abbot Anderson nodded.

"But you're so young!" David exclaimed in amazement. He instantly regretted his surprised reaction, not wanting to imply that the Abbot wasn't qualified for the job. "Sorry." he offered to the man.

"Ah, you flatter me young David." Abbot Anderson smiled, waving away his apology. On closer inspection, his eyes didn't look young at all. They had the patina of wisdom and experience. "Truthfully, I am a hundred and two years old."

David's brain got fuzzier with the Abbot's revelation. *A hundred and two years old*? David felt a surge of anger, certain that he was now a victim of a prank. And he wasn't in the mood for pranks. Not after what he had gone through.

"Is this a joke?" David's tone was clipped. He knew he was being rude but he was past politeness. If he didn't hear the truth from the Abbot soon, David was going to lose it. "Where are the Littlefields? Where am I and who are you really?" David demanded.

"David," Doctor Vitalis soothed him. "You are safe here. The Littlefields are gone and they can never come here."

The Abbot was nodding. "You are with your own kind now, David. You are with us and we will protect you. That we guarantee."

David only felt trepidation. "My kind? What do you mean?" His eyes were huge in his face, very much afraid of what they were going to tell him.

"I cannot reveal everything to you at this moment, to do so

would take years." said Abbot Anderson. "But answer me this David, have you observed that you are stronger than other young people your age? Faster?"

David shrugged, not wanting to share this secret when he had no idea of their intentions. They may appear harmless, helpful even, but the bottom line was, David didn't know them and he didn't know this place.

Abbot Anderson gazed at him intently, his piercing blue eyes pinning David to the hospital bed. "It is because we are different." and his next words almost stopped David's heart. "Not completely human."

Not like the Littlefields! David wanted to blurt out. Please say we aren't like them!

Instead David carefully said, "I don't feel different." and in a bitter voice, continued, "I'm just a fifteen-year-old who's had to survive on his own."

"And that is the truth." Abbot Anderson agreed. "But there are also other truths that will be opened to you here in the Monastery."

"Like what? What are you? And what am I?"

Abbot Anderson's voice was solemn. "You are a Nephilim. We all are. What that means David, is that you are half-human and half-angel."

4 The Enemy Revealed

Yeah right. David thought, quite cynical and unaccepting. He wasn't some ignorant kid sequestered away in the suburbs. But he was willing to hear them out, get all the facts first.

"Nephilim? Half angel?" he asked the Abbot. "So my parents, who was -"

"Your mother was mortal, your father is an angel."

David shook his head to clear it of the cotton haze that blanketed his mind. Come on, was any of this even real? Maybe he was in a psychiatric facility. Maybe all of *this* was David's psychotic delusion. *Okay, play along*. David advised himself.

"If my dad is an angel, then where is he? How come he's not here? And where has he been all these years?"

Both Abbot Anderson and Doctor Vitalis looked uncomfortable. "Only your father would be able to answer that." said the Abbot gently. "And he will. He will come to you in his time."

David fell silent, pondering the Abbot's response. He realized that nagging them about his dad would be useless, so instead he asked, " So, I'm half angel? How does that work exactly?"

"You embody both the qualities of your mother and father." Abbot Anderson replied, warming up to the subject. "As half angels, we are stronger than humans. Indeed, we are capable of great strength and we have excellent reflexes. We can move extremely fast if we so desire and we heal quickly."

"Heal quickly?" David frowned, still feeling quite sore. "I don't think I'm healing quickly."

"Oh but you are!" expressed Doctor Vitalis. "You did. If you had seen the condition you were in when you arrived! Head trauma, a fractured cheek, broken nose, bruised neck and throat, a dislocated left shoulder, five broken ribs, a punctured lung, bruised kidneys -"

It was like a grocery list.

"- a fractured femur, lacerated spleen, some internal bleeding, contusions, cuts and abrasions, some lacerations.........and despite all that you managed to fight back, still throwing punches. David, you have survived in a condition where most humans would be dead!"

"Ah, thank you for the inventory Thomas," Abbot Anderson said. "I very much think David has gotten your point."

Doctor Vitalis looked mildly abashed.

"I went through all that?" David asked in wonder. "I wasn't even thinking about the pain. I just had to.......fight."

"And that you did. Most admirably." Abbot Anderson added approvingly.

"But how did I get here? Who brought me here?" David wanted to know.

"You called us." revealed the Abbot.

"No, I didn't." David protested. "I didn't even know half-angels or this place existed!"

"You see David," Abbot Anderson explained, "You uttered a prayer. You asked for help and we came to help you. Well, not me personally, but two very brave Nephilims came to your aid."

David frowned, "Yes, I did ask for help. Now that I think about it, it was the very first time I did that." Then he looked at the Abbot. "You mean to tell me, that if I had asked for help before -"

23

"Then you would have been with us sooner." nodded Abbot Anderson.

Doctor Vitalis turned to the Abbot and said, "Sir, I think in a few minutes David will have to rest...."

"Doctor Vitalis, please." David implored. "Just a few more questions. How can I even rest when I have been resting for four days."

Doctor Vitalis smiled, "You have been *healing* for four days. And you really needed it too. Fortunately, as a Nephilim, our healing process is rapid."

"Plus, our Doctors and Healers are extremely gifted and efficient." the Abbot stated with undisguised pride. "and this Infirmary, although isolated from the outside world, is state-of-the-art." he added. "Go ahead David, just a few more questions and then I defer to Doctor Vitalis' suggestion that you rest."

"My foster parents......." David hesitated. The thought of them sickened him and he realized how narrowly he had escaped from them. "Mr. And Mrs. Littlefield......what are they? They said -" he paused, unwilling to repeat their words, "they said.....that they are the opposite of us."

Abbot Anderson clasped David's shoulder in an attempt to comfort him. His intense blue eyes blazed with sympathy and conviction. "For once they have uttered the truth. They are the opposite of us, and they are our eternal enemies. They are Demons."

David scoffed. "Demons?" *How ridiculous!* This delusion was way out of control. "I'm sorry Abbot Anderson, but why should I believe anything you've just told me?" David didn't want to be defiant or disrespectful, but questioning their story was necessary. "How do I know any of this is real? I mean, I only have your word for it, and I don't even know you."

Abbot Anderson pinned David with his unnerving eyes once more, as if truth transference could occur through penetrating gazes. "Oh it's real David. It's very real. We are half-angels and our eternal enemies are demons. Outside the safety of these walls, a war is going on. Yes, even at this very minute. Constantly, we are at war. Always and unceasingly."

Did they all speak like this? David wondered to himself. Like very very old people from a time of armors and horses and swords? "I'm sorry Abbot Anderson, but I need proof. And words aren't enough anymore."

Abbot Anderson nodded to Doctor Vitalis on some silent signal. Doctor Vitalis stood in front of David, closing his eyes in gentle concentration.

Slowly but determinedly, Doctor Vitalis' body started getting brighter and brighter. White light emanated from every part of his skin, radiating a brilliance so tremendous that David had to shield his eyes.

Then, with a loud rumble like the unfurling of a giant sail, a pair of enormous, powerful, white wings opened at Doctor Vitalis' back.

Here was proof unfolding before him.

And for once since he met them, David had absolutely nothing to say.

The following morning, David was declared well enough to be discharged from the Infirmary. Doctor Vitalis looked in on him, going through David's chart and latest test results and announced him fit and recovered. "I am very certain that you will love residing in the Monastery. There is so much to learn, David, and so many new friends to be had."

Doctor Vitalis beckoned to Liz again, the Healer that David had met the previous day. "Liz will assist you with the discharge process and you will be escorted to your room before class starts."

Liz approached David cautiously, a bit miffed with him for his abrupt attitude the day before. She kept pursing her lips and shooting disapproving glances at him while she fiddled and scribbled with his chart. Now that David was feeling much better, Liz was beginning to grow on him.

"Why do they call you a Healer?" David asked. "Is that like a nurse or something?"

"Not at all." she replied with a bit of frost. "We have nurses and assistants here in the Infirmary and I am neither. I am a Healer because that is what I am."

Sheesh! She was really confusing.

"So your job is to heal people?" Liz nodded at David's question. "How exactly?"

This time Liz broke into a genuine smile, lighting up as she explained. "Some Nephilims have special gifts and one particular gift is the power to heal."

"Like magic?" David teased. He was intrigued but quite amused at how serious she was for a ten-year-old.

"Like power." the frost was back in her voice. "Here, I will show you." She stood in front of the bed and asked him. "Are you still sore anywhere?"

"My left shoulder." admitted David. "That's the one that got dislocated."

Liz positioned herself so that her palms rested on his left shoulder. "I have been healing you while you were unconscious. This, plus the latest in medical care, plus our natural ability to heal quickly, has produced your miraculous recovery in just four days." She took a deep breath. "Prepare yourself." was her pompous declaration.

She sounded like a very prim old lady.

Liz closed her eyes and liquid warmth spread from her palms to his shoulder and the surrounding muscles. The point of contact between her palms and his shoulder gleamed an incandescent yellow as if a light bulb was stuck there. Then the glow diminished and vanished completely.

Liz opened her eyes and just like that, the soreness was gone.

"Incredible!" David looked at her in amazement. "That is one insane gift! Liz, you have super powers!"

Liz blushed at David's compliment. "And that is why I am a Healer." she said simply.

"You really are."

Liz handed David a white robe to put over his hospital gown and David frowned at the garment. "This is what I'm wearing all the way to my room? You're kidding, right?"

"Not at all." was Liz's unruffled reply. "That is standard protocol for post hospitalization and is the only garment available for you to wear. The rest of your clothes will be in your room."

"Do you all talk that way here?" David had to ask.

"What way?"

"Well, no offense Liz, but you sound like a forty-year old professor. I mean," said David apologetically, "you sound really.....old, but really really smart too." he added lamely.

Good thing Liz didn't say that in comparison, David sounded really really stupid.

She smiled again. "Not to worry, not all of us talk *that way*, as you put it. It actually depends on what age you were when you start here. For instance, I was here since I was seven, so most of my conversational influences were from older Nephilims. But we're very diverse here."

"Seven? So kids just keep arriving at different ages?"

"In a manner of speaking." Liz nodded, clearing David's bedside table free from medical supplies. She was methodical and efficient in her movements. "But more often than not children begin early here. You see, in most cases, the mortal parent is aware that his or her child is a Nephilim and as soon as the child is seven, which is the earliest age of entry to the Monastery, they bring the child here. As we grow older you see, the outside world becomes quite perilous for us." Liz continued in a hushed manner, "In fact David, you are the very first one to enter the Monastery at fifteen years of age."

David felt a chill down his bones. "What happens to the other kids? Those who don't make it here?"

Liz made a helpless shrug,"I can't really say. All I know is that they get attacked.....by demons."

David clenched his fists, now sitting-up upon hearing this piece of information. "We should be doing something. We should be helping them."

"Oh we are." she assured him, a little alarmed by the quick fierceness of his manner. "We're really trying David. We have missions precisely for that with Scouts and Warriors whose job it is to search, protect, and rescue." she laid a hand lightly on his arm. "We also have Warrior Training for those who want to be out there fighting. There are many options and careers here in the Monastery."

David felt a slight relief, already thinking about Liz's words: *Warrior Training*. Maybe being in a Monastery won't be so bad after all.

"But now, you really must go, David. You are to meet the Prefect after breakfast for a quick orientation."

David looked at the robe again, closing his eyes in defeat. How humiliating! His first trip through the Monastery was going to be in some darn bathrobe and slippers. "Can you at least take me through a short cut?"

Her wide eyes danced with mischief. "I would if I were escorting you. But I'm not. Tatiana is. Oh, and here she is now."

"Tatiana?" David queried, putting on the robe and slippers and turning around to face his escort. When David saw Tatiana, he unconsciously sank back down on his hospital bed, caught in jaw-dropping surprise.

Coming towards him was a flying chubby baby.

5
Making Friends With Puttis

"*Cheerio!*" a sweetly syrupy voice called out to them.

David didn't know what to say, so surprised at the sight of a flying baby now hovering near him. "Uh, hello?" was his weak greeting.

"David, meet Tatiana." Liz introduced, thoroughly enjoying David's reaction. "and Tatiana, this is David."

David moved towards the floating baby and couldn't help but laugh. She was incredible and he had to admit, very cute.

"Tatiana is a Putti, David." Liz explained. "Putti's are very friendly and helpful. In the outside world they're more commonly known as cherubs. Not to be confused with Cherubims of course."

The cherub had light curly hair, big beautiful eyes and dimples everywhere. She had little feathery wings on her back, fluttering constantly. David couldn't fathom how those tiny wings could support a fifteen-pound looking baby, but the cherub seemed to be doing well.

He reached out and touched it gently on the foot. He couldn't help himself, he had to know if they were real.

The cherub giggled, its round tummy jiggling, "*That tickles.*"

"They're adorable aren't they?" Liz grinned. "The Monastery is full of Puttis, so, just look out for them, I guess."

"*Time to go David.*" said the cherub. She smelled of freshly baked cookies. "*I'm the one showing you to your room.*" she was obviously very eager for the task, considering it important as she preened with her proclamation.

David got to his feet, cinching his robe tightly. He had shuffled along the Infirmary last night to test out his legs and all had gone well. He felt even better today. Yes, still mildly sore but considering the extent of his injuries, *mildly sore* was something to be thankful for.

"Thanks for taking the time to show me to my room." David thanked the cherub. "And you have a very pretty name, Tatiana."

"*I know.*" she giggled again, wafting the scent of cookies everywhere. Now David was getting hungry, and he wondered where people ate around here. Well, half people. He would have to get used to the thought that he was only half-human.

Suddenly, two more cherubs joined them. "Hello." they chirped at David. "*Are you new here?*"

Tatiana nodded. "*His name is David, he's our new friend.*"

"Cheerio David." the other two cherubs squeaked. "*I'm Cinnia.*"

"*I'm Zoe.*"

David said hello to the newcomers.

"*Do you like chocolate? We can bring you chocolate. Do you like hot chocolate at bedtime?*" asked Cinnia

"*How about tea?*" said Zoe.

"*Or books?*"

"*A platter of cookies?*"

"*Or someone to talk to at night?*" Zoe and Cinnia chimed after each other.

Tatiana zoomed in front of David and glared at the other two cherubs. "*David is my friend. Mine.*"

"Uh oh." Liz muttered, throwing David a warning glance.

"*Mind your own business Liz.*" Tatiana said, even more sweetly.

"That's right." the other two cherubs agreed.

The three babies were batting their long lashes at David, big eyes gazing at him in obvious adoration. David flushed in embarrassed discomfort, uncertain on what to do. He cleared his throat, red in the face. "Uh....you're all my friends."

Zoe and Cinnia cheered while Tatiana pouted. *"Very well, but I'm the one taking David to his room."* she finished in triumph. Then looking pointedly at the other cherubs, *"Don't you have your own work to do?"*

The cherubs consulted their miniscule watches and said, *"Sorry we have to leave David, time to follow our schedule."*

"It was thrilling to meet you." Cinnia gushed.

"We'll be watching out for you." Zoe promised.

"Don't hesitate to call us for anything!"

"We'll bring you chocolate. See you...."

And the two cherubs fluttered away, leaving a glowering Tatiana behind, her tiny hands on her tiny hips.

David grimaced at the two departing flying babies in white diapers. Their goodbyes didn't sound so good. Creepy actually.

"Let me have a word with David." Liz said while Tatiana acquiesced reluctantly, flying slowly out the Infirmary doors.

When she was certain Tatiana was outside, Liz said. "The cherubs won't hurt you, or anything in that category. But be warned, they are extremely enthusiastic and are not afraid to show it."

"Yikes." muttered David. "And are they all girl cherubs?"

Liz grinned, "No. I think we have an even population here at the Monastery. Male and female."

"Thank God for that." said David, appreciating Liz's kindness. "Thanks a lot Liz. I really mean it. And thanks again for being my Healer."

Liz beamed at him, her baby blue eyes sparkling at the compliment. "Very happy to help. Oh and David, don't get on the bad side of the cherubs. When angry, they can play very nasty tricks."

David groaned. "Thanks for the heads up. I'll really keep that in mind."

Tatiana chatted with David non-stop from the Infirmary all the way to his room.

She was overly eager, overly upbeat, and overly enthusiastic.

David didn't know it was possible to be amused and annoyed at the same time.

The halls were deserted – which David was thankful for – because most Nephilims were at breakfast. Although they did see a grown-up wrapped head to toe in white: sweater, pants, and even boots.

"*The Monastery is a Training Facility for Nephilims. Here, you are educated and trained for warfare. You cannot re-enter the outside world unless qualified to do so. For that, you must become an accomplished Warrior.*" jabbered Tatiana.

"*The Monastery is a harmonic fusion of old and new structures. At the moment, we are in the modern building, an immense edifice of glass and steel. It is an architectural wonder and incomparable with any human-made construction. This is Nephilim ingenuity at its height.*"

"*The original building though is very old. I believe it predates the Crusades and contains antiquities and artwork to rival any museum of note here on earth. Also, the Monastery is an extremely large and sprawling compound hence a map will be provided for you in your room. That way, you can arrive to your classes and visit other areas with full directions.*"

David remained incredulous through-out Tatiana's

monologue, still grasping the reality of a flying baby and trying to understand her words beyond the squeaks and high-pitched voice. Tatiana was right though, the building really was an architectural wonder. As for Warrior Training, he wanted to get into that right away.

Tatiana led him through tall and wide hallways, all hushed and bright, with only David's footsteps shuffling on the pure white marble. The Monastery's interior was minimalist and very modern. It was all windows and natural light with a smattering of furniture in unique shapes. There were only three color schemes: white, silver, and glass – if glass were a color. David's gaze was constantly drawn to the world outside. Nothing but snow and mountains.

"Where are we?" David asked with wonder.

"Alaska." chirped Tatiana. *"The Far North. We are surrounded by a vast space of nothingness. Completely isolated from the outside world. And our view of the Aurora Borealis is superb!"*

She continued, *"Lukas Hackett will be by your room in half an hour. He's your age and will be in most of your classes. He's to be your guide today."*

"We are here!" she announced with ceremony, stopping in front of a plain white door. With flourish, she produced a fine silver key from her pocket and opened the door.

"Welcome home, David." she beamed at him.

David thanked Tatiana for her kindness, humbly accepted the silver key to his very own room, and waved away her offer of help to settle in. What he really wanted right now was to be alone to get his bearings and explore this new shelter.

After promising to bring him treats and to *'watch over him'*, Tatiana dimpled her goodbye and fluttered away.

David stepped into the room, walking around slowly,

touching surfaces.

Temporary or not, today and for several days, this was his space.

Sure, he still had no idea what his life would be like here, but the Monastery was offering him a home, training, and answers about this half-angel business.

Besides, what were his other options? He had nowhere to go and no one to go to.

David had no family, and his mother died giving birth to him.

This knowledge was a burden of guilt for David. He knew it was irrational and yet he still wallowed in it. David was haunted by the realization that because of his birth, his mother had died. And she shouldn't have died. She was healthy, young, alone yes, but seemingly strong. She had given birth to him in a hospital and it wasn't the dark ages of hideous medical practices. The doctors did their best to save her but it was as if she had given up. For no pinpointed reason, she died.

Babies like David who were orphaned or abandoned at birth had a high percentage of being adopted. And by all means, David should have been part of that statistic; adopted and then growing-up with a family desperately in need of a child. But circumstances frowned on his existence and conspired the prevention of a happy adoption.

First of all, David was born premature and sickly. There was something wrong with his heart – a murmur or an arrythmia of some sort that the doctors couldn't figure out. What this meant was he yoyoed through the years between hospitals and the Gardner Foundation Children's Home which was the name of his orphanage.

And before David knew it, he was six years old and no longer prime candidate for adoption. Children below five years old were.

Then, when he turned seven, something wonderful but sad happened. David was given his mother's personal belongings – the ones she had with her in the hospital when she gave birth to him. An overnight bag containing change of clothes and toiletries, a couple of soft baby blankets in a light blue color with his name embroidered on it, some baby pajamas and shirts, a cap and booties. She had gotten ready for his arrival!

There was also her wallet with twenty two dollars and some change, one credit card and her driver's license:

> Cross, Rebecca Bethany
> Date of Birth: 06-18-73
> Height: 5 feet 4 inches
> Eyes: Blue

And there was an address for an apartment in Mesquite, Texas.

She was pretty, his mom. And even in a driver's license picture, she had a beautiful smile. Her strawberry-blond hair fell in soft curls around her face and her blue eyes twinkled as if she had a funny secret in mind.

But David looked nothing like her. For one thing, he had shot-up like rushing bamboo over the summer and now towered over six feet despite being just fifteen. Also, his hair was a dark blond, almost brown really, and he had gray eyes, not blue. His facial features were different and there was nothing in his mom's picture that he could own up and say "Oh, my nose is just like hers. Or, "We have the same smile." They didn't look related at all.

But since there were no family pictures, no other personal items, no photo of his father, David had no idea who he looked like and if his mom had any family out there somewhere.

David sighed. *His father...............*

Who was he? Where was he? Did he even know that David existed?

David allowed himself to sometimes daydream about his dad, but mostly he was angry and completely pissed at the guy. If his father was still alive, where had he been all these fifteen years? And why had his mom been alone?

But questions like these were dangerous and unproductive, so David chose to pack-up these questions, bury them deep into his brain and maybe look at them again on Christmas or Thanksgiving. *Maybe.*

The thing to do now was to grab the opportunity to stay in this Monastery where he would be safe (hopefully), to arm and educate himself, and to find out what being a Nephilim was all about.

His room was small but awesome. One wall was made entirely of glass, offering more view of the powdery whiteness outside. There was a bed by the glass wall, quite low and very japanese. Some distance from it was a desk made entirely of metal paired with a cushy chair. Everything was colored white.

Obviously, the Nephilims were white-obsessed.

The wall opposite the glass one was made of flat panels that turned out to be a closet. It was full of clothes: shirts and pants, sweaters – some softly knitted, some made of wool; fiber-fill vests, thick puffy coats, streamlined jackets, and a selection of sneakers, comfortable indoor boots and insulated outdoor boots. They were all white.

Everything was obviously cold-climate clothes. Very cold

climate. The last panel on the closet wall was a mirror and as David caught his reflection, he noticed that at least his gray eyes didn't look miserable – they usually did. His dark blond hair was a bit long, but haircuts weren't priorities when finding food was the number one goal. He looked somewhat gaunt and malnourished, but this past year hadn't exactly been a vacation.

He was about to rummage through the contents of his desk when a knock sounded at the door.

"Come in." he called out, and a lanky boy of David's age entered.

He wasn't really tall, just average height, but he seemed to be all arms and legs. He also had a choir-boy look to him with his neatly-trimmed hair combed and parted precisely, without a hair out of place. His clothes were the whitest David had seen so far, as were his shoes and his smile.

"Hi, I'm Lukas Hackett. Great to meet you David." They shook hands.

"Hang on while I change my clothes." said David, eyeing Lukas' outfit. "Does everything have to be white?"

"Yeah, it's the regular uniform here. But you'll be surprised at how comfortable everything is. I got used to it pretty fast."

"And the hair too?"

"Nah," chuckled Lukas. "I'm just a neat-freak. You can leave your hair alone."

David grinned with relief, but became serious as he saw the mountains from his glass wall again. "You know, they rescued me from Texas, and I still can't believe I'm in Alaska right now."

"Yeah, incredible isn't it? They had to find a remote place to build the Monastery on. Far away from regular people. It's for their protection and ours too. Let's just say we're so far north that we're not even on the map." Lukas chattered on, "And, cities are full of demons so we have to stay away from those places, unless we're on missions. Also, I heard demons get crazier when half-angels are around and they hurt people more because of us."

"Oh man, that sounds bad."

Lukas nodded solemnly in agreement.

David started taking out clothes from the closet and tossing it on the bed. "Have you ever been on a mission?"

"Nope. Not allowed yet. You have to be sixteen to start going on missions. And you train really hard for those."

"I can't wait to go on training and then go back outside and kick some demon butt." David said. "They owe me for this year."

"Dude, you are so lucky to be alive. Our oldest late-comer was a ten-year-old and she had her dad with her the entire time before she came here. And even then the demons gave them so much trouble."

"Dude?" David straightened up. "Hey, Lukas, great! You talk like a normal person."

Lukas was laughing. "Oh yeah, they sound kinda weird, don't they? The ones who grew up here. It rubs off on you though so if next time we're *conversing with precision and proper diction*, don't be surprised."

"How old were you when you came here?"

"Nine, and I still talk the way I used to because I figure, if I'm going back outside, might as well sound like a normal kid."

David grabbed a pair of sneakers from the closet. "How come you started late?"

"My mom," Lukas' smile was sheepish. "She couldn't let me go yet, said she'd miss me too much." he reddened. "but she had to let me come here eventually. It just got too hard, we got chased too much."

They both fell silent, remembering their ordeals.

"It's a blessing and a curse, I guess." added Lukas.

"I'm still waiting for the blessing part." David replied.

Lukas glanced at his watch, a nifty sundial which didn't need the sun to tell time. "We better get going, we've got a busy day ahead. First, breakfast at the coffee shop -"

"Where?" asked David in amazement.

"You'll see." Lukas promised. "Then you have a meeting with Prefect Macarius, he's in charge of all the school stuff. And then, depending on your class schedule, that's where you'll be the rest of the day."

He handed David a palm-sized gadget which David thought was a cellphone at first.

"It's like a local GPS of the place, in other words, a map." and Lukas said seriously, "Always take it with you. You're gonna need it in this place."

Lukas led him to the older part of the Monastery through a confusing maze of corridors and hallways. The walls were now rough-hewn chunks of stone and the floor was yellowed with age. David saw half-angels everywhere, and a couple of times, he saw a grown-up walking around with wings.

They finally came to a stop in front of heavy rustic doors with a glowing sign on top which said, *Pearly Gates Cafe*.

When Lukas led him inside, David's jaw dropped.

The cafe was enormous. And yet, despite the vastness of its space, it still managed to feel homey. Tables and chairs were grouped together in cozy clusters. There were inviting sofas and wingback chairs before coffee tables, snug sectionals, tall tables with equally tall chairs, lounges, wooden dining tables and heavily-cushioned chairs, and David even saw some daybeds thrown into the mix.

Some areas were partially screened-off to provide a bit of privacy, while other chairs faced hearty fireplaces lining the walls. Thick rugs layered the floor so that you could just sit back, put your feet up or dig your toes into the soft carpet.

In the middle of the room, buffet tables were set up and on it were every breakfast treat imaginable.

Pancakes and waffles, platters of bacon and fat sausages, eggs prepared in different ways, hotdogs, ham, warm rolls, croissants and muffins, bagels and donuts, sandwiches and wraps and a lot more. It was mind-boggling!

There was a table topped with fresh fruit slices, puddings and flans, and a separate table loaded with desserts – coffee cakes and tarts, tiny pastries and big round cookies, trays of chocolate, delicious cakes on stands. There was even a freezer with ice-cream and yogurt and other cold goodies. Tureens of warm soup wafted beckoning aromas beside baskets of different kinds of breads and plates of cheeses.

The coffee you had to order at the counter so the staff could prepare it for you fresh and of the kind you wanted. David, who had been hungry and poor most of his life, had never even tasted any of it. *Latte's, espressos, mochachinos, frapuccinos, iced-coffees* - and many more exotic-sounding choices. There was also hot chocolate, a variety of teas, fresh juices and smoothies.

"I may never leave." David announced.

"I know exactly what you mean. When I first came here when I was nine, I thought my eyes would pop out of my head. I swear, the entire room must have heard my stomach rumbling."

David laughed at Lukas words. "Let's grab a plate."

After piling their plates with whatever they wanted, David and Lukas cornered an empty table for some serious breakfast work. David even returned for second and third helpings. He washed it all down with freshly squeezed orange juice and delicious cups of *Nebulatte* – a mocha and chocolate infusion with a touch of mint. Even though he wanted dessert, there was just no room for it.

Now that his hunger no longer gave him tunnel vision, David was able to observe his surroundings.

Students of different ages were finishing up their breakfast amidst carefree chatter and loads of laughter. Some were packing-up school bags and preparing to leave. Others had their noses buried in laptops or books, muttering and mouthing words as though preparing for a test. It looked like any regular school, actually. Except for the all-white wardrobe, the unbelievable cafe, and the fact that each one of them were only half human.

Across David, three eight year-olds were receiving their fresh cups of coffee from the counter.

He pointed them out. "Should they be drinking coffee at that age?"

"Yeah, coffee doesn't really affect us the way it does normal people. We can drink plenty of it and be okay. We're caffeine proof, I guess." Lukas shrugged. "But they-" he pointed at a cherub, " -can't have any. Drives them nuts."

Sure enough, as soon as the cherub stole a sip from leftover coffee, it began squeaking and shaking and started zooming around the cafe like a deflated balloon.

"*Help!*" the cherub squealed.

Several students chased after it until a tall and powerful looking boy of about seventeen spread his wings and flew after the out-of-control cherub. He made an impressive rescue and carefully handed the jittery baby to a grown-up, who proceeded to make the cherub drink plenty of water to neutralize the coffee. The winged teenager was smiling good-naturedly at the applause.

"That's Caian James." said Lukas, in obvious hero-worship. "He's an Alpha Warrior and leads others to missions. He's on his last term here, well, if he decides to go on the outside when he graduates. Which I bet he will. You'll get a chance to see him during Warrior Training." promised Lukas. "He's just an amazing fighter. Really amazing."

"I can't wait until Warrior Training." said David. "I bet it's incredible to see half-angels fight and I'm itching to learn all those stuff."

"Warrior Training is crazy hard, but I'm absolutely sure you'll love it." Lukas affirmed, standing up. "Time to go. I have to take you to Prefect Mac for your class schedule. Although I'm certain since we're the same age, we'll have the same classes. That's how it works here, same age kids are grouped together."

"And I bet you all just get along, huh." David teased.

"This isn't heaven, David." said Lukas. "We may be half-angels, but we're also half-human. And that comes with what all a person is about. Good and Bad."

"Hey, are you trying to scare me?"

Lukas shook his head. "Just a warning." But he looked quite grim.

6 The Burning Ones

Prefect Martial Macarius was a jolly, rotund man who had an unhealthy love for candy. On his desk were many small and circular crystal bowls filled with colorful treats of different shapes and sizes.

He had sparse white hair, a generously jovial attitude, and a raspy voice.

"David Cross," he beckoned heartily. "Come in, come in. Have a seat and rest that backside." he pointed to one of the two plush leather chairs in front of his desk.

When he himself was seated, he stared at David with a huge grin on his face. It seemed a cross between a smile and a sneer. "Candy?" he offered.

David shook his head. "No thank you sir, I just had breakfast."

"Hmmm," Prefect Macarius smacked his lips. "Pearly Gates Cafe. Quite delightful, isn't it? Yes, yes, just had breakfast there myself. But *I* wouldn't say no to candy." He tinkered a bit at the candy bowls until he made his selection.

"A pumpkin and toffee crunch in celebration of the fall season." the Prefect announced, as he popped the candy in his mouth. "Now, on to serious business." he grinned again.

David squirmed slightly in his seat. He wasn't used to grown-ups grinning so much at him and he really suspected that underneath all the smiles, Prefect Macarius was a strict disciplinarian.

"Well David, I have your Class Schedule here for you," said the Prefect, holding a thick and crisp paper in his hand. "-which you will be perusing shortly. But before that, let me share the structure of our school system and an overview of our school calendar."

"Just like any regular school, our term starts every September and ends in May. Since it is October now, you do have some catching-up to do. Or should I say, some *years* of catching-up to do." he popped another candy in his mouth - a bright blue one. "But not to worry, David. Not to worry. No pressure here. All the teachers have been duly informed that this is your first year. And at fifteen years of age! They will give you more time to learn." he assured David.

That completely sucks. David worried. He didn't want the teachers to give him any special attention, or to think he was stupid. He just wanted to be treated like everyone else.

"Ah, they don't have to do that sir," David hastily replied. "I don't want them to go to any extra trouble for me."

"How endearing, dear David." gushed Prefect Macarius. "So considerate. So humble. But really, it will be no trouble at all. Everyone understands your special situation perfectly."

David cringed in his chair.

"We celebrate Thanksgiving of course, and Christmas holidays definitely. After all, He's our boss." the Prefect pointed a finger heavenward, along with a wink.

"We also have Spring Break and certainly, summer vacation. Although all students remain in the Monastery at all times of the year, during the summer, we plan small group excursions to different destinations so that our students can at least leave school, even for a little while."

He handed the Class Schedule to David.

"There you have it. Take your time to study your Class Schedule, and never hesitate to ask me questions."

David looked at the paper as Prefect Macarius rummaged through the candy bowls again.

~ Class Schedule ~

Essential Angelology
Sciences of the World
-   Chemistry, Biology, Botany
Warrior Training (Beginners Class)
Elementary Guardianship
Heavenly Art
Angelic Chorale

Elective Classes:
Latin
Carpentry and Metallurgy
Celestial Culinary Delights
Garments – Design and Execution

"Sir," David hesitated, "What is Angelology?"

"Well, that's the study of Angels, David. Everything concerning us. Our history, important Beings and events, even our modern life."

"And Angelic Chorale sir?"

"Ah, one of my favorites." Prefect Macarius smiled-sneered again. "Music. Singing."

"Singing? But I can't sing." David couldn't stop himself from blurting out.

"Of course you can dear boy!" boomed the Prefect with gusto. "We all can. After all, we are half-angels."

David swallowed. Perhaps he would be the very first half-angel in history to not carry a tune. Would croaking count as singing?

Determined not to worry about it until he was actually being made to sing, David asked another question. "What about these elective classes sir?"

"You just choose one from the list. And for your age-level, these are the classes being offered. So, young David, what would it be?"

He looked at the choices again. "Definitely Carpentry and Metallurgy, sir."

The Prefect nodded his approval, his head bouncing like a bobble-head. "Very good choice my boy. Very practical. I believe Carpentry and Metallurgy will be quite useful skills to have at hand, later on."

"And now David, a few disciplinary reminders." Prefect Macarius loudly cracked and chewed another hard candy.

Were his teeth not breaking at all from all the crunching? David wondered in amazement. They must have a premier dental plan in the Monastery.

"Wrongdoing is not tolerated here, so be aware and be forewarned dear boy. Anyone caught doing so is punished direly." He allowed some time for his words to sink into David's brain. "Questions?" he asked silkily.

David shook his head mutely.

"Good! Here is your Handbook. It will be your guide to the Monastery's Rules, Policies and Regulations."

David accepted the thick, hard-bound book with nervous fingers. Already, he was inching towards the door.

"Very well, very well. If you have no more questions David, off you go. Classes would have started by now."

David stood up, clutching his schedule and his handbook. "Thank you sir." he remembered to utter.

"Oh and by the way, dear boy," Prefect Macarius said. "Kindly watch your language here. Swearing and cursing is instantly punished."

"Instantly sir?" David asked with trepidation. Who didn't swear and curse once in a while?

"Yes, instantly, David. You'll see for yourself." smiled-sneered the Prefect. It seemed an ominous promise.

David muttered his thanks again and hurried out the door. There was something really weird about the Prefect and David decided that the less he saw of the guy, the better.

Outside the office door, David was surprised to see Lukas waiting for him.

"Hey, I thought you'd be in class by now."

"I have a special pass today." said Lukas. "I'm your guide, remember? Let me see your schedule."

Lukas quickly read David's schedule and smiled. "Knew we'd have the same classes. Okay, first up, Essential Angelology.

Essential Angelology was actually very interesting.

Their teacher, Prudence Celestine, was a petite and animated woman with the face of a saint. She was persuasive and perky and seemed capable of making the mother of all pep talks. She could be heaven's Head Cheerleader.

Class had begun by the time David and Lukas arrived, and thankfully, Teacher Celestine just waved them to their seats as she continued with her lecture.

"Now, who can tell me the nine Angelical Hierarchy in descending order?"

A hand shot up from the front of class and a willowy redhead answered. "Seraphims, Cherubims, Thrones, Dominions, Virtues and Powers. Principalities, Archangels and Angels."

"Very good Miss Connelly."

Another hand raised up, this time from the back of the class. Teacher Celestine peered at the girl. "Ah, Miss Pierce, you have a question, no doubt."

"Teacher Celestine, where are we in this equation? Why aren't we historically included in the hierarchy? Is this exclusion deliberate? Aren't we wholly angel enough to warrant a place on the list?"

David looked at the girl in surprise. He didn't know how they went about things at the Monastery, but, coming from the outside world, for him these were bold questions to ask. He had to admire her guts though. Whenever David was in school, he preferred existing below radar.

"The answer to all your questions, Miss Pierce, is that the Angelical Hierarchy pertains only to Pure Angels. Those without any mortal descent." Teacher Celestine said patiently. "Be assured though, that in the course of our lesson, we will be discussing the unique hierarchy of Nephilims and how we are in symmetry with other Angelic Beings. Anymore questions Miss Pierce?"

"Yes please." her voice rang clearly and confidently. "Why is there a separateness in the first place? I *get* that we aren't Pure Angels. I understand perfectly that we are half-human. But still I'm compelled to question why we must be 'officially' divided from the Angelical

Hierarchy. Why can't we be listed under Angels?"

"Very good question, Miss Pierce." Teacher Celestine acknowledged, she seemed to flit as she walked the room. "It is undeniable fact that we possess human blood. Our Angel ascendants do not. We have free will because of our mortality. They do not. We are, in essence, unique and as such cannot be placed in the same category as our Angel parents from whom we only share half traits." she peered at the vocal Miss Pierce again. "I hope I have satisfactorily answered your questions. Do you have anymore?"

"Not right now Teacher Celestine, but I'm sure I'll think of something later." the girl replied cheekily.

"Impudent behavior young lady, but your interest in the subject is admirable." Teacher Celestine retorted back.

This was apparently a common occurrence because the other students seemed unsurprised by the exchange. David was intrigued though and he couldn't help but look curiously at the girl.

Even while seated she appeared – rebellious. Although her uniform was neat and correct, she had paired it with rugged outdoor boots. And instead of a sweater, she was wearing a thick and taut body suit as if ready for immediate combat. She had pulled her long black hair back into a tight braid, but this only revealed her striking good looks – a narrow face, high cheekbones, and the palest green eyes David had ever seen.

"Alright, who can tell me more about Seraphims?" asked Teacher Celestine.

A boy raised his hand in reply and from then on the entire morning was devoted to learning about Seraphims.

David was furiously taking notes because he really did have a lot of catching-up to do and truthfully, he wanted to learn about this new world he had stumbled into. He also found it unnerving that his classmates came prepared for class, readily able to answer Teacher Celestine's questions.

Lukas had given him a sleek and slim laptop to use for all his classes and David almost convulsed in ecstasy as he accepted it. It was top of the line and too beautiful for words. David had never owned anything so.......magnificent.

"No internet though." Lukas apologized.

"What?" David was surprised. A laptop without internet capabilities? It was like owning a car without wheels – going nowhere. "Why not?" he wondered.

"The Monastery is a fortress of parental control." Lukas grimaced. "We are our own island, dude. Sorry."

"So, this is just for copying down notes?" David wanted to cry.

"Hey, it's not that bad. It's loaded with cool games. I'll show you later." Lukas promised.

But for now, the laptop was David's data bin. He was surprised to discover an eagerness to learn. Or maybe his classmates were extremely contagious. Or maybe he just didn't want to appear absolutely moronic. Honestly, it wasn't like him to wish to scoop up knowledge. But in this room where everyone was running so far ahead, David didn't want to be left behind.

In Angelology that morning, David learned that Seraphims or *The Burning Ones* were the caretakers of God's throne and that they had to shout praises all day long. Since they were also the ones closest to God, they were very powerful and burned extremely bright.

He discovered further that the Seraphims were so powerful that no one else could look at them – unless they wanted to be disintegrated – not even the other angels.

David was astonished by this fact. He was amazed to learn of angels so powerful that other angels could not even look at them.

"Tell me," said Teacher Celestine, "How many wings does the Serephim have?"

Lukas raised his hand to answer. "They have six wings, ma'am. Two covering their faces, two covering their body, and two more for flying."

"Well said, Mr. Hackett." the teacher smiled at him and Lukas flushed in delight.

Six wings! David thought. He imagined them to be very spectacular although a bit scary and intimidating. He certainly didn't want any Seraphim visiting him and calling him out for, say, misbehaving in class, or failing to follow Monastery rules. Not that he would survive the encounter. They'd be sweeping the floor to gather the dust he had become.

Teacher Celestine also discussed the most famous of the Seraphims - Seraphiel and Metatron. In an artwork that she showed them, Seraphiel had the head of an eagle.

David encoded all this information into his laptop, hoping that some of it would stick to his brain. He was feeling quite overwhelmed, like he had stepped into an alternate universe and he didn't know which was which and what was what.

Actually, he did step into an alternate universe and his mind was screaming: *Information overload!*

"You look like you've been clobbered." Lukas observed at the end of class, waving adoringly at a departing Teacher Celestine.

"I have been clobbered." admitted David, smiling at Lukas' teacher-worship. "And I can't believe it's only lunchtime. This morning was like a whole week already."

As David and Lukas packed away their things in standard issue messenger bags, someone approached them.

"Well, if it isn't the Nephilim of the Year, Lukas Hackett." drawled a voice behind David. "Is he your *boyfriend*, Lukas? Or your *only* friend." snickers followed the boy's insults.

David turned around and stood face to face with a boy his height. The boy had a tough, angular face and his body was an assemblage of packed muscle. He appeared capable of grabbing David by the neck with one hand, holding him up, and letting him dangle to death. He probably could.

Lukas was red in the face. "Get lost, Zachary."

"Or what? Girl face." Zachary growled. He extended a hand and clenched his fist, making all his knuckles crack loudly. David didn't even know it was possible to crack your knuckles with just one hand.

"What are you going to do about it, choir boy?" Zachary goaded again, chuckling at Lukas in amusement. "Hey Giles," he turned to the boy beside him, obviously his pal, a steroid specimen gone wild. Were the teachers sure these boys were only fifteen? They could pass for double their age. "Did you know that Lukas is really a *girl* angel? When he gets his wings, it'll be pink."

Giles the steroid freak laughed with a rotweiller rumble. He really shouldn't be allowed to run loose or be a half-angel with that face. Weren't angels supposed to look good? Decent?

David had to step up.

"I'll do something about it." he said calmly. It was probably suicidal and stupid but he couldn't just let them bully Lukas.

"You will?" Zachary grinned evilly. "Aren't you the new kid? So new here you want some breaking in, huh?" He drew in menacingly, obviously enjoying the thought of pulverizing David.

David didn't want any trouble but he wasn't going down without a fight. He was going to defend himself and tensed to do so.

As Zachary motioned to go in for his first attack, a blur of a person came between them. A stunning girl with pale green eyes.

7 A Piercing Rescue

"Boys, boys. How troglodytish is all this testosterone showdown!" she smiled at them, all relaxed and nonchalant. "We might as well call with rotary phones and listen to cassette tape music. Although," she mused, "I wouldn't say no to some cassette tape music."

She was the one asking bold questions in class - the rebellious Miss Pierce.

"Get out of the way, Rafaella." Zachary was staring her down, but Rafaella only smiled back at him, using her prettiness to full effect.

"Sure, I could do that." she shrugged. "But, you know, a teacher could walk in any minute. Won't it be absolutely, excruciatingly, boring to get punished? There are so many other things to do around here." she smiled at him again

Zachary seemed completely mesmerized by her. "Hmmm, you have a point, Rafaella. Know what? You do make sense sometimes."

"Thanks." she flashed her full wattage smile. "Just trying to help."

Zachary cracked an arrogant grin, then looking at Lukas and David, he glowered again.

"As for you dork drones," he laced each word with contempt,

"There will be a next time." It was an obvious threat.

"See you at lunch, Rafaella." Zachary and Giles walked away.

"Sure." she replied breezily, a smile still tacked to her face. Once they left the room, she turned to Lukas with a worried frown. "You okay?"

"Yeah, thanks again Rafaella." Lukas sighed wearily. "And who was he calling a drone?" he added in mock-indignation, "I may be a dork but I'm not a brainless drone."

Rafaella laughed, "You're fine alright." Then she turned serious. "Honestly, I don't know why Zachary keeps coming at you Lukas, but just do your best to stay away from him, ok."

She glanced at David. "You too, new angel."

David nodded at her. "Thanks for cooling things down, you were really great. I'm David by the way."

"Yeah, I heard. I'm Rafaella."

"Yeah, I heard too." David smiled at her. "You don't have to worry about us though. We can take care of ourselves. Right Lukas?" David nudged him.

"Huh?" was Lukas' reply. He had already moved on, his brain wrapped around the next class. Lukas did appear like an overachiever.

The truth was, David appreciated how Rafaella had prevented a fight, but he also didn't want someone else fighting his battles for him. Especially a girl. It didn't sit well with his very independent self.

Rafaella gave another shrug. "Suit yourselves. Just trying to prevent a nuclear-warhead explosion."

Lukas thanked her again enthusiastically, paying attention once more. "Believe me, I'm really grateful." Turning to David, he continued, "You don't know how many times she saved me from those two. Just because Zachary and I started here the same year.....he has been picking on me the second we met."

"That's because you keep beating him at everything!" Rafaella realized, an epiphany dawning on her. Then for David's sake she revealed, "Lukas really is the Nephilim of our year level. Zachary wasn't joking about that."

"But not in Warrior Training." Lukas lamented. "I suck at Warrior Training."

"No you don't." Rafaella punched him in the arm in protest. "You just haven't beaten Zachary yet. That doesn't mean you suck."

She slung her messenger bag over one shoulder. "Okay boys, I'm off to lunch."

Since David and Lukas were going to lunch too, they trudged out of the classroom together, walking in the direction of the Cafeteria.

Lukas lagged behind David and Rafaella, fidgeting with his notes and bag. When they turned into the corridor with wide pillars, David and Rafaella heard a loud smack behind them.

Lukas had walked hard into a pillar, his nose and forehead an angry red. As Lukas rubbed his sore forehead – all the while muttering muffled curses under his breath – he was suddenly spitting and gagging as bubbles began coming out of his mouth.

"What's happening?" asked David, completely alarmed. He held on to Lukas, afraid that he was having an epileptic fit.

Rafaella, surprisingly, was only laughing, nearly crumpling to the floor in hilarity. "Aw, come on Lukas. You know better than that. You've been here six years."

Lukas spit and gagged some more. "Bad -" spit, "habit." gag and spit. "Been trying to get rid..." he gasped, "trying to get rid of it." he spit again.

Rafaella looked at David's clueless expression. "Swearing and cursing." she explained. "No foul language allowed here, remember?"

David caught on. "You mean, if you say swear words, soap bubbles will come out of your mouth?"

Lukas nodded sheepishly, wiping his mouth on his immaculate sleeve. "I'm telling you, those soap bubbles taste even worse every year. Whoever's mixing them has a sadistic sense of humor."

David couldn't help grinning. "Thanks for the warning Lukas. So that's what Prefect Macarius was talking about." then he added teasingly,"You know, I wouldn't have expected it of you – *choir boy*."

"Hey," Lukas protested laughing. "That bump hurt."

They continued walking, cracking-up about the incident all the way to The Cube – which was what they called their cafeteria.

"Oh, I almost forgot." Rafaella exclaimed. "We hardly had any time this morning." Then she gave a loud and piercing whistle.

Something came bounding towards them. A huge something.

David couldn't grasp what he was seeing. It looked like a dog, but it wasn't flesh and blood. It wasn't a ghost either.

"Rafaella, what is that?" he asked in confusion and amazement.

"This is Wolverine. My essence pet." she gushed, her green eyes glowing with joy.

"Essence pet?"

Lukas explained to David. "Essences are animals who lived in the world and then died. They usually go straight to heaven, but since we're kind of in the middle of both worlds, they can come here."

"They usually find their owners." added Rafaella who was kneeling down and vigorously massaging wolverine. "Especially if their owners miss them a lot. They can only visit half- angels though, that's why they can come here."

Wolverine gave her a wet kiss, slobbering all over her as Rafaella basked in his canine affection. "I lost him when I was ten and when I arrived here -" she looked overcome with emotion, "- Wolverine was waiting for me."

She cupped and rubbed Wolverine's face. "You were waiting for me, weren't you boy? You're such a good doggie, do you know that?" she cooed at him.

David was still trying to wrap his mind around the existence of an essence pet, admiring the massive siberian husky built like a steel tank with mounds of fur.

"He really is a great looking dog." David breathed, "Can I pet him? Is he – solid?"

"Sure, you can pet him." Rafaella replied. "He's very friendly, well, except when he feels that I'm in danger. Then he can be very protective and fierce. As for the solid part – you just have to experience it for yourself. It's kinda hard to explain."

Lukas was nodding in agreement.

David approached Wolverine and held out his hand to him. The dog sniffed at his palm and fingers, then looking at Rafaella, he nudged his head against David's palm.

"Why, you're just a big baby, aren't you." David chuckled, rubbing the dog's head, face and soon, exposed belly. He and Rafaella had a fun time just pampering the rolling and grinning Wolverine, his tongue lolling at the side of his face.

Essences really were strange and hard to explain, David thought. Wolverine was solid, but not our idea of solid. Not the skin and muscle and bones kind. But you could touch him and feel him. You also have the weird feeling that your hand could go through him as though he were a ghost.

Wolverine was all white now, like a spirit, and there was a shimmery glow about him.

"So crazy!" uttered David.

Standing up, he exclaimed further, "Man, do I have a lot to learn about this world."

"Eh, don't worry about it." Lukas attempted to lessen the pressure. "You don't have to take everything in at once. Look at me, six years here and I'm still spitting soap scum."

"Too true." drawled Rafaella.

"And on that thought, we really have to go you guys." Lukas reminded them, rather urgently. "I badly need to hose down my mouth. I can still feel bits of soap stuck to my throat."

8   Pets and Peers

When David walked into the Cafeteria, he stopped in his tracks. "Whoa!" he exclaimed, stepping back into the corridor, half-afraid he would tumble off the mountain they were on.

The cafeteria was made entirely of glass.

The floor was glass, so were the ceiling and the walls.

David drew nearer, peering intently on the floor, his mouth hanging open as he beheld the sheer drop of the mountain from the see-through glass. The cafeteria jutted-out from the mountain wall, so it seemed as though the entire space was floating on air. When his momentary surprise passed, David noticed the metal struts and support that held the glass dining hall in place.

"How?" David gushed.

Lukas' eyes brightened with pride, as though he had done the architecture himself. "Nephilim Engineering."

Lukas led the way to a food-engorged buffet table at the other end of the room and David followed gingerly, his eyes glued on the floor, absolutely mesmerized by the illusion of walking on air. There was nothing underneath him. Nothing! The edge of the mountain gave way to a plummeting fifteen-thousand feet drop.

"We're not as high-up as the highest peak of Mt. Mckinley, which is Alaska's tallest mountain at more than twenty-thousand feet," said Lukas, "but this height is pretty awesome, right?"

"It's unbelievable!" David breathed, frowning at the body of water beneath them, so very very far away. "Is that a lake?"

Rafaella, who had joined them by this time, nodded. "Wait 'til you see the glaciers, David. It's incredible." She handed him a plate and encouraged him to start piling it with food.

David was too amazed to do something as mundane as eating, allowing himself a minute or so to observe what was around him. No wonder they called it The Cube!

There was the regular commotion of many people having lunch, but there was also the light, soothing strains of live music. David craned his neck to locate the performers and zeroed in on a trio of cherubs strumming musical instruments with gusto. One was playing the harp, another playing fluidly over piano keys, and the third one sawing on a miniscule violin. They were a merry assembly of musicians.

David also saw Liz, his Healer, at a table of ten year olds and she gave David a friendly wave. He smiled in return.

He also saw Caian James, the helpful warrior, at a table in the center of the room. He was surrounded by incredibly good looking kids his age.

Ah, the cool and popular kids – didn't every school have a set? David mused. Apparently even a Monastery wasn't immune to this dynamic.

Still, there existed the broad spectrum of students who looked like Caian James to students who looked like Giles the slug and the regular looking people in between. It was heartening to realize that even Pure Angels had a varied preference for human mates.

Another surprise for David was the heavy traffic of fluttering cherubs. Even more surprising was the fact that they were helping with lunch – serving drinks in fact, and carrying small pitchers of juices or milk or sodas.

Forewarned by Liz at how tricky they could be, David was pretty wary of them.

At the buffet table, an impressive feast was laid out before them again, and David helped himself to perfectly cooked steaks, fried chicken with loads of gravy, mashed potatoes, and even some bright and fresh vegetables. He was famished again despite the coronary-inducing breakfast he had earlier.

But this time, David promised himself to save room for the decadent chocolate cake he saw, the spongy layers of tiramisu, and some cheesecake.

When they had finished piling their plates with food, David, Lukas and Rafaella seated themselves at a table with other fifteen-year-olds already enjoying their lunch. Best of all, the table was located far from where Zachary and Giles were gulping down their meals.

As soon as David sat down, a cherub zoomed happily beside him.

"Remember me, David?" she smiled coquettishly, her blond curls bouncing.

"Of course." David smiled back, secretly on guard and embarrassed to be singled out. "Hi again, Tatiana."

"Oooohh." she cooed. "*You do remember me! How very flattering. I can't wait to tell Cinnia and Zoe. You also met them this morning.*"

David was grateful when Lukas cleared his throat to get Tatiana's attention.

"Ah, Tatiana," said Lukas. "Can we ask you for our drinks now?"

"*Oh, I'm sorry. How irresponsible of me. Of course!*" she turned to

David instead and winked at him. *"What will it be David?"*

"Just a soda, thanks." he mumbled and Tatiana happily poured him a glass.

She also gave Lukas his order of soda, and freshly brewed iced-tea for Rafaella. Thankfully, Tatiana left them to eat in peace after handing them their drinks. Of course, she had to deliver a parting shot of *"See you tonight, David."*

"Don't frown so, David." the girl beside him said. It was the red-haired girl from class, the tall and willowy one. "Cherubs really are quite nice, so long as they don't get mad at you. I'm Consortia, by the way."

David nearly snorted his drink out of his nose. Consortia? Really? Poor girl, he thought.

She must have guessed what he was thinking because she added defensively, "I'll have you know David, that I was named after a saint."

"Nice to meet you Consortia." he replied weakly, a little ashamed that he had made her feel bad. "What were you saying about the cherubs?"

"Oh yes, the cherubs. Actually, they're extremely helpful. They're very handy at delivering messages. If you want a message sent to anyone at the monastery, they will hand-deliver it for you. Isn't that *sooo seventh heaven*?" she waited for David to nod.

As Consortia prattled on, David slowly ate his lunch.

"Also, they're very good with the younger Nephilims, poor dears. Especially those who begin their lives here at seven years of age."

Consortia played with her food as she continued, "I myself started at that age, and I can emphatically say that it was such a tremendous change. Certainly the daytime was fun with all the school activities but it could be quite lonely during night-time. Which is why the little ones have dormitories instead of their own rooms. This way, they have company."

"And how do the cherubs help?" wondered David.

"In such an adorable way!" Consortia exclaimed. "They snuggle with the little kids at night. Isn't it *supreme*? They are our substitute teddy bears. Oh, they're so cuddly and sweet. *Sooo seventh heaven.*"

"That is nice of them." David agreed.

Consortia was right. It must be especially hard on the younger kids to be separated from their human parent at such an early age.

He glanced at several tables where the seven-year-olds sat. They had an adult Nephilim for company who helped them with their lunch. They were hyper-active chatterboxes and the grown-up had to repeatedly remind them to sit down and eat their food. She looked a bit frayed and exhausted.

He also noticed Abbot Anderson seated at the front of the room. In his table were Prefect Macarius, Teacher Celestine and a bunch of other people who David assumed were teachers or Monastery staff.

As David continued to look around the room while digging into his lunch, he saw that Wolverine was not the only essence pet around. Wolverine was contentedly plopped down beside Rafaella's chair, almost half-asleep.

At the table next to them, a girl had an essence cat on her lap, and a teenage girl had one of those tiny dogs sticking out of her bag. Strangest of all, a few tables away, was an essence fish swimming in a bowl of water. It was on the table beside a boy who was eating his lunch with determination.

"David," Rafaella claimed his attention. "I'd like to introduce you to our other classmates."

Seated beside her was a girl named Gertrude Greer. She had a beatific smile and a quiet manner. She instantly made David feel wonderfully calm.

Beside Gertrude was a boy named Joseph Santos who managed a hurried wave in between big bites of chicken.

"Missed breakfast." Joseph mumbled through his full mouth.

Next to him was an asian boy named Isaac Yu. He had a friendly and enthusiastic demeanor and welcomed David with a big smile.

"Isaac and Lukas are the top brains of the class." Rafaella shared. "I swear they must be competing with each other even when asleep."

"Most of all, we compete with each other for Zachary's attention." Isaac grinned.

"Yeah, good thing he's far away from us right now." Lukas said darkly. "Almost got in trouble this morning."

"Sorry he got to you, but I'm kind of grateful that I had a break from him today."

"Don't celebrate too soon kid," Lukas warned. "there's still Warrior Training this afternoon."

Isaac groaned.

Rafaella was frowning. "We really should do something about Zachary and his troll buddy Giles."

"Oh, surely they're not as bad as you imply." said the girl beside Consortia. "Hi, I'm Katherine Morgan." she said to David. "They're quite nice to Consortia and myself."

"That's because you're girls." Rafaella snapped at her. "And they're trying to impress you. Of course they're nice to you. Have you seen what he does to Lukas and Isaac?"

"Yes, at times I do." Katherine admitted. "But is it really as terrible as you say?"

"Yes!" replied Rafaella, David, Lukas and Isaac.

"It really is." added Joseph.

But Katherine only shrugged, not overly concerned about the matter. "Consortia, have you seen the trimming which I plan to incorporate in my design for our Garments class?"

And unbelievably, the two girls started jabbering about designs and materials, patterns and styles, completely lost in their own world.

Rafaella gaped at them in disbelief, her eyes blazing with indignation and anger. She looked ready to smack them on the head with her plate.

"You know," said a quiet voice beside her, "We may not agree with other people, but they have every right to be wrong."

"Thanks for the reminder Gertrude." Rafaella breathed deeply, trying to compose herself.

Gertrude gave a softly serene smile once more and everyone at the table felt – calm.

Later on, as David was slicing into his cheesecake – after demolishing servings of chocolate cake and tiramisu – he was reminded of a question he had been meaning to ask.

"Lukas, what did Zachary mean about getting your wings? How do we get our wings?"

Lukas pondered the question before answering. "It's different for every person, the timing, I mean. But our wings just literally grow overnight. One day you don't have wings, and next morning – boom – a pair has sprouted on your back."

"Really?" David was amazed.

"Yeah." said Rafaella. "Plus, they're fully retractable too. If you're not using them and you don't want to walk around with them, you just will it to retract – that's what they say anyway."

"So you guys -" David looked at them questioningly.

They both shook their heads.

"We're still young." Lukas said. "Most half angels get their wings when they turn sixteen. It's also a sign of maturity, you know, of being battle ready."

Rafaella nodded. "You can't go on missions without wings. We have to fly towards our assignment and we have to be exceptional in using them."

"Yup. You have to remember David, that demons have wings"

"I know, I've seen them." David interjected.

"- and they're expert flyers. That's what I hear in Warrior Training. So, when we do grow wings, we have to fly better than them."

"So how come nobody uses their wings that much." David asked. "I mean, take right now. I don't see any wings out."

Lukas chuckled. "That's just practicality. Adult Nephilims have impressive wing spans. You'll just end up bumping into everything."

"Yeah." agreed Rafaella. "Pretty tricky to maneuver wings indoors."

"And what about the color? Does it come in different colors? Could you really get – pink?" David fearfully wondered.

Rafaella and Lukas laughed.

"Nah, Zachary was just messing with me." Lukas grinned. "As far as we know, all angel wings are white."

"But you know," Rafaella teased. "There's a first time for everything. You're the very first to enter the Monastery at fifteen – who knows David, you just might get pink wings."

David shuddered at the thought. "Don't even say that."

9 Test of Twenty

At two in the afternoon, David and his classmates headed outdoors for Warrior Training.

It was brutal.

In preparation, Lukas had shown David where the locker rooms were – conveniently situated near the Monastery's side entrance – where they donned stretchy and sturdy sports gear.

The training arena took up an entire side of the monastery. It was a wide and complex lay-out of obstacle courses, archery ranges, arenas for weapon-maneuvers, plus a whole bunch of other gears and constructions that David had no idea what for.

It was suitably divided into sections: seven, eight and nine year-olds were grouped together with their own courses and challenges. So were the ten to twelve year olds. Then, thirteen years and older had the extreme and intense-looking arena.

From a distance, David could see some older kids zooming and flying through an incredible aerial obstacle course. David was thrilled and bursting with excitement. He had been waiting for this all day!

Their group was met by a tall, powerfully muscular Nephilim with keen and cunning eyes. He had a stern face that seemed to say – *Take this seriously! Your life depends on it! Or else....*

"Good afternoon class. Ready for battle?"

"Yes, Teacher Peregrine." David's classmates replied.

Teacher Peregrine nodded at them. "Alright. Let's pummel you into shape."

He wasn't kidding.

First he ran them through some warm-up exercises that were too intense to be called warm-up. When they were done, David was already covered in sweat. He was grateful to observe that he wasn't the only one. Isaac was wheezing and Consortia was smudgy and fretting about her hair. Rafaella though looked unaffected by the drill.

"Okay!" barked Teacher Peregrine. "Now that you're suitably warmed-up, let's challenge your agility, speed, strength and endurance. Group yourselves – five to a group."

David, Lukas and Rafaella grouped themselves and Isaac and Joseph joined them. Zachary and Giles were in a group with three more boys that David had not met yet. All of them looked tall and muscular. They were also incredibly psyched about the exercise, high-fiving each other and looking ferociously determined.

Teacher Peregrine led them before an obstacle course – extended version from the looks of it. It was far more difficult than David had anticipated.

"That is insane." he muttered under his breath. How was he supposed to do the obstacles, much less finish the entire course? It seemed impossible.

"Listen up." the teacher called their attention. "You will be timed individually, but the first group to finish wins a prize. Today's coveted prize is front and center seats to this afternoon's battle at the Combat Circle. The winners will really be able to see the fight up close and visualize the strategies satisfactorily."

"Sweet!" crowed Zachary, and their group started patting each other on the back with full-sized grins as though they had already won.

"This obstacle course can have five persons at one go, so all groups will have one member going at a time. Now," he looked at them craftily, "put your heads together and decide who goes first, second, so on, and fifth. You have one minute."

David's group huddled together.

"I'm going first." Rafaella said. "You boys know that I make good time in this course and I want us to have an early lead."

The other boys nodded. David was still concerned about finishing.

"I think I should go next." said Isaac. "I'm the weakest of the bunch and hopefully, the guys after me can, you know, make up for our time lost."

Nobody protested.

"I also think Joseph should go next." Isaac continued. "He may be the laziest slug sometimes -"

"Hey!" Joseph reacted.

"- but he's excellent in Warrior Training."

Joseph smiled, slightly appeased. "True."

"Then I go next." Lukas said. "Then you David. This way you'll have time to observe how we tackle the course."

David nodded, finding it hard to swallow all of a sudden.

"Time's up!" Teacher Peregrine announced. "First representatives of the group, take your places. Oh, and my dear cherubs," he smiled with relish, "we're doing this Angel Mode."

The five students to lead the race nodded. They had been expecting nothing less.

"What on earth is Angel Mode?" David whispered to Lukas.

"Super speed only." Lukas replied.

"Super speed!" David croaked. How was he supposed to do

that?

Lukas patted him on the back. "You'll be able to do it. I bet you've done it before and just haven't noticed. Don't worry about it, we can all do it. We're born with it."

It didn't help at all.

David imagined himself as this heavy, giant slug, moving with all his might and energy and realizing that he had barely moved an inch.

"Ready," Teacher Peregrine called out. "Set........Go!"

And they were off!

The first five students to tackle the course were Rafaella, Giles, Katherine, and two other boys.

They were facing a whopping twenty obstacles and they had to super speed through it to place their teams on the lead.

First up was a belly crawl on slushy snow under wires with wickedly long spikes. It wasn't a regular barbed wire, it was piercingly murderous barbed wire.

Rafaella was a blur as she crawled under the wires, her face almost pressed to the snow, her body hugging the ground to prevent snagging herself. She was first to get through and instantly leaped on a rope to wall climb. Giles followed closely.

In an instant, Rafaella was over the wall and rapelling downwards then she was off to the hopping posts. David had to marvel at her nimbleness as she balanced carefully on top of a post, then jumped to the next one, and the next without falling off. At the back of his mind, he also noted that as half-angel he must be able to see clearly through Angel Mode because at the rate they were going, they must have only been a blur to regular humans.

The fourth challenge was a tall, single bar over water and you had to swing through it with your hands. Rafaella monkeyed her way through the bar with Giles overtaking her as he managed to cover more ground with each swing. Still, they finished closely with the other two boys at their heels and Katherine only a little behind. Once again, Rafaella took the lead on the long balance beam, her arms struck out on her sides, her feet running neatly over the beam.

Then, incredibly, they were zig-zagging their way through a minefield wherein a set-off mine exploded a cloud of noxious yellow sulfur, and each explosion was a point against the student. Rafaella blurred across the minefield without setting off a single one. Giles meanwhile, set one off. David could hear Giles roaring in fury.

Seventh on the list was a twenty-foot tall chain-link fence that the challengers easily climbed and scrambled down on, speed being the skill that mattered.

Rafaella was still in the lead and she gracefully crawled on her belly once more, disappearing into a tight tunnel. She came out of the other end, bursting into a run as she zig-zagged through tall and thin marker posts.

Then it was a dizzying tall spiral staircase next, and David watched as Rafaella ran up the steps into even tighter and dizzier circles. At the platform on top, she grabbed a rope to begin her inverted descent, with Giles and the rest still trying to catch up with her.

David and the rest of their group were yelling their encouragement at Rafaella.

The twelfth challenge required both brains and speed as the challengers had to figure out the rhythm of pendulously swinging weapons in order to cross it without getting bumped off, sliced off, or clobbered into unconsciousness.

Rafaella rocked back and forth on her heels as she prepared to go through multiple weapons – swinging hammers, a club, a scythe, a mace, cruelly spiked balls, sharp clanging swords, thick and heavy metal chains, and pounding anvils.

Rafaella was amazing as she wound her way through the killer weapons, narrowly escaping being sliced clean by the scythe, but receiving a gash from the trickily swinging swords.

One boy was completely bumped off the path by the huge hammer, while Giles suffered severe lashing from the metal chains which he entered wrongly. Then, with a clean leap and roll under the anvils, Rafaella was on to the next challenge.

It was a jigsaw puzzle made from heavy concrete.

She had to carry or drag the puzzle pieces to an empty slab ahead of her and form the puzzle there. It took her several trips to transfer the pieces, but once she had all of it, she made quick work in assembling the puzzle.

Giles, steroid freak that he was, took no time at all in carrying the pieces, but was considerably slowed down as he tried to figure out how to assemble the puzzle. Each challenger had a different puzzle, and soon, even Katherine and the other two boys were alongside him. Zachary was screaming furiously at Giles as the clock ticked on, making Giles even more nervous and panicked.

Meanwhile, Rafaella was on an impressive lead, having gone on to the next step, entering a sealed and transparent square, about the size of a small room. From the outside, the interior looked smooth on all sides.

"That's the Weather Chamber." Lukas informed David. "They can create any kind of weather inside, usually foul or extreme conditions that you have to cross. There's an exit door at the other end."

Today, Teacher Peregrine had decided on hurricane winds accompanied by brutally lashing rain. They could see Rafaella being buffeted inside the chamber, scrambling to get a foothold and trying to fight her way to the exit. She came out at the other end, ragged, drenched and windblown but still very much determined and still in the lead.

Giles had finally figured out his puzzle and had entered the weather chamber too. Katherine and the other two boys entered their chambers at the same time Giles did.

The fifteenth challenge was another belly crawling one. Rafaella crawled under a metal mesh which hummed and pulsed menacingly as low voltage electricity passed through it.

You touch it, you get electrical shocks.

To up the level of difficulty even more, Rafaella was crawling on sharp and jagged gravel, the crumbled rocks and pebbles digging and scratching her entire front. Still, she was a blur under it, crawling with such dexterity that soon she made it out from under the mesh. David heard a few zaps though, and knew that Rafaella had brushed the metal mesh a few times.

David also heard zaps from the other challengers as they struggled between the electric mesh and the sharp gravel. Katherine shrieked now and then, and Giles, being bulkier, got zapped even more.

One boy challenger was spitting and coughing under the mesh, apparently having mouthed off some swear words, and David imagined what a terrible time it was to be foaming with soap in the mouth. Still, the half-angels plowed on.

There were only five obstacles left. Rafaella, a true warrior, leaped onto the next one with enthusiasm. It was a dangerously high rock-climbing wall and offered zero harness or rope. Insanely, the challenger was expected to make it to the top with mere footholds and a strong grip. Sure, if they fell there was a wide net waiting to catch them – but still, David was astounded at how extreme the obstacle was.

He held his breath as Rafaella climbed the wall as fast as she could. Twice she slipped and had her feet dangling in the air before they could find purchase. Incredibly, she continued to be the first one to reach the top which was a small wooden platform. Cherubs fluttered around Rafaella with ankle harnesses and a long cord.

"Is she supposed to -" David uttered in surprise.

"Yup, bungee jump." replied Lukas. "That's the next challenge and the only way to get down."

"That is so sick!" exhaled David, his tummy doing flip-flops at the thought. Not that he was terrified – okay, maybe he was terrified – but he was also a little excited. He hadn't done anything like that before and he wanted to try it, too bad it had to be in a race.

Rafaella went into a graceful swan dive and before she even stopped swinging as she landed some feet from the ground, she released her ankle harness and back-flipped neatly on her feet.

Then, she was waist deep in a long pool of mud – sloshy, sticky, sucking mud – which she had to wade through. It was hard, sluggish work and David knew she must be tiring. Giles had landed from the bungee jump, so did the two other boys. Katherine, meanwhile, was screaming her head off as she jumped from the platform.

It was amazing really how Rafaella remained in the lead and was beating the dignity off Giles.

She reached the end of the mud pool and clambered out, diving immediately into a pool of water – another long stretch that she had to swim this time. She did fast and determined strokes, a speedy streak in the water. Before they knew it, Rafaella had emerged, dripping and gasping from all the exertion.

She was on to the last and final challenge!

It was a lengthy track to run spiced up with twelve burning hurdles. Literally burning hurdles! The flames were flickering and leaping with the breeze. It certainly was a persuasive incentive to jump high.

David, Lukas and Joseph were yelling themselves hoarse as they cheered Rafaella on to the finish line. Isaac was already positioned at the starting point since he would begin as soon as Rafaella crossed the finish line.

She was a force to be reckoned with, covering the hurdles in strong leaps.

A buzzer sounded.

Rafaella had finished first. They were in the lead!

Even more amazing was that she had finished the obstacle course in under a minute!

She stayed on the benches beyond the finish line – singed, battered and exhausted, but with a huge grin on her face. She was also shivering from the cold but a helpful cherub was present to wrap her in a blanket and offer her a warm drink.

Rafaella wouldn't be allowed to return to her teammates. Coaching and tips were strictly prohibited and her tips would really help. Although some of the obstacles were familiar to the students (except David of course), there were new challenges thrown in. It was Teacher Peregrine's policy to always change things up. There would be no relying on comfortable familiarity.

David now turned his attention to Isaac who had already started. Despite what he had said earlier, Isaac was no slowpoke. He also was a blur as he tackled each challenge, although David soon noted that despite the lead advantage Rafaella had given him, the other students soon caught up with him.

Next in the bullies team was a boy named Dominic who was soon head to head with Isaac. The leaping posts slowed Isaac down a bit, who sometimes went almost too far on the posts that he had to balance and scramble in place, or not leaping the required distance, hence all the wood gripping and trying to get back on top. Then he would pick up his momentum and try to make up for the time lost.

He sailed thru the bar and balance beam, but set off two explosions of noxious yellow gas in the minefield. By the eleventh challenge – the inverted rope descent – Dominic had taken the lead and Isaac was in third place.

Fortunately, Isaac recovered and gained advantage during the swinging weapons and the puzzle obstacle. And yet, despite his best efforts, Isaac finished in third place. David thought that wasn't bad at all. Third place was a great spot, and this from a boy who had humbly declared himself the weakest in the group.

David didn't want to feel anxious, but he did. He was undetermined after all. Untested.

He didn't know what his capabilities were. Could he even do Angel Mode? Super speed?

He did his best to block out the giant slug image that kept popping in his brain.

Soon, David and Lukas were cheering Joseph on.

Joseph proved to be a secret weapon after all. He appeared lazy and sleepy and in perpetual torpor, but he was fast and a surprisingly determined competitor. He crawled and climbed and jumped and evaded, ran and solved, waded, swam and sprinted.

Incredibly, Joseph managed to put their team back into the competition for first place as he finished the same time with the boy from Zachary's team.

It was a tie and when the buzzer blared, Lukas and Rusticus

threw themselves into the course. The other teams were some seconds late before starting up.

David realized with a sinking feeling and increased nervousness that Zachary himself had chosen to be the last player in their team. David was going to go up against Zachary, and even as they waited their turn, Zachary was glaring at him furiously and cracking his knuckles single-handedly.

David chose to ignore him and focused on Lukas instead.

Once again, despite the humble declarations of weakness, Lukas was performing very well. By the eighth challenge – belly crawling in the tight tunnel – he was still tied with Rusticus from Team Bullies, while the other three competitors tried to catch up. It was on the next obstacle that Lukas lost his place as he tripped while running through the zigzag.

Amazingly, now in second place was Gertrude. Quiet and calm Gertrude.

David promised himself never to take appearances at face value again as he watched shy Gertrude compete with fierce resolve. He wanted to root for her but also reminded himself that he was rooting for Lukas and their team. David wanted badly to win and give Zachary's team a good kick in the face. A peg or two down their high post would do them a lot of good – if that were possible.

Lukas redeemed himself especially when it was time for the swinging weapons and the puzzle, beating Rusticus soundly during those challenges. Gertrude was excellent in those too, but got slowed down in the Weather Chamber.

Rusticus handily muscled his way through the more physical challenges and it was once again him and Lukas in the lead.

The rock-climbing wall was another difficult obstacle for Lukas and he lost his place in the lead. Rusticus was soon climbing on the platform on top of the wall and bungee jumping his way back to the ground.

Lukas did the best he could to catch up, but Rusticus powerfully tankered his way through the mud, swam like a hyper shark through the pool of water and bounded relentlessly over burning hurdles. To his credit though, Lukas still finished in second place.

The instant Rusticus crossed the finish line, Zachary was off.

In those tortured seconds while David was waiting, time seemed to expand and stretch like pulled caramel candy.

He was at the starting point, ready – or desperately hoping to be ready – watching Zachary crawl and claw his way in the first challenge. He wanted to pull Zachary back, he wanted to protest – to have a fighting chance. Zachary was already a blur in front of him.

He was waiting.........waiting............

Then the buzzer sounded.

Finally, it was David's turn.

10 † The Gothic Sword

David remembered that when he was eight years old, something unexplainable happened.

It was Christmas Day and he was still in the orphanage. He was also very angry that day. He was angry that his mother was dead, angry that he didn't know who or where his father was, angry that he was spending Christmas in some orphanage.

He had rummaged furiously through his meager belongings until he found his mother's old apartment address in Mesquite, Texas.

It seemed that one minute he was reading the address and when he had looked up, he was facing a row of neat, but tiny apartments. He didn't know how he got there, or how long it took, but David remembered the feeling.

That was what he was doing today.

He was remembering the feeling.

His heart started to beat faster and his vision sharpened as if there had been netting covering them before.

His ears throbbed as sound became amplified, the sensitivity and acuteness increasing a thousandfold. And yet, the world seemed to have come to a stop. There was a vacuum, an eerie silence – a hushed anticipation.

David felt his limbs warming up. He was absolutely still and crouched in a runner's stance, but his body felt like a motor revving up. Warmer and warmer, his body was – pulsating.

Then the buzzer sounded and every other thought left David. There was only the challenge ahead of him. There was only the obstacle course.

Nothing else existed.

Nothing else mattered.

He pushed himself down under the spiky barb wire, his face almost touching snow. He crawled and propelled himself, not feeling a sting on his back indicating that he was low enough. Then he was done and his hands were clasping the rope as he climbed up and down the wall.

He felt the excitement explode in his brain, the happiness. David knew he was born for this – training, competing, and soon fighting.

"I belong here." his mind said. "I belong here!"

He jumped posts, swung hurriedly across the bar, zoomed over the balance beam and minefield. He was giddy and laughing and enjoying himself.

He climbed the chain-link fence and crawled under the tight tunnel. He streaked through the zigzag and ascended the spiral stairs then descended head first with the rope. The swinging weapons were his friends, telling him when to pass and the puzzle challenge offered a quick solution. He tornadoed his way across the weather chamber and crawled as low as he could under the metal mesh, not wanting to receive electric shocks, the gravel pressing into his hands and knees.

Then he was rock-climbing the tall wall. Grabbing and holding on, finding footholds and going up and up until he reached the platform. The cherubs secured ankle straps on him and then David was soaring as he bungee jumped, yelling his head off in great fun, having an incredibly good time.

He sloshed through the mud, and sliced through the pool of water. Then it was the burning hurdles and he was leaping over them, happy that he was finishing the course and hoping that their team wasn't far behind.

The buzzer blared as David crossed the finish line – what a joyful sound it was – and David came to a stop, facing his bunch of tattered and ragged teammates.

There was a huge grin on David's face and a questioning look in his eyes.

He was met with silence.

Gaping, shocked silence.

Lukas was the first to recover, screaming "We won! We won!"

And then they were around him and slapping him on the back, and jumping crazily up and down.

"We did?" David was yelling back. "We won?"

"How did you do that?" They were exclaiming in return.

"Incredible!"

"Awesome! Just amazingly awesome!" Lukas was gripping him.

David was a little confused and extremely happy at the same time. His teammates made him turn around towards the finish line and everything became clear to him.

Unbelievably, Zachary was still in the eleventh challenge with the other teams behind him. David had accomplished the obstacle course so quickly that he had passed them all. They weren't even finished yet!

David's team was in first place and David himself was the declared winner of the race.

He had set a record!

Of course David was very happy that their team had won, and he was even happier to realize that he knew what he wanted to do now – what he wanted to be.

And that was to be a warrior, a protector.

But he was also uneasy about all the attention he was getting.

Teacher Peregrine had declared him the winner of the race, and most astonishingly announced that David was the very first Nephilim ever to set such a record.

His classmates were congratulating him on his win – and on his first try too! Of course, not everyone was happy for him.

Zachary's face was a tug of war between a scowl and a cry. He looked about to pull all his hair out in frustration and anger. He was also bearing down hard on Giles, berating him for *allowing* Rafaella to take the lead.

There was a calculating look in Teacher Peregrine's eyes, and he kept saying *'hmmm'* thoughtfully whenever he looked at David.

Lukas, Isaac and Joseph were the most jubilant, recapping David's undertaking of the obstacle plus their own adventures. Today was also the first win for them.

Rafaella kept looking at him measuringly – sizing him up as an opponent. But she did slap him on his back with a smile saying, "Great job, newbie. And once you get the basics of Weapon Maneuvers, I'm looking forward to taking you on."

"Oooooh........" the other boys reacted to Rafaella's challenge.

"Can't wait." David grinned at her, and it was true. He could hardly wait to get his hands on a weapon and begin training.

David immediately got his wish that same afternoon. The obstacle course was only the first activity of the training. There would be no resting yet.

Next on their list was Weapon Maneuvers. This time, they were divided into smaller groups, or in David's case, all by himself.

There were many other Nephilims present to oversee student training, with Teacher Peregrine as head instructor of their class.

Since it was David's first day, he was escorted to the Armory – by Teacher Peregrine no less – so that he could familiarize himself with the different weapons, handle them, and select one that he would train with.

"As you can see, you're all by yourself this afternoon. The rest of the class already have their training schedules and goals – you'll be getting your own too." Teacher Peregrine assured him.

"Now, through the course of your entire training, you will learn how to handle all the weapons you see here." the teacher's eyes became fierce. "This will be to your advantage. When you're battling demons you will have to use any weapon at hand. Any weapon!" he barked, "So, the more you master, the better your chances of winning the fight."

He turned to David, his face deadly serious. "You just came from out there, David. You, more than anyone else in your class, know that this is not a game. We train to protect humans. We train to survive." He took a deep breath. "We train to kill."

"So, take a good look at all the weapons here. Choose one. This will be the first weapon you will train with." Teacher Peregrine instructed.

David looked around the impressive array of weapons. Teacher Peregrine was right. This wasn't a game and the school was only a temporary haven for all of them. The obstacle race may have seemed like a game, but at its very core, it was preparing them and honing them to be warriors.

The armory was divided into sections – knives and daggers,

swords (broadswords, long swords, sabres, scimitars, arming swords, cutlasses, to name a few). There were blunt weapons such as clubs, maces, war hammers, morning stars and flails. There were whips, spears, lances, battle axes and other huge and menacing weapons. There was also a fine selection of bows and arrows.

David circled the armory twice but the same weapon kept calling to him, kept catching his attention. He walked towards it and reached out his hand, his fingers itching to feel it.

It was magnificent – a long sword possessing a powerful, twenty-seven inch, double-edged blade of sharpened steel. David noted its classic cruciform style, its sculptured cross guard and the spiral handle curved exactly to fit his hand. The sword felt almost – familiar, like a great friend he hadn't seen in a long time. And the second he grasped it, again there was that sense of homecoming.

"Sir!" uttered David in surprise. "The sword sir………it's glowing!"

"Ah yes," Teacher Peregrine nodded. "It's how the forged metal reacts to our substance. You see David, ordinary metal will not kill demons. Definitely it can hurt them, but not kill or vanquish them."

"Then what can kill them sir?"

"It is our *angelic substance* that empowers the weapon. Whenever we touch a blade, a sword, whatever weapon we choose to employ – that weapon will burn with our substance and only then can demons be killed."

David studied the sword he was holding again. It was white hot and impressively burning. *Too Cool!* David thought. He could definitely slay demons with this weapon.

"Hmmm...." Teacher Peregrine said. "Fascinating choice David. Most fascinating."

"Sir?" David was puzzled.

"The name of that weapon is the Gothic Sword. That particular make of long sword is the favorite weapon of a certain class of angels." Then Teacher Peregrine shook his head. "But it's impossible of course. Impossible. They would never – so I'm not going to bother you again with my improbable conclusions. So, how does the weapon feel?" he asked.

"Just right sir." David said.

"Good." nodded Teacher Peregrine. "Let's begin."

For the next two hours Teacher Peregrine hammered David with instructions and corrections. The proper stance in sword fighting, the exact way to hold and handle the weapon, how to prepare his limbs for the fight, basic attacks and lunge sequences, and primary defenses.

David could hardly believe that he was training with Teacher Peregrine. The guy was so tall and ripped that David couldn't help feeling like a toothpick against a giant redwood tree. Their swords clanged and clashed relentlessly and even with angel strength, David's arms felt like lead at the end of their session. He had also never felt more excited or exhilarated.

"I'll hand you your training schedule at the end of class, David." said Teacher Peregrine. "Now, let's get going. It's time for some battle demonstration."

They walked towards the Combat Circle where David took a seat with his ecstatic teammates in the front row. Apparently, the front row were seats of honor reserved for students doing extremely well in Warrior Training and again, it was Lukas', Isaac's and Joseph's first time to be seated there. They were as giddy as teenage girls on a celebrity sighting and David was carried along by their happy spirits. Rafaella was pleased to be there too but it wasn't her first time in the seats of honor. She was after all, a very daring and accomplished warrior.

Teacher Victorinus, the senior instructor, walked towards the middle of the Combat Circle and addressed the entire assembly.

"Welcome to the Combat Circle for another afternoon of Versus Battle. Our competitors today are senior classmen – Jerome Gallagher and Caian James. This afternoon's fight will be a weapons combat. The first to disarm his opponent and place in endstage submission hold will be declared the winner."

"Let us begin."

Jerome and Caian walked to the center of the Combat Circle and readied themselves. They were like night and day – Caian, tall and fair and handsome, Jerome, dark and fierce and compelling. Both wore combat gear and protective metal chestplates.

Caian was armed with an unusual looking sword – curved at the handle, it began as a narrow blade then broadened towards the tip. Its double-edged blade was stylized and gleamed majestically.

"That's a Persian War Sword." Lukas whispered to David. "It's Caian's favorite – an exact replica of Alexander the Great's sword."

Jerome, on the other hand, was wielding a heavy looking, long sword. Its blade was about thirty inches in length. It had a cast metal pommel and a leather-wrapped handle.

"That is a wickedly powerful Viking Sword." said Lukas. "Darn thing's heavy too, so unless you have the muscle power for it, just forget trying to use it."

"Even in Angel Mode?"

"Well, yeah we have super strength, but so do demons. And the student warriors who have been on missions say that going head to head with demons really take its toll. So if you're not used to a heavier weapon -" Lukas left his words hanging in the air as the buzzer sounded.

It was fight time.

Caian and Jerome unfurled their wings. They faced each other with impressive wing-spans and glowing, burning swords. Slowly, they circled each other, looking for the opportunity to strike.

Jerome was the first to attack. He thrust his sword powerfully at Caian and Caian deftly parried the sharp move.

Caian countered with precise slashes and managed to cut Jerome on his arm. David was shocked.

"They're allowed to actually draw blood?"

Lukas nodded. "Extremities yes, not on the chest. That's why they're wearing protective gear. No decapitating allowed of course."

"I'm so relieved." David drily replied, but Lukas' attention was only on the fight.

Clanging sounds reverberated across the Combat Circle as Caian and Jerome's swords connected again and again. They were incredibly fast, attacking and parrying, offense and defense.

Jerome was backing away with reverse hovering leaps as Caian came at him with bold strokes. He defended himself admirably from Caian's cutting siege, but was unable to counter all attacks and once again, Caian's blade sliced across Jerome's skin – this time on his cheek.

David could see the burst of fury in Jerome's eyes and in a retaliatory move, Jerome flew towards Caian with quick, determined slashes, but Caian expertly countered Jerome's advances.

They continued circling each other, moving in on every opportunity to render their opponent weaponless, trying again and again to draw blood and score points.

With four gashes in, Jerome was able to gain an advantage

and seized an opportunity to cut Caian on his upper arm. At the last second, Caian's wings closed around him and Jerome's sword cut Caian's wing instead. A few feathers dropped to the floor.

There was a collective gasp from the onlookers.

Caian's wings opened again and he took Jerome by surprise with a rapid sequence of attacks. With the flat of his blade, he hit Jerome's sword hand and with an upward thrust, successfully sent Jerome's sword flying away.

Jerome was now weaponless but he still wasn't done with the fight. He looked for a way to make Caian weaponless too.

Again, they circled each other, Jerome moving cautiously without his sword. It was already out of the Combat Circle and deemed irretrievable. He would have to fight Caian with his hands.

Seeing an opportunity, Jerome lunged at Caian, but Caian evaded his hold with an overhead backflip and he landed behind Jerome. With a powerful kick at Jerome's back, Caian sent Jerome sprawling on the floor.

Jerome didn't even have time to get up. Caian was already on him, pinning him down and holding him at sword point.

The buzzer blasted again. The fight was over. Jerome was weaponless and defenseless.

Caian had won.

There was enthusiastic applause for the victor and also for the fight itself, which had been thrilling. Caian, good-natured as ever, helped Jerome to his feet and the two warriors shook hands.

"Good fight buddy." Jerome said graciously at Caian, who smilingly slapped him on the back.

"You too Jerome."

It was the end of Warrior Training and David and his new friends trudged back to their rooms to freshen up for dinner. It had been quite a day, and already, David was beginning to feel the onset of fatigue. He had been bombarded with a multitude of physical and mental surprises that all he wanted to do was crawl into bed and shut down into sleep.

Back at the Cube, dinner was a more formal seven-course event. The buffet tables had been put away, instead cheerful servers placed course after delicious course on every table.

David was seated with his victorious team and they were contagiously euphoric. They didn't even mind Zachary's never-ending glower some tables away.

"I wonder how he can eat if he keeps scowling and muttering like that." Rafaella observed absent-mindedly, fondly stroking a sleepy wolverine beside her chair.

Lukas and Isaac were chuckling and grinning from ear to ear.

"Let's just ignore the sore loser." said Lukas.

Isaac was nodding beside him. "We may have to pay for it tomorrow or the day after, but today -" he closed his eyes in joyful appreciation. " - ah, today........we definitely kicked his butt."

"Priceless!" chimed Lukas again. "Best Day Ever. And next time that he gives me a hard time, I will be replaying his look of defeat inside my head."

"We may even have some zingers and comebacks that we can throw in his face now." Isaac added.

"You really shouldn't put up with him anymore." David suggested. "And, we can do the strength in numbers play – you know, with the five of us. Maybe he and Giles will leave us alone."

"Hah, fat chance." Isaac said. "He and Giles have more cavemen buddies they can reel in anytime. Like the ones on their team."

"I can't understand though why he keeps Innocent in his

group." Rafaella wondered.

"Innocent?" asked David.

"Third guy on their team during the obstacle course. He's their weakest link, also tall but scrawnier than the rest of them." Lukas answered.

"Maybe he's the brains in the group." Isaac offered.

"Well, they could certainly use some." snickered Lukas.

"Dream Invader." Joseph simply said.

David was surprised. Joseph had been quiet throughout the meal, almost asleep as he munched down his food. David had never seen eating while sleeping being done before and he had been amazed at Joseph's capabilities. He hadn't missed a fork or swallowed the wrong way.

"That explains a lot." exclaimed Rafaella. "So that's why they're keeping him in the group."

"What's a Dream Invader?" David asked.

"Well, as Nephilims, we have the capacity to invade dreams. This is how we inspire regular people with ideas – either for inventions, or art, or some such thing. Pure Angels are better at it of course and it's really tricky to do." Rafaella explained.

"Not everyone can do it." Isaac said. "Some half-angels have the extra sensitivity for it, you know, like how some people seem more psychic than others."

"Like having ESP." David noted in understanding.

"Precisely." said Isaac.

"Lukas, remember the time that you were quacking like a duck?" Rafaella reminded him.

"What?" David almost choked on his food.

Lukas was frowning angrily as he remembered. "Yeah, I was Dream Invaded. That I was a duck and could only talk like a duck. I was quacking half the day until the teachers realized what must have happened and they had to Dream Invade me back."

"I remember that day." Joseph woke up laughing. "It was so funny."

Seeing Lukas' mutinous look, he mumbled a hasty apology. "But, couldn't you remember who Dream Invaded you in the first place?" David asked, aghast at the thought that you could be so vulnerable in your sleep.

"The Invader could make you forget he was there. You wouldn't even remember him. All you'll remember is the message." Lukas replied.

"That was a nasty trick." Rafaella was shaking her head. "And to think Innocent is being taken advantage of by those primates. He's a very powerful weapon."

Joseph opened his eyes again. "I don't think he's being taken advantaged on, or used. I think Innocent himself likes it. Heard him laughing his head off with their other buddy Dominic about it. Don't know who they targeted that time. Anyway, Innocent was going on and on about someone he Invaded. Boasting about it actually. They thought I was asleep when they were rambling on about their joke."

"Everyone thinks you're always asleep." Rafaella said drily.

Joseph only grinned. "Works to my advantage."

"But, can you, I don't know – lock your mind or something? Be protected from it?" David was asking.

Lukas only shrugged. "Haven't met a Nephilim yet who is impervious to it."

Everyone resumed eating but David continued to worry about the conversation. Being Dream Invaded! That sounded horrible. And you couldn't even remember who did it to you. What if he woke up the next day running around school naked, or dressing and talking like a little girl, or whatever crazy thing the Invader would make him do. David revolted against the idea of it.

"*Coffee, David?*" a syrupy voice breathed in his ear, startling him out of his thoughts. It was Tatiana again, floating and smiling prettily at him. David reminded himself to be extra nice to her. After all, as he had learned earlier, cherubs liked to snuggle. He had to repress a shudder at the thought and made a mental note to make sure he locked his room before sleeping.

"Thank you Tatiana. I'd love some."

Tatiana giggled and proceeded to pour him some coffee.

11 T377SF

The very first thing that David did when he woke up the next day was to make an inventory of himself. He practiced talking – still normal, walking – the same, and after racking his brain and insanely testing his reflexes, he heaved a sigh of relief that he had not been Dream Invaded by Zachary and his evil minions.

He bathed and dressed for the day and smiled a goodbye to the picture of his mom – a driver's license – which he had carefully propped in a place of honor on his study desk.

After consulting his electronic map of the Monastery, he headed to the Pearly Gates Cafe for breakfast. Lukas and Rafaella were already there and had saved him a seat.

"How are you both?" was his greeting to them. "Everything normal?"

Lukas nodded fervently. "Luckily. We have to watch our backs though. I just know Zachary has something planned -"

"Will you both just relax." Rafaella rolled her eyes at them. "You're killing my caffeine buzz and you're acting like pathetically paranoid schizoids."

David winced at Rafaella's assessment. She sure wasn't one to mince words.

"Besides, if they retaliate, then we'll worry and figure something out." she added.

"We don't get a caffeine buzz." David retorted lamely back at her, but he shrugged in agreement anyway and loaded his plate with breakfast food. Once he had finished gorging himself with a magnificent calorie fest and knocking back glasses of juice and coffee, he turned to Rafaella.

"Actually, you have a very good point. I don't want to walk around worrying if Zachary has set a trap for us, so, he's officially banned from inside my head for now."

Lukas was more reluctant. "I'll.......try?"

"Sounds good enough to me." David said. "Okay, what do we have today?"

First period was Sciences of the World, and today was Chemistry. Their instructor, Teacher Tellurium, had a mad scientist look about him, but he endeared himself to David right away with his generous attitude toward his students, his passion for the subject, and his infectious enthusiasm. He looked old-school, but David was pleasantly surprised to learn that he wasn't.

"Today we continue with 'Whatever You Feel Like Doing Day'." Teacher Tellurium announced, his voice full and robust. He looked like a tall, thin, and manic Santa Claus.

"Therefore, feel free to browse through your manual and choose the experiment that suits your fancy. Be daring! Discover and explore! No new invention was ever created without bravery and imagination."

He walked around the room.

"But, I would very much like a finished work at the end of class. So, rifle through those pages and get cracking. Get cracking!" he encouraged vigorously. "Just a reminder though, there are fire extinguishers under each table. Use them efficiently when needed."

There was the crisp, snapping sound of book pages being

flipped through as everyone took time to select what experiment to do for the day. Soon beakers were filled with chemicals, burners were fired up, masks and protective goggles snapped on.

David was having a hard time choosing which experiment to do, not that there was a lack of interesting choices. In fact, he could hardly believe that they were allowed to undertake such experiments in the Monastery.

To his right, Rafaella was already engrossed in reproducing Kevlar fibers, her pale green eyes gleaming with determination behind her goggles.

Kevlar was made of polymer fibers which were five times stronger than the same weight of steel for bullet resistant vests. It was also a handy protection against other weapons.

To his left, Lukas was furiously muttering under his breath as he measured and very carefully added chemicals to a solution that had something to do with genetics and the DNA. It was all very beyond David at the moment.

Katherine and Consortia had their own sweet and heady corner as they concocted lotions and shampoos, while Gertrude happily formulated her own flu medicine, incorporating natural herbs with the usual pharmacological mixture, hoping to create a better and more effective remedy.

David also couldn't help glancing occasionally at Innocent, the boy whom Joseph had pointed out as a Dream Invader. He looked harmless enough, slightly on the thin side, with a prominent nose and a nest of unruly curls on his head. David had to remind himself about what Joseph had said – that Innocent liked Dream Invasion. That he relished it and boasted about it.

Hard to believe from a quiet looking boy.

As David flipped through more pages, something caught his

eye – T377SF.

Type 377 Synthetic Fiber – Acid Corrosion Resistant

It sounded promising.

He still had a nasal memory of how Mr. And Mrs. Littlefield smelled – very strongly of sulfuric acid. Concentrated amounts of sulfuric acid.

David had found his experiment.

He glanced at the detailed formula and step-by-step process and proceeded to lay out the materials he needed on his work table. For the more sophisticated parts of the experiment, half the room of the large chemistry lab was mounted with all kinds of equipment that would be the envy of any advanced chemical laboratory in the world. David was pretty sure whatever equipment he needed would be found there.

The next couple of hours were quite engrossing and stimulating.

Teacher Tellurium walked about the room – brimming with energy – and observed everyone's experiment, throwing in a comment or a criticism as he went along. One time, a lazily floating cherub wandered inside the lab (they were forbidden from interrupting classes) floating on its back and happily drinking milk from a baby bottle.

"Oh my dear Putti," said Teacher Tellurium. "Hurry back outside before you're accidentally burned to a crisp in here."

The girl cherub was startled enough by Teacher Tellurium's words that she choked on the milk she was drinking and began coughing and spluttering. The teacher had to gently slap her on the back to help her breath again. She threw her milk bottle at Teacher

Tellurium's head and weaved angrily out of the lab.

"Tsk,tsk." said the Teacher. "What very bratty children they are."

The class had only been mildly disturbed by the exchange and continued on with their work.

"Quite an accomplishment, my dear." Teacher Tellurium nodded at Rafaella's work.

At Lukas' table he exclaimed, "Formidable!"

David looked up and caught Zachary's jealous scowl at the compliment and he couldn't help but grin. Another score for Lukas.

At Isaac and Joseph's experiment, Teacher Tellurium actually laughed. "What audacity! I don't quite recall this being in the manual."

"It's not, sir." was Isaac's sheepish reply.

"Very classic though." acknowledged the teacher. "Well, carry on and good luck with that."

Isaac and Joseph had apparently tackled the age-old alchemical fantasy and debacle of turning metal into gold. Of course, it had never been done.

Teacher Tellurium continued his way around the room, smiling kindly at Zachary's work and saying, "Well, at least you tried."

David and Lukas looked at each other and grinned.

Finally, the teacher made a stop at David's table and looked over his experiment. "Is it acid-resistant yet?"

"Yes sir, but only in room temperature and small doses of acid." David replied. "When the temperature changes and the concentration of acid increases, the solution is not as resistant." Wow! Did he just say that mouthful?

"And that is why there are several layers to the experiment."

shared Teacher Tellurium. "Explore them as much as you can in the time left – taking into consideration the factors of change. Good work, young man."

David beamed at the compliment.

When class was almost over, there was a sudden commotion in the middle of the room.

"Oh no! No! Ouch! Stop! STOP!" Giles was yelping.

It was the most words David had heard him say.

Teacher Tellurium was instantly at Giles side assessing the botched experiment. Giles was working on an ultra-industrial grade corrosive which he had 'tweaked' with additional compounds and was now melting his table and the floor. Some of the solution had also splashed across his front robe and was smoking and burning away the cloth.

The students backed away from the corrosive which was determinedly eating the floor while Teacher Tellurium powerfully yanked Giles away from the creeping solution.

"Just your average idiotic mistake, dear boy." Teacher Tellurium cheerfully announced. "Better Angel Mode it to the Infirmary. If that corrosive reaches your skin, it'll melt your skin, muscle and bones away."

Giles made another panicked yelp and zoomed out of the room.

Teacher Tellurium also zoomed – to David's side and grabbed his beakerful of T377 solution.

"Let's see if this works, shall we?" he jovially mused.

Teacher Tellurium, although bizarrely buoyant about the accident, expertly poured David's solution to Giles corrosive crater.

Instantly, the sizzling and hissing stopped and the creeping corrosive halted in its tracks. The area seemed to be blanketed in foamy snow.

"Good show!" exclaimed Teacher Tellurium. "Look class, Resistant trumps Corrosive. Good show David! And a fine Acid-Resistant Solution you have produced. Well done!"

There was a round of applause for David's solution and when the applause had died away, David once again heard Zachary's knuckles cracking.

This time, the cracking sounded more ominous than usual.

By the time David, Lukas and Rafaella arrived at the Cube, lunch had already started, so they opted for an empty table with Wolverine lumbering behind them, wagging his tail happily.

He had been waiting for Rafaella right outside the Chemistry Lab and he had even given a friendly bark at David whom he now recognized as Rafaella's friend.

Although he was still getting used to how Wolverine appeared – silvery and kind of ghostly but not – David was happy to see him too and proceeded to pet the massive dog. He had always wanted a pet, but he never had that luxury growing up in an orphanage and foster homes later on.

As expected, the food was heavenly and David, still mentally and habitually starved, stuffed himself with succulent paper-thin slices of roast beef, perfectly grilled baby back ribs, creamy and buttery mashed potatoes, and exquisitely fried and flavored chicken – the Colonel must be crying in envy somewhere.

David knew he would eventually get used to food being always available, but for now he was filling himself to the brim, topping it off with the homiest, yummiest apple pie he had ever tasted.

When he was done eating the lunch of a lifetime – so full he could hardly move – he finally resurfaced to reality and noticed Rafaella and Lukas grinning at him.

"Finally full?" Rafaella teased.

"Maybe." David laughed, holding down a giant burp. "My body thinks it's always starving."

"Yeah, I went through that phase too." Lukas admitted, a bit absentmindedly, "When my mom and I were on the run from the demented demons, there were times when we couldn't even get to food........" Lukas trailed off then he started mumbling confusing chemical terminologies, questioning his lab work and second-guessing himself. They only caught bits and pieces of it. "..........methyl methane sulfonate........ why the display of morphological aberrations?.......... hydrogen cyanide..........."

"Huh?" asked David.

"Ah, my favorite geek." Rafaella sighed at Lukas, then she turned to David and asked, "What was it that Teacher Tellurium said about Lukas work?"

"Formidable." David and Rafaella chorused.

"You did great completed work." she reminded Lukas. "Now, stop worrying your halo away."

Then, her eyes brightened at someone she could see approaching.

"Hey Lukas, look who it is."

"Here comes my favorite cherub." Lukas waved, motioning to the mentioned Putti to come to their table.

"Hey Froggy, where have you been? I haven't seen you in a while."

"Kitchen Duty." the cherub grunted.

David was surprised to meet a cherub who was different from

the regular mold of chirpily cheerful and indecently cute bunch. Froggy was actually frowning and he had the raspy and surly voice of a bad-tempered henchman.

"Froggy, we'd like you to meet our friend, David. He's new in school."

David smiled at Froggy who only sneered and grunted.

Maybe we should call him Grouchy, David thought. Or Grumpy.

"His real name is Frogarian." Lukas told David, "but we call him Froggy."

"Yeah, yeah, because I sound like a frog." Froggy snapped. When he saw Rafaella though, his face brightened, and as impossible as it seemed, his sour face cracked into a smile.

"Hi girlfriend." Froggy winked at her, tossing his blond curls in an invisible breeze.

"Oh Froggy, I bet you say that to all the girls." Rafaella could only smile indulgently. "You're such a flirt. I know you have lots of girlfriends in this place."

The cherub shrugged, his wings continuously fluttering. "Sorry angel, but I'm too good-looking to remain a one-woman cherub. But don't worry mi Rafaella, you're at the top of my list."

"Promises, promises." she sighed in pretend dramatics.

"Hey Froggy, what's the latest news?" Lukas interrupted their banter. "Anything hot?"

"You betcha kid." He looked around to make sure no one else was listening except the three of them.

"Abbot Anderson is about to lay an egg. He was so angry yesterday I thought he'd give himself an aneurysm."

"Why? What happened?" Rafaella asked.

"Some overeager senior students went out on a mission. Think there were four of them. Anyways, I heard that everything went okay during the mission. It was the getting back that something came up."

"What?" David, Lukas and Rafaella chorused.

Froggy checked around them again. "They saw a hellhound lurking outside these walls – and the idiots brought it inside. They freaking brought it inside! Thought they were being useful or resourceful or some such idiotic reason."

"A hellhound!" David was stunned. He really was in an alternate universe.

"Where is it now Froggy?" Rafaella asked, concerned but obviously excited.

Froggy looked at her slyly.

"I know what you're thinking Warrior Princess. But you're not getting any chance to slaughter it. Prefect Mac was all for having the students make a combat demo of it, so were the other warrior trainers. But the Abbot put his foot down. Absolute no on the subject."

Rafaella sighed. "What a challenge that would have been."

"Where is the hellhound now though?" Lukas wondered.

"Tucked away somewhere maybe." Froggy guessed. "Or maybe vaporized. Haven't heard the buzz about the outcome yet."

David was still processing Froggy's information. A hellhound just outside the walls! Who knew what else was lurking immediately outside the Monastery. It was like stepping outside your home and getting run over by a truck – right on your front porch. Of course, this was much worse.

"What exactly is a hellhound Froggy?" David inquired.

Froggy frowned again. "David is it? Not exactly the sharpest knife in the kitchen, are you?"

David reddened.

"A hellhound is what it is. A hell. hound. Sheesh!" With an exasperated huff, Froggy zoomed out of the Dining Hall.

"Are you sure he's your favorite cherub?" David looked at Lukas, still smarting under Froggy's insult.

Lukas and Rafaella were laughing. Apologizing and laughing.

"He likes you." Rafaella assured him. "That's how he shows approval."

"By insulting me?"

"Yep." said Lukas. "I think he was just waiting for the opportunity."

Rafaella added, "He just takes getting used to, but really, he's okay."

"He's our eyes and ears in this place." Lukas nodded.

"If you say so." was David's doubtful reply. He still thought Froggy too abrasive and downright rude. But on the upside – he was a well of knowledge and information. Intellectually speaking, it really was a smart relationship to cultivate.

12   Nocking With Patience

Every afternoon and the whole day of Friday was devoted to Warrior Training. Many of his classmates, especially Consortia and Katherine, moaned and complained about this – how it was exhausting, how it bruised them, how they could be creating *celestially supreme* garments instead.

David thought the school was right – which was a first for him – about the schedule. What could be more important than surviving living outside the Monastery walls and helping other Nephilims and regular people who needed rescuing?

You wouldn't be creating music, or clothes, or inspiring people with ideas if you had been slashed to pieces. What you'd get was an early admission to the real Pearly Gates.

Rafaella agreed with him too. Lukas, not so much. He also would rather spend more time on other subjects than do Warrior Training.

Teacher Peregrine scheduled David to practice sword-fighting again. This time, he was paired with Joseph to clash blades with.

Joseph's blade of preference was a fifty-four inch full tang Samurai Sword. It was a pretty lengthy sword to wield and its carbon steel blade was quite impressive.

"I especially like how it curves just so……see?" Joseph demonstrated, slashing the samurai in the air. "And the blade is slim, which in my opinion is easier to maneuver."

Joseph and Isaac had apparently bonded over their love of oriental swords. They didn't have many other interests in common, but they were frenetic fanatics of oriental swords. Isaac's favorite sword – David learned – was also a Katana.

Soon it was time for their training to commence.

David and Joseph bowed to each other, the opening courtesy of any fight. David was clutching the Gothic Sword again, still his favorite despite trying other blades, and already his mind was leaping to calculating how Joseph would be as an opponent.

David knew Joseph was stealthily strong but he didn't know Joseph was also an aggressive fighter. He came at David fearlessly and with amazing technique, cutting and slashing, his feet on a forward motion as David retreated from the continuos onslaught.

David was able to parry his attacks and even though he was a new learner, David managed to hold his ground, eventually putting in some aggressive attacks of his own.

He could see Joseph's eyes widen in surprise and admiration.

They continued with the fight for some time – always in Angel Mode, blurry and quick, their hands a whirlwind of slashes and thrusts.

David learned that when it came to fighting, they always had to be in Angel Mode because demons, being pure evil without a drop of human blood, were incredibly strong and fast. They also had no mercy whatsoever.

Three cuts each later, David and Joseph's fight ended in a draw.

"Man, that's really impressive!" Joseph gasped, a bit breathless from all the exertion. "Two days in and already the fight ended in a draw."

Joseph crumpled himself down on the floor, resting his back on a wall with his sword beside him. David did the same.

"I'm not one to boast, David, I'm too lazy for that -"

David laughed.

"- but honestly, I'm not such an easy opponent. You're really good. I mean, instinctively, in-your-bones, good."

"Aww Joseph." David reddened. "You're making me blush."

"I mean it." Joseph earnestly replied. It was the most energy he had exerted into a conversation. "I bet your angel-parent is a warrior. It must be genetics. Your responses are instinctive. You move like a warrior and after only two days of training. Two days! I've been training for four years now."

"Wow! That's brutal." David said. "You know, this is the first time I've heard about the angel-parent affecting fighting skills. Does that mean what your angel-parent does can determine what you become?"

"Oh sure." Joseph nodded. "Genetics definitely play into what we decide to be and how good we are. But, we're not forced to follow in their footsteps. That's what's so great about free will. You get to choose what you want to do." Joseph studied his Samurai Sword.

"What does your angel-parent do?" David asked.

Joseph smiled. "He's a Messenger."

"Like Angel Gabriel?" said David, recalling an Angelology lesson.

"Exactly." Joseph affirmed. "He makes announcements, delivers important messages. It can be in person or through dreams and visions. This duty is what many Pure Angels do because it's one of the ways that God can deliver messages to people."

"Awesome."

"But it's not for me." Joseph shared in all honesty. "I just don't see myself doing that. Not interested in being a Messenger at all."

"You'd rather be a Warrior." David concluded.

Joseph nodded, getting to his feet. "It's the only activity that wakes me up. This and eating."

They both laughed.

"C'mon, it's time for our next training schedule." Joseph said.

They headed to Teacher Peregrine to find out what was next on their training list. It was Archery for David while Joseph went off to Weaponless Combat.

David had never tried archery before and the two persons to help him start off were Lukas and Gertrude.

As it turned out, Lukas was seriously good at archery. He was an excellent archer and he demonstrated a few shots for David on a regular target so David would have an idea on how it was done.

"He's one of the best." Gertrude praised him. "And I don't just mean in our class, but in the entire school."

Lukas looked flustered as he threaded his arrow into a bow.

"Let us show you how it's done." Gertrude continued and they proceeded to demonstrate the proper techniques of archery.

Gertrude handed David a recurve bow, explaining, "A recurve bow is my top choice. It delivers more power and energy compared to the traditional 'D' longbow. Plus, with a recurve bow you can make the bow smaller and still deliver the same impact. That makes it a lighter and less cumbersome choice when you travel. Or in our case, when we go on missions." she ended solemnly.

She showed him the proper shooting stance with feet shoulder width apart, one foot in front of the other.

"Technically, your feet should be five to ten inches apart, but you really must adjust it to what's comfortable for you."

Gertrude lay an arrow on the ground in front of David.

"Visualize a line from you, to your target. This will be your shooting line. I simply placed this arrow in front of you as a temporary guide while you're practicing."

She patted him on the back for encouragement. "Soon enough, with constant practice, you won't need an arrow guide."

She made David wear a protective glove and showed him how to nock the arrow in the center of the bowstring.

David couldn't help but notice how great she smelled – like spring flowers or a bouquet of roses, (there had been a delivery at the orphanage where David had grown up).

Dementia! What was he thinking?

David made himself focus on the archery lesson. This wasn't the time to be a.......*boy.*

Get a grip! He told himself. *Demons, weapons, archery. Combat. These are what's important.*

David held the bowstring with his first three fingers – just like they showed him - settling the string in the crease of his last joint. He used his thumb to keep the arrow stable.

Then he gripped his bow firmly, arm locked straight, and Gertrude adjusted his elbow so that it rolled slightly outwards.

"Now, face your target." Gertrude instructed. "Draw the string back until your index finger is almost touching the corner of your mouth."

"Aim." Gertrude continued.

"Remember to use your back muscles and shoulder to pull the string." Lukas reminded him.

David narrowed his eyes on the target some distance away, training his eyes to follow his arrow guide and shooting line.

"You are to take a deep breath, hold it, and release the arrow, alright?" Gertrude said.

And just as David was about to follow Gertrude's instructions, Lukas began jabbering about the Archer's Paradox, Power Strokes, and Tiller Rotation.

"Dearest Lukas," Gertrude smiled sweetly at him. "Please shut up."

Then turning to David she said, "And David, just shoot the darn thing already."

David released the arrow and held his shooting position until he saw his arrow hit the target. He made a whoop of delight.

Sure, it was at the very periphery, but at least he didn't miss.

"Wonderful attempt, David." Gertrude praised him. "Let's do some more, shall we?"

David nodded eagerly. He never thought archery would be so much fun.

David picked up an arrow and noticed something on it. He looked at it more closely. Etched on the metal was the word *Hope*. On another arrow, it said *Love*. Another arrow said *Joy*.

"Hey!" David exclaimed. "A word is written on each arrow."

"It makes the arrow more powerful." Gertrude explained. "What you see here are *Words of Life*. It increases the power of our weapon and is more fatal to demons."

Lukas picked up an arrow and showed it to David.

"This one is the most powerful yet. Look."

The arrow had a cross etched on it.

"One of these, just one, will make a demon explode. Boom! Completely annihilated to bits. The other arrows, the *Words of Life* ones, will make a demon burn and will kill the demon certainly, but a cross-arrow..........instant dust." Lukas gestured excitedly with his hands to prove his point.

"And like our other weapons, look how our angelic substance

affects the metal." Lukas went on.

"I did notice." David said. "The arrow is burning up, lighting up."

"Double effectivity, I must say." Gertrude commented. She looked very pretty in her sports gear, her dark blonde hair up in a ponytail, a constant smile on her lips. David inexplicably felt lighter and happier next to her.

Lukas punched a code into a sleek remote control and David heard the whoosh of things popping up.

"Now for our real target." said Lukas excitedly.

"Argh!" David yelled, startled.

Right in front of him were life-like replicas of demons. They looked like the evil incarnates who had cornered him – Mr. And Mrs. Littlefield – in demon form.

"Lukas!" David clutched his chest. "Some warning would have helped!"

"Oh no, I'm such a nano-brain." Lukas apologized. "I'm so sorry David!

David looked at the demon targets again. It was creepy how they looked life-like. "They look so real.......what are they made of?"

"Silicone, latex, resin and some such thing." Lukas replied. "The Weapons Master make them look too real, doesn't he?"

David could only nod silently.

"I'm really sorry David. I forgot to warn you. And to think that these creeped me out the first time I saw them. I'm such a moron."

"Yes, you are." Gertrude replied in somber agreement. "The demon targets require time for familiarity, but you will become accustomed to them. It's better this way you see," she gently told David. "It is in the hopes that when we combat them, their appearance will no longer be frightening nor intimidating to us. They will be, how do they say it?......blah?"

David couldn't help but smile at Gertrude's attempt to be current. She was right, of course, he acknowledged. The more they all got used to how the demons appeared, the less strange, weird, and intimidating they would look.

He stared at the targets again.

They varied in height but there was a commonality about them. Tall, bony but broad, an expanse of wings – some unfurled, others tucked behind them. If their eyes glowed yellow, how even more real they would become.

David could feel the anger and bloodlust tightening his chest. His facial features turned cold and stony.

Gertrude, ever empathic and insightful, touched him on the shoulder. Very quietly she said, "In archery, and in any battle, you must always be master of your emotions. Anger, although a great motivator, will only make you lose focus and ultimately defeat you."

She handed him a cross-arrow. "Remember, aim carefully. Take a deep breath, hold it, and release the arrow."

David nocked the arrow in the bowstring, his fingers trembling slightly. Once again he gripped the bow firmly, adjusting his shooting stance. Then he pulled the string, his index finger brushing his face.

He could remember them. Their hisses and taunts. Their awful, cruel faces. Their fangs. Their glowing yellow eyes.

David took a deep breath, still unsettled by the sight of demons – even silicone ones – and released the arrow.

It went too wide and didn't even hit a target.

Gertrude calmly handed him another arrow. "Try again."

David looked into her serene eyes, her quiet attitude, and

began to feel calmer, more clear-headed.

He nocked the arrow (*Patience*) into his bow and tried again. This time he hit a target-demon, squarely in the chest.

Lukas and Gertrude cheered at his victorious shot.

David looked at the silicone figure, feeling an intense satisfaction in seeing his arrow lodged deeply into it. He tried picturing an actual demon burning from the fatal hit.

Lukas was studying David's facial expression. "Feels great doesn't it?"

"Explosive." David replied. "Let's shoot more demons."

Gertrude could only shake her head in disbelief.

"Boys." she muttered. "Would you rather talk about how you're feeling, David? How these figures affected you initially?"

"No way." David shook his head vigorously. "I'd rather shoot them to bits."

He turned to Lukas. "C'mon Lukas, load up."

Lukas was already nocking an arrow into his bow-string, grinning in anticipation.

It was one satisfying, arrow-flying lesson.

In a small way, David felt that he had a little revenge on his evil foster parents. He was still savoring the sight of his last arrow shooting a silicone-demon on the forehead.

"Once you really get the hang of this, then we'll move on to moving targets." Lukas promised.

"Moving targets?" David gaped. "Sweet!"

Warrior Training ended with this exhilarating thought and they returned to the Monastery to wash up for dinner.

After dinner, David, Rafaella and Lukas lounged around at the Pearly Gates Cafe for some coffee and dessert.

Rafaella had kicked off her boots and was comfortably curled-up on a day bed amidst a sea of fluffy pillows. David and Lukas sat across from her, each one sprawled on a plush wingback chair, their feet propped on top of fat, circular foot stools.

David was inhaling the fantastic aroma of his chocolate latte with a hint of pumpkin spice, while Lukas carefully sipped his rosemary and orange tea.

"You're such a girl, Lukas." Rafaella laughed, her pale green eyes bright with amusement as she observed Lukas' prudent and scholarly manner. His little finger was carefully lifted and crooked as he gingerly sipped his tea.

"This is a very healthy combination, you know. Much healthier than your latte and espresso choices." Lukas scoffed at them. "Espresso Rafaella? Really? Before bedtime?"

She stuck her tongue out at him. "Doesn't matter to us how much caffeine we pour down our throats. No effect whatsoever."

David raised his cup to them. "Thank God for that. This stuff is great and I can have as many cups as I want. For free!"

He was about to bite into a warm blueberry muffin when the lights began flickering rapidly for several seconds.

"What's going on?" he asked.

Lukas and Rafaella glanced at each other, looking both pleased and worried at the same time, which was a weird combination of facial expressions.

"Angel visit." Rafaella murmured.

"A Pure Angel." Lukas disclosed. "When they visit or appear in their true form, they really mess up electrical connections and gadgets too."

"I wonder who the angel is visiting?" David thought aloud. "Do you think it's the Abbot? An official visit? Wow – straight from heaven! How cool is that?"

"They usually come during office hours when it's an official visit." said Rafaella, surprisingly in a small and miserable voice.

It was only then that David realized what they weren't saying.

"It's a parent visit isn't it?" he asked flatly. "Some kid right now is being visited by his angel-parent."

Rafaella and Lukas could only nod mutely.

"Great. That's just great." was David's angry exclamation.

"But you've only been here a few days." Rafaella protested. "I know your father will visit you. He will! Everyone's angel-parent does!"

"If you're trying to make me feel better, it's not working." David snapped at her. "Yeah, everyone's angel-parent comes to visit. Maybe except mine. I don't even know who that....that....."

Lukas was shifting uneasily in his seat. "Careful David – they can hear you."

David looked around them. The cafe was pretty quiet and their next neighbor was some tables away.

"Who can hear me Lukas?"

"Everyone in heaven can." Lukas whispered. "They can hear us anytime, all the time."

David's eyes were a furious, stormy grey. "Then that's even better! That's just absolutely perfect! My father can hear me all the time? Anytime?"

Lukas and Rafaella nodded.

"He knew all along what was happening to me.........knew what I was going through – and he just........he just.....and what about losing my mom? Whoever the scumbag my father is -"

Lukas and Rafaella winced.

"- he knew I was all alone! And this year when I had to live on the streets........." David just couldn't go on. He was mute with anger. His jaw was clenched so hard he thought his teeth would break.

"David," Rafaella tried to calm him down, "I don't know what's going on with your dad and why he hasn't shown himself to you yet. They work in a different way, you see, and they're on a completely different time structure."

Lukas was nodding earnestly. "When they say time is relative and a millennia for us is a blink of an eye to God -"

"Tell me this though," David interrupted. "When you arrived here, how long before your angel-parent came to visit?"

Lukas fidgeted before he could answer. "My first night here."

David could feel his head burning up and he had to swallow several times before he could speak again.

"What about you Rafaella?"

She was glaring at him as she replied, "The same. My first night here too but - "

"Then spare me the homily." David cut through her words.

"Look, you jerk." Rafaella snapped at David. "We all have issues – yes! We all do!" she emphasized at his sneer.

"But we try to understand their world too and their responsibilities. The sooner you come to terms with the fact that they do love us in their own way, but they can't be with us, then the sooner that you'll be at peace with yourself and with our world. It's the only way that you'll know who the real enemy is."

"How do you know?" David blasted at her. "How do you know what I'm going through? What did you really have to live with to be *at peace with yourself*?"

David knew he was being snide and ugly, but he was just too angry to care. "Mommy not give you enough money? Not enough dresses or toys before you came here?"

"Hey guys, come on, let's not do this -" Lukas tried to pacify them but David and Rafaella ignored his attempts.

Rafaella stood up, her stance becoming more rigid and her tone colder and colder, reaching sub-zero temperatures. "My mother is my angel-parent. My father was human. Was, David." she continued, her voice as brittle as icicles.

"I say *Was*, David, because my father is dead. The demons killed him right after my tenth birthday. My angel mother didn't do anything about it. She let him die. So yes," she hissed in barely controlled, roiling anger, "I do know what I'm talking about. I do know something about living with the truth and trying to find peace."

She turned around and abruptly left them. She didn't even bother picking up her discarded boots. Rafaella speeded away in a blur, leaving only David's colossal feelings of shock and guilt behind.

Back in the cozy privacy of his bedroom, David was tossing and turning on the bed, the sheets all tangled up and messy around him. He couldn't sleep, he felt like a putrified fungus for all the mean things he had said to Rafaella.

He had tried to apologize but she had locked herself in her room and refused to open the door. In the end, he and Lukas had to leave because it was curfew time.

Yes, he was angry at his father and even though Lukas and Rafaella tried to explain and justify his actions and his pure-angel responsibilities, David would still be angry at his father.

His dad had a lot of explaining to do.

Unfortunately, his dad was not making any personal appearance.

And this hurt even more.

David punched his pillow into shape. Where was his father?

Actually the bigger question was, who was his father? David didn't even know. And it hurt to know that most kids had an angel-parent visiting on their very first night here. A parent who would welcome them, explain things to them, and continue to visit as they grew up. Regularly or sporadically, to David that hardly mattered. The crucial point was that they visited.

"Oh mom," David sighed to the silent room. "Who did you get caught up with? And where is he?"

As expected, there was no answer.

Still, whatever anger he felt towards his father should be directed towards – his father. He should have never blasted his frustrations to Rafaella. It was unfair of him.

He did admire how she blasted him right back. She had also hurled a heavy truth at him. The truth about her past, her hardships, and most of all, her father.

She had been with him when he died.

The demons had killed her father, right in front of her.

David could feel the guilt pressing heavily upon him. It was as if an anvil, a grand piano, a loaded crate, and a humungous truck had fallen on top of him, and he was underneath it all, flat and smeared on the pavement.

He would apologize to Rafaella first thing tomorrow morning.

He turned off his bedside lamp. It really was time to get some sleep, or at least try doing so.

When David did drift off to a restless slumber, he dreamed of a dagger.

It was an incredibly vivid dream, full of detail and instruction.

The dagger gleamed before him and when he reached for it,

he could touch its cold strength. He felt the shape in his hands, the length of it, the angles and planes.

The dagger was seventeen inches long with a double-edged blade in a mirror finish. Its cross-guard and pommel were made of fine cast metal extending to a five-inch handle of powerfully wrapped leather. As the dagger slowly rotated in his dream, David noted a potent insignia etched exquisitely on its hilt – a blazing sun with rays radiating outwards. The dagger itself emitted a strange but glorious light.

The Hand of God.

That was the name of the dagger.

Tomorrow, David knew what to do.

13 † Elementary Guardianship

David's first priority the following day was to apologize to Rafaella, but she wasn't making it easy for him.

Now that David knew where her room was, he went there first, hoping that she would still be there and hopefully open the door for him this time.

No such luck.

When he went to the Pearly Gates Cafe for breakfast, she wasn't there too. Lukas was also non-plussed as to her whereabouts.

Their first lesson for that Wednesday was *Elementary Guardianship* and David finally saw Rafaella in class. He was about to approach her and take the opportunity to say he was sorry, but her glacial warning look, fierce frown, and determined headshake, told him to STAY AWAY.

"Better not push it, buddy." Lukas advised, also witnessing Rafaella's frightening refusal.

"I can see that." David murmured, deciding that it really was best to let Rafaella thaw a bit more. "Let's find seats."

The classroom for *Elementary Guardianship* was an unconventional set-up. It was a combination baby nursery and play-place with the cheerful décor of bright, primary colors. Large windows let in loads of sunlight and there was the merry assortment of baby toys and activity centers.

Their teacher was a large, solid bulk of a woman who looked like she could throw every one of them single-handedly. She would blend right in with some hulking members of the Women's Olympic Team.

She had a big voice to go along with her big persona, and she heartily greeted them a good morning and welcomed them to class.

"We have finished discussing the Basic Tenets of Guardianship and today, we move forward to the Practical Application of Guardianship." Teacher Romana boomed. She turned to David, which somewhat alarmed him, and said, "To our newcomer, Mr. Cross, I'll hand you a copy of what we have already discussed in class so that you may keep up with the lesson."

"Guardianship, as I have emphasized before, is an important and primary duty of Nephilims and Angels alike. Whether you pursue it as an eventual career or not, you must still be knowledgeable and equipped to act as Guardian."

Teacher Romana looked about the room. "There may be instances when our Guardianship services are mandatorily called upon. What this means, ladies and gentlemen, is that when you are called to act as Guardian Angel, you will perform your duty whether you like it or not."

David could see Zachary and Giles frowning at this information. God really should discount those two from the Guardian Angel list, David thought.

"We have very special visitors this day and for the next several days." continued Teacher Romana. "Our visitors come directly from heaven, and they have wonderfully accommodated us to assist in our Guardianship Skills Development."

Teacher Romana opened an adjacent door and in came crawling twenty – babies.

"Welcome dear Puttlings. Welcome!" she effusively greeted the gurgling, cooing bunch.

The babies were newborn cherubs. So newly born that they didn't even have wings yet. They could crawl and hold on to furniture, but they couldn't talk yet and could only communicate like a human baby, with squeals of delight and laughter or incessant crying and bawling.

It was mayhem.

Each student was given a Puttling to watch over and Guardianship meant that the newborn cherub mustn't come to any injury or harm. The Puttling must also be introduced to play activities and other helpful tools to improve their motor and cognitive development.

It was a baby-sitting meets covert operations scenario.

Poor Joseph failed miserably with Puttling Guardianship. His attention kept wandering and his baby cherub fell off a chair twice, smacking hard on the floor and crying non-stop afterwards.

Rafaella morphed into a queen-mother/warrior-goddess, and she attacked the training like a battle ground, fiercely protecting her Puttling to the point of insanity, glaring and growling at anyone or anything that came near them. She was successful, ferocious and fearsome.

Lukas seemed tentative and out of sorts. He appeared to like babies, he just didn't know how to act around them or how to take care of them. At first, he carried his Puttling awkwardly, looking as though the baby might tumble out his arms any minute. He did get the hang of it after a while and spent an enjoyable session playing with his happy newborn.

The Puttlings looked like human babies but they exhibited cherub qualities. They were stronger than normal babies and were pushing furniture around when someone's attention wandered, or lifting heavy objects which invariably fell on them or someone else. They also loved grabbing just about anything and putting it inside their mouth – thankfully not swallowing it, but crunching it to bits – a watch, a ball, Katherine's necklace, a pen, and incredibly the leg of an activity table. That Puttling belonged to Giles who frequently left his newborn to fend on its own until it was chewing the leg off the table. Teacher Romana gave Giles a scolding and low marks for his neglect.

Isaac was great with his newborn, admitting to taking care of his human brothers and sisters who were younger than him. Katherine and Consortia were giddy and excited, exactly like schoolgirls playing mommy. They pampered and hugged and squeezed their Puttlings, raining kisses on the adorable babies and wishing constantly out loud that they could dress their charges in fashionable baby outfits.

Gertrude, who had a calming effect on everyone, had an expectedly calm Puttling who happily followed her instructions and played baby gym and other toys when asked to do so.

David also had experience with taking care of younger kids from his orphanage days so he was comfortable with his Puttling, letting the newborn explore his surroundings but keeping a close watch on him to prevent injury.

His newborn was a mischievous one who tried to get away with things and David had his hands full stopping his Puttling from throwing furniture to other Puttlings, or attempting to jump on other newborns, or chew on David's shoe! His newborn liked clambering all over David and he happily settled sitting on David's shoulders where he could view the entire room, making and blowing bubbles with his own spit.

When the Guardianship Training was over, everybody heaved

a sigh of relief – except for Consortia and Katherine who began crying earnestly at the thought of being separated from their babies.

Zachary was in trouble. His Puttling had broken a wrist from a bad fall and he had to accompany Teacher Romana and his newborn to the Infirmary. After which, David learned, Teacher Romana was marching Zachary to Prefect Macarius' office for disciplinary action.

Everybody was chattering about how fun but exhausting it was to care for Puttlings.

"I was so afraid something would happen to my newborn, I had to really guard him!" exclaimed Rafaella to Lukas.

"Don't worry, not even a fly could have approached your newborn. You were like a lioness with a cub – to the nth level." Lukas laughed. "You looked positively insane, Rafaella."

"Yeah," David tried to chime in but he quieted down when Rafaella only glared at him. He had forgotten that she was still mad at him and before he could begin to apologize, Rafaella had walked away again.

David tried to hurry off after her but Lukas stopped him. "Give her more time. She won't walk away when she's ready to talk."

Next on their schedule were elective classes. Lukas had Latin so he and David went separate ways. David's class was *Carpentry and Metallurgy* which he had been looking forward to all morning.

Their Carpentry and Metallurgy shop was located on the ground floor of the Monastery. It was a large, bright room with high ceilings and tall windows. The shop also opened to the Monastery grounds for those students working on large-scale projects that required outdoor space, or for students who simply enjoyed working in the brisk, frigid air.

Teacher Coppersmith was a burly and capable Nephilim with precise and callused fingers, carefully dressed in protective gear. He was the kind of person who was happiest in his workshop, handling tools, crafting projects and supervising students.

David's classmates were working on ongoing projects and upon arriving in class, they proceeded to do so. Most of the boys had opted for *Carpentry and Metallurgy* except Lukas and Isaac. Although David was not surprised to see that Rafaella was taking the class (where else would a devoted warrior be?), he was surprised that there were hardly any girls in it. There was only Rafaella and one other female that David didn't know.

Teacher Coppersmith approached David and welcomed him.

"Is there any project in particular that you wish to undertake?" the teacher asked him. "If something is of interest to you, then we can start there."

"I want to make a dagger sir." David decisively replied.

"A dagger. Very well then," Teacher Coppersmith nodded. "let's get you started."

He directed David to a room where he could change his clothes for sturdy, protective gear, and also handed David thick and fitted work gloves, goggles, and a welding mask.

"Goggles are a must. You must protect your eyes at all times when you're working. We don't want any accidents here." the teacher seriously reminded David.

Then he proceeded to discuss with David the basic steps of making a dagger, handing him an instruction manual for further reference.

"And when it is time to work on any machinery," said Teacher Coppersmith, "you must call me so that I may show you how it is done properly."

David's dream about the dagger remained vivid in his mind, as though the image had been seared into his brain. When he closed his eyes, he could picture every detail of the dagger from the tip of the blade, to the edge of the handle.

First he familiarized himself with the tools he would need: the anvil, various hammers such as cross and straight peens, a sledge hammer, set hammer and flatter. He explored chisels, punches, hardies and drifts; files, a vise, torch, grinder, buffer and drill press. He studied the forge, the quench tank, the slack tub and handled tongs until they felt like an extension of his own hand.

David was ready to begin creating the dagger so he carefully chose his metal of carbon steel with a carbon rating of 80 points to ensure a blade that would be superior, resilient, and tough. With his selected metal to work with, David carried it to the forge – basically a super-sized oven – in order to start the heating process. Once the steel was heated to a burning red, David dived into the process of drawing-out: increasing the length of the steel and reducing its thickness. This was achieved by hammering at the glowing metal and David diligently pounded away until the shape of a dagger took form.

Next he began tapering the blade to create the tip and the tang, the noisy clangs of his hammer hitting at an angle to accomplish the desired result. David worked on the blade a section at a time, heating small portions until it was red-hot, then shaping it with hammers and other tools. He flipped the would-be dagger repeatedly during the hammering to ensure that both sides were evenly worked.

Several times during the forging, David normalized the steel – placing it back to the forge to be reheated, then cooling it down to smoothen the structure of the blade. This was succeeded with annealing of the blade, the purpose of which was to make the steel soft and easier to grind or cut. Annealing required for David to heat up the metal again, then cooled-back down gradually. This process took several hours to more than a day in the outside world, but thanks to Nephilim ingenuity and a nifty insulating material, annealing was completed in half an hour, which was a great help to David since he wanted to finish his dagger right away.

David consulted Teacher Coppersmith every so often to ask questions and in turn, the teacher checked in on his work to ascertain that David was performing the sword-making process correctly.

Now that the metal was soft and pliant, it was time to engrave the insignia on the dagger. David fervently etched the blazing sun design, his eyes narrowed in concentration as he carved the symbol onto the dagger. He then dunked his still-evolving dagger into the quench tank filled with oil, for reheating. This would harden the steel once more and prepare it for cutting. Then David proceeded to temper the steel, doing this process several times until he achieved the desired level of hardness; producing a tough blade that would be strong, but not too hard that it would be brittle.

When he was completely satisfied with the blade he had made, David went on to make the crossguard, pommel, and then the handle. He measured his almost finished dagger, smiling as it hit the correct length in his dream – twelve-inches, full tang, double-edged blade with a five-inch handle. Seventeen inches total.

Next, David made quick work in strongly wrapping the handle with exceptional leather, following the wrapping pattern in his crystalline dream. After doing so, David studied the dagger he was holding in his hand.

He had done it! He had actually finished the dagger!

Well, almost finished. There remained the buffing and

polishing to be done.

He fitted the buffer attachment to the bench grinder and brightened the blade to a mirror-finish. Finally, David turned to the whetstone to sharpen the blade. David was even more grateful for Angel Mode as he angled the blade against the whetstone, sharpening his dagger to a beautiful but deadly finish.

David felt an overwhelming responsibility to re-create the blade as he had seen in his dream, and he was pressed with an unexplainable urgency about the project. He just knew that he had to finish the dagger during this class.

David studied the finished dagger. The shiny blade glimmered with the sunlight, the handle fit perfectly into his hand. The weight and substance of the weapon was comforting, like a security blanket, or like a hidden stash of emergency money.

He needed a temporary sheath for the dagger, until he could make a handsome scabbard for it. So for now, David settled for a leather sheath which he held together with rivets. He also fashioned a belt that he could wear to secure the sheath with. That way, he could always carry the dagger with him, just hidden beneath his clothes.

"You have made quick work, young David." observed Teacher Coppersmith. "A finished dagger! And on your first day in the shop. What was the hurry though, I wonder?"

David shrugged. "I'm not sure sir, but I just really wanted to finish it."

"May I see the dagger please?"

David handed the weapon to Teacher Coppersmith who looked at it closely, his nose almost touching the blade.

"This design looks very familiar." he murmured gruffly. "An older design......I'm sure I've encountered it before. I simply can't recall right now............most unusual of me to forget........" he turned the dagger around, inspecting every inch of it.

"This is impressive work, David." complimented the teacher. "You certainly seem to have the passion for shop work. This insignia-" he mused, "I know this insignia. Where have I seen it before?"

Teacher Coppersmith handed the dagger back to David. "Well, you have given me quite an interesting puzzle to solve. Frankly, I will be spending my free time searching the archives for the origin of this dagger design." he held up a hand. "Do not tell me where you copied it from, David. I'm very much anticipating the challenge of the hunt."

David breathed a sigh of relief. Thank God Teacher Coppersmith decided not to ask him questions about the dagger. For some reason, David felt a compulsion to keep its origins secret. He also didn't want to discuss his dream and how clear the detail of it was. He just knew that he must keep the existence of the dagger to himself.

David sheathed the dagger and kept it with him.

The Hand of God.

Why had he dreamed about it? What was its purpose?

14 Blade versus Sticks

David wolfed down his lunch beside a worried Lukas. Rafaella had chosen to sit far from them, her faithful Wolverine nuzzling against her hand. Apparently, she was still mad at David.

David was eager to get to Warrior Training and find out what was in store for him that afternoon. Yesterday's sword fight with Joseph and arrow slaying of the target demons had been hugely satisfying.

Teacher Peregrine started David off with sword practice once again, reminding David that he must master the elements of one weapon before moving on to the next. David picked up what he considered to be an old friend by now, the Gothic Sword, which truly felt like an extension of his hand.

When he turned around, David was surprised to face a stony and aloof Rafaella. She was holding a shiny silver Nunchaku in her hand.

"Let's see you fight a weapon besides a sword." she boldly challenged.

"Are you here just to pick a fight with me, Rafaella?" David frowned at her, but she only scoffed at the question.

"Careful David, your ego is showing." she mocked. "Teacher Peregrine assigned me as your opponent today, so we don't have a choice."

"I don't want to fight you when you're angry with me." David said.

"Well, I do. So shut up and start fighting." then she warned him, "Don't hold back because I'm a girl, David. I won't hesitate to pulverize you."

Before David could protest anymore, Rafaella began swiveling and whirling her nunchaku around her body. She was lightning fast, and the whooshing and slapping sounds of the nunchuks were impressively intimidating.

Rafaella swung the nunchakus in repeated L-strikes and X's, then she held a fighting stance and locked her nunchuks into a defensive x.

She was obviously waiting for David to make the first move.

David made bold figure eights with the Gothic Sword and moved in for sharp slashes at Rafaella. She calmly blocked his move with the locked nunchuks, forcefully deterring his sword and then quickly moving in for a counter-attack on his chest.

David staggered backwards as the hit plowed him powerfully on the solar plexus.

Rafaella resumed her defensive pose and waited for David to attack again. David had to rethink his strategy. She was obviously an expert in her weapon, and her footwork was fast and impeccable.

David moved in again, this time, swinging and slashing his sword rapidly, looking for an opportunity to score a point with a direct hit.

Rafaella, in turn, executed rapid swing through moves to block David's sword. Even while engaged in combat, David had to admire how phenomenal she was as she did shoulder swings and spin combos, constantly changing the direction of her nunchucks to repeatedly rebuff his attacks and to confuse him at the same time.

Again, as Rafaella did rapid upwards and downwards swings, David wasn't fast enough to block the nunchucks and the silver metal hit him smack on the face.

David could feel the pain exploding at the side of his face as the nunchucks solidly connected, but he was a Nephilim and he ignored the injury and pressed on.

Rafaella fought with intelligence, quieting down to defensive poses and delivering brutal counter-attacks when David moved in on her. She successfully blocked his sharp jabs and cuts with the Gothic sword, swinging her nunchakus in insanely rapid combinations.

David learned to quiet down as well when she made these rapid moves and was finally able to attack in time when her nunchuks were on one side and her other side was vulnerable – for less than a split second. David lunged with full control and slashed Rafaella on the arm, drawing blood.

He could see her eyes widen in surprise and her nostrils flare in increased anger. She was a fireball of emotions and David had to admire how she kept herself in check and remained in control of herself. Based on the short time he'd spent with her, David knew Rafaella could be volatile.

David deftly slashed his sword but could no longer find the opportunity to close in on Rafaella. She continually blocked his every attack, her clever side spins, strikes and reaching throws scoring points as she inflicted body blows and hits on David.

As David boldly encroached on her space with a barrage of slashes, Rafaella crouched down to a knee squat and repeatedly flailed the nunchuks on David's knees, hitting them hard.

David felt himself crumple to the ground as his weakened knees buckled under him.

In a flash, Rafaella was over him, holding him down with a pressing knee then she locked her nunchuks on his neck in a hard x.

She had won. Rafaella had taken him down and beaten him soundly.

"You win." David croaked against the nunchucks pressing on his throat. "And don't kill me today, if you don't mind."

Rafaella stood up, her pale green eyes glittering with the joy of her victory. "How does it feel to be whipped by a girl?"

"Extremely painful. And I don't just mean my body." David grimaced.

Rafaella helped him to his feet, grinning ruefully. "I was pretty hard on you, wasn't I?"

"I appreciate it." David said, stretching gingerly in order to assess his injuries. The good news was, Rafaella was smiling at him now.

"Got it out of your system or are you still mad at me?" he asked.

She shook her head with a smile. "Not anymore. Not after that beating you took." she ended with a laugh.

"Fun-ny." David winced. "But really, wow, you were incredible Rafaella. You have to show me those moves next time, when I graduate from the sword, that is. As we've seen today, I still have a lot of sword technique to learn."

"I'm really sorry for being such a pain to you yesterday and today -"

"Don't worry about it," David said. "I was such an unfair mud scum myself, I'm the one who should be apologizing. I'm sorry too."

She looked at him seriously. "I want to make it up to you David, for being a good buddy. Tell you what. Meet me outside my room before dinner. I want to show you something."

David nodded. "I'll be there."

Then they made their way to Teacher Peregrine for their next training schedule.

As promised, David showed up outside Rafaella's door right before dinner. He had showered and changed – a must after every brutal warrior training, knocked on her door and waited for her to answer.

She emerged a few seconds later, fresh and smiling with a bounding Wolverine at her side.

"I've always wondered," said David, "Does Wolverine still eat regular food? Do essence pets eat?"

Rafaella shook her head. "Not anymore. He's basically an essence – a spirit, and doesn't need the usual sustenance. But sometimes, he likes to pretend to eat...... it's so funny when he does that, and a little bit gross." she made a face, "You can actually see the food being munched and tumbling around inside him."

"Now that would be something to see." David laughed, imagining food being digested in Wolverine's stomach – in full view. Rafaella meantime seemed furtive, darting glances on both sides of the corridor.

"What did you want to show me?" asked David, intrigued.

Rafaella checked to see that they were alone (they were), but she still whispered anyway. "It's a secret place, but I want you to see it."

David felt a jolt of surprise and a – thrill? Rafaella was letting him in on a secret? He wondered what place it was.

Rafaella led the way to the upper floors of the Monastery until they reached the topmost level. David had no sense whatsoever of where they were now, hopelessly lost from all the twists and turns, corners and corridors. Wolverine had already abandoned them some floors ago, preferring to run off with other essence dogs rather than join their circuitous journey.

"Don't worry," assured Rafaella. "We'll be at the Cube in time for dinner."

Then, she stopped in front of a plain and ordinary white door (another one) and said, "This is my most favorite place in the Monastery. I call it the Stratus Stairway."

Rafaella opened the door and David stepped inside.

He stopped in his tracks, his mouth gaping open. "What the....."

He was in a room of floating clouds.

Clouds!

There were clouds low enough to touch and clouds that reached the dizzyingly high, glass domed ceiling. David could see the still light sky outside and felt as though he were outdoors, on a mountain top that had reached the heavens.

"What is this place?" he breathed.

"I don't know exactly." Rafaella replied, holding out her hand to play with a cloud. "A reflection of heaven? A Nephilim playground?"

She looked solemnly at David. "This is a secret place, David. Not many students know about it, and the ones who do........well, we'd like for it to remain a secret."

"I promise not to tell anyone." David solemnly said as well. "It's not on the Monastery map?"

Rafaella shook her head. "Not a blot. And don't worry about Lukas. He knows about this room."

David gave a sigh of relief. "I'm honestly relieved. He's been such a great friend, I don't want to keep secrets from him. Not about something like this room."

Rafaella gave a mischievous smile. "You ain't seen nothing yet, David."

Then, she ran and made a flying leap on a cloud.

David expected her to fall flat and go through its mist, but instead, she landed on the cloud as though it were a huge floating cottonball.

Rafaella was laughing loudly at David's shocked face. "Yes, you can actually climb on it. Come on!"

"You've got to be kidding me!" David yelled in excitement. "This is insane!"

David lost no time in leaping on a cloud himself.

He could feel it's cool mist enveloping him. It felt as though the cloud couldn't carry his weight, like he would just go through it, but he didn't.

It really was inexplicable.

David didn't waste any time trying to figure out how it worked, instead, he lay back and enjoyed the cloud carrying him luxuriously across the room.

Rafaella was already climbing the clouds, going higher and higher, jumping from one cloud to the next and just laughing with absolute joy.

"I love this room!" she yelled.

"Me too!" David yelled back.

He had to try cloud climbing and see what it was like. *Cloud Climbing!* David shouted in whoops at the crazy idea.

It wasn't as easy as it looked but it was incredible fun. The tricky part was that the clouds were in constant motion, gliding slowly and dreamily all over the room. David and Rafaella clambered up and down and down and up the floating clouds, until they both reached the top most tier – a large, fat bed of a cloud. They were so high up and so close to the glass-domed ceiling that they could see nothing but the sky outside.

It was unforgettable.

"Thanks Rafaella for sharing this room with me." David quietly told her, as they lay sprawled and lazy on the cloud.

Rafaella turned her face towards David, her pale green eyes luminously beautiful in the light of the setting sun.

Her lips curved in a smile. "You're welcome, David."

They lay there in silence for a while, just enjoying the slow drifting of their cloud, looking up at the sky as it changed colors from a light pink, to a deepening mauve blush, to the purple hues of twilight. As the first stars began to emerge, Rafaella sat up grabbed something at her side, and threw it to David's face.

He felt the cool puff of mist of a small cloud ball.

Rafaella grinned at him. "Cloud ball fight!"

David scooped up a palm size cloud ball and lobbed it at Rafaella. She easily evaded the throw and her laughter rang out as she jumped down their cloud to escape.

Their descent became a game of throwing and evading, puffs of cloud balls streaking and zooming as David and Rafaella tried to hit each other. By the time they reached the ground, they were breathless from laughter and slightly disheveled from all the cloak and dagger tactics.

"It's time for dinner." Rafaella sighed, turning slowly towards the door.

"Wait." David said, holding on to her shoulder, making her face him. "You have cloud mists on your cheek." Then, boy that he was, he smacked a handful of cloud balls to her face.

Rafaella shrieked in surprise, automatically transforming into a warrior and attacking David with a powerful jujitsu maneuver.

Before David even knew what happened, he was on the floor flat on his back, the breath having left him during the hard landing.

Rafaella was laughing and contrite at the same time. "Sorry David. Defensive reflexes. Can't help it."

That was twice in one day that she had felled him. He smiled ruefully at her. "Ouch, lesson learned.But I did get you in the face with that cloud ball."

She rolled her eyes at him. "You're such a little girl."

Then she pulled him up his feet with an impatient, "Come on! I'm starving."

Needless to say, dinner was totally tame compared to their Stratus Stairway adventures.

Someone was shaking him awake. A very persistent someone.

David tried to swat the hand away, but the shaking became even more vigorous.

"Wake up, David. Wake up!" squealed a high pitched voice.

It sounded like a cherub.

David groggily opened one eye and was startled to see a cherub fluttering by his bed. It was Tatiana.

"Wha -?" David mumbled.

Tatiana shook him again. She was really relentless.

"Whaddyadoinmyroom?" David asked incoherently. "How'd you geddin?"

"I have a master key." Tatiana showed him a shiny gold key. *"It's not important at the moment. Wake up, David. You have to wake up."*

"Huh?"

"Someone's in trouble, David. She needs your help!"

David shook his head awake at Tatiana's words. Already he was leaping out of bed and belting a robe over his pajamas.

"Who's in trouble Tatiana?" David whispered urgently at her. "And where?"

Tatiana was fluttering outside the door, impatiently beckoning to him. *"I'll lead, David, and you follow. You have to use your Angel Mode. We have to hurry! It's your friend. Your friend Gertrude. She's hurt inside the catacombs."*

Before David could ask another question, Tatiana zoomed away and David transformed to Angel Mode to catch-up with her.

Tatiana weaved her way around the Monastery, through empty rooms and corridors, leading them lower and lower to the very bottom level of the ancient wing of the building. Finally, she came to a halt in front of a massive but narrow stone door with a wrought iron design at the front.

It was an eerily silent and isolated place, and the catacomb door looked unopened for ages. David was beginning to have doubts about Tatiana's claim.

"Are you sure about this Tatiana?"

She looked him straight in the eye and said. *"I'm certain of it, David. This is one of my evening routes before bedtime – a routine check of different sections of the Monastery as part of my duties. I heard her – in there. She was calling for help and I answered her. She said to get someone. To get you, David. That you're her friend and that you would readily help her."* Tatiana finished in a rush, urgently pointing to the catacombs.

Tatiana was right, he would readily help Gertrude if she was in trouble.

"Gertrude!" He called out through the thick door. "Can you hear me? It's David! I'm coming in to help you!"

He pressed his ear against the door, the decorative iron work icy against his ear. He could hear movement inside, some shuffling and a muffled sound.

Someone really was in there.

"Why didn't you go in and help her right away Tatiana?" David asked, checking his robe pocket for his dagger.

"Me?" squeaked Tatiana, *"I'm very sorry, but I am not entering the catacombs by myself. I'm too.......I'm too..........."*

"Sorry Tatiana," David hastily interrupted. "We're wasting time. I have to go in and help Gertrude."

He pushed the door open and it creaked and screeched in resistance. From the light of the corridor he could see curtains of cobwebs hanging from the low ceiling. Other than that, the catacombs stretched out to complete darkness.

"Gertrude?" he called out. "Can you hear me?"

As David cautiously stepped beyond the door, Tatiana shoved him hard from behind, pushing him inside the catacombs in a stumble.

Before he could turn around and ask her what she was doing, David heard the door slam with dreadful finality and heard the lock click loudly into place.

He was trapped!

David rushed towards the door in the blinding darkness and began feeling for a door-knob or handle, anything that he could pull the door with. His hands only met the flat and cold surface of polished stone.

"Tatiana!" he yelled. "Open the door! Open the door! Why are you doing this?"

As he quieted down to listen, he heard soft footfalls behind him and the hair-raising sound of unearthly growling.

David was not alone in the dark catacombs.

15 The Hand of God

David felt his body thrumming as he switched to Angel Mode, instinctively locking himself in a defensive stance.

As he morphed to Angel Mode, the most surprising thing happened. It was like someone had turned on the light switches in the catacombs and David could see clearly.

He had night vision!

In that millisecond of clear sight, the creature sinisterly approaching made a bounding lunge towards David.

David twisted away in time, barely escaping, and felt gaping jaws and hot breath next to his face. David zoomed away from the door, turning around to face the creature, shock registering in painful waves as he realized what was in front of him.

Hellhound!

It was huge. Built like a bear with a massive bulk of a body. It had paws that could kill him in one powerful strike, with cruel talons wickedly flashing at him.

David stared immobilized at the hellhound's burning red eyes, glinting with undisguised evil and intelligence. David knew to his bones that this was a creature with a sharp mind, keen instincts, and a lust for blood. His blood.

He turned from the creature and ran as fast as he could away from it, putting as much distance he was physically capable of between them. He needed to think, to come up with a battle plan, to find another exit!

David felt for the dagger under his robe.

Thank God! Thank God it was with him.

David carefully unsheathed the dagger as he ran, his hand clenching tightly around the handle, and he watched the blade glow in a familiar white light as he held the weapon. He drew strength and sustenance from it, feeling as though it were a friend, ready to protect him.

Even as he ran through the catacombs, turning sharp corners in the underground labyrinth, David realized that there wasn't any other exit. He would have to make a stand. To battle the hellhound and fight for his life. His best choice was the circular room in the middle of the catacombs, a room large enough to fight a hellhound in.

There was nothing to do but wait.

David drew in deep and steadying breaths, willing himself to remain calm and to think like a warrior. He readied himself, the *Hand of God* gripped tightly in one hand.

David didn't have to wait long. Just like them, demons and their kind had super-speed too. David also bore in mind that the hellhound would be preternaturally strong.

He heard the thunder of enormous paws pounding closer and from where he was standing, he smelled the acrid stench of sulfur becoming stronger and stronger.

David flattened himself to the wall, guarding the entrance to the circular space. As he saw the quick blur of the hellhound streaking by him, David sharply slashed his dagger and felt it slice into demon flesh.

The hellhound gave a yelp of pain, bounding past David across the room then swiveling around to face him.

Foul black blood dripped from its flank, the hellhound growling in hatred and anger, yellow clouds of sulfur coming out its nostrils with each breath.

Then, before David's very eyes, he saw the gash on the hellhound's flank heal and close-up in an instant.

The hellhound bared its long fangs at him in a leery smile, mucus-like saliva dripping from its pointy sharp teeth.

This wasn't going to be easy.

Boy and beast faced each other, circling slowly, looking for an opportunity to strike.

The hellhound attacked first, lunging at David in an attempt to pin him down. David deftly evaded the frontal attack and crouched down for another slash of his dagger at the hellhound.

But he didn't want to wait long enough for the evil incarnate to heal quickly.

David jumped at the creature, landing on its broad back and stabbing his dagger at its neck.

The hellhound howled ghoulishly in pain, so loudly in the underground room that David thought his ears would bleed from the deafening sound.

David stabbed its neck again and again, anywhere and everywhere he could strike.

The hellhound furiously turned its head towards him, eyes burning like hot coals, and David slashed its face as well.

The evil beast deviously managed to clamp its jaw on David's arm, crunching down into it so that David acutely felt each bone breaking, and each of the hellhound's fangs sinking into his skin, piercing him like red-hot pokers.

Then the hellhound threw David powerfully across the room, slamming him hard against the wall.

Every inch of David's body was in pain and his left arm was a concentration of burning and flaming agony. Thankfully, the hellhound had not gotten hold of his right arm – his weapon arm.

David had no time to lose. He felt the small nicks and cuts healing quickly, but his broken arm remained broken. He jumped to his feet to face his enemy and lunged at the beast again.

What would it take to kill this thing? David wondered, even as he furiously attacked the hellhound. Wasn't his dagger and angelic substance enough? Shouldn't it be disintegrating by now?

David could see that the hellhound's neck wounds were slowly closing, frightfully aware that in no time the monster would heal itself again.

"No you don't!" yelled David, going at the hellhound with his dagger.

The hellhound met his attack head-on and David had to spin and writhe rapidly away, barely escaping the hellhounds wide-opened jaws. It could swallow David's head in one bite!

The hound savagely landed a blow at David's side, talons out, ripping through David's robe, skin, and muscle.

The explosion of pain was excruciating! Blood dripped from his wound in rivulets, but there would be no giving up. David's only choice was to keep on fighting.

The hellhound came at him again and this time David ran towards the wall, the demon beast close at his heels.

David had to find a way to get close to the monster and inflict absolute injury.

David continued his path to the wall, running up on its cobbled surface with the demon behind him. He back-flipped tightly and landed on the hellhound's back once more.

Again, he stabbed it repeatedly with his dagger. The blade

burning brightly with each thrust, slicing through malodorous fur and rubbery skin, cleaving through muscles from hell itself, and David was spattered with oily, rancid, black blood.

The hellhound shrieked and roared in enraged savageness and pain but still it held on, spewing bursts of sulfur in defiance.

"Die you hell scum! Die!" David was shouting with each stab.

The heart! Stab it in the heart! A voice echoed in his brain.

As the hellhound crumpled to its side, growling and spitting, hissing furiously, David nimbly escaped being pinned down beneath its hulking weight.

As fast as he could, David aimed his dagger to the hellhound's chest, straight to its large and thirsty heart, embedding the glowing steel to the hilt.

With a last attempt of a biting snap, along with an eerie, ululating howl, the hellhound exploded and disintegrated into black ash.

David's dagger clattered victoriously on the stone floor, its white light slowly going out.

He was bruised, bleeding, and broken, but the hellhound was gone.

It was mercifully over.

David could barely Angel Mode it back to the catacomb's doorway.

He may have won the fight, but he was still underground, trapped inside the catacombs. He still had to figure a way out.

Nobody knew where he was – except the traitor, Tatiana – and David knew no help was coming. There would be no rescue.

When he arrived at the sealed entrance – limping and bleeding, clutching his side in agony – he gathered his strength and used his night vision to maximum capacity.

Now that he could explore the entry way without the urgency of an enormous hellhound intent on killing him, it was logical to assume that there must be a button/ pedal/ lever/ switch – something – to open the solid door from the inside. He was hoping that whoever built the place had the foresight to prevent getting locked in and be in David's exact position.

He patted and pushed on the walls, banged and felt edges, until finally his perseverance paid off. Handily – and again logically – situated on the first niche away from the door, was a small cobwebby lever. It was a small, narrow and deep niche, wide enough for a human hand but too small for large hellhound paws. No wonder the Abbot chose this place to lock the hellhound in.

David cranked the lever upwards and the stone door slowly opened with its customary creaking and screeching.

David felt the most wonderful and intense feeling of relief as he glimpsed the corridor outside, the overhead lights still on, but expectedly deserted of Tatiana's treacherous presence.

He could feel his strength ebbing and he was starting to wobble on his legs, but David knew he wasn't out of danger yet. The hellhound may be gone but he had been lured to this place. David knew Tatiana wasn't the true culprit.

She had been used.

Also, he could very well bleed to death in this underground, his wound at the side not healing yet. David suspected that the hellhound's talons contained some potent poison against quick healing. And yet, he didn't want to go straight to the Infirmary. He needed a friend, someone he could trust.

Lukas.

But David didn't know where his room was. But he knew another good friend who would help him.

Rafaella.

David pulsated into Angel Mode again, climbing upwards away from the lowest level of the Monastery until he reached upper floors that he recognized. From there, he made fast work to Rafaella's room.

"Rafaella." David knocked weakly on her door. "Rafaella!" he called out again.

Her door opened and she gasped in shock when she saw him and the state he was in.

"Ran into a hellhound……" David smiled weakly before the world tilted weirdly and Rafaella caught him in her arms.

When David awakened, he was already at the Infirmary with Rafaella sitting anxiously on the chair beside his bed. He was no longer in pain and his broken arm was in a cast.

"Why is it that I'm always falling flat on my back when I'm with you?" he croaked raspily at her.

"This time, I caught you." she smiled worriedly at him, holding on to his hand. "How do you feel, David? What happened?"

David tried to sit up but couldn't muster the strength for it. He hated feeling weak, especially in front of Rafaella. He was beginning to feel like an absolute wuss.

Before David could reply, he saw Abbot Anderson striding towards him, a troubled look on his face. Even though it was the middle of the night, the Abbot was immaculately pressed and dressed in his customary suit.

"David," said the Abbot. "Miss Pierce called for me saying that you have encountered the hellhound. I have in fact checked where we had imprisoned the beast -"

"At the catacombs, sir." David rasped.

The Abbot nodded, surprised and worried at the same time. "Yes indeed. At the catacombs, and there is no longer any hellhound within. Please tell me what happened, and how you came to battle the dangerous creature."

David asked for a bit of water before he began his tale, and after taking sips for his parched throat, he told them how Tatiana had come into his room, luring him falsely to the catacombs with the story of rescuing Gertrude, pushing him inside and locking him in with the hellhound.

David wearily recounted how he fought the hellhound and how fortunate he was to be carrying his dagger with him.

"May I see the dagger, David?" Abbot Anderson asked.

Rafaella stood up and handed the weapon to the Abbot. "We removed it from him, sir, when he was being treated."

"Of course," acknowledged the Abbot, slowly removing the dagger from its leather sheath. He looked closely at the impressive weapon, turning it every which way, the light catching on the blade's gleaming finish. The blade had returned to its undefiled state, as though it had not disintegrated a hellhound that very evening.

Abbot Anderson also examined the etched insignia thoughtfully. Then he looked somberly at David. *"The Hand of God."*

"You recognize the dagger, sir?" David was surprised.

"It is an ancient weapon, a very old design and rarely in the archives. But yes, I do recognize it, David. It is quite a famous dagger."

David waited for Abbot Anderson to continue but he seemed reluctant to discuss the dagger's history. Instead, the Abbot asked David.

"Where and when did you acquire it?"

"I dreamed about it, sir. A very clear dream.......and also the feeling that it was very important that I make the dagger right away.......and to always carry it with me......" David trailed off.

"I believe it wasn't just a simple dream, David. I think it was an Inspiration, a message from a Pure Angel." Abbot Anderson continued contemplatively. "You have been very brave tonight and I commend your combat skills and all that you have learned in the few days that you have begun training. But I must reveal to you, David, that this very dagger saved your life."

"You see, no amount of great skill would have finished off that hellhound without such a mighty blade. Its demise required our angelic substance and a weapon powerfully imbued to kill it. This dagger is such a weapon. And yet, I think, even then, the hellhound was tremendously difficult to kill?"

David nodded at the Abbot's words.

"It was a grave mistake on my part for not having terminated the creature immediately upon its entrance to the Monastery." Abbot Anderson said in consternation. "Truthfully, it was scheduled to be terminated this coming morning by not just one, but a team of Warrior Trainers, headed by Teacher Victorinus."

Abbot Anderson gave a weary sigh, lines of anxiety marring his young and handsome face. "Please forgive me for my error in judgement, David. Because of my unwise decision, your life was put in peril."

"But sir," David protested, "It wasn't your fault at all. I was trapped into it. Someone else is responsible for it."

"And we will get to the very core of the lie, until we uncover the truth." Abbot Anderson promised. "Still, I feel quite responsible for agreeing to harbor such a dangerous creature among innocent students. We had taken precautions, certainly, and measures of safety. Its location was kept secret and guards were posted round-the-clock outside the catacombs."

The Abbot shook his head in self-beratement. "I take very seriously the safety of my students, and it is in fact a miracle that you have survived that most terrible confrontation with the beast. You see David, that was no ordinary hellhound."

"What do you mean, sir?" David was puzzled.

The Abbot gravely explained. "In hell, three extremely powerful hellhounds guard the throne of their Dark Prince. You, David, have just encountered and killed one of them."

16   Interrogation

Despite the fact that it was almost dawn, Tatiana was brought to the Infirmary for questioning. She was accompanied by Teacher Victorinus, the head of the entire Warrior Training Program.

Tatiana appeared nervous and bewildered, as though she had no idea why her presence was required.

"Tatiana," Abbot Anderson looked at her intently. "Please, take a seat. We have some extremely important questions to ask you."

"Of course, sir." said Tatiana tremulously. "Anything I can do to be of service to you and the Monastery."

"Do you know why we have called you here?"

"No, sir." she shook her head. "I am puzzled by the summons, but please be assured, that I do not mind being here. What is it you need from me, sir? What questions need to be answered?"

From his hospital bed, David could see Tatiana's face very clearly and it was really difficult to imagine her betrayal, how she had pushed him to certain death had it not been for the dagger he was carrying.

And yet, even more difficult to imagine was her having a hand in the plot. She was looking at all of them with wide eyes, her blond curls bouncing around her face, her tiny wings tucked neatly behind her as she sat on the chair in her diapers and candy pink pajama top.

She was a cherub for heaven's sake. A baby! How are you going to interrogate a baby?

"Do you remember going to David's room tonight, Tatiana?" Abbot Anderson asked gently, sitting across her.

"No sir. I have no recollection of going to or being in his room"

"Do you remember leading him down to the catacombs?"

Again, she shook her head. *"The catacombs sir? Oh no, why would I visit that underground, much less bring David there? No, Abbot, I have been with my seven year old Ward, Sarah, the entire evening."*

"What do you know about the captured hellhound? Anything at all that you've heard."

Tatiana flushed guiltily at his words. *"Ummm......I have heard something......the other Puttis were conversing about it. It certainly was the gossip of the day sir. That the students had captured a hell -"* she shuddered. *" - a hellhound. Also that it was imprisoned in the catacombs. But, that is the extent of my knowledge regarding it, sir."*

Abbot Anderson nodded slowly. "I guessed as much. Thank you Tatiana, for answering all my inquiries most patiently."

He nodded towards Doctor Vitalis who was witnessing the proceedings unobtrusively, and the Head Healer approached Tatiana with a goblet.

"Drink this, Tatiana." Doctor Vitalis instructed. "It will calm your nerves and ensure a better night's rest."

"Thank you Doctor." she smiled up at him and obediently drank the concoction he gave her.

David was confused about the interview, so was Rafaella. They kept looking at each other questioningly and David was about to sit up and voice his protest but the Abbot, sensing David's unrest, shook his head warningly to silence him.

In a matter of seconds, Tatiana closed her eyes, slumped gently on the chair and slowly breathed the rhythm of deep slumber.

"Ah, here she comes." the Abbot said as footsteps approached. Explaining to David and Rafaella, he said, "If my initial conclusions are correct, we will be certain of the truth in a short while. You see David, I do not believe that Tatiana acted so falsely, so criminally by her own will. She had been Dream Invaded. Quite powerfully, I might add, and instructed to do everything that you had reported to us, *and* made to forget her actions. We have a strong Dream Invader in the Monastery, one who is unknown to us, and we must find out who the culprit is."

Teacher Peregrine came into view accompanied by – Gertrude.

What's she doing here? David wondered. Were they going to ask her about the excuse Tatiana had lured him with? About her being in the catacombs? David was pretty sure that Gertrude had no idea of the night's events.

"Thank you Miss Greer for accommodating us at such a late hour." Abbot Anderson greeted Gertrude. "As you can see, we are in great need of your assistance."

Gertrude glanced at the sleeping Tatiana and bit her lip in doubt. "Certainly sir. I wish to be of help at any time. Ummm.....I have never attempted to perform this on a cherub before. I'm not so sure it would work."

"We have confidence in your abilities, Gertrude. Please, just do the best you can."

Gertrude nodded and seated herself across Tatiana. Doctor Vitalis handed her a goblet as well.

"Just a mild mixture of sedatives. I have incorporated some herbs to make the elixir act instantaneously." explained Doctor

Vitalis, more for David and Rafaella's benefit.

As Gertrude sipped from the goblet, Abbot Anderson explained. "Gertrude is a very accomplished Dream Invader. We ask for her assistance whenever there is a need. There are other Dream Invaders in the Monastery of course, and when the matter being dealt with is not so important or so delicate, then they come to our aid. But during events of urgency and significance, we call for Miss Greer. She is the unparalleled Dream Invader here."

Gertrude would have blushed at the high praise if she were awake, but before the Abbot finished talking, she was already under.

There was complete silence in the room as everyone observed Gertrude and Tatiana.

What now? David thought. Was it just a matter of waiting?

Then Gertrude inhaled deeply and began in a flat, somnambulent tone.

"Tatiana, did you go to David's room tonight?"

"*Yes.*"

"Did you lure him to the catacombs?"

"*Yes.*"

"How?"

"*I told him you needed help......I lied to him. I told him you were trapped in there.*"

"What did you do next?"

"*When he opened the door, I pushed him inside. The hellhound was waiting for him.*"

"Why was he brought there?"

Tatiana started breathing more rapidly. "*To die! To die by the hellhounds' savageness!*" She began shaking and quivering, tears were running down her baby cheeks.

David was shocked at what was transpiring before him. He

wanted to interrupt, to say something, but he knew he shouldn't.

"Did someone come to your sleep, Tatiana? Did someone order you to do this?" Gertrude continued.

"Yes."

"Who was it? Who Dream Invaded you?"

"Innocent. Innocent Reichenberg."

Everyone in the Infirmary who were awake were staring at each other, some in shock, some in satisfied confirmation.

David had been expecting no one else. Of course it was Innocent. He was Zachary's mob underling and would carry out Zachary's thuggish commands. Deep down though, David never expected them to be capable of attempted murder.

"What about the guards at the door? What did you do with them?" Gertrude asked the cherub.

"*I offered them food and drinks. It was drugged. Then I carried them to an empty room and locked them in. They're still sleeping.*"

"Do you know who ordered Innocent Reichenberg to Dream Invade you? Do you know who's really behind this?"

"No." Tatiana shook her head.

There was silence again as Gertrude ended her questions. She had asked what they needed to find out. Then, with deep inhalations, Gertrude slowly opened her eyes and looked expectantly for Tatiana to do the same.

Instead, Tatiana, still in deep slumber began muttering, "*Arepo.....Arepo.......*"

When David woke up some hours later, it was midday. The Abbot had instructed him to rest and forgo classes that day. He was still in the Infirmary but was itching to return to his room and to his regular schedule. He felt well and mended already.

"You again." a voice called out.

It was Liz, his healer when he had first arrived at the Monastery.

"You know, you should stop being admitted here just to annoy me." she teased.

David couldn't help grinning at the sassy ten year-old. "Yes Liz, I broke my arm especially for you."

Her baby blue eyes widened at his comeback and her pale skin colored. "Ah...ummm......" she stammered.

David, oblivious to her reaction as any boy his age would be, said, "Am I completely healed? Can I leave now? Oh, and don't you have classes?"

"Yes I have classes." she frowned, "but it's lunchtime and when I finish my meal, I come to the Infirmary to carry out my duties. And yes, you are completely healed. Your bones have mended, you'll still feel bruised........but you may be discharged today. I'm to take your cast off."

David lay still and quiet as Liz went about removing his cast. Despite his light banter with Liz, the truth was he remained troubled about last night's events.

When Tatiana had awoken, she had full memory of what she had done – Gertrude having restored it to her – and the poor cherub was overwhelmingly aghast by her actions even though it had all been under some kind of hypnotic persuasion.

Tatiana had cried and went into hysterics and was inconsolable until Doctor Vitalis calmed her down with another concoction, and Abbot Anderson repeatedly assured her that none of it was her fault.

The Abbot had concluded the gathering by scheduling a

Tribunal for the coming morning wherein Innocent and whoever else was involved would be called to explain themselves and be justly tried for their actions.

Tatiana, of course, would be the principal witness. As such, Doctor Vitalis was keeping an eagle eye on her to ensure her safety with the additional protection of Teacher Peregrine.

Teacher Victorinus had initially volunteered to be her protector, but his presence was more needed at Warrior Training. He was the head trainer after all.

David could see how the Abbot was deeply affected by the events. This wasn't some mischievous conduct to be tried, or a teenage prank.

It was attempted murder.

If David had failed to defeat the hellhound.............

"Hey, David." a voice interrupted his thoughts and he saw a worried Lukas and Rafaella approaching his bed.

"Man, when Rafaella told me what happened last night, I was just blown away. Blown away!" Lukas said. "I thought she was joking at first."

"How are you feeling, David?" Rafaella asked, hovering worriedly over him. "How's your arm?"

"I feel better actually. Look, my arm has healed and Liz is taking the cast off."

They exchanged hellos.

When Liz had finished removing his cast and cleaning his arm, she excused herself to put things away. David remembered to thank her for all her care and attention and Liz smiled brightly in reply, red in the face once more.

"What's the news?" David looked at Rafaella. "Did they do the Tribunal as scheduled?"

"We think so." she looked seriously upset. "Tatiana will witness against Innocent, but it'll be up to Innocent if he'll witness against the real mastermind of the plot."

"And we know who that is." Lukas interjected.

"This is just all so worrisome." Rafaella continued. "It's obviously Zachary who's behind all this, but David, nothing like this has ever happened at the Monastery before. Sure, pranks and nasty tricks, but not....."

"Attempted murder." David finished for her.

They silently contemplated things for a minute and then Rafaella asked,

"Are we missing something? Do you think Zachary is really that psychotic?"

"Well, I can definitely attest to the fact that he has aggressive tendencies, but I never expected him to take it to the next level." Lukas admitted. "I thought his expertise was limited to bullying and a fist-fight now and then."

"Look, I haven't been here long so I don't really know what's normal around here, and what Zachary and Innocent are capable of," David said. "but I do remember what you guys always tell me about free will. We all have a choice."

David continued. "And that we have our Angelic and our Human side. There are many screwed up things in the outside world, things our Human side is capable of. I'd never have guessed it about Zachary and Innocent, but the evidence is pretty convincing."

"I'm sure when the trial is over, Abbot Anderson will let you know what happened, David." Lukas said. "He knows that you'll be worried and wondering about it."

David nodded, agreeing with Lukas. He was hoping for that too, that the Abbot would let him know the outcome of the Tribunal.

Then, he asked Rafaella about something that had been bugging him from last night.

"Rafaella, do you remember that last thing Tatiana was saying?"

She frowned in recollection, "Arepo?"

David nodded. "I was wondering what it meant."

"Arepo?" Lukas asked too. "That's Latin."

"It is?" David was surprised. "Do you know what it means?"

"Yes. It means *Trust*."

Lukas was right about Abbot Anderson. In the afternoon, a cherub approached David at the library, delivering a message from the Abbot, calling him immediately to his office.

David had been very eager to leave the Infirmary, return to his room and put on the regulation white clothes, and return to class. He had missed the morning schedule of *Angelic Chorale* (thank god! David couldn't carry a tune even under coercion, duress or torture) and he had also missed *Heavenly Art*. That would have been a fun class, David thought, and he was sorry he missed that one.

Teacher Peregrine also excused him from Warrior Training despite David's protests that he was fine and ready – total bummer! - and so, he had been left with an entire afternoon free of classes.

What was he going to do?

Nagging his mind was the word Tatiana uttered before she awakened.

Arepo. *Trust.*

But was that what it really meant? It was like Tatiana was speaking in code or delivering a clue. David was convinced that there was greater significance in what she had said.

And so he trudged towards the library, marveled at its immenseness and dazedly wondered where to begin as he spied rows and rows of thousands of books.

The librarian, Miss Theophila, helped him out. She was an ancient and motherly Nephilim who was amazingly strong and sprightly despite looking five hundred years old. She effortlessly lifted stacks of books for David and zoomed him to *Turn that Page* – the library snack bar.

Yes, the library had a snack bar.

David happily whiled away the hours munching on whatever snack beckoned him, but he was having second thoughts about his research venture. His books were getting more complex by the minute and most of it were in Latin.

He didn't know Latin.

In the end, David was relieved when the messenger cherub interrupted him with summons to the Abbots office.

Abbot Anderson's office featured glass walls that had a sweeping view of majestic mountains and streaming afternoon sunlight. The entire room had a spartan feel, an unclutteredness of objects chosen precisely for their functionality rather than decorative value. Every object had its place and its owner knew where its place was.

The man himself was an enigma. His beautiful desk held no pictures or personal mementos. Did he have a family? What were his interests? Well, if David was waiting for the office to give him a clue, he would have a very long wait.

And yet the Abbot didn't come across as cold or standoffish. On the contrary, he was kind and charming with a quiet assurance and confidence to his manner. He made David feel very safe and centered.

The Abbot motioned for David to sit down. Today, he seemed weary and deeply saddened.

As David took a seat in front of the Abbot's desk, he saw a prominent red phone sitting squarely on the desk. Was it.....?

"Sir," he couldn't help asking, "Is that phone a direct line to........God?"

The Abbot smiled. "Not to God exactly, but to heaven yes. As you will see, the phone has no cord and is not plugged into any device, and yet Pure Angels manage to call just fine. The phone also rings to inform me when someone is about to visit."

"Like a doorbell, sir."

The Abbot chuckled. "Exactly David."

A quick thought entered David's mind. "Sir," he hesitated. "If they could call you........could you call them? Could you call anyone in heaven?" he couldn't help the hopeful note in his voice.

There was understanding and empathy in the Abbot's eyes. "Sadly no. It's more of a one way means of communicating. But you can talk to anyone in heaven anytime, David."

"I can, sir?" he was startled.

"Yes David, through prayer. When you pray, every time you pray, God and everyone else in heaven can hear you."

David shrugged, a little disappointed. "Well, I do know that sir........"

"But the phone idea was more exciting." Abbot Anderson finished for him, and they both smiled.

Then Abbot Anderson became serious and somber. "And now David, may we discuss what transpired this morning as I am sure you're wondering about the result of the Tribunal and who the real perpetrator is."

"I think I have an idea, sir." David admitted.

"And so did we. I am sorry to inform you David that the true culprit has not been discovered."

"What do you mean, sir?"

"Well, as expected, Tatiana witnessed against Innocent Reichenberg. Incredible as it seems, Innocent did not witness against anyone."

"He didn't?" David was surprised. "He took the fall?"

"Yes. He admitted to the Tribunal that it was his idea. His plot. And his alone. According to him, no one had ordered him nor coerced him into such actions."

"Sir, I don't believe that. I don't think Innocent is the one behind all this. I mean, yes, he's guilty for his part in it. For Dream Invading Tatiana and hypnotizing her to do all those stuff. But someone else is behind it, and I think it's Zachary Spencer."

"So do we, David." Abbot Anderson affirmed. "But at the heart of justice and fairness, is proof. We need proof, David, or else we'll simply be pointing fingers."

David silently mulled over the Abbot's words and then asked, "What happens to Innocent?"

"He has been found guilty and will be punished for his wrong-doing. As a juvenile, he will not be sent to prison but will be sent instead to *Kalvarium*, a Nephilim Juvenile Correctional Facility. He will matriculate there for six months of disciplinary education and intense labor, after which, an evaluation will be conducted."

David was shaking his head in sadness. He remembered Innocent – the tall, gangly boy with the unruly mop of hair. He didn't seem capable of such actions and here he was now, being sent to a Correctional Facility. "I can't believe it."

"It is grievous indeed." Abbot Anderson quietly said. "It pains me, severely, that such wrongdoing has occurred here. I never thought it possible.........." he trailed off in sorrowful contemplation.

"What about Zachary, sir? Is he just getting away with what he's done?"

"Innocent until proven guilty, David. We have to follow that rule. But certainly, he is suspect and will be under investigation."

It wasn't enough. Hardly enough. Innocent was being carted off to *Kalvarium* while Zachary would continue his privileged life at the Monastery. David thought it was monstrously unfair.

But at least something was being done.

"Sir, I really believe he masterminded the whole thing and I can't understand why Innocent didn't witness against him. But Zachary should be taken out of this school to protect the students........he bullies kids, sir." David was amazed that he was being so outspoken to the Abbot, but he knew he had to say something. "Even for that alone he should be punished."

The Abbot nodded. "Thank you David. Your outrage and concern is justified. I know that it is not enough, but let me assure you that Zachary is being investigated and we hope to uncover proof against him. As Prefect of Discipline, Martial Macarius is heading the investigative committee, aided by other staff members."

David felt his heart sink. *Martial Macarius*! He wasn't reassured at all. There was something odd about the man, and he didn't know why exactly, but David didn't trust him.

"Keep your senses sharp, David." Abbot Anderson advised.

"Be constantly on guard. This is not over yet."

17  A Secret Shared

When David entered the Cube for dinner, he was startled by the resounding applause that greeted him. Several students approached to shake his hand or pat him on the back.

"A hellhound! Incredible David!"

"Impressive." a senior said.

"Sooo Seventh Heaven!" Katherine and Consortia chorused.

Sixteen year olds congratulated him, ten year-olds lavished him with over-the-top praises.

David was in shock. He was also uncomfortable from all the attention.

"I thought it was supposed to be a secret." he hissed at an approaching Rafaella.

"Tatiana blabbed. No one instructed her to keep silent about what happened and she was super eager to relate her part of the drama. You should hear her courtroom scene." said Rafaella wryly. "It plays out like a movie."

"This does not help." David muttered. "How is Zachary going to react?"

David and Rafaella looked around the room and clapped eyes on a sullen and silent Zachary. His eyes were as cold as steel and he remained unresponsive to Giles who was trying to engage him in conversation.

"Oh David, how proud we are of you for vanquishing the hellhound." two cherubs chimed at him. It was Tatiana's friends, Zoe and Cinnia.

"Poor Tatiana, she was so ashamed for what she had done."

"So ashamed!"

"Unforgettably ashamed!"

"Embarrassed"

"Terribly, terribly embarrassed!"

David had to put an end to their high-pitched chirping.

"Tatiana has nothing to be ashamed or embarrassed about. She's only a victim like me. She was Dream Invaded to do all those things, after all."

The cherubs fluttered their wings even more excitedly. "Ooooh David, how romantic! You are defending Tatiana. You are her champion!"

"Champion!"

David was groaning in embarrassment and shaking his head at them.

"We'll be sure to tell Tatiana, David. She'll be so thrilled."

"Apoplectic with shock! But how romantic!" they sighed.

"Help!" David whispered to Rafaella.

"Thanks Cinnia, Zoe." said Rafaella. "Oh look, that table is signaling you. I think they need your help with something."

The two cherubs flew away in ready assistance.

"Thanks for the save." David said. "Where's Lukas?"

"Getting us a table. And I think he found one for us already." Rafaella pointed to a waving Lukas. Thankfully, the other students were returning to their tables and resuming dinner.

On their way to Lukas, David was intercepted by Caian James so David motioned for Rafaella to go ahead.

The good-looking senior was smiling easily at him.

"Well done, David." Caian complimented. "Taking on that hellhound. Must have been quite a fight."

David was quite flattered, especially with compliments from a warrior of Caian's caliber. He was also embarrassed by the sudden spotlight. All the emergent attention was giving him the hives.

"To the death, actually." was David's quiet reply. "But I was only defending myself. It wasn't like I had any choice."

Caian seriously responded. "We were just astounded when we heard about it. It really is staggering that you survived that encounter, David. You are a true warrior."

Then he continued. "Spoken by someone who has repeatedly gone into battle outside these walls, it always is a fight to the death. And you, David, only fifteen and yet you have defeated that hellhound, single-handedly. And I heard it was no ordinary hellhound."

Caian lowered his voice. "I also heard that Innocent Reichenberg is being sent to *Kalvarium*."

David nodded, again feeling exposed. Was nothing at all sacred in that Tribunal? A gag-order should be imposed on Tatiana.

"I could hardly digest the thought that a boy his age would commit attempted murder." Caian frowned. "I never knew him, of course, since we have no frequent interaction with younger Nephilims. But I did hear that he is a powerful Dream Invader. To have Dream Invaded a Putti……..the audacity of the idea………."

David couldn't think of any reply.

"Do you believe that it was all his *plot*, though?" Caian asked him.

"I can't really say." David replied in all honesty. "Maybe you also heard that Innocent didn't witness against anyone during the

Tribunal. If there was someone else behind it, we have no proof."

"Of course." Caian acknowledged. "Well, I'm keeping you from your dinner. I just wanted to say well done, David. And I'm really looking forward to sparring with you in Warrior Training. Your instincts would be a challenge to pit against."

"Oh, please don't." groaned David. "I bet you'll just whip me senseless in under a minute."

"I don't believe that." Caian brushed off. "When you fought that hellhound, all you had were your wits, your will, and a ready dagger. You triumphed over that monstrous beast and you should be proud of your victory." Caian added pensively, "Some words of caution though, now you have drawn firstblood and slain evil. We know in our hearts that we are in the right. Still, it is not so easy to kill. Be warned, David, I no longer sleep the deep slumber of innocents. No, not anymore. In my sleep I see the demons that I have slain."

David gulped loudly in reply.

Caian clapped him cheerfully on the shoulder. "Every rescue is an honor, David. You, even more so. See you around, Warrior."

And with that cryptic parting shot, Caian returned to his table.

David remained standing where he was, a puzzled expression etched on his face. What did Caian mean?

"You okay?" said someone beside him. It was Jerome Gallagher, the boy that had been Caian's opponent at the Combat Circle.

"You're Jerome." David said, still mildly befuddled.

Jerome nodded, towering over David. He was the dark to Caian's light.

"I heard what Caian said to you just now. You look confused."

"I am confused." David confessed. "What did he mean by

that?"

"Has no one ever told you? About your rescuers when you were attacked by your foster parents."

David shook his head. "I always thought Pure Angels came to my rescue."

Jerome smiled. "Well, you're half right. A Pure Angel came to your aid. He was accompanied by a Nephilim, and it was Caian."

David's eyes widened in surprise as Jerome added in confirmation.

"Caian rescued you that day, David."

The next morning, David woke up to a bright and sunny day. It was Friday and David could hardly believe he had only been at the Monastery for a week.

Well, actually, it was already more than a week now, but since he spent his first four days passed out and unconscious in the Infirmary, it didn't count.

He felt like a time-warp victim. So much had happened already it could have been stretched into a month. Or many months.

Suffice it to say that when David joined Lukas and Rafaella for last night's dinner, they too were astonished with David's news about Caian. They were also fully impressed that Caian had been his rescuer that fateful day.

David was certainly very grateful. He owed Caian his life! And the Pure Angel who had been with him that day. David would have to ask Caian who that angel was.

Last night's dinner was spent percolating ideas on the best way for David to show Caian his complete gratitude. Lukas jokingly suggested for David to be Caian's slave for a month, while Rafaella thought a weapon would be a more appropriate gift.

But really, how can you repay someone who saved your life?

And just as Caian had warned, it took David a while to push off into deep sleep. His mind kept tumbling over his horrific combat with the hellhound. He remembered the matted fur beneath his fingers, the slime of tar-like blood and the beast's malodorous hot breath.

David kept patting the reassuring presence of his dagger which he was wearing everywhere, even to bed. He had learned his lesson – the hard way.

Today, he was looking forward to class.

It was an all-day Warrior Training. David expected it to be brutal and yes, he was still the tiniest bit sore and his arm twinged occasionally, but other than that, he was as fit as an infomercial personal trainer – minus the bulky muscles of course.

When David opened up for a morning stretch, something popped out behind him and struck the bed and his desk. It was as if he had hit both his shins on something. Only, it wasn't his shins.

OH MY GOD!

HE HAD WINGS!

YES! YES! YES! YES! YES! YES!

David punched the air in joy.

When his initial surprise was over, he turned his head this way and that to study his wings.

WHAT?!!!

It must be some trick of lighting. David thought.

Was he seeing shadows? What was going on?

David faced the window fully so the morning sun could wash over him. As he did so, he looked at his wings in mortification.

His wings were not white!

David mouthed off a swear word in complete shock and started foaming at the mouth. Coming out from his throat in frothy profusion were the bitter and most disgusting taste of punishing soap bubbles.

After David had repeatedly rinsed his mouth of soap scum – gagging and shuddering while doing so – he studied his wings in confusion.

Had he missed something? A comment maybe that Lukas and Rafaella had made? An offhand remark or an implication?

But he did remember clearly.

They had said all wings were white. That wings only came in one color.

So why were his wings black and grey?

David looked at his wings again.

Wow! They really had impressive wingspans!

David had to stand obliquely in the small room in order for his wings to fit and not hit anything.

He could feel their weight at his back, but it wasn't heavy or uncomfortable. No, nothing like that. It was more of an awareness that something was on his back.

It was like he had grown a second pair of arms, only, they weren't arms.

He could feel every sensation on it though, just like his arms – how the feathers ruffled whenever he moved, how the very air felt against it.

David also knew that he could easily control them, as he could his every extremity.

Fold! He thought, and the wings folded neatly behind his

back.

Open.

The wings expanded once more in a stunning display.

When he thought about stretching, his wings expanded even more, like fingers opening wide and elongating to its fullest.

David remembered Caian's protective maneuver and he ordered his wings to close around him.

It instantly did, forming a feather cocoon around his body.

It was too cool!

David opened his wings again, making them angle closer to the front so he could look at the color once more.

He had not been mistaken.

The feathers really were black and gray.

The upper part of his wings was jet black, slowly lightening downwards into deep shades of gray.

Was it demon-influenced? David wondered in fear. Had the hellhound perhaps tainted him or poisoned him? He was bitten after all.

David could still clearly visualize and feel the hellhound's piercing fangs crushing down his arm. Perhaps he had been poisoned.

But he had seen real demons and their wings didn't look like his. They had been thin and rubbery with bony protuberances – like bats.

David had to show Lukas and ask him. Maybe he would know.

But what if he really had been tainted. What if he was an aberration in the Nephilim world. What if his wings were strange abominations?

What if he got expelled because of the color of his wings?

Look. David told himself. You're not expected to get wings anyway until you're sixteen. So there's no rush of exposure here. Think David, *think*!

He would have to hide his wings for now.

Keep it a secret.

The library! David shouted in his brain. Maybe he could find some reference there. Some obscure book or something. Miss Theophila had been very helpful before and that's exactly what he needed now. Help.

David closed his eyes and willed his wings to retract.

They did, disappearing into his back to who-knows-exactly-where. David looked in the mirror and saw only his smooth back. No scars, no pouch, no increasedly prominent shoulder blades. No sign of his wings.

Insane! David thought, still trying to grasp where his wings had gone.

He unfurled his wings again.

Then he retracted them.

Again, no sign or identifying mark for his wings.

He was lucky it could be hidden for now. The real question was, for how long?

18 ✝ *Protectors of Men*

David was completely distracted during Warrior Training. Hiding wings was not easy as it seemed.

David was afraid that if he sneezed, his wings would pop out, or if he exerted himself in training, his wings would emerge in defense.

As his assigned sword-fighting opponent that day, Lukas was getting frustrated with him.

"Aw, C'mon David. Don't make it too easy for me. You haven't even realized that I've been pulverizing you for the last minute."

"Sorry, sorry." David apologized.

Lukas was right. He had to get his head in the fight or Lukas just might decapitate him by accident. David mustered up enough effort – just enough to defend himself, but he knew he was performing poorly.

Lukas finally gave up his aggressive moves, having decided that David had taken enough beating for the day.

They hunkered down on the floor, weapons on the ground, killing time before their next training session.

"Okay, spill. What is it?" Lukas asked in concern. "Is it the fight with the hellhound? Are you suffering from Post-Traumatic Stress Disorder? Because that's absolutely understandable and normal."

David shook his head. "No, that's not it. It's something else. Although now that you mention it, should I be suffering from Post-Traumatic Stress?"

"Not if you don't want to." Lukas chuckled, then abashedly apologized. "Seriously though, I heard that it's a common occurrence for warriors after their first mission, that's why we have counselors for that. It's only logical, right? Theory is not exactly the same as the practical application. Honestly, if it were me, I think I'd be peeing my pants the entire week after my first mission."

David grinned at the thought. "Nah, I think you're made of much stronger stuff than that."

"So, what's bothering you?"

"I'll tell you at lunch." David decided. "You and Rafaella. There's something I have to show you."

David was looking at their incredulous expressions, from Lukas' open-mouthed gaping to Rafaella's bulging eyes.

David had brought them to his room – locked the door and checked repeatedly – made them promise not to scream, then unfurled his wings for both of them.

"Please, please don't tell anyone until we've figured it out." David begged. "I don't want to get expelled."

"Why would you get expelled?" Rafaella frowned.

"Umm, hello, have you seen the color of my wings?"

Lukas tentatively touched a feather, so cautiously as though it may attack him. "I haven't seen wings this color before. They're always..........white."

"How about reading about it? You go to the library a lot,

right? Ever read about it? Or heard about it?" David asked, almost desperately.

Lukas and Rafaella shook their heads.

"Don't worry, David. I'm going to do research on it. After dinner tonight, I'll hit the library and coax Miss Theophila on much older works. Some tucked away book may have the answer." Lukas promised.

"You know, I could chat up Teacher Celestine and ask her – casually – about wings. Like I'm just completely curious and eager about it, which I am by the way." admitted Rafaella. "She's our Angelology teacher. All things regarding Angels, pure and half. She's bound to have an idea."

"Thanks Rafaella, that's a great suggestion. Just make sure it comes off as a 'hypothetical discussion'." David pleaded.

"Easily done." she shrugged.

Rafaella looked at his wings again, hand extended. "May I?"

David nodded and she reached out to touch his wings.

"I just hate you right now, David. I really do. First you get to fight with the hellhound, and now you have wings! Wings at fifteen!"

"Are you crazy?" David gasped. "They're black and grey! And, I almost died fighting that stupid hellhound, Rafaella. It wasn't fun."

"Still." she stubbornly replied. "I'd give anything to have wings right now. I might even accept pink if I get my wings early." Then she looked heavenwards. "Uh. No, cancel that. Erase that thought, axe that request. I do not want pink wings, do you hear me? No pink wings!"

Lukas and David were laughing at Rafaella's monologue.

"Let's grab some lunch. Sheesh," said David ruefully, glancing at the back of his torn shirt. "I sure am going through clothes fast.

Think laundry will notice the ripped clothes?"

"We can always blame Warrior Training." Lukas suggested.

"But we don't wear these to Warrior Training."

"Then you'll pretend to be a moron and say that you wore regular clothes to Warrior Training." Rafaella snickered.

"Gee, thanks."

"Don't worry, you can pull off looking like a moron. I see the expression crossing your face even if you're not aware of it." Rafaella countered.

"Ha. Ha."

"Is that your robot laugh now?"

"Oh, shut up, Rafaella. You sure are an annoying girl."

She batted her eyes at him. "I do try."

Lukas was laughing at their verbal warfare while David was thankful that they kept him sane and relatively normal. He was also relieved that they hadn't freaked out on him.

In the afternoon, Teacher Peregrine started Warrior Training with a lecture on *'Knowing Your Enemy – How to Spot a Demon Instantly'*. He also handed out pamphlets for them to study and David carefully read the following Tips:

— 1 A Demon can appear in different forms – animal, human, false angel, metaphysical disturbance (eg. Smoke, fog, lashing wind, etc...), natural form.

— 2 No matter how they try to disguise it, clues of their true nature will appear. (eg. Sulfurous breath or essence, glowing red or yellow eyes, pervasive evil).

— 3 Not all Demons are created equal. Some can be easily vanquished with a touch or injury from a Nephilim weapon, others require more fatal blows, and Rare Demons require special weapons.

— 4 They have potent powers of persuasion. They can be very charming and deceiving. (If you are average looking and is approached by a gorgeously stunning boy or girl, be suspicious!)

— 5 Trust your instincts. As Nephilims, we are wired to recognize them right away.

A raucous and lively discussion followed as students volleyed questions to Teacher Peregrine. Isaac asked, "Sir, is it true that they have acid for blood?"

"No it is not. They have foul and odorous black blood, not damaging like acid, but disgusting nonetheless. As for acid blood, when I was in the outside world, I happened to see a movie featuring an alien with acid blood.........." Teacher Peregrine trailed off with a smile.

"Do they all have fangs, sir?" asked Joseph, who was surprisingly awake.

"Yes. They may hide it at first, but when they combat, it almost always come out."

"Do they really have a poisonous bite?" a girl named Mary asked.

"Some of them. Not all of them do, but it's better to refrain from being bitten during combat. Others may also weaken you with a bite and hinder your powers of fast healing."

David jolted in his seat at Teacher Peregrine's words. Poisonous! Maybe he really had been poisoned! Plus, he knew the hellhound had weakened him when he was bitten. He really should do research on demon bites after dinner.

"Sir," said Dominic, one of Zachary's friends, "I'm not average looking, so if a gorgeously stunning girl approaches me, that doesn't mean she's a demon right?"

His question was met with loud boos and snickers. David and Lukas in particular enjoyed the booing.

"In your case," said Teacher Peregrine with a laugh, "she might very well be. Look at every girl approaching you as a demon, or a moron."

The class laughed at his words.

Lukas asked, "Are they faster than us, sir? During superspeed?"

"Again class, it depends on the demon. Just like Pure Angels and Half-Angels, most are strong and incredibly fast, but others prove even stronger and faster. Always expect an enemy to be stronger than you. That way, you never underestimate your opponent. Thus in combat, you will use the best weapon in your arsenal and you will always fight as though your life depends on it, because your life does depend on it."

The class was silenced by Teacher Peregrine's words. Once again they were all reminded that this wasn't a game, that Warrior Training wasn't only a subject, it was their lifeline and they were at war.

David raised his hand. "Sir, do demons have weapons? Do they use weapons in combat?"

"Yes, Mr. Cross. Not all of them do since they all possess long, razor-sharp claws, but it has been observed that their favorite weapon is the Scythe."

Katherine asked a question as well, a question that fearfully lurked in everyone's mind. "Sir, if they are Pure Demons and we are Half-Angels, are we not at a disadvantage already?"

"To be sure Pure Angels are stronger than us, but that does

not automatically imply that we are weaker than Pure Demons. We have the capabilities of Angels and have inherited the power to slay demons. Do not look upon your mortality as a disadvantage, rather accept it as a challenge to be better and to do better."

While the class pondered his words, Consortia came up with a question which was perhaps David's favorite in the entire afternoon.

"Sir, is it true that music will calm then obliterate demons? Perhaps if I sing to it sir?"

Teacher Peregrine did his best not to burst out laughing, although some chortles and choked laughter erupted from the class. "Uh, I'm sorry to say Miss Connelly that music has no effect whatsoever on demons. It was a nice thought, though."

"Now," said Teacher Peregrine. "It's my turn to ask you warriors a question."

He cast a beady eye about the room. "Why are we fighting demons? Why are they our enemy?"

Gertrude raised her hand to answer. "We fight them, sir, because they are evil. The purpose of their existence is to harm humans and to harm us."

"Perfectly phrased Miss Greer." said Teacher Peregrine. "Another question please, what then is the purpose of our existence?"

Rafaella answered, "To protect humans and to protect our kind."

Teacher Peregrine nodded. "Thank you Miss Pierce. And that, my dear warriors, is the reason why we are here today. We, Nephilims, are Protectors of Men. It is our duty. It is our vocation. Never forget that."

19 Nighttime Visit

David did a quick pass to the library after dinner to borrow a book on demon bites but decided to read in his room instead. It was only his first day hiding his strange wings and already he was tiring from the effort. He thought it was safer to hole up in his room and lessen his chances of discovery.

David plopped down on the bed with his book, but he had hardly turned the first page when the lights in his room flickered.

Way to go kid, he thought, his mouth set in a grim line. At least the lucky someone was getting a parent-visit.

David sighed. He really should stop hoping and secretly waiting.

Without warning, the lights went out.

David heard screams coming from outside so he knew it wasn't just his room having a black-out. Instinctively, he grabbed his dagger and was about to morph into Angel Mode so he could have night vision, when just as abruptly, the lights came back on.

David yelled in surprise.

Standing right beside his bed was a complete stranger.

An Angel.

"How – how did you get in here?" David gasped. "Who are you?"

The Pure Angel smiled at him, his very skin glowing

luminously of his essence. He didn't look like any of the half-angels David had met. He wasn't wearing the usual clothes of their kind, instead, he was battle-ready in all-black combat gear.

A Gothic Sword was strapped to his side and the Angel exuded such power and magnificence that David felt a crazy urge to cower before him.

This is a Warrior, David gazed in awe.

"Hello David." the Angel said. Even quietly speaking, his voice reverberated around the small room.

"My name is Michael. I'm your father."

David didn't know if he had heard correctly but his eyes were bulging out of their sockets in absolute shock. He was at a complete loss for words, sitting on his bed, seemingly paralyzed and unable to move or think.

Then, with a rapid rush of adrenaline, David leapt off the bed and started attacking his father.

He didn't care.

He didn't care if his father was a Pure Angel. If he could swat David away like a pesky bug.

If he would retaliate and cut David down in half with his Gothic Sword.

All David felt was anger and the overpowering need to lash out.

His father stood still as David hit him everywhere. He didn't even stop David.

"Get out!" David's voice trembled with rage. His body was vibrating with crackling anger as if he were a tightly pulled string that had been rudely strummed. "You can't just walk in here.....show up like the past fifteen years didn't happen."

"If I could explain -"

"You let my mom die!" David yelled at his father. "You let her die and left me all alone!"

Michael nodded, his piercing gray eyes flooded with pain and guilt.

Perhaps it was that expression on his father's face that made David pause. He lowered his arms, suddenly very weary. With the most contempt he could muster, David said, "Just get out of here."

"No." Michael replied. "Sit down David, and let me explain."

David stubbornly remained standing up.

"Please, David." his father asked gently. "I know you are angry. But I also know that you want answers. Please, let me give them to you."

Reluctantly, as though he would die if he just easily gave in, David sat down on the bed. He remained rigidly angry but as much as he hated to admit it, David needed answers.

His father sat across him

"If I could have done anything to prevent your mother's death from this earth, then I would have. But I had no choice, David. It was already her time."

"You could have prevented her death – I don't know, asked God for a miracle or something." David insisted. "Just..........something."

His father was shaking his head sadly. "It is God's law and even I could do nothing about it." He tried to reach out and touch David's hand, but David pulled away.

"Believe me, David, that it pains me greatly that you and your mother are not together. But she does live on. And you will see her again."

"Yes, I know." David's voice dripped with sarcasm. "In heaven – a place that I can't visit."

"Not yet. But someday you will. And you will see her again."

David looked at Michael, unable to believe that this Angel before him was his father. He looked too young to be a father for one thing, more like a young man in his early twenties, off to fight the war of the world.

Michael's eyes gave him away though. They were the knowing, astute, and ancient eyes of someone who had seen so much and lived so long.

"Do you see her?" David couldn't help asking.

"Yes, but not as often as I'd like. Of this I am certain, she misses you deeply and she watches over you constantly."

"I miss her a lot too." David felt somewhat of a sissy for saying it, but it was the truth. Still, he also had to find out another truth from his father.

"Why was I left on my own? In an orphanage?" David's voice hardened with each word. All the memories of loneliness and misery, of uncertainty and fury were crashing down on him.

"Why didn't you do something? Bring me to this place earlier?" David's gray eyes burned with pain and resentment. "You must have seen that I needed help! Why didn't you help me?"

"David, please forgive me that you were on your own for a long time. Truthfully, I have been keeping an eye on you even though I never intervened nor interfered in your life." his father stood up and walked towards the window, facing the dark night.

"It had been designed that way, you see, to ensure your independence, to make you more aware of the world outside – and not closeted immediately in the protection of this Monastery." he looked at David. "It was designed to make you stronger, because you need to be."

David stood up as well and faced his father. "We all need to be. Everyone here. And yet other parents brought their children as early as they could here. I could have trained earlier, learned sooner..........be with my own kind."

"You, my son -"

David flinched at the acknowledgement.

" - need to be stronger than others."

Michael solemnly asked David. "Do you know why the color of your wings is different?"

David's gaze locked with his father's in surprise. His dad knew about his wings?

"It is because we are different." his father said.

In a flash, his father brightened with such overpowering brilliance that David had to close his eyes. When he felt the light fading from his lids, he opened them in awe to look upon his father's wings.

They were black and gray – just like his own.

"I am the General of God's Army." his father said. "I have battled Lucifer and sent him and his minions to the depths of hell. I am Michael, the Archangel, and you are my son."

David felt his mind electrify with the force of this truth. He was the son of an Archangel? Of Michael – the General, the Triumphant Warrior who had been defeating demons since before man?

His father held David's face closely, their identical gray eyes staring into each other in recognition, locked in an elemental bond. "This is why you need to be stronger than others. I have crushed countless demons beneath my feet and they will pursue you in retaliation."

Michael's eyes were sad as he admitted to David. "You have inherited a timeless feud, David. As my son, you will be a target for their vengeance against me."

Michael drew out a dagger from his right side. It was exquisite – gleaming with a mirror-finish, twelve inches of double-edged steel with a five-inch handle of worked leather. The blazing sun insignia winked at David with reflected light.

"The Hand of God." David quietly murmured. "The original dagger."

Looking at his father, David realized something.

"It was you!"

Michael nodded in confirmation.

"You gave me the Dream Inspiration! You sent me that vision of the dagger and the message to make it as soon as I could."

David frowned in puzzlement. "Does this also mean you knew? You knew about the hellhound and about the planned attack?"

"Yes, I did." his father said. "But David, this is another matter that I came to warn you about." he sounded weary. "I will not be able to keep a constant watch over you. Nor will I be able to warn you every time danger is approaching."

Michael placed his hand on David's shoulder and while he felt he wasn't ready, David let him.

"Forgive me my son, but my time is not my own. As God's faithful soldier, I go wherever he sends me. Therefore I entreat you, David. Be always on your guard. Be vigilant!"

He continued. "As we have seen, even here – inside these walls – you are under attack. I show you this dagger to remind you. Keep your weapon close and be on full alert."

David silently contemplated his father's words, not only regarding his encounter with the hellhound, but also on future attacks if he left the seclusion of the Monastery. His father had revealed a disturbing truth. As Michael's son, David would be targeted, singled out for revenge.

"I'm going to train as hard as I can." promised David. "I'll make myself ready."

"I know you will." his father replied. "David, please let me say this," his father paused, uncertain. "I have watched you from the moment of your birth -"

"No!" David harshly said, turning away from his father. His mind or heart could not open to the idea.

He had never felt as if someone was watching over him. He had never felt the presence of a guiding force in his life. David had always felt alone, going through his young life knowing that he only had himself to rely on.

"I don't believe you." David gritted out. He couldn't believe it. He couldn't stand the thought that his father had been watching and yet, had done nothing.

"It is the truth." was Michael's quiet reply. "Whether you like it or not, the truth is I have been watching over you every chance I could. You, David, have been sown in a land of thorns, and yet, you have grown up strong, honest, intelligent and an outstanding warrior."

David could feel the ice around his heart thawing just a little bit at his father's words.

"I am so proud of you, David." his father said.

Coming from him, from this Archangel, David thought his heart would burst at the compliment and at his father's obvious pride. He felt himself growing warmer, burning hotter, and David saw his entire being brighten with his father's approval.

He was glowing! Pulsating with the life force of a giant sun. And he felt his wings open behind him, taking in the moment of precious connection with his father.

David knew that he had not yet forgiven his father. Not entirely. And he knew that he was still angry. But this minute, this second – it was their time. They were linked, strongly and faithfully, by blood, essence, and spirit.

20  Halo Attack

There was a brief knock on the door and Rafaella came bursting in.

"David! Your father must be an Archangel! That's why your wings are black and gray -" she froze mid-stride when she realized she was interrupting.

When Rafaella's gaze landed on Michael, she gave a loud gasp.

"Michael!" she shrieked. It was the first time David had ever seen Rafaella shriek. She was swooning like a teenager before a favorite popstar. Then, unexpectedly, she grabbed Michael in a crushing hug, babbling insanely as she did so.

"Oh my God! This is just crazy! You're my favorite, most absolute hero! I mean, I'm just dying right now, absolutely dying. And I don't usually babble, right David? I'm not like this. Oh my God! Such an honor. Such an honor to meet you!"

Rafaella was actually curtsying.

"I must have your autograph, something, anything......David!" she shrieked again. "Give me a pen, a paper, a shirt......whatever. Please, please can I have your autograph?"

When she finally allowed herself to breathe, Rafaella looked at David and his father, their wings were unfurled, their striking gray eyes stared back at her, they had similar facial expressions and were even standing the same way.

Rafaella's eyes widened like never before, her pupils dilating in realization.

"Michael, sir, are you..........are you David's father?"

When Michael nodded, Rafaella sat weakly on the bed, just staring at them. For once, she was speechless.

The next day was a Saturday. David woke up to a sharp and clear morning and he felt wonderfully free of his burdens.

What did half-angels do on a weekend? David mused.

He gazed outside his window and saw several cherubs playing tag, their tiny wings fluttering madly as they chased after each other, bouncing and tumbling in the air with infectious giggles. They sure were a happy bunch.

The essence pets had also come out to play and he could see several frolicking outside on the lawn. Wolverine was there, dragging himself across the snow in simple canine pleasure.

David showered and dressed for the day and when he was about to go out, a familiar knock sounded on his door. Before he could open it himself, Rafaella came barging in again, this time dragging Lukas with her.

"Hey!" David protested. "You can't just barge in here anytime you want to Rafaella. I could have been changing!"

"Lock your door then." she sassed at him. "Oh my God, I still can't believe I humiliated myself that way last night with THE Michael. THE Ultimate Archangel." She hurled herself on the bed, punching David's pillows in frustration.

"Did I really act that way? Was I really babbling and being insane?" she looked at David pleadingly. "Please tell me I wasn't as pathetic as I remember."

Lukas sat down on a chair. "I still can't believe Michael is your father." he was shaking his head looking quite stunned. "Wow, David. This is so – ungraspable. I'm not even his son and *I'm* reeling from the news."

He looked at David. "How do you feel?"

David shrugged. "I don't think it's sunk in yet."

"It explains a lot of things though." Lukas commented. "Your warrior skills, your instincts,"

"Your incredibly super speed." added Rafaella.

"It's not all good, you guys." David said quietly. "I may have inherited those things, but I also inherited Michael's burden."

Rafaella sat up on the bed. "What are you talking about?"

"Demon vengeance." David grimly replied.

The three of them became silent, processing the implications of David's inheritance, until Lukas – forcing to be cheerful – stood up and said, "Well, you don't have to think about that today. We signed up for Halo Attack, you included, and it's going to be wild."

"Halo Attack?"

Rafaella grinned. "You'll see."

David groaned. "I hate being a newbie."

They headed outside into icy morning air after an artery-clogging breakfast at the cafe and Lukas and Rafaella led David to an outdoor section that he had never been to.

This area was fenced in by immense metal bars and coming from the inside, David could hear roars and snarls.

"What exactly is this place?"

"This is one of our arenas for sporting events or team combats, and this is also where we play Halo Attack." Lukas replied.

They climbed up some stairs until they reached the entrance of the arena and when they did, David just stood there, taking it all in. Now he knew what was making the snarling and roaring sounds.

It didn't look like it from the outside, but the arena was huge and sprawling, fencing in an impressive acreage of blindingly white land. All around it were spectator seats, sloping upwards for a fantastic view of the grounds.

Most amazing of all were the creatures in the middle of the arena, lumbering gracefully in their majestic power.

Polar Bears.

Before David could even react, he saw some students walking up to the polar bears, as if it wasn't the most idiotic and suicidal thing to do.

"Relax, warrior." Rafaella teased, knowing David was about to morph into Angel Mode and rescue some witless students.

"The polar bears are part of Halo Attack. We ride on them."

"Say that again?"

Lukas explained as they descended towards the bears. "Halo Attack is Team Battle. Usually with four teams competing against each other. We each have a polar bear to ride on and the objective of the game is to make all your opponents fall off their bears. Last man – or woman – standing, or should I say, still astride a bear, wins."

"Quick question," smiled David. "How do we make the polar bears not have us for breakfast?"

"They already ate." Rafaella replied with a straight face. Then with an impish grin she answered, "We're Nephilims, David. One of our abilities is power over animals. Any animal. We can communicate with them."

"You guys! You have to tell me these things way before we do them." David exclaimed. "So, how do we communicate with them, exactly?"

"Incredibly easy." said Lukas. "You just transform into Angel Mode and for some supernatural reason, they understand us. They can understand what we're saying."

"We just ask them, *nicely*, what to do, and they follow." added Rafaella.

When they reached the bottom of the stairs, they bumped into Consortia and Katherine who were on their way back up.

David noticed for the first time how Lukas pinkened a bit as he smiled at Consortia.

"Ah....uh....Did you sign up for Halo Attack today, Consortia?" Lukas squeaked.

Consortia grimaced at Lukas' suddenly squeaky voice and flipped her long red hair back. "Ugh, never. I have no desire in volunteering for activities that will only result in myself becoming sunburned and sweaty and completely unladylike."

Katherine nodded in agreement.

"I will be much better off indoors where it is nice and cool and very calming."

"I'm sure we'll all be better off with you indoors." muttered Rafaella, but she was drowned out by an enthusiastic Lukas.

"Oh, but it's so nice out here today, and don't you find Halo Attack exciting?"

Consortia only stared at him cooly. "Remember recently when the Crab Nebula spurted mysterious flares?"

"Oh, yes. I read about it in the news. Isn't it quite thrilling?" Lukas beamed.

"It is indeed, for all the geektellectuals interested in such events. As for me and Katherine, we find it as exciting as watching our nail polish dry."

"And that's how we feel about Halo Attack." she fake yawned.

"We only came down to say hello to the polar bears." cooed Katherine. "They're so adorable."

"Shall we have tea at the museum?" Consortia asked Katherine. "Ooh, we can gaze at my favorite Renoir and read poetry all afternoon."

"Splendid!" gushed Katherine and the two girls continued their way up the stairs, oblivious to Rafaella's murderous stare and Lukas' gooey eyes.

"How I hate that condescending twit!" said Rafaella.

"Well," defended Lukas, "She's just being herself and being truthful about it."

"Honestly Lukas, for a smart boy, you can be incredibly thick. Don't you even say that you like Consortia or I will beat you right now until you come to your senses." Rafaella threatened, then she huffed down the remaining steps toward the polar bears.

David was pleased to discover that their team of five members consisted of Lukas, Rafaella, Joseph, Gertrude and himself. He had been wanting a chance to thank Gertrude for her help in uncovering Tatiana's innocence and in revealing Innocent's part of the plan. Perhaps, after the game, he would be able to thank her properly.

They had changed into fitted white sports gear with a bold blue, slightly padded vest. Their leader for the morning's game was Lukas, who, though not as swift and nimble as Rafaella, propelled himself with the brains for strategy that should help their team fight their daunting competitors.

The Red Team was no other than Caian James' group. He was another person that David needed to thank. He had not forgotten what Jerome had told him. Caian saved his life. He was standing here because of Caian's quick rescue.

Jerome, as expected, was in Caian's team, along with two good-looking senior boys, and a stunning girl. Attractiveness was apparently a contagious magnet since David had never seen a plain looking Nephilim in Caian's group.

The Yellow Team were tough-looking sixteen year-olds headed by a boy named Abraham, while the Green Team consisted of Zachary, Giles and three of their troll buddies. Zachary had apparently recovered from his sullen stupor as he scowled menacingly at David once again.

David felt his body clench with anger. He could barely digest the evidence of Zachary's absolute absence of remorse. The slippery criminal was openly mocking him when David knew he was guilty.

Zachary was guilty of attempted murder and he was getting away with it. Worse still, he had allowed his supposed friend, Innocent, to take full blame for the crime. The injustice was almost enough to make David run towards Zachary and take matters into his own hands.

"Something is being done about it." a soft voice said beside him in an attempt to calm him down. Amazingly, Gertrude was again perceptive of his thoughts.

"That's beginning to get creepy, you know." David said, accepting her effort to calm him. She was right. This was not the place to pick a fight, and fighting Zachary would not prove his guilt.

"Just keep your mind on the game." Gertrude said. "Who knows, you could be the one to stun that maggot Zachary immediately. Although such a tiny consolation, it will be quite satisfying."

Soon they were sitting astride the polar bears, each bear equipped with a harness and a saddle, waiting for the shrill rip of the whistle to signal the start of Halo Attack.

As his teammates had explained to David, the objective of the game was to take out their opponents and be the last team standing.

Their weapon?

Their halos.

"We have a halo?" David laughed. "I thought only Saints and everybody else in heaven had those!"

"Yeah, surprisingly, we do too." Lukas said. "Although ours doesn't mean that we're holy or anything like that. Ours is more like a weapon."

"Seriously?"

They all nodded.

Rafaella demonstrated. "It's very easy to conjure. All you have to do is close your eyes and think of a halo on top of your head."

She did so, and right before David's eyes, a halo formed, floating at the top of Rafaella's head.

"Watch this." she said. Rafaella grasped her halo, which became suddenly solid at her touch, then she deftly spun it from her like a frisbee and it arced forcefully towards a metal fence, clanging loudly upon impact. Then, her halo boomeranged back to her waiting hand.

It was beyond words.

"But they'd also be throwing their halos at us." David concluded with a frown. "Does it hurt?"

"It'll stun you and knock you out cold, like you've been sucker punched." answered Lukas.

"Oh great."

"When you get hit, remember to hold on to your bear." Joseph advised. "You don't want to fall off and get trampled."

"What?" David thought they were joking, but they clearly

weren't.

Gertrude added her reassuring bit. "Don't worry David. We heal quickly, remember?"

At her words, the whistle sounded.

The four teams entered from different portals of the arena, and for David it was a riveting sight – twenty Nephilims riding on huge polar bears, bounding towards each other, their colored vests identifying their teams as the bears roared and reared in excitement. The spectators cheered as the players came into view.

Then the four leaders met in the center of the arena. It was time for alliances. They were buddying up. Theirs and Caian's team, versus the Yellow and Green team.

With alliances in place, the teams thundered towards their opponents in a blizzard of spinning and zooming halos.

David ducked close to his bear, thankful and amazed that the bears were impervious to the halos. Twice, David felt halos whirring near him. The first one was a fast spin from a glaring Zachary which nearly caught David by the ear. A quick evasion had saved David from being stunned.

The second one was from a leering and idiotic Giles, whom Zachary had very obviously influenced. It was clear that David was their primary target.

David was furious with both of them and was itching to stun them out of the game. He decided to target Giles first. Time to remove the simian side-kick.

All of the players were in Angel Mode and David's senses were on full throttle. His vision was sharp and telescopically clear, his hearing acutely sensitive. His body was thrumming with awareness, noting vibrations in the air whenever a halo streaked close to him.

With all the players in a high state of awareness, the game

wasn't easy as it seemed. Halos were flying everywhere but the players were fast and adept at evading the attack.

David grasped his halo, it was disc-thin and cool to the touch, then he spun it towards Giles.

Giles was also crouched low over his bear and when he saw David's approaching halo, he changed directions but ran right smack into the halo's curving trajectory.

David yelled out in satisfaction as his calculations paid off. He knew Giles would change directions, happily, towards where David guessed he would.

Giles was out cold. David's halo had caught him right at the rib and David barely noticed as four medic cherubs fluttered over Giles inert body. The cherubs slowly led the slumped Giles and his polar bear out of the arena.

As David surfaced from his combat with Giles, he took the opportunity to scan the arena and investigate how his team was doing.

Lukas was signaling for David to join forces with him since a double attack would be more aggressive and effective in taking out opponents. Gertrude and Rafaella had teamed up, slowly but surely eliminating players from the Yellow and Green team with their spin fast halo throws and imaginative escapes.

Joseph was nowhere in sight and David had to assume that he was out of the game. Already, the players in the field had dwindled to half the original number. Caian's team was lightning fast, steadily gaining advantage over the other teams.

David nudged his polar bear to where Lukas was, but halfway there, he was intercepted by an avenging Zachary, this time teaming up with Rusticus, another fifteen-year-old buddy. They simultaneously threw their halos at David and as David saw one halo streaking towards his face, he let himself slide sideways on his bear, almost cartwheeling backwards but holding on to the saddle to keep from completely falling off. The second halo barely cleared his leg.

Using his polar bear as shield, David countered with a snappy throw of his halo towards Rusticus who had not been expecting his quick comeback. David got him full on the chest and the boy tumbled off his polar bear as he got knocked out.

David heard Zachary's furious roar and he couldn't help but smile grimly. This time he was going for Zachary.

David sat astride his bear again, still crouched low and on the lookout for attacks. As Zachary waited for his halo to boomerang back to him, he ran off from David's line of fire, hugging his body flat on the polar bear.

Pointing at Zachary, David nudged his polar bear to pursue and they zigzagged their way across the arena, making nano-second swerves to avoid being knocked-out by incoming halos. He could see Zachary looking over his shoulder at David every now and then.

As they neared the opposite end of the arena, Zachary faked a turn and as David switched directions to follow, something unexpected happened.

Zachary turned 180 degrees so that he was abruptly facing David. In that click of a finger, Zachary had the advantage of surprise and had spun his halo at David before David could even register what was happening.

The halo was almost an inch to David's face when his superspeed reflexes saved him. He twisted away in time, grasping his own halo as he did so and spinning it forcefully at a triumphantly smiling Zachary.

The halo caught Zachary right in the face, and his expression of triumph quickly changed from utter surprise, to disbelief, to beginning outrage before the force of the halo knocked him over backwards, making him fall off his polar bear in an unconscious heap.

"YES!!!" David punched the air repeatedly in satisfaction. He had finally gotten his bit of revenge to the inexcusable slime which had set the hellhound on him.

David turned his bear around and headed back to his teammates. *Now*, he could buddy-up with Lukas.

21 Paper Trail

By the time David joined Lukas, the entire Green team had been eradicated and only two members from the Yellow team remained. Caian and his group relentlessly went after one Yellow player while Rafaella, Lukas and Gertrude zoomed their halos at the other surviving member of the Yellow team.

Even as David caught up with them, his three friends had successfully stunned the Yellow player and immediately, all four of them turned towards the still intact five-member Red Team.

The alliance was over. Now it was Blue versus Red.

"I'll go with Rafaella. David, you go with Gertrude." instructed Lukas. "It's time to split up."

They paired accordingly and commanded their polar bears into different directions. Already, halos were whirring at them and as David and Gertrude rumbled off, they heard the clanging sounds of halos striking the metal fence where they had previously been.

Jerome plus the stunning girl and another senior were chasing after them.

"Move forward on your bear." Gertrude yelled over the noise of the fight.

David immediately followed her instructions and to his surprise, Gertrude executed an acrobatic leap and landed on David's bear, right behind him, facing towards their opponents. She twirled her halo at the three chasers and managed to hit the other boy who had assumed from Gertrude's aim that she was going to take down Jerome.

His guess was wrong and he paid for his mistake with a tumble off his polar bear as he got knocked out.

"By the way," Gertrude yelled over her shoulder. "Our Choir is having a concert tonight after dinner, and I'm singing -"

"What?!"

"I would love for you to come and watch. It will be at Saraqael Hall – the performance center-"

"Yes! Yes!" David screamed at her as he maneuvered their bear in swerving and circuitous motions just to evade a determined Jerome and pretty girl. "Are you insane? Keep your eyes on them and keep attacking!"

"I am." replied Gertrude as she grabbed David's halo and snapped it at Jerome.

She missed.

"Time to split up." Gertrude gaily exhorted and with a sharp whistle, her polar bear bounded next to them. Once again, she gracefully leaped and landed confidently astride her bear.

"I'll see you tonight, David." she called out, moving away from him with the pretty girl at her tail. The pretty girl's halo almost nicked Gertrude at the shoulder but amazingly, Gertrude escaped.

David decided that it was time to stop running.

He couldn't defend himself with his back turned to Jerome. He had to face him instead.

He commanded his bear to turn around and with a flick of his wrist, his halo twisted towards Jerome. Jerome threw his halo at David and the two weapons forcefully collided, tainting the air with the scent of burnt ozone and the sizzling crackle of electricity. Their halos ricocheted back to their owners and as soon as David grasped his, he sent it flying back to Jerome.

Jerome was still in the act of catching his own halo when David's halo hit him by the midsection. He looked at David in utter surprise then collapsed on top of his bear.

"Sorry Jerome." David muttered. "But we play to win."

Looking around him he saw that Lukas was out of the game. So was Gertrude.

At the other end of the arena, Rafaella was battling Caian and another Red team boy. David hoped to reach them in time to help Rafaella.

Even from a distance, David saw a halo strike Rafaella on the chest and she swung limply atop her bear. Surprisingly, and soon after, the other Red team player collapsed too. Rafaella must have thrown a parting shot that had hit her opponent.

"Way to go, Rafaella!" David cheered, along with the amazed and clamoring onlookers.

Then a hush fell as Teacher Victorinus, the Halo Attack Referee, announced over the speaker system.

"Final players of this morning's Halo Attack – Caian James and David Cross!"

The spectators cheered and yelled in anticipation of the showdown. Some were yelling David! David! David!

But mostly, the crowd was chanting for Caian – Senior Warrior extraordinaire, Monastery poster boy and over-all hero.

From almost opposite ends of the arena, Caian and David looked at each other.

The game was on!

David's and Caian's bear rushed towards each other as their riders commanded them, their massive paws thundering over the hard ground, covering huge spaces in single bounds.

Defensively, David was using his bear as armor and he was hanging off its side, making sure he was angled away from Caian.

Caian was doing the same, hanging off the side of his bear but plodding on to meet David's approach.

Suddenly, Caian sat atop his bear, but hugging his body as flat as he could to the bear's fur and he aggressively made a beeline for David.

Seeing Caian on top of the bear, David took the opportunity to attack. He carefully aimed and spun his halo to Caian's body, but as expected from such a skilled warrior, Caian veered away with seconds to spare.

The watching crowd oohhd at his escape and a loud applause followed as Caian remained unscathed.

Caian continued on a frontal assault at David, appearing unfazed that their polar bears were about to butt heads. Caian looked pretty determined for a collision to occur so David gritted his teeth and plowed on, wondering at the back of his mind what Caian was up to.

Just before a collision could happen, Caian nudged his bear to change course but he himself made a leap for David, his halo already spinning away, its aim true as David saw it headed straight towards him.

David allowed himself to cartwheel backwards, tumbling off his bear and landing on the hard ground. He had escaped!

Surprisingly, the spectators burst into applause, cheering David on. David heard his bear grunt and pause a bit as it took the full brunt of the striking halo.

Immediately, David whirled his halo at Caian who had just landed on his bear, this time almost nicking Caian at the arm. The experienced warrior dodged the attack and countered with another beautifully aimed halo at David.

David had expected to be clobbered instantly by Caian, lasting mere seconds in the arena with him, so David was happy that he was holding his ground.

They continued to fight – hurling fire bright halos at each other, delivering rapid throws and executing clever foils. Finding ways to be creative in an attempt to catch the other off guard.

The arena was roaring with excitement, the spectators tremendously pleased by the thrilling match. David knew that he had to find a way to outsmart Caian. How was he ever going to hit him with his halo when Caian managed to escape every time? David also knew that while he had luckily eluded Caian's spinning halo so far, it would only be a matter of time before Caian's skills would defeat him. Eventually, experience would trump luck.

He could only think of one thing to do.

Whispering to his tiring bear, David began running around the arena, hanging off the side of his bear and protecting his body from Caian's sight.

Around and around they went, running in circles with a bewildered but focused Caian at the middle. Caian estimated David's trajectory and continued to spin his halo at them, sometimes hitting the poor bear, or the metal fence behind David. One time, David almost got it in the face as he took a peek at Caian. Still, he didn't attack, continuing instead to run in tighter and tighter circles, getting slightly dizzy as his bear obediently ran continuous laps around the arena. David encouraged his bear, praising the faithful animal and asking it to hang on and just keep going.

Finally, Caian lost patience as he stood in the middle of David's running circle. He could see that David was closing in, slowly hemming him in from all sides. Caian knew better than to get trapped inside the tightening circle.

In a decisive move, Caian and his bear made a bounding leap to break free from the circle and as he did so, David threw his halo at Caian, carefully calculating the path Caian would take and where he would be most vulnerable.

As David's halo spun away, appearing ahead of Caian as though missing its mark, Caian ran towards the rapidly rotating halo, trying desperately to change his course. With a deft twist of his body and a testament to his tremendous skills as a warrior, Caian barely cleared David's halo through an impossible-looking feat. And as David once again gaped in surprise at Caian's stunning evasion, he didn't see the warrior's sharply spun counter-attack.

The senior's halo made a definitive impact on David, hitting him surely in the chest, caught off-guard as he was from assuming certain victory. Blunt pain bloomed from David's solar plexus, his body folding from the blow, his face momentarily frozen in surprise and disbelief.

"Oh." were David's last words before everything blacked out.

His final view was of Caian's triumphant face and the thundering sound of the arena bursting with yells and applause.

That night, David fidgeted with his bow-tie as he and Rafaella walked through the glass corridor in the direction of Saraquel Hall. He had just learned that concerts were dressy affairs in the Monastery and he had been unpleasantly surprised when Rafaella knocked on his door earlier that evening carrying a tuxedo for David.

"What's that for?" he had asked bug eyed. "I'm not wearing that!" he might as well wear a straightjacket.

"You have to or you can't watch the concert." Rafaella said matter of factly.

David thought for a minute. "Fine. I'll stay in my room tonight."

"You can't. You promised Gertrude you'd watch and Lukas is also performing."

David groaned and reluctantly accepted his tuxedo. "Where did you get this anyway?"

"The illustrious Garments Class, otherwise known as the Monastery Closet. Any outside clothes you want, they have there. And you can order other stuff too."

"Jeans and shirts?" David asked hopefully. "Not in white?'

Rafaella laughed. "Yes, that too."

And so with much trepidation, David had donned the formal suit – complete with shiny black shoes – and even draped the white scarf thing over his shoulders, forcing himself not to laugh at his reflection. He'd seen grown-ups on TV wearing such outfits and he had always thought the men looked as though long towels were hanging down their necks.

David kept glancing at Rafaella as they walked to the concert. She was all dressed up too and looked, well, very pretty. David was having a hard time not staring at his friend. She was beautiful before but tonight in her gown and heels with her hair flowing and loose down her back, she looked amazing. Was she wearing makeup? Whatever it was she did, David was beginning to feel uncomfortable around her.

Suddenly he was very aware that he was a boy and she was a girl. A very pretty girl.

As they entered the lobby of the performance hall, David stood rooted on the spot, gazing around the impressive décor of the place. It was as if he had stepped into another world, or more appropriately, stepped back into the outside world.

Saraquel Hall mirrored the beautiful theaters of large cities. David had never been in one of course, but he had seen enough television to recognize it. The lobby had an old-fashioned charm with very high and gilded ceilings, enormous and cascading chandeliers, deep carpets and arrangements of plush sofas and chairs.

Teachers and students hovered around concession stands manned by cherubs who served champagne (for grown-ups), lemonade and sparkling cider for the underage masses, and platters of hors d'oeuvres or those tiny appetizers that you could swallow in one gulp.

David was adjusting to how everyone looked in tuxedos and dresses, never having been to anything so formal before. Yet somehow, the normal world setting only underlined the fact that they were not normal people who would live regular lives.

"That was a very well-played game today, David." Caian greeted him. David was impressed by how goodnatured the senior was. "Congratulations."

David reddened at the compliment and muttered thanks. "I lost and you were really amazing."

"So were you." acknowledged Caian. "I do believe only my far longer experience saved my neck today." he added generously. "You would have beaten me otherwise."

David reddened even more at the Alpha Warrior's belief in him. "Uh....I still have a very *very* long way to go before I'll even be in league with you. And saying 'I'll be in league with you' sounds ridiculous. And impossible."

Caian shook his head at David, on his face an I-believe-in-you expression. "Certainly you will be at my skills caliber." assured Caian. "and sooner than you expect, I imagine."

Turning to the girl at his side, Caian said, "By the way, I would like to introduce you to my girlfriend -" David almost gave an embarrassed snicker "- Antonia Tremont."

It was the stunning girl who also played Halo Attack. She gave them a cool nod and looked bored with their company. She certainly appeared snooty and contrasted to Caian's friendliness.

David introduced them to Rafaella as well, who was disturbingly gazing at the handsome Caian with worshipping eyes. She was even oblivious to Antonia's disapproving frown.

"Well, we'd best return to our group. Good game, David, Rafaella. Until next time." Caian waved off.

"Isn't he amazing." she breathed. "Top of his class from what I hear and the best student warrior in the Monastery. And to think that he's also nice and friendly."

David felt irritated by her gushing commentary. "Yeah, yeah, he's absolutely perfect. Come on, let's get a drink." and he strode to a nearby concession stand.

He almost bumped into a hurrying Liz who seemed in a rush to leave. She was pale and waxy and looked likely to vomit anytime.

"Are you okay?" David asked.

Liz managed a nod. "Must have ingested something that's not agreeing with me."

"I'll help you to the Infirmary."

"No, no." she blushed. "Two Puttis are accompanying me. Please David, I'll be fine. Really."

And with the last of her reserve, she zoomed out of the Hall along with two cherubs who were half carrying her.

"Oh, I really hope she feels better." Rafaella murmured, catching up with David.

"Me too." said David, worrying for his little Healer.

Later, as they seated themselves for the concert, David didn't know what to expect of the show, it being his first one. A whole night of choir singing? It sounded so fearfully boring and he had in fact asked Rafaella to wake him up when it was Lukas or Gertrude's turn in case he fell asleep. He also asked her to make sure he didn't snore.

She only shook her head at him in disapproval.

David was happily surprised that the show caught his attention from the start. The music was powerful and vibrant and the show transitioned seamlessly from one act to the next.

Lukas performed a heartfelt duet with Consortia (!!!), their harmonized voices soaring through the hall.

But the star of the evening was Gertrude.

She was incomparable.

David had no background knowledge of music or theater, but it was extraordinary how undeniable real talent was when one was faced with it.

Gertrude rendered a breathtaking performance, her voice capturing his imagination with its beauty. She also looked incredible in her elegant white gown that sparkled each time she moved. She performed three solos during the concert, each one more jaw-dropping than the last.

As the curtain dropped to a close, everyone in the audience, David included, stood up in applause. The curtain opened again and the choir took their bows and curtsies amidst shouts of bravos and a thundering ovation.

When the show was over, David and Rafaella made their way back towards the lobby, taking their time as students and teachers comfortably chatted along the aisles, simply enjoying the festiveness of the evening.

They were in no hurry themselves, it was a Saturday after all, and so waited patiently as the throng moved at a snail's pace to the exit.

Abruptly, someone bumped David from behind, accompanied by a growling. "Out of the way booger brain."

It was Zachary in all his crass and primitive glory.

Without waiting for any reply or acknowledgement, he plunged through the crowd away from David and Rafaella, a square white something fluttering down behind him.

David didn't hesitate to pick it up, very curious as to what Zachary had dropped. When he saw what he was holding, he beckoned excitedly at Rafaella.

"Come look at this."

They both stared at the card David was holding. It was a puzzle of sorts with different words inside a boxed square. Most significantly was a word David and Rafaella had heard before.

S	A	T	O	R
A	R	E	P	O
T	E	N	E	T
O	P	E	R	A
R	O	T	A	S

"Arepo." they both murmured.

They had found a clue!

"What else is written?" Rafaella asked.

"Nothing else on the front." said David. Flipping the card

over, he saw a hastily scrawled word at the back.

Tonight.

He and Rafaella looked at each other.

What was going to happen tonight?

22 The Puzzling Palindrome

As planned, David and Rafaella met up with Lukas and Gertrude after the concert. They managed to get a table all to themselves, which was a miracle considering how crowded the *Pearly Gates Cafe* was.

David and Rafaella had already decided on their way to the cafe to trust Gertrude into their confidence and to ask her help in solving their newfound clue. She could also provide more details as to what she and the cherub, Tatiana, had seen inside Innocent's questionable brain during that terrible night of the hellhound attack.

As the four settled down with their cakes and coffee, David and Rafaella plunged into enthusiastic praise for Gertrude's and Lukas' performance at the concert. Admittedly, David was somewhat star-struck with Gertrude at the moment, unable to comprehend that the Gertrude he was talking to was the same shining girl on stage.

"Remember that night when you were called to Dream Invade Tatiana?" Rafaella dived in purposefully after their preliminary niceties. "I'm not sure if you recall but at the end of your interview, Tatiana said an unusual word -"

"Arepo." Gertrude nodded.

"Yes, exactly. Did you see what she saw? What she remembered?"

Gertrude frowned in concentration. "If my memory serves me

correctly, I had already pulled out of her mind when she mentioned the word. Sadly, I never saw what she did that time."

"What did you think of it at that time?" asked David.

"To be honest, I merely thought Tatiana had uttered a random word, that there was no significance to it. Or that perhaps she was feeling guilty for betraying David and everyone else. I do know what Arepo means. It's Latin for -"

"Trust." Rafaella and Lukas finished together.

"We've discussed it before, Gertrude." Lukas nodded. "But I think tonight, David and Rafaella has more to tell us."

Rafaella handed the crisp white card to Lukas, Gertrude peering over his shoulder.

"Zachary dropped it." Rafaella solemnly revealed.

Lukas and Gertrude studied the card intently, Gertrude following the words with her finger and making vertical and horizontal excursions on the paper.

"It's obviously a palindrome." Gertrude said. "a Latin palindrome. Look how clever it is. It can be read top to bottom and vice-versa. It may also be read left to right and right to left and the words will remain the same. What a clever word square this is!" she finished in amazement.

"I did notice that." said Rafaella. "and I thought it was incredibly smart for the person carrying it. Too smart in fact. Sure, he's not as dim as Giles, but what's Zachary doing with a word square? It's not exactly his style, is it?"

"Wait, wait." David said. "What exactly is a palindrome? You guys may be getting it, but I'm not."

"Well, a palindrome is a word, a phrase or numbers that can be read the same way in either direction." Gertrude explained. "For example, the word RADAR, which if you read from left to right or right to left would still be read as RADAR. Another example is LEVEL, or CIVIC. You get the general idea. It can also be a phrase such as 'STEP ON NO PETS' or it can be a sentence."

"Thanks Gertrude, that helps me a lot. And this palindrome we have here, all the words are in latin?"

Lukas and Gertrude nodded.

"You're the ones taking Latin." said Rafaella, "why don't you translate it for us."

"Sator means a sower, or a farmer." said Lukas

"It can also mean a founder." added Gertrude. "Arepo means trust but it can also imply movement, or to move."

"Yes," Lukas agreed. "Tenet is to keep or hold and Opera means work."

"Really?" said Rafaella. "I always imagined it to be theater related. What about Rotas?"

"That's the easy one." Gertrude said. "Rotas or to rotate or simply, a wheel."

"That's great!" David interjected. "So we've translated it! We know what it means, right?"

Lukas and Gertrude shook their heads. "Latin is pretty tricky." Lukas professed, slowly sipping his tea. "The truth is, it can mean a lot of things."

"Such as, the Farmer Keeps Working on his Wheels or plough." Gertrude murmured. "But in that translation, Arepo is lost and excluded. Not unless the name of the farmer is Arepo. Therefore the translation would become: the Farmer Arepo Keeps Working on his Wheels. But even then, it is such a plain and insignificant message when translated in that manner."

David shook his head. "I find it hard to believe that Zachary would be interested in farmers and ploughs and hard work."

"Me too." said Rafaella. "Do you think it's just a.....game? A puzzle maybe that he was working on?"

Lukas snorted. "I can't imagine Zachary spending his free time working on puzzles."

"Besides," David reminded them. "We can't forget that there's a message at the back of the card."

Lukas flipped the card over. "Tonight?"

"I wonder what he's up to tonight?" Rafaella wondered out loud. "Should we go scouting around the Monastery right now and find out where he is and what he's doing?"

David sat up straight. "I have a better idea. Tatiana!"

"What about -" Rafaella began to ask but David was already off and headed to the cherub.

"I'll be right back!"

A few minutes later, David was back at their table greeted by curious and questioning looks from his friends.

"I asked Tatiana to look for Zachary. It's only logical, right? Don't cherubs know the Monastery inside and out?"

"Great idea." Lukas agreed. "I just hope she does find him so we'll know what this tonight business is about." he tapped the word square card, lost in thought. "Something's nagging me about this palindrome, it's like I've seen it before or have come across it. I just can't remember where. One thing's for sure, I'm digging into the library tomorrow and see what I can find."

"I'll join you." Gertrude volunteered. "Although I must admit, I've never laid eyes on that word square before."

David looked at the card again, staring deeply into the rapidly scrawled *tonight*. Somehow he knew that this wasn't some puzzle or game that Zachary was playing with. Tatiana had uttered Arepo when she was remembering her Dream Invasion by Innocent. And now, the same word had turned up again, this time in a mysterious latin palindrome, and somewhere in the Monastery, at this very moment even, Zachary was meeting a person or persons and was up to something.

"What are we doing?" David smacked his forehead. "You're right Rafaella! We shouldn't be sitting here just talking about this card. We have to look for Zachary. It might be our only chance to find out what this Arepo is all about. And what if he's out there tonight hurting someone else? What if he had set another trap?"

They were instantly on their feet and rushing out the Cafe.

"Let's meet up at the Cube in five minutes." Rafaella said.

"First, let's get out of these crazy clothes."

They decided to split into pairs and search for Zachary at each level of the Monastery beginning at the very ground floor where the catacombs were. David and Gertrude streaked alongside each other through the maze of their designated half of the lay-out, but came up empty handed each time.

No sign of Zachary.

They did interrupt a couple of fourth-year students kissing in an underground room and they both blushed and stammered their way out from the young lovers tryst.

At each level, David and Gertrude met up with Lukas and Rafaella, who shook their heads as they too saw no shadow or self of the hidden Zachary. The problem was, the Monastery was huge and even in Angel Mode, it took quite some time to explore every nook and crevice of the place. And what if there were secret passages or rooms that they were not aware of?

By the time they sweep-searched the third floor, it was well past midnight and the chimes of curfew had long since sounded. Now, they were breaking school rules and David had a painful flash of a smiling-sneering Prefect Macarius gleefully doling out a more than suitable punishment for the four of them.

Up the next level, they ran into an exhausted Tatiana who tearfully informed them that she had not been able to locate Zachary. David felt incredibly guilty for having requested what now appeared to be a herculean task for the small cherub. She was an infant, after all.

David apologized profusely for having inconvenienced Tatiana but he was met only with *"Not at all!"* and *"So very happy and honored to help."* and a disturbing, *"Anything for you David."*

By two in the morning, they were resigned and defeated. Even during that time, they had still failed to search the entire Monastery and could only marvel at the vastness and intricacies of the place. In normal speed, they cautiously made their way back to the rooms, hoping to arrive safely and not get caught prowling the Monastery after curfew.

Just as they turned into the second-year rooms corridor, they almost smacked into a frantic Froggy who seemed worried and agitated.

"Shhh...Froggy," Rafaella reassured him. "It's just us."

Froggy peered at them in the semi-darkness. "Hey, girlfriend." he croaked. "What are you doing wandering the Monastery at this time?"

"We were looking for someone." Rafaella admitted but didn't go into the particulars.

"Well, you'd better get your behinds straight into your rooms. It's not safe just walking about on your own right now."

"What do you mean?" David asked.

"I've just been to the Infirmary and was ordered to search a boy's room for any unusual items. Not that I found any." he breathed in deeply, his face a ripple of worry and anxiety. "Something unheard of in the history of our Monastery has happened."

"What?" the four of them asked as quietly as they could.

Froggy looked around as he always did before delivering news. "A student has been poisoned. Deliberately. One of your own."

"One of our own?" asked Lukas.

Froggy nodded. "A second-year boy named Zachary Spencer."

23 An Unlikely Savior

By the time Monday morning rolled in, David and his friends still had no clear idea as to what really happened to Zachary.

To be honest, David wasn't weeping over Zachary's fate – he wasn't ecstatic either, but he was worried that Zachary had been poisoned. That someone had plotted, deliberated and incubated ideas to harm a fifteen-year-old. Sure, Zachary was a bully, and his being one was another hurdle to the investigation of the matter. A lot of kids had wished for his injury; only they simply had no courage and intention to actually do the deed.

But this time, someone did.

David spent his Sunday, which was a Prayer Day, scouring the Monastery for Liz, his opinionated Healer. But she was elusive as ever. She was either locked in her room for an all day prayer and meditation session, or she herself was in the Infirmary; she wasn't looking well during the concert.

David attended his very first Mass then met up periodically with Lukas, Rafaella and Gertrude for frequent updates. Lukas and Gertrude immediately immersed themselves in the Library to research the word square, while Rafaella chatted with every cherub she encountered, her faithful Wolverine at her side, for any tidbit or gossip they might have heard about the circumstances regarding Zachary.

Attuned and creative as ever, Froggy once again picked up some information for them. Froggy revealed that Zachary was lucky to be alive. And he was only alive because he had been immediately found by a worried Giles who knew his whereabouts. The poison that Zachary ingested was lethal and it was only Giles' quick thinking (surprisingly) that had saved him. Giles had lugged his friend over his shoulder and Angel Moded him to the Infirmary.

When Giles was questioned for further clues, he could reveal none. He didn't see anyone, he didn't know who Zachary was meeting – only that he was indeed meeting someone – and he couldn't remember a cup, bottle, or any container at the scene that might have been the poison receptacle.

Giles was commended for his heroism – David didn't know whether to cheer or vomit – and he was to be awarded for his life-saving rescue.

In response to the still unsolved crime, curfew was pushed back from midnight to ten pm., and students were discouraged to go anywhere on their own. The little ones were always escorted by cherubs or teachers.

One thing was certain, for the first time ever, there was an atmosphere of suspicion and distrust among the students. It was as though the serpent had entered the Garden of Eden, had once again broken trust and ruined relationships, and until the perpetrator was discovered and brought to justice, the serpent was here to stay.

After breakfast on Monday, David was again summoned to the Abbot's office where Abbot Anderson expressed his happiness over David's reunion with his father. Michael had met with the Abbot shortly after his life-altering visit with David, and it was to be public knowledge that David was the son of Michael, the Archangel.

In addition, David would begin *Dynamics of Aeronautics*

classes each afternoon in conjunction with Warrior Training. He was quite excited to test his wings in actual flight.

David also mustered up the courage to inquire about the investigation related to the hellhound attack (in the hopes that there would be a connection with Zachary and his current status), but Abbot Anderson only shook his head sadly and informed David that Prefect Macarius continued to look into the matter and had no new leads so far. The Abbot gave him reassuring news though. Monastery security had been increased and they were now Protected Ground. It meant that no demonic being may enter the Monastery and live. The very air would repel the demon.

Again, the Abbot verbalized his guilt and sense of responsibility over what happened to David and David hastily but firmly reassured the Abbot that he had not been at fault.

Finally by lunchtime on that same day, David spotted Liz and he eagerly sought out her company in order to ask about Zachary.

Liz still looked slightly wan and remained pale, her pin-straight hair seemed more limp than usual and her baby blue eyes lacked their trademark sparkle. She also looked exhausted and was puzzlingly monotonic during their entire conversation.

"Yes, I was at the Infirmary during the weekend. I have not been feeling well."

"I'm really sorry to bother you Liz, and you look like you're still recovering, but did you see Zachary at the Infirmary?"

She startled for a split-second before replying, "He's in the Intensive Care Unit so no, I haven't seen even a glimpse of him. Don't worry so, David. He's in excellent care and fortunately for us, we heal rapidly."

It wasn't the conversation he had been hoping for but still David thanked Liz for her time and peering worriedly at her he asked, "Are you sure you should be up and about? Honestly Liz, you look like you need more rest."

Liz merely shrugged away his concern. "I'll be fine David."

During the following days, David concentrated on adjusting to the rhythm of his Monastery schedule and putting more effort in doing well academically. He had immediately noticed how garnering top grades was prized and honored by every Nephilim and intellectual achievement ranked first in everyone's list of priorities. Even the most skilled student warriors made earning excellent grades a must. David guessed that everyone wanted to be Caian James – first-rate warrior and Class Valedictorian. Rafaella had broken it down for him during Warrior Training.

"It's like this, David. No matter how good you are as a warrior, if you don't have the brains, the quick-thinking and chess-format comprehension of combat, you are going to get slaughtered out there. Caian is an impressive fighter not only for his skills, but most especially for his battle strategies. You just know that with him, you can expect the unexpected."

It became even clearer to David that he was in another world as he witnessed his classmates tackle each class with mind-bending enthusiasm and vigor that seemed plain wrong when it came to kids his age and education. Weren't they supposed to be pouting and slouching their way to learning? Being dragged, gagged and trussed-up in the corridors of academia?

But no, his classmates argued their way through lessons and voiced their opinions decidedly. Rafaella continued to ask thought-provoking questions while Lukas consistently answered every question the teacher directed or misdirected his way.

David's jaw slammed to the ground a thousand times as he watched their intellectual tennis match, with knowledge as the yellow ball hurtling from one player to the next.

Amidst all this, he was still the boy who had just arrived, the newcomer with loads of catching-up to accomplish, holding an invisible placard that said – spectator.

After an exhaustive study of Seraphims (of course there was still much to learn about them and their mysterious make-up) in Angelology, Teacher Celestine led them into the world of Cherubims. These Cherubims were nowhere alike the adorable, baby cherubs with tiny fluttering wings. Oh no. Cherubims were known as Protectors. In fact, they were the ones who stood guard at the Tree of Life in the Garden of Eden. They were also the Guardians of God's Throne.

David closed his eyes as he pictured the fierce protectors: with four faces each – a man, an ox, a lion and a griffon vulture; four conjoined wings covered with eyes! David shuddered a bit at the mental picture. Four wings and it was covered with eyes? It sounded impressive and terrible all at once.

These Angels were unbelievably powerful and so mighty that David couldn't even imagine that he had anything in common with them. Of course, Seraphims and Cherubims were at the top tier in the Angelic Hierarchy and with no missions on earth or interactions with humans, they produced no offsprings. Only the lower-tier Angels were known to intermarry with humans and David certainly had no idea whether other Archangels also had sons and daughters. Since wings his kind was not easily recognized, David deduced that Archangels did not produce children as frequently as Angels did. And even then, they were all in the Third Sphere of the Angelic Hierarchy – the Principalities, Archangels and Angels.

If the top-tier of Angels produced any half-mortals, they would truly be forces to be reckoned with, but David guessed no human would survive encounters with them.

Every afternoon in Warrior Training, David flourished under the strict and military guidance of Teacher Peregrine. He continued to instruct David with the Gothic Sword with intervals of Archery and an immersion in hand-to-hand combat beginning with Brazilian Jujitsu. Looking at the list of disciplines to master, David sometimes felt overwhelmed but steadily challenged knowing that if his fellow classmates could master them, so could he.

Right now, Brazilian Jujitsu was first on the list and later on he would succeed to Muay Thai, Taekwondo, Capoeira, Hapkido, Aikido, Judo, Krav Maga, and other different vehicles that would prime and prepare him to be the strongest version of himself.

His body and his mind were being honed and conditioned on a daily basis and David stumbled his way into Biology, still under the hyper and creative methods of Teacher Tellurium who headed all subjects under *Sciences of the World*. Thankfully, Lukas took the time and had the patience to tutor David, ever since he started walking around with a shell-shocked expression, crawling into bed each night in absolute exhaustion.

In *Elementary Guardianship*, they continued to guard their newborn cherubs, who only after a week of life were already showing signs of speech. Rafaella was ecstatic that her cherub started calling her Ella while Lukas teased his newborn into saying pneumono-ultramicroscopic-silico-volcano-coniosis, just for the heck of it.

David found his cherub soothing and secretly languished in the baby's coos and first-word attempts, although by the end of the lesson, his cherub had only progressed to Da.

Zachary was still in the Infirmary but even in his absence, Giles, Dominic and Rusticus made sure petty rough-housing and menial meanness continued without their dictator. They wreaked havoc whenever they could in devious ways but got in trouble anyway when Teacher Romana discovered them teaching their newborns forbidden swear words which resulted in the poor infants gagging and coughing-up soap bubbles while their supposed guardians crumpled on the floor in hilarity. Suffice it to say, their punishment from this act made them seriously sorry for ever considering such wrongdoing.

Wednesdays *Carpentry and Metallurgy* class was always a welcome break for David. It was only his second session but he discovered that he had a passion for weapons – studying their make, honing and shaping the metal and losing himself in the craft of building things. Of course the class wasn't only about weapon making, fortunately Teacher Coppersmith allowed David to finesse another weapon after he had gruffly but heartily clapped David on the shoulder to personally inform him that he now knew the name of the dagger that David previously created.

"I was right, I had to search the archives." he professed gleefully, happy at the thought of exploring the archives for the challenge. "I must admit young man, that it took me some time to locate the design of that particular weapon, but find it I did."

He looked at David measuringly. *"The Hand of God*, that is the name of the dagger and it is quite a rare design. Did you know that only Michael, the Archangel uses the original?"

"I've heard about it, sir." David admitted.

"Well, that is very good of you." he blustered. "You had created a rare challenge for yourself and even knew of its origins. I'm impressed. So, today, Mr. Cross, what is of interest to you?"

"If you'll allow me sir, I'd like to make another dagger. It's a gift for a friend."

"Not going to stab him with it, are you?" Teacher

Coppersmith guffawed at his own joke. "Very well, very well. Let me see the design."

David handed the chosen design to Teacher Coppersmith. He had spent last night at the library looking for a dagger design that would suit Caian. It was his thank-you gift to the senior warrior for coming to his rescue on that terrible day in the streets.

"Ah, this one I recognize." said Teacher Coppersmith, sounding pleased with himself and at the same time disappointed that there would be no challenge from David today. "A Royal Stylet, favored dagger of the nobility. Twelve inches total length, with a seven inch steel blade. It has a particularly unique triangularly-sectioned blade, sharp and slender much like a stylus – hence its name. An appropriate choice for someone who appreciates the classics and the glamour of the old world."

"That's what I thought too, sir."

"Did you also know, Mr. Cross, that this weapon was favored by royals because it was easily concealed, could penetrate through chain mail, plus a single thrust could deliver a piercing wound which at that time meant absolute infection due to its unique triangular blade? The shape of this blade ensured that the wound would heal with difficulty and that even just a single wound could prove fatal." Teacher Coppersmith shook his head. "Blood thirsty savages they were, those *royals*."

Satisfied at the inspection and stamped with his approval, Teacher Coppersmith sent David off to work and he happily but silently greeted his fellow companions for the day – his hammers and shaping tools, the enormous forge, the vise, grinder, files and whetstone for sharpening the blade. This time, David was in no hurry to finish the dagger in one lesson. He wanted to enjoy the process and make certain that he gave a high quality gift to Caian James. Without that rescue, David wouldn't be even present for today's activity.

It was also on that Wednesday night that an exciting clue presented itself to David and his friends. Lukas and Gertrude had tirelessly and diligently searched the library for any single information on the word square they had found and it was Lukas who discovered it in a small book entitled, *The Early Christians – Depictions of Daily Life.*

Lukas had speedily sent for David and Rafaella via an over-eager cherub who had practically dragged them to the library to hear Lukas' urgent news. David and Rafaella found Lukas almost buried in books with an excited Gertrude beside him, reading over his shoulder.

"Lukas found it!" she exclaimed as loudly as she was allowed in the tomb-like silence.

As David and Rafaella cleared some space on the table to better see Lukas, he began reading passages that he found significant and relevant to their research.

"Known as the Sator Square, it was first discovered in the ruins of Pompeii which was buried in the ash of Mount Vesuvius in 79 A.D. Its later appearances reached as far as Syria, England, Siena, and the Benedictine Abbey in Abruzzo, Italy."

S	A	T	O	R
A	R	E	P	O
T	E	N	E	T
O	P	E	R	A
R	O	T	A	S

"A Sator Square?" David wondered aloud. "So that's what it's called."

"Yes, taken from the first word on the square. There are also translations for each word, but we basically got the translations right the first time." Lukas showed them.

"Sator means a sower or a founder or a farmer." Gertrude read. "Arepo is trust, but it could also be a name -"

"And it can also mean to move, like we've said before." added Lukas. "Tenet is to keep, possess, or create, and Opera means work or effort -"

"Or trouble." nodded Gertrude. "And Rotas can either be a wheel or to rotate."

"What is different here though that we've never thought of before is that in the christian context, Arepo can mean Alpha and Omega."

"As in, The Alpha and The Omega?" asked Rafaella. "Hmmm.....so the Sator Square is known to be christian in origin and has been appearing all over the place.......even in a Benedictine Abbey. But does it say what it really means though?"

Lukas flipped to the next page. "Yes, that's one of the more exciting parts. When the words are strung together, the basic translation is still – The Farmer Arepo Keeps Working on his Wheels. But the early Christians also translated Rotas to mean Life, and more importantly, for ArepO to significantly mean The Alpha and The Omega – who is God, of course."

Lukas looked at them to make sure they were following his line of thought. "And so, the Sator Square actually means *Life full of good Works are Held by God our Creator.*"

The four of them fell silent as they contemplated the meaning of the Sator Square. Then Lukas continued, "And get this, it was an early code for Christians."

"Code?" asked David. "Code for what?"

"It was their safe and hidden way to signal their presence to each other." said Lukas.

Gertrude explained. "You see, the early Christians lived in a time of persecution. They couldn't walk in the streets of Rome and declare themselves to each other, nor were they allowed to conduct meetings or gather as a group."

"Yes, that I know." Rafaella said. "We're talking about the time when Christians who were found out were being thrown into the arena to fight and be eaten by lions."

"Exactly." said Lukas. "And the Sator Square was their way of identifying themselves to each other, secretly. It appeared as a word game about a farmer, but actually meant something completely different. For the early christians, it was brotherhood, and refuge and even help."

"Look, this is really great that we now know what it means," David said. "But how does the Sator Square connect to Zachary?"

"That's what we have to figure out." Rafaella agreed.

"Zachary had the Sator Square and he got it from someone who knew about it. Someone he was meeting that night of the concert." David formulated. "And Innocent must have known about it because we actually first heard it from him but through Tatiana."

"So, what do we have here?" David continued. "Three people who know the Sator Square and have been using it to..........signal each other?"

"That's absolutely right!" Rafaella excitedly acknowledged. "They must be using the Sator Square as a code, just like the early christians."

"But who are they? And what are they up to?" David frowned. "And unlike the early christians, whoever Zachary met that night, whoever gave him that Sator Square, also poisoned him."

24 Introduction to Aeronautics

David stared at his feet and the thin plank that was holding his weight. It was the only thing separating him from the hard ground which right now appeared so far away. It was his first lesson in *Dynamics of Aeronautics* and as excited as he was, David was also a tiny bit apprehensive about jumping off the diving board and just letting his wings do the work. This was warrior land – no net was under him or any water either. If he fell and just spiraled like a crashing plane, he was sure his rapid healing powers wouldn't save him from certain death.

"You will be able to do it, David." Caian encouraged, hovering in the air next to him. He was assisting in David's lesson today, while the Aero instructor – Teacher Xystus – waited patiently down below for David to jump.

"Just open your wings and leap. Instinct will take over, I promise." added Caian.

David willed his wings to unfurl and like twin sails, his wings flapped open majestically, their wingspan impressively broad as it expanded outwards. From below, David could hear gasps as the color of his wings was revealed – deep black feathers lightening to grey. His wings were a dark beacon in a sea of white. He could see students from below pointing up at him and his strange wings.

David closed his eyes and shut the outside world from his

mind, readying himself.

Looking up to heaven, he murmured, "Here's to you, Mom." then he stepped off the plank and leaped.

He felt the wind rushing up to meet him and at the same time felt his wings open even more, keeping his body buoyant and soaring. It was the most freeing and liberating experience of his life.

He was actually flying!

David didn't even realize that he was yelling and whooping in joy, a huge smile beaming from his lips to his entire body as he flew over the sprawling grounds of Warrior Training. His body and his wings were so attuned that it seemed to have a mind of its own. As he swerved and dipped, changing directions, adjusting to the oncoming force of the wind, so did his wings automatically make the necessary increments to maintain flight.

Beside him, Caian flew with an approving nod, encouraging David to continue. "You're doing excellently." he shouted over the rush of wind and the flap of their wings. "We're to circle the Monastery then return to Teacher Xystus."

Although the Monastery covered a lot of ground, David and Caian easily circled the place as they flew with great speed. David completely embraced the power and wonder of flying and even on his first run, he pushed and tested his abilities.

He soared up in the air as high as he could then he zoomed in a steep dive towards the ground, the pale earth just inches from his body. Then he came up again and this time propelled forward in spirals and twists. He was yelling his head off almost the entire time, zoning out in the absolute bliss of flying.

"Awesome!" David called out to Caian and as he once again soared higher and higher, the wind speed picking up and the air growing colder, he heard only fragments of Caian's words over the deafening wind.

"Don't........Wall.........Wait.........."

"What?" David yelled back, unable to hear the senior.

Caian pushed off after David. Don't……..near……..wall ….."

Before the implication of Caian's words registered in David's brain, he smelled the danger.

Sulfur!

"DAVID! DON'T GO NEAR THE MONASTERY WALL!" yelled Caian. "DEMONS!"

David backpedaled and tried his best to halt his momentum. The wall was miles beneath him and although he had not gone over the boundery yet, David could hear the screeching and hissing of demons who had suddenly appeared on the other side.

Five demons flapped their wings furiously, clawing their way towards David but unable to approach him as an invisible wall prevented them.

Although David did his hardest to prevent further movement, his wings working overtime to pull him backwards, he continued to press close to the Monastery border, the invisible bubble mere inches from him. From what he could see, the demons could not enter their protected airspace, but did it work vice-versa? Would the protective bubble prevent him from flying outside or would he in fact careen straight into the grasping claws of five slobbering and snarling demons.

"Come this way little boy." one demon taunted, its voice gravelly and sinister, its eyes glowing a disturbing yellow.

"Look," another demon jeered, its leathery wings slashing the air, "a son of an Archangel." The other demons cackled and growled, their unearthly voices raising the hairs all over David's body.

"Who is your father?" asked another one in a sickly syrupy

voice. "Want to come out and play with us Nephilim? Want to show us what a great warrior you are?"

David ignored them all, concentrating instead in moving backwards, refusing to rise to their taunts and the overpowering temptation to cross over the border and fight them.

What would happen if he just flew over the protective bubble and started bashing some demons around. Would he survive against the five of them? Probably not, but boy would it feel good to pummel their monstrous faces with his fists and to slash them with his Gothic Sword.

"Scaredy cat." a demon called out to David in provocation and much to David's absolute shock he was staring into the faces of his friends.

The demons had transformed!

They were hideous copies of Lukas, Rafaella, Gertrude, Joseph and Isaac. Exact replicas except for the burning yellow eyes and evil smiles, peppered with the horrible stench of sulfur around them.

"Scaredy cat. Scaredy cat. Scaredy cat." The five evil clones chanted, bringing David's blood to a boil. He wanted to fight them even more. The wrongness of their appearance threatened to push him to the edge. It was an intimidating display of their powers – that they could easily read his mind and pick his memories and channel them into weapons. Instantly, they had used his weakness against himself, automatically capturing how he valued his new friends.

"Don't." an arm grabbed him, pulling him determinedly backwards, further away from the chanting doppelgangers.

"It's alright David, you're safe." said a firm voice. It was Teacher Victorinus. "Don't allow them to control you. Don't give in."

David's breathing was shallow and rapid as anger clouded his brain. He wanted nothing more right now than to actually battle with the demons but the logical part of his brain alerted him to how stupid this would be.

His eyes flashed at Teacher Victorinus and Caian as they dragged him further away from the diabolical quintuplets. He tried to stop the blistering words from erupting out of him, but he uncontrollably exploded. "Why wasn't I warned? How come nobody told me about flying too near the wall? Or over the wall? Or over the protective bubble?" his voice was near growling. "This is a flying lesson! Why didn't anybody tell me about this!"

Caian's handsome face flushed with guilt. "I really am sorry David, but all the while I thought Teacher Xystus had instructed you. He should have before you even started flying. Did he not deliver a briefing? Prepared you in some way?"

David could only shake his head mutely, afraid even to answer and open the doorway to shouting rage. He was angry at them, at Teacher Xystus, at himself! He hated being a newbie and forever catching-up and being the last one told, the only one who *didn't know*. If someone said to him right now that *you'll see or you're about to find out*, David would punch that person in the face.

"Caian is right." said Teacher Victorinus, gently guiding David back to the Aeronautics Center. He knew that David was incoherent with anger and not thinking straight. "Xystus should have prepared you. And you are correct, David. You should have been warned about our bounderies and told what to expect when overstepping it. This was highly irresponsible of Xystus and I will speak to him about it."

David was trembling with suppressed anger about the surprise attack and gritting his teeth, he muttered. "Let's just forget about it sir. I don't want any trouble."

"Forgive me David, but I must speak with Xystus regarding

this. His negligence placed your life in danger. But do not worry, there would be no trouble."

There was no deterring Teacher Victorinus.

Back at the Aeronautics Center, David watched silently as Teacher Victorinus berated a shame-faced Teacher Xystus for his irresponsible action. David couldn't hear their conversation since they had moved away from the students, but their gestures and facial expressions spoke volumes. He didn't want anyone chastised because of him but it honestly felt great to be justified and championed by the likes of Teacher Victorinus who was Head of Warrior Training. David felt an increased respect for the instructor.

For the rest of his Aero Training, David quietly acquainted himself with flying rules and safety measures. This time, an apologetic Teacher Xystus carefully instructed David on Flight Prerequisites, Checklists, and their allowed Airspace – marking off Monastery borders and the extent of their protective dome.

David paid concentrated attention to all the facts. It was another lesson learned the hard way, one he didn't want to be repeated.

One of the things that David loved most about the Monastery was how everything was provided for and how he didn't have to worry about money and how to come up with his basic needs. He had food, shelter, clothing, and for a young man like him who grew up in poverty and who later had to fend for himself in city streets, this was his closest brush with heaven.

He loved the simplicity and sparseness of his room, the wall of glass beside his bed that offered an astounding view of Alaskan mountains. He gazed now and then at the picture of his mother and wondered how she and Michael had met, before drifting off to exhausted slumber. For David though, it was a good kind of tired. A satisfying kind of tired born from hard work and sweetened with daily achievements.

His other favorite pastime was tracing the Monastery map and absorbing the twists and turns, floors and passages outlined in the map to his brain. He would like nothing better than to go exploring on his own but with the strict curfew and a still unknown murderer on the loose, it wasn't the brightest idea of the moment. There was a particular room of interest to him and he asked Lukas about it.

"How does the gift shop here work exactly?"

"Who are you getting a present?" a curious Lukas asked.

"I want to get Gertrude something, you know, as a thank you for getting the truth out of Tatiana."

"Oh yeah. Gertrude must be an excellent Dream Invader. Imagine, Dream Invading a cherub........impressive! What a skill that must be."

"According to the Abbot, she's the best one in the Monastery. How about you? Ever tried Dream Inspiring or Invading?" David asked.

"Oh sure! You know me, I'm such a geek, of course I'd be trying to do it. Sadly, I'm not very good at it. I've tried countless times but it's always murky and I don't have any control and sometimes I have a hard time just going inside the dream. Not as easy as it sounds buddy." Lukas shook his head ruefully.

"Hmmm....I'd like to try that sometime." David decided. "So, the Gift Shop – how do you buy a present?"

"You don't. You pick which one you like and you get it for free."

"For free? You're kidding right?"

"Nope." Lukas laughed at the incredulous look on David's face. "But there are limitations. You can only get one item a week, you know, so there's some control over it and no rampant buying or 'getting' happens." Lukas added. "And the great thing about the Gift Shop is you can recycle. If you get an item and later on, no longer want it, then you just return it so other kids can use it too. The Monastery encourages that so nothing goes to waste. Even when the thing is broken, they just repair and refurbish it."

David wanted to get a present right after dinner so that he could give it to Gertrude the following day. He and Lukas headed for the Gift Shop while Rafaella went off to polish her knife collection before bedtime.

Most items in the Gift Shop were unique and David wished he had all the time in the world to explore each one. He and Lukas drooled over a Build-A-City kit complete with Weather Control – cool spring, winter blizzard, windy fall, scorching summer plus different weather elements such as rain: drizzle, afternoon shower, cats and dogs; hail, hurricane, tornado and earthquake. It all served as a study of weather changes and the damage caused by natural forces, but for David and Lukas, it was just calamity cool. Best of all, after every disaster, the city simply reconstructed itself!

They spent half an hour playing with the store model while the weirdly silent and immobile shopkeeper, Mr. Rembert, stared broodingly at them. Lukas pelted the city with soccer ball size hail while David gawked at an F5 tornado winding a destructive path over the city. They let gentle snowflakes fall and watched as the city got blanketed in snow, then hypered it up to a whirling blizzard.

After that, David leafed through intricately hand-painted books and stared hypnotically at poster-size pictures of outer space taken by pure angels. It certainly wasn't from the Hubble Telescope and David wondered how far up the earth's atmosphere he could fly without any damage to himself. How insane that would be! He reminded himself to ask Caian about it when he got the chance. Maybe the fourth-year had tried it already.

Then he and Lukas suited up in authentic medieval armor and engaged in a noisy and clanging sword fight complete with a ton-like shield and an equally heavy longsword. After some bashing with swords glowing with their angelic substance, plus a lot of idiotic pushing and shoving, David and Lukas guffawed and laughed their way to being scrap metal heaps on the floor. They would try to help each other up, only to fall down again in the heavy and awkward armor, and all their laughing didn't exactly help their predicament.

Finally, David protested that he really had to look for Gertrude's present and after extricating himself from the medieval armor, he reluctantly asked the assistance of the eerily quiet Mr. Rembert, who turned out to be a fountain of knowledge about his wares. You just had to suffer through his clipped but whispering responses.

David chose a music sheet in curled and yellowed parchment, which was – according to Mr. Rembert – an original composition of Sandalphon, the Angel of Music himself. The notes of the song appeared complex to David but he was sure Gertrude would have no difficulty in reading the notes and translating it to song. And as much as he wanted to stay and tinker with every item in the store, it was nearing curfew so he and Lukas headed back to their rooms. David did promise to get the Roaring Rollercoaster set for himself next time. It was a large-scale model that actually worked and you could re-design it and add your own ideas while miniature figures screamed with joy when the design pleased them, or booed throughout the ride when the design didn't meet their expectations. David couldn't wait to design his own ride and see how the miniatures would react to it.

As he and Lukas got near their rooms, they passed an almost empty student lounge where Caian sat in silent contemplation of his chess game. He brightened considerably when he saw David and immediately asked, "David, may I interest you in a game of chess?" gesturing at the empty seat in front of a finely crafted chess set.

"Umm..." David hesitated, "I don't really know how to play chess."

"Well then, today is the day." Caian stated solemnly and firmly pushed David down the empty seat. With a reluctant look at Lukas, David signaled his friend to continue on without him.

"It really is an essential game, David. Vitally essential for us who are set to engage in constant warfare." Caian said, arranging the chess pieces back to their starting positions. "Our goal is to always be several steps ahead of our opponent, and chess is the exercise that will sharpen your mind to such awareness."

"Well, I do know the basics – you know, how each piece moves and what their roles are." admitted David. "but that's about it."

"That is a good place to start." nodded Caian. He set about a pared-down and shortened summary of how chess was played just to make sure that David did know the simple rules, and as they delved into the game, Caian also engaged David in conversation.

"How are you liking your stay at the Monastery?" Caian asked.

David pondered the question a bit before answering. "It's an incredible place. I mean, if someone had told me before that this kind of place existed and that there were real angels and demons running around, of course I wouldn't have believed it."

"Yes, it is quite unbelievable isn't it? And yet, here we are."

Caian moved his bishop. "Are you looking forward to going on actual missions?"

David frowned at the game, contemplating his next move, "I am but I don't think I'm ready for that yet. I've barely scratched the surface of my training goal. I've only been handling two types of weapons so far and I've just started with hand-to-hand combat. My friend Rafaella – a girl – can beat me in all those things."

Caian smiled, "And yet despite all that, you successfully vanquished the hellhound."

David only shrugged.

"I know you're destined to be a great warrior, David, you absolutely have the instincts for it. Plus, you have an enviable lineage – an archangel parent – the color of your wings certainly herald it. May I ask who it is or is it a secret? I'm assuming your father is the archangel. Archangels are invariably male."

David's hand paused on top of his rook, uncertain about answering. "Well.....it's not actually a secret and I guess other people would know about it soon enough, but to be honest Caian, I'm not really comfortable talking about my father." David breathed deeply, put on the spot but not wanting to be coy about the truth. "He's Michael, the Archangel."

Caian inhaled sharply at David's announcement, looking at David in a different way, with awe and a hint of envy in his deep blue eyes. That's what David was afraid of. He didn't want people looking at him differently because of his father. Michael's accomplishments were his own, not David's. And what would they expect of him now? To be as good as his father?

"Very impressive David." Caian said. "Michael – the Commander of God's Army, Vanquisher of Demons. Did you know that it was Michael who defeated Lucifer in the Battle of Angels?"

When David shook his head, Caian continued with his story.

"Before man was ever created a rebellion occurred in heaven. A group of angels led by Lucifer – the Morning Star – raised their arms against God, questioning his authority. They wanted to be God's equals, you see."

David was listening intently, forgetting that it was his turn to move.

Caian continued. "And so heaven was divided; Lucifer and his army of fallen angels, versus God's army led by no other than Michael the Archangel himself. Michael brought victory to God and he was tasked with bringing Lucifer and his minions to the depths of hell. That is how magnificent your father is."

David swallowed at this comment. "Kind of hard to live up to that."

At this Caian grinned. "Don't even try. Just be the best version of yourself and that would be more than enough." Then he reminded David, "It's your move, by the way."

Leaning back in his chair, Caian asked David, "What do you think our role should be in the outside world?"

It was a no brainer. "We're Protectors. We protect our own kind and humans from demons." David sacrificed a horse in order to gain an advantageous position.

"Yes, and it is a satisfying and noble task, but, do you think we should be doing more?"

David looked at Caian. "What do you mean by more?"

"According to the laws of the Nephilim Heirarchy, we are prohibited from directly affecting human affairs, especially on a global scale, such as holding important government positions or being an economic influence. We are to be their protectors but we must never interfere or decide their course."

"But, don't Pure Angels intervene a lot?"

Caian looked extremely pleased by David's question. "Exactly. Why should Pure Angels intervene in human history while we are forbidden to do the same? Why are we forever relegated to be protectors when we are half-human ourselves? What if we can lead mankind to a better and more just world?"

David studied Caian's recent move and thought of his question at the same time. "I guess it comes down to the biggest difference between us and Pure Angels, doesn't it? Free will. We have it, they don't. So, it's safe to say that whatever intervention they do is a direct order from God."

"You're very right David, and you're very smart. That is the most unique and priceless difference between us and Pure Angels. We have free will. As such, I personally think that if by holding office or by having an influence in the world we can help mankind create a more honest, fair and happier world, then we too should be given that right." Caian looked a bit abashed by his impassioned speech. "I'm a confessed crusader David. The truth is, I was never one to stand aside and just let others do the work."

"I understand where you're coming from." David said, admiring Caian's zest and honesty. "I guess if the time came for me to go on missions and to see the world a lot, I'd also like to change things. Who wouldn't want a better world?"

Caian smiled in relief. "My sentiments exactly. I'm so glad you understand." Then he added with an apologetic smile, "Checkmate."

As they carefully returned the chess pieces to its original position, Caian casually said, "I'm a member of a club here in the Monastery promoting such ideals of a better world – our 'heaven on earth' so to speak, and we're always keeping an eye out for promising new members for our select group. Tomorrow, we're having a meeting at Uriel Lodge – why don't you come? Oh, and bring your friend, Gertrude Greer. We hear that she's a very talented Dream Invader."

25 The Elite

When David awoke the following morning, snow was falling in determined swirls outside his window. It didn't take a genius to assume that the temperature had dropped even more and David patted his warm glass wall appreciatively, grateful for the temperature controlled Monastery. It appeared to be always winter in their Alaskan hideaway, only today, winter had leveled-up.

Over breakfast, David kept his friends up to speed about his interesting conversation with Caian James and his and Gertrude's invitation to this select 'club' which Caian had not named.

"What do you think?" he asked around the breakfast table, trying to gauge his friends reactions. "Could he be talking about the Sator Square? Maybe there is an organization here connected to the square."

"It's possible......" Lukas nodded in agreement, a little lost in thought. He had gone awfully quiet when David had mentioned Caian's invitation. "And Caian said the meeting would be at the Uriel Lodge?"

"Yes, and of course, as usual, I've never heard of the place."

Lukas was looking at David weirdly, as if he was carefully assessing him. "It's a very exclusive, supremely elite club – known to have a carefully selected roster of members. I hear they have a very tough selection board and chooses only what they consider 'Par Excellent' students. You can't even apply for the club. It's by invitation only."

"Par Excellent sounds right up your alley, Lukas." David said in all honesty. "I bet they'd be knocking your door down with an invitation."

Underneath the table, Rafaella gave David a silent but painful kick. "Who cares about exclusive clubs." Rafaella archly announced. "It's the very antithesis of democracy. I think the people who create such societies only do it to make themselves feel special and superior. It goes against our very nature."

"I didn't even know the Monastery allowed it." Gertrude added. "Rafaella's right. Such organizations should be banned, especially here. It is the kind of society that only fosters negative elitist concepts and cruelly inspires envy and demoralization of non-members. How could Abbot Anderson allow this?" She sounded particularly betrayed, in clear disbelief that the Abbot could be so careless.

"Hey, we could be talking about the Monastery itself." Lukas defended. "It's not like we're letting humans live here."

"But we're of different species who require different learning processes and training. Can you imagine if we all went to one school? How would humans compete against our Angelic gifts? It should be this way for their own growth and ours." Gertrude calmly argued.

"I bet that was a powerful racial argument before." Lukas countered.

"Hey, you guys - " David interrupted, " - this is all very noble and interesting and we could argue this issue for hundreds of years, but this is not the point today. Could we just focus on the Sator Square and if Caian's club has a connection to it."

"I don't believe it." Rafaella expressed. "We're talking about Caian James here. He's our intelligent and highly skilled warrior who's ready to swoop in and rescue anyone who needs help. How could he even be connected with the Sator Square and what happened to Zachary? I just can't believe it." she shook her head. "I think we're digging in the wrong spot."

David frowned, suddenly irrationally angry. "Maybe you're hyper-crushing on him and its blinding you."

Rafaella glared in reply. If she had a weapon, she probably would have sliced David with it.

Gertrude cut through their hostility and said, "Whether or not this club is involved with the Sator Square, David and I must investigate it. We have to be intuitive to new clues and hopefully step closer to the truth regarding Zachary's poisoning."

David and Lukas nodded at Gertrude's suggestion while Rafaella's opposing silence spoke out for her. There was an underlying yet unspoken disharmony in the group and most of their wondrous breakfast had gone uneaten.

Lukas stood up abruptly. "I have to go somewhere before class. I'll just see you later." then without looking at any of them, he walked off.

They were left staring at Lukas' departing back, Rafaella in a frown, Gertrude in silent contemplation, and David just plain confused. This was not how he thought his news would be received.

Underneath the table, Wolverine was happily munching on brightly colored dogfood which visibly rotated inside his clear stomach like a bizarre tornado.

David envied their canine friend his simple doggie cares and blissed-out sprawl. If only life were that simple. His day was starting complexly and David had an unsettling suspicion that it was about to get more complicated.

As it was a Thursday, their first lesson was Heavenly Art under the eccentric guidance of their art instructor, Teacher Verrocchio. She had the gaunt and ascetic look of a starving artist but she strode about the room purposefully and with the vibrant joy and energy of a person fully immersed in art.

She was wearing a beautiful and striking red scarf over her artist smock and her long and wild, pure white hair, was kept away from her face by ropes serving as head bands. It was as though she couldn't and wouldn't be bothered by the mundaness of dressing but had thrown over the red scarf just to brighten up the day.

"Art is the imprint of the longings of the soul. The emotion that consumes you must be channeled onto your canvass in a controlled infusion of truth and your version of beauty. Forget what is ideal! Forget what is common and expected. Look into the heart of your subject and draw that into your work." Teacher Verrocchio walked about the room, keeping an eye on their progress or in some cases, royal messes.

David was surprised at how he enjoyed doing artwork, finding the creative expression satisfying. In regular school, he had done the customary art class but it was his first foray into oil painting and Teacher Verrocchio's level of expectation. His teacher in the outside world had been nice but disinterested, grading his work with diligent obligation but not really *looking*.

As it was his first exposure to oil painting, David chose an uncomplicated but important subject – the Gothic Sword. He wanted the sword to look powerful and energetic on canvass, despite its stillness.

Beside him, Rafaella painted with a certain beautiful fury, her strokes bold and deliberate. David would never have pegged her for an artist, but she was, and an accomplished one. She was way ahead of David in terms of technique and skill and was in fact painting a fierce battle between an angel and a demon. It was riveting.

Near the large windows, Gertrude was a sea of calm, painting a peaceful and dreamy landscape. Even her painting style was languid and graceful.

Today Lukas had chosen a spot far from David, and seemed determined to ignore him too. David knew that he could be insensitive at times – and he had been at breakfast – but never in a million years would he deliberately hurt his friend. He knew Lukas was upset about the invitation. How could David have known that such things would matter to Lukas?

Every now and then David glanced at his friend who approached his canvass with utilitarian perfection. If he could have ruled and penciled everything beforehand, Lukas would have. He was happiest when everything was neatly parallel, dedicatedly stacked-up and in their proper place.

"Get dirty! Get messy! Dive into those colors and wallow in it. You must not be afraid of smearing your canvass. Translate your subject, this is not copying! Otherwise you may just as well take a photograph and leave this class."

Lukas frowned at Teacher's Verrochio's words and David couldn't help but smile. He too couldn't imagine Lukas going heavy-handed with globs of paint. There were hardly any spots on his extra pristine smock.

For more than an hour they labored on their paintings and then it was time to put their work away – finished or unfinished and head on to *Angelic Chorale*. David was dreading this particular class because he wasn't downplaying the fact that he couldn't sing. He really couldn't! He was definitely tone-deaf and was not looking forward to being made fun of.

Angelic Chorale was the only class being taught by a Pure Angel. David stared mesmerized as their instructor, Teacher Irayazel, stood before them in a pool of luminescence. His very skin seemed to be glowing and there was brilliance to his countenance that repeatedly rendered David awestruck.

While his classmates took their assigned places and leafed through their sheet music, Teacher Irayazel motioned for David to join him in a secluded corner for his audition. This was to determine whether David was a tenor or bass. David was more nervous than ever and kept wiping his now damp palms to his white clothes.

"You may sing any song you wish." said Teacher Irayazel. Amazingly, every time he spoke, chimes accompanied his voice, making his very words melodious. It only made David even more nervous.

He didn't know many songs but he remembered one in particular which he learned in grade school – Swinging on a Star. Somehow, the words brought him comfort especially during those times when his life seemed unendingly bleak.

David started singing the song, his voice wobbling and warbling through the melody and before he finished the second line of the song, Teacher Irayazel smiled kindly at him, clasped him on the shoulder and said, "Mr. Cross, you are a natural Mouther. Truly I could feel your emotions in that song but sadly, you were never meant to sing. Perhaps privately or in the shower?"

That said, and to David's complete relief, he was asked to join a small group of his classmates – all Mouthers – whose job it was to mouth silently with the song but to make sure not to sing. To David's surprise, Rafaella was in the group.

"Apparently, I'm a warrior, not a singer." was her unabashed explanation. David grinned in reply, feeling much better that he wasn't the only monotone in their group. True enough, they mouthed (silently) beautiful words to the music and every now and then one of the Mouthers would get carried away and belt-out a most awful rendition much to the goodnatured hilarity of the class. Mostly it was Gertrude's and Lukas' time to shine, along with Consortia and unbelievably Joseph. He seemed to be sleepwalking but sang with such warmth and goose-bumps enducing smoothness that had David gaping at him. Sometimes David forgot that he was in the company of half-angels but it was during moments like these that he was delightfully reminded of their gifts.

This must be what heaven sounds like, David thought to himself, carried away by the music his classmates were creating.

As expected, grunting Giles was in their group of Mouthers along with another girl named Isobel. David didn't know why they had to take the class, given that they didn't exactly blend in, but perhaps it was to learn and appreciate the songs more than anything. Despite their non-participation, it was still an entertaining class.

For the rest of the day, Lukas started thawing bit by bit towards David. He wasn't as open and friendly as before, not yet anyway, but at least he wasn't aloof either. Lukas did fall silent again when David and Gertrude left their group after dinner to attend the 'club meeting'.

As hard as David and Gertrude resisted at the meeting, they actually had a great time. From what they could see, the meeting was more a round-up of possible candidates to join the mysterious club –

whose name was never mentioned throughout the entire night. So it was more party than meeting.

The energy was up in the very posh Uriel Lodge and the excitement of all possible candidates was quite contagious. Their shining eyes and giddiness shouted how fortunate they felt to have been invited and *considered* for the very hush-hush and exclusive club. An orchestra of very pretty cherubs played onstage, dressed in floaty white garments. The food, as always, was excellent.

"How happy I am that Caian invited you David, and you too, Gertrude." Antonia beamed beautifully at them. "I certainly hope you'll find the festivities this evening to your liking."

Antonia was Caian's girlfriend. The stunning but aloof girl, who tonight was shockingly friendly. David and Gertrude couldn't help but shoot amazed glances at each other as Antonia continued to chat them up.

Caian, of course, enthusiastically welcomed them and worked his way around the room, greeting and thanking everyone for being present. He was affable and charming as ever and even Gertrude who was always calm and cool, blushed a little at Caian's attention.

Each person in the room had an identifying bracelet on – gold for club members and silver for candidates. Only a select few, like Caian James, had double-strand bracelets which signified that they were officers. David committed these persons to memory, his instincts flagging them as important. Caian was an officer, so was Antonia, Jerome, and another senior named Samson.

David was shocked to discover that Consortia was a member and he would have bet anything that Zachary was a member too and would have been strutting around were he not still unconscious in the Infirmary. He was puzzled about Consortia's membership though. Did she have a secret skill? An extraordinary talent? Zachary was the top warrior in their class so it wasn't a surprise that he was recruited – although David thought brawn alone was poor recommendation. Lukas, who was smartest in their class should have been recruited too and Rafaella as well. She was, after all, one of their best warriors and very intelligent, to top it off. But Consortia? Did singing count? Nah, scratch that thought. If singing counted then Lukas would be here also.

In the end, it was a game of 'Who's That?' with Gertrude, as David asked her the names of the other members. He did recognize Abraham, a third year, from Halo Attack. They weren't sure if all members were in attendance but their meticulous counting turned up the following results: 12 seniors, 10 third years, only Consortia representing second years (why?), and 2 first years. David and Gertrude didn't see anyone younger present. Then it was a matter of memorizing and remembering the officers and members of the club.

The cherubs played a series of catchy, uptempo tunes and although David had never danced before, nor did he have any intention to, it was hard to say no to a persuasive Antonia who plucked him from Gertrude's side and led him to the dance floor. Gertrude too was asked to dance, by Caian himself, and even under the soft lights of Uriel Lodge, David could see his friend blushing from the warrior's attention.

Soon David and Gertrude were dancing with each other and when the music slowed down to a dreamy melody, it only seemed natural for David to continue dancing with Gertrude, holding her closer as her arms comfortably settled on his shoulders.

David hoped his face wasn't red from embarrassment, but looking around the room, everyone was simply preoccupied with their own partners or for those not dancing, chatting with each other.

David thought Gertrude looked even more beautiful and he

liked that she wasn't self-conscious at all, dancing with David with utmost ease and later, resting her head on his chest. She must hear how hard his heart was beating, it was impossible not to! Even David could hear his pounding heart with his own ears. His rational side of the brain was yelling – *You're here on a mission! You're here to find out about the Sator Square!*, but then the other side of him argued – *You got some information, you know who the officers and members are. Relax. Enjoy the moment.*

In the end, David got tired of arguing with himself and just allowed himself to have fun. He let the music wash over him and appreciated the beautiful girl in his arms. It may not be the right place, but it was definitely the right girl. The truest thing that David learned tonight was – he liked Gertrude. He liked her more than just a friend.

26. Jasmines and Seraphic Butterflies

David felt the soft pressure of Gertrude's hand in his as she slowly led him to a secluded spot in the Monastery. They were alone outside with the bright moon as their light and from what David could see, they were in some secret garden that he had never been before. The ground was blanketed in snow and yet he didn't feel cold and despite the descent of winter, multitudes of flowers were in bloom all around them. There was the heady scent of jasmine in the air.

Gertrude led them to a deeply cushioned loveseat in the middle of the garden and some distance away, David could hear the soft trickle and splash of a water fountain.

As he faced Gertrude, ever more lovely in the moonlight with a sweet and shy smile on her face, she whispered, "I like you David."

David gazed solemnly into her deep blue eyes and replied, "I like you too."

Then their faces drew nearer each other, David's gaze locked onto the soft curve of Gertrude's lips, then as he closed his eyes, David felt the soft touch of her lips on his and it was heavenly. It was exciting. A jolt of electricity coursed through his body, nudging him to open his eyes, to take in the moment. As he did, David looked around in confusion.

He wasn't in a garden. He wasn't with Gertrude.

He was in his room and on his bed.

It had just been a dream.

The following day, despite the vividly disturbing dream of the previous night, David set about preparing the gifts that he would give to Gertrude and Caian James. The aged music sheet was in a soft leather satchel while the Stylet Dagger and it's matching scabbard was tucked safely in David's messenger bag.

At breakfast in the bustling cafe, David handed his gift to Gertrude in the most economical manner without any ceremony whatsoever, but hopefully managing to convey how thankful he was for her help in the Tatiana affair.

Only Rafaella's eyebrows were raised although she and Lukas knew that he had been intending to give Gertrude a thank-you gift.

"What is this?" Gertrude asked in her soft and soothing voice.

"Just a small thank you gift. You know, for helping with Tatiana." David said, his voice barely audible. He kept darting furtive glances at Gertrude, unable to look her in the eye when each time he did so, all he could think of was his dream last night.

David could see that Rafaella was frowning at him. Obviously, he was acting weird.

"Thank you David." Gertrude smiled, clasping at the leather bindings of the satchel. "May I?"

At David's nod, she opened the leather ties and slowly pulled out the sheet music. "Why, it's an original composition by Sandalphon!" she exclaimed.

"The guy who makes shoes?" queried Rafaella.

"The *guy* who is the Angel of Music." Gertrude replied with a slightly sharp glance at Rafaella. It was the first time that David had seen Gertrude annoyed.

"It's exquisite David. Thank you very much." then Gertrude got up from her seat and kissed David softly on the cheek. "Already I'm looking forward to singing the song."

"I...ah.....um...." David was stammering, "I thought you'd like that........seeing that you like music a lot." he could feel the spot of her kiss burning his skin. Was it all red? Was his face all red?

"What an intelligent deduction David." Rafaella drawled. He knew she was making fun of him and while Lukas nudged her for her unwarranted crabbiness, David chose to ignore her remark.

"I have some errands to run before class, so I will see you later then." Gertrude said, methodically putting away her things. She carefully returned the music sheet to the leather satchel and carried it close. Then with a secretive smile she turned to David. "Did you know that my favorite flower is the jasmine? Its perfume is strongest when the moon is near its fullness. You should see it sometime."

Then with a graceful turn, she walked away, but not before she saw David's astonished and dumbstruck face.

As David slowly sat down in bewilderment, he could hear Rafaella tartly saying, "So now she wants you to give her jasmines? Soliciting flowers now is she? You know, for a very nice girl, Gertrude is beginning to get on my nerves."

A non-committal and equally confused Lukas simply brought his cup to his lips and drank his herbal tea.

David carried out through the day in a mild haze of confusion. Had the dream been real? Did it really happen? Or had he – for the first time ever – been Dream Invaded? Somehow he couldn't reconcile the thought of Gertrude Dream Invading him and having that kiss happen. Not calm and sweet Gertrude! He felt guilty for even entertaining such a thought about his friend, the one he liked more than a friend.

David shook his head to clear it from the cacophony of circulating thoughts. Frankly, he was getting a headache from all the thinking.

He became even more confused with every additional encounter with Gertrude who acted as though nothing had happened and proceeded to treat him like a close friend. She made no more mention of jasmines or full moons, nor did she even mention that she had mentioned such things before. If only she gave more hints to David. Or maybe she thought her comment at the cafe had been hint enough? What if it had only been a casual remark and David was reading too much into it? He felt like the stupidest person on the planet.

So with Gertrude's nonchalance, David too pushed away all the did it/did it not debate in his brain and focused on his lessons, which was an all-day Warrior Training. He successfully walloped a haughty Consortia with his Gothic Sword while she screeched and screamed at every impending attack. David tried to scale back his moves but Teacher Peregrine shouted at him for slowing down and he shouted at Consortia for her half-measured and hysterical fighting, threatening to punish her if she didn't do her best.

Consortia was a member of Caian's club and David was even more puzzled how she could be, considering her poor fighting skills. Her weapon of choice was laughable – a Cutlass that had been rendered nearly useless by its heavy styling and over decoration. Clearly she had added a lot of embellishments to her weapon.

Their fight ended with a gash on Consortia's thigh wherein

she quickly conceded defeat. She put on a brave face while Teacher Peregrine was with them but burst into tears when he left, calling David a cruel, cruel boy. Fortunately, before David could think of any expected response, she ran off.

There was more sword practice in store for David and next on his list of opponents was Rafaella again. She was minus her nanchuks but wielded an impressive weapon all the same. Two impressive weapons – the Seraphic Butterfly Swords.

Rafaella approached David holding the twin swords in her hands. They were shorter than the average long swords and yet gleamed menacingly of shining forged steel. The Seraphic Butterfly Swords had unique handles that could cunningly trap a long sword and yank it from an opponent. David whistled in awe at Rafaella's choice of weapon, feeling a thrill at how particularly blood thirsty she looked today. It was going to be a challenging fight.

"Ready to get your butt kicked again?" she taunted saucily.

"Don't be too sure about that." David warned in reply.

With customary bows, David and Rafaella clashed into their opening maneuvers. David was taking no chances. He knew what a spectacular fighter Rafaella was – she had beaten him soundly with her nanchuks – and while this was their first sword fight, David expected her to be an expert swordsman.

Rafaella was dauntingly fierce today. Whatever was bugging her was being projected into her fighting style – determined, focused, but brutal. She wasn't showing David any mercy or making allowances for his beginner status. She was giving the fight all her intrepid and creative moves, going in for quick slashes and lightning fast cuts. David, in intense Angel Mode, parried her every attack and boldly countered with his own sly maneuvers. Both were unforgiving and driven to win.

Several minutes in, David had cuts on his face and arms. Rafaella also had slashes on her arms plus midsection gashes that bloomed blood on her clothes. Still, they were unrelenting.

Teacher Peregrine watched them closely as they battled on, monitoring their fight's progress and being simply present to witness them go head to head. He neither interrupted their concentration or meddled in their technique. He just allowed them to fight.

It was exhausting warfare.

Rafaella added leaps and somersaults to her offense and defense while David continued to hold his ground, sorely tempted to use his wings but refusing to indulge in unfair combat. He compensated with creativity and rapid responses to Rafaella's more experienced fighting. In the end, David managed to overcome her, successfully making Rafaella lose her weapons and holding her at neckpoint with the tip of his Gothic Sword.

She was breathing heavily, denial clear in her eyes as she realized her defeat. Teacher Peregrine gave the fight to David and announced him the victor, while Rafaella yelled out a frustrated "Nooooo!"

Suffice it to say, she wasn't a graceful loser and didn't concede defeat with good humor or sportsmanship. Instead she blasted him with a freezing stare, continued to scream in frustration and walked off the training area. David didn't know whether to be mad, sad or fall down laughing. It should have been a moment of sweet victory but was considerably dampened by the fact that Rafaella walked out on him.

Later on in the day though, she slinked embarassedly to his side and apologized for her 'abominable behavior' as she called it. David was grinning at how hard it was for Rafaella to articulate the words, but in the end she did congratulate him on his win, almost choking on the words as she said them.

As for Caian's gift, it was over the weekend that David found a chance to hand it to him – for saving his life and bringing him to the Monastery. Their now habitual foursome of David, Lukas, Rafaella and Gertrude were roaming around the Monastery in search of Caian when they espied him and his girlfriend Antonia talking earnestly with Prefect Macarius.

The sight alone stopped them in their tracks as they curiously wondered what the hushed business was about. They watched as the three conversed quite seriously, Prefect Macarius continually making furtive glances every time he uttered whispered statements. What was more surprising to David and his friends was how Wolverine, who was running around with them, was growling in the direction of Prefect Macarius.

David and his friends decided to hang around the periphery and when Prefect Macarius left at last, with a cursory nod of acknowledgement to them, David approached Caian, taking out the dagger he made from his trusty messenger bag.

Caian was effusive in his thanks for the gift that David made him, admiring the Stylet Dagger from all angles and complimenting David's precise workmanship. He also showed his appreciation for the matching scabbard emblazoned with intruiging designs. David was disappointed though when Caian and Antonia made no mention about the club. Except for a friendlier attitude towards David and Gertrude, Antonia acted like last Thursday's club meeting never happened.

With the entire day free at their disposal, Rafaella suggested a snowball fight and they trudged outside to a frigid Alaskan October. For David who grew up in texan climes, snow was a rarity, and he plunged gamely into the fight that soon became a battle between the boys and girls.

He and Lukas craftily built a fort and Angel Moded their way into creating as many snowballs as they could. Soon, a barrage of snowballs were being lobbed back and forth between their engineered hideouts. Rafaella and Gertrude upped the ante as they managed to fashion (although Lukas and David were dumbfounded at how they accomplished it) an automatic weapon from sculpted ice – shooting a rapid succession of snowballs at them.

David succumbed to sneaky tactics and used his wings, flying over the girls fort with his black wings spread out, and ceaselessly hurling dozens upon dozens of snowballs at them. Soon they were shrieking *"Unfair!"* and shaking their fists at him. But with Lukas covertly nearby plus David's unending snowball missiles, the girls got plastered in an obliterating storm of snowballs.

Come Monday morning, David and Gertrude received matching invitations on crisp and stiff paper for another club meeting. It was a post dinner arrangement for the following Friday at the esteemed Uriel Lodge. While David was excited for the opportunity to investigate the Sator Square again, he also dreaded Lukas' reaction to the invitation. Although his friend put on a brave and unaffected face, his mood was soured by the new missive.

David's friendship with Lukas was beginning to feel like a rollercoaster ride and the week felt like a repeat of the previous one with David walking on eggshells around Lukas, determining the mood of his friend on a daily basis. At least by Tuesday, Lukas appeared to be over his brooding and oppressive mood and was his cheery, overachieving self once more.

The big news of the week was the seven year old newcomer whose pet tiger died trying to save him from demons. Over the PA system, Prefect Macarius joyfully announced the presence of the tiger essence pet and exhorted everyone to watch out for it. He ended the announcement on the not so comforting note that essence pets didn't need to eat, so he was quite certain that no Nephilim would be eaten by the newly essenced and still voracious tiger.

The week passed by in a blur of schoolwork and punishing Warrior Training, with David's thoughts constantly dwelling on Friday's upcoming meeting and the occasional puzzled but secret glances at Gertrude. She looked serene as ever but electrified David now and then with beautiful and meaningful smiles – or maybe he was just imagining it. He did notice himself staring at her when she wasn't looking, admiring how her eyes lit up when she talked, how smooth and shiny her hair was and how he wanted to reach out and feel it himself. He thought she looked prettier every day and he secretly inhaled each time she was near to enjoy how she always smelled of flowers.

By the end of the week though, David was also stumped by the drastic change in Rafaella. She became crabbier and crabbier with each passing day and answered questions waspishly, living up to her surname as she pierced everyone with her sharp and biting comments. Lukas and David wanted to line her up with the wax demons and shoot arrows at her for being so annoying. At least, Rafaella's surliness improved Lukas' mood and he and David became co-conspirators in avoiding Rafaella when they could.

At last, Friday evening arrived and after dinner, with more urgent instructions from Lukas and a grudgingly mellow Rafaella, David and Gertrude again made their way to the elegant Uriel Lodge.

But not before a bombshell dropped on them.

As the four friends prepared to go their separate ways for the evening, a furtive Froggy urgently beckoned them. They followed the cherub to a less crowded spot away from the Cube and when their informant was satisfied that they were by themselves, he whispered croakily at them.

"I had to tell you as soon as I learned."

Lukas leaned closer the cherub to ask, "What did you find out, Froggy?"

"Good news. A breakthrough to our dangerous case." glancing at his rapt audience, Froggy gleefully revealed:

"Zachary Spencer is awake."

27 A Golden Necklace

Uriel Lodge appeared exquisite and imposing as ever, but this time with a hushed solemnity and palpable sacredness that to David was daunting and yet inviting at the same time.

A very pretty third year ushered David and Gertrude to a formidable antechamber where three students already waited. David guessed that they were fresh recruits just like him and Gertrude. Two of them were beautifully pale and faery-like with ash blond hair and the palest blue eyes he had ever seen. Although one was a boy and the other a girl, they were obviously twins. They introduced themselves as Perez and Zarah and were third year students in the Monastery. Both could not contain their animation and excitement. They repeatedly confessed how they have heard of this elite society for so long and now they were about to become actual members of it!

The other occupant in the room was a very confident first year girl with vivid eyes and warm honeyed skin. Her name was Sabeena Safavi and she boldly declared that she had always expected an invitation to this select group.

Soon someone collected them from the antechamber and led them to the main hall of Uriel Lodge where an assembly of charismatic students gathered. David, Gertrude and the other three recruits were led to the front of the room, facing a solemn Caian who awaited them on a raised platform of flawless marble.

"You are here because you are special. You are here because you rise above the rest. You have a skill like no other, abilities uniquely your own, intelligence at genius levels." Caian gestured around the respectfully still room. "Look around you and see that you are in the company of the excellent. Each person here has been chosen because of their power and prowess. Only the best may enter this room. Only the best may be invited. Welcome Primo Angelus, peerless and unrivaled, superior and without equal. This is your family now. A family of incomparables, bound by faithfulness, loyalty, and sworn to secrecy. If you are prepared to become our brother, our sister, then do so now. If not, leave while you can."

David could sense Gertrude hesitating and he had to discreetly signal an encouraging nod to prevent her departure. They were at the point of no return.

When it was apparent that no one was leaving, Caian continued.

"To know the true name of our society is an oath to secrecy. Do you pledge to protect the identity of this Brotherhood?"

David and the other neophytes murmured, "I do."

"Do you pledge to honor and uphold our Vision and Mission with the purest of intentions?"

"I do."

"Do you pledge to obey the Governance of this assembly and strictly adhere to its Constitution?"

"I do."

To David's left Perez and Zarah were leaping from their skin in excitement and anticipation. David meanwhile, was mentally crossing his fingers and wondering how on earth he was going to get out of this secret society craziness that he was diving deeper into. To his right, David could sense Gertrude's twinges of anxiety and it was even more alarming because he had never seen her anxious before.

Caian breathed deeply and uttered, "This is the Society of the Sator Square. Welcome. I am Caian, your brother."

At his words an ornate and medieval banner unfurled behind him and at last the Sator Square was revealed. Just like the card they had discovered, the mysterious palindrome beckoned to David, its words almost shimmering and floating from the enormous banner.

S	A	T	O	R
A	R	E	P	O
T	E	N	E	T
O	P	E	R	A
R	O	T	A	S

A fourth year boy came forward. "I am Rotas – the Wheel. Welcome. I am your brother, Jerome."

"I am Opera – the Worker. Welcome. I am your brother, Samson."

"I am Tenet – the Keeper. Welcome. I am your sister, Antonia."

"I am Sator – the Sower. Welcome. I am your brother, Caian."

The ruling Governance of the Society of the Sator Square stood on the marble platform. Each one resplendent and awe-inspiring, standing tall with an outpouring of pride and courage. David couldn't help but feel admiration for them.

Surprisingly no one mentioned or questioned the absence of Arepo and what that person stood for. But at least, for now, David had to content himself with the revelation of the Sator Square, the secret society.

Samson came forward once again. "Sabeena Safavi, by your talent, I call you into the service and protection of Opera, the Worker." Sabeena happily sauntered to Samson's side.

Antonia was next. "Zarah Parnevik, by your talent, I call you into the service and protection of Tenet, the Keeper."

Then it was Jerome's turn. "David Cross and Gertrude Greer, by your talent, I call you into the service and protection of Rotas, the Wheel." David and Gertrude walked to Jerome's side, this time facing the assembly and being extra careful not to reveal a hint of reluctance or resistance.

Lastly, Caian stepped forward. "Perez Parnevik, by your talent, I call you into the service and protection of Sator, the Sower."

Then three students came forward, the middle one cradling a velvet pillow on top of which David caught glimpses of gold.

"Satorians, this necklace shall be your mark of membership and must be worn next to your skin, hidden from plain sight. You may only reveal it to a brother or sister of our society."

David saw Sabeena bowing her head as the two students very carefully placed the necklace on her as if performing a sacred rite. They moved to Zarah next and then they were in front of David. David also bowed so they could put the necklace on him and as they continued to Gertrude, David discreetly inspected his necklace. It was quite long and would be easily hidden beneath his clothes. The chain was thin but sturdy and made of burnished gold, but it was the pendant that was of interest. David had been expecting a Sator Square pendant but instead it was a small rectangle with the word *Rotas* on it. He guessed that each necklace would spell out what Service you belonged to, and he thought it actually clever that they didn't brandish the Sator Square about.

So that's how they've been protecting their secret society, David realized.

An oath to secrecy, carefully mentioned only among members and kept hidden from other Nephilims. He realized now what a grave mistake Zachary had committed when he carelessly lost the Sator Square card. A grave mistake that David and his friends fortunately and luckily discovered.

He looked at his necklace again. Rotas – the Wheel, and he wondered just what he had gotten himself into.

Although it was close to midnight when David and Gertrude emerged from Uriel Lodge, the four friends still met up in Lukas' room – which was impeccably neat and freakishly clean – so that they could trade information on the night's events. David and Gertrude made quick work of describing their bizarre evening with the finally revealed Society of the Sator Square while Rafaella and Lukas listened raptly to every detail and delved for more data by asking numerous questions. When they had finally exhausted the recruitment topic, Lukas grimly said,

"We have something to tell you too."

They had been successful in infiltrating the Infirmary.

"It was thanks to Rafaella here really that we managed to get in and see Zachary." said Lukas.

"You saw Zachary!" Gertrude exclaimed. "However did you manage that? And at such a late hour?"

Rafaella's face flushed and there was a fierce expression on her face. "I just did what I could think of. I went to Doctor Vitalis, told him Zachary was my –" she breathed deeply, hardly able to utter the word, " – that Zachary was my boyfriend –"

David choked on his drink.

Rafaella glared at all of them as though daring any idiot to laugh and promising repercussion with her icicle emerald eyes. " - and that I had heard he was awake. I had to beg Doctor Vitalis to let me see that disgusting piece of garbage."

"Oh she begged prettily alright." Lukas confirmed. "I never would have imagined it of you, Rafaella. She actually teared up! Teared up, if you can believe it. I swear if I didn't know how much she disliked that bullying cockroach, I would have believed her to be in love with the guy. Terrific acting Rafaella. Can I just bow to you right now?"

Rafaella flushed even more. "Well, Doctor Vitalis believed it and he let us see Zachary."

"Now here comes the weird part." Lukas continued. "When we came near Zachary, he was still sleeping, or he looked like he was sleeping. His eyes were definitely closed. Then without warning, he was staring wildly at us. Just wildly, like he was scared and panicked."

"We don't even know if he recognized that it was us."

"Then he grabbed Rafaella and said – *It wasn't me! I didn't do it!*" said Lukas. "He was slobbering all over the place and just completely agitated."

"That is expected though, isn't it?" Gertrude commented. "After all, he had been poisoned, by someone he knew to top it off."

Lukas nodded in agreement. "He kept saying it over and over: I didn't do it. I didn't do it."

"And we kept asking him, what didn't you do?" Rafaella added. "I kept reassuring him that he could tell us. That he could tell us anything and we would keep his secret safe. Then Zachary said: Hell -, and then he looked over my shoulder and just lost it. Total panic! He was thrashing on the bed, trying to get up, trying to yank his I.V. out. It was pandemonium. Doctor Vitalis made us leave that instant."

"But who was behind you?" David demanded, quite impatiently. "Who did Zachary see?"

"Doctor Vitalis was there, and Liz. But coming towards Zachary was another person -"

"Maybe he was just investigating. Of course he wanted to ask Zachary questions-" Lukas interrupted.

"Who was it?" David yelled.

"Prefect Macarius." Rafaella answered grimly.

28 ✝ Prefect and Pebbles

"How the heck are they doing that?" exclaimed David in amazement.

It was Archery class for him and Lukas and they had moved on from the intimidating but stationary demon targets to the Archery Arena – a training dome filled with huge and life-like demon figures that were *moving*.

"Superior animatronics and highly complex robotics." Lukas replied.

The scenario had also changed. The demons were no longer sitting ducks of a target practice that were lined side by side. This time around, David and Lukas were in the middle of the arena and they were surrounded by menacing demons that closed in on them.

"Ready?" Lukas looked at David.

David pulled an arrow from his quiver, nocked it (*truth*) into his bow and nodded at Lukas.

When Lukas pressed the remote, the demontronics came to life.

The technology behind the robots was unlike anything David had ever seen and he was sure it wasn't anything the outside world had seen either. The demontronics were not some clunky and chunky robots that moved in slow motion. They were agile and fast and looked unbelievably real.

They were crouching and growling towards David and Lukas, some were swooping in from the ceiling, their terrible wings extended.

David felt the adrenaline coursing through his body as he deftly switched to Angel Mode.

Combat Time!

He shot two arrows into a tall and hulking demon before it fell down, turned around and aimed at a sly and crouching one who he pierced in the head with *fortitude*. The demons fought back too. They swiped at David with their sharp claws but in Angel Mode, they were no match for him as David quickly side-stepped their advances.

Behind him, he heard the repeated twang of Lukas' arrow as his friend zeroed in on the other demons with perfect precision. He really was a formidable archer.

"Reload! Reload!" Lukas was shouting at David.

David grabbed a handful of pencil-sized sticks from his pocket and dropped it into his quiver. He heard the sticks lengthening to full-size arrows when it came in contact with the quiver.

David pointed at the flying demontronics and signaled to Lukas. "I'm going up!"

His black and grey wings unfurled and David shot up towards the demons in a heartbeat. Soon he was having his own aerial combat zone which proved to be a tricky feat when the demontronics were in constant motion. David struck down three, but he missed the other two demons as they evaded his arrows.

David flew after them, chasing them beneath the ironwork of the dome's ceiling. One demon turned around abruptly and swiped its metal claws at David. He backtracked to escape but the demon successfully ripped into David's shoulder and drew blood. The demon didn't get to do anymore injury though. His swipe was rewarded with an arrow between the eyes and a long fall to the ground. As it was training and the demons were expensive pieces of equipment, they had back-up parachutes to soften their fall and not break them into a jumble of scrap metal.

Only one flying demon was left in front of him.

David knew he could easily outfly the demontronic, but he also wanted to practice shooting the flying rat from behind. David grabbed an arrow and aimed at its flapping wing. Missed!

He grabbed another arrow and aimed at the wing again. This time his arrow found its target, clipping the demon's wing and throwing off its balance. The demontronic still tried to fly, sometimes spiraling wildly before regaining flight.

David shot another arrow to its other wing and as the demontronic hurtled towards ground, he shot it in the heart for good measure. With no more flying demons to target, David descended beside Lukas who was now sporting a gash above his left eye and a bloody claw swipe in the back.

Even with Lukas' shooting power, he had been outnumbered.

And the fight wasn't over yet. Three towering demontronics were muscling their way to David and Lukas.

"I'll get those two, you get that one." Lukas motioned.

David knew that Lukas was a formidable archer, but was he fast enough? Under this archery dome, the only weapons allowed were bows and arrows. If the demons swooped down quickly on them, they wouldn't have any swords or daggers to defend themselves with. That was the point of the training – attack with bows and arrows, defend with bows and arrows. If cornered and outnumbered: *think fast*!

As the three enormous demontronics closed in on them, Lukas knelt down and aimed, hands steady as ever, blood dripping above his left eye. In rapid succession, Lukas shot down the two demons, his aim straight and true, while David – stance shoulder-width apart, arms slightly curved – shot a streaking arrow at the third demon's forehead. The three menacing equipments fell down almost at the same time and David and Lukas high-fived each other for a job well done.

Later, as they were sprawled on the floor, catching their breaths after their energetic fight with the demontronics, Lukas asked, "What are you spacing-out about?" observing the frown and faraway look on David's face.

"Arepo." David muttered. "Who is he? And how come we've never seen him?"

"It's actually highly intelligent of them." Lukas observed, wiping the sweat from his eyes with sticky fingers. "It's obvious isn't it, that Arepo is the high commander of the group, and they're protecting his identity……."

David was nodding, "By not making his identity public knowledge, especially to us new members." He flexed his feet, feeling the slight soreness of his muscles. "This society, Lukas, they are just layers and layers of secrets. So, with what we've concluded – that not everyone knows who Arepo is – then who does? Who has access to him? Who does he give his orders to?"

"The officers." They both answered in unison.

David fell silent again, letting his mind work on the puzzle of the Society of the Sator Square. When Caian had invited him to that very first meeting – the meeting that turned out to be a party – the society's name was never mentioned. It was only when he and Gertrude passed that first screening and were sworn in as members that they even found out the name of the group. And yet from the start the officers had been bold in declaring their status. They had worn special bracelets, then they had introduced themselves during membership.

Arepo had been conspicuously absent, and yet no one had mentioned it. Not a hint, not a side comment. The officers and members acted as though he didn't exist.

But there was, *is*, an Arepo. And he was Alpha and he was pulling the strings.

Students would come and go. Officers would change, graduate, leave the Monastery and take on the outside world. But Arepo had to be constant. He must always be present to guide the society towards their goal. He must be the one to groom the officers, to control everyone – but behind a curtain of secrecy. And he must have the freedom and the capacity to do all this.

David abruptly sat up. "He's a teacher. And I think I know who it is."

"I have a bad feeling about this." Lukas whispered at David. He was fidgeting and jittery and sweating like a stream.

They were crouched outside Prefect Macarius' office, with David fiddling the ancient doorknob with the help of two hairpins and a metal file. In Angel Mode, they didn't need any flashlights to see in the dark and it was as visible as being in morning sunshine as to how pale Lukas was. He looked about to vomit at any moment.

Earlier that afternoon, David and Lukas discussed in earnest the identity of the mysterious Arepo. David was convinced that it was Prefect Macarius and he had diligently connected the dots to Lukas.

"Who was Caian and Antonia talking to *secretively* in that deserted corridor? When you and Rafaella talked to Zachary at the Infirmary and he panicked, who did he see? And why are there no further clues to the hellhound case? Who is in charge of the investigation? All the answers point to one person – Prefect Macarius."

David continued. "Don't you see, he's in the best position to manipulate the people in charge of this Monastery, and to manipulate the students. He's in between the divide! He has access to important information but as Prefect of Discipline, he also has power over all students."

Lukas contemplated David's deductions, running the information through his mind. Soon he was nodding in agreement. "You're right David. It makes perfect sense. Arepo, as you said, must be a teacher. Someone in authority, someone who has lived and will live in the Monastery for many years. We've seen Prefect Mac a couple of times in suspicious circumstances, I say, let's investigate further."

It was David's idea to snoop into Prefect Macarius' office after school hours, preferably after curfew, in the hopes that they would find some evidence connecting the prefect with the Society of the Sator Square. When Lukas heard the plan, he whitened and balked at the thought.

"I'm top of the class.......I'm going to be expelled..........we'll end up in Kalvarium just like Innocent Reichenberg......."

"No we wouldn't." David protested. "He committed attempted murder. We're just breaking and entering. Perhaps detention, tops."

But Lukas was pacing and muttering in nervous spasms. The poor kid was a wreck!

"You know what, you have too much to lose." David said. "You're right, they would probably string you by the ankles, hang you upside down and make an example of you. I'll go by myself. I can manage." he took a deep breath. "I can't let it go, Lukas. I have to find out for myself. I have to get evidence against Prefect Macarius."

Seeing how serious David was and how important it was to him, Lukas stopped all his spastic blathering and looked at David in the eye. "No, you're not going by yourself. You're right, this is important. I'll...." his jaw set determinedly, "I'll go with you."

And so here they were tonight, outside Prefect Macarius door. Lukas had suggested that they enlist the help of Rafaella and Gertrude, but David refused. If they got caught, he didn't want many people punished because he led them to delinquent behavior. No, two persons were enough, and even now he was feeling quite sorry for Lukas. David hoped his friend wasn't going to faint on him.

He totally understood Lukas, of course.

Up to this point in their investigation about the hellhound and the Sator Square Society, they had not broken any rules. Tonight was different. David was beginning to feel sorry for dragging his friend along. Lukas did have a lot to lose. He was class valedictorian and an all-around good student. He was the Nephilim of their year!

Still crouching by the doorknob, David shifted his position, mentally cursing the new jeans he was wearing. Thank God there was no punishment for mental cursing, because if there was, David would have soap bubbles coming out of his ears, leaking from his brain. That was an experience he would willingly pass-up on.

Even their getup tonight had been difficult to procure. Most of their clothes were white. Glaringly white. Not exactly the color for nightime criminal activity. After sweet-talking Katherine into letting them have access to the Garments Class, David and Lukas scoured the gigantic and bewildering closet of clothes, had almost given up on their plans, until they found black jeans and shirts tucked away in an obscure drawer.

With another twist and slight jiggle, David felt the lock give way. He wiped off the beads of perspiration on his forehead and slowly turned the knob and opened the door. Breaking into locked doors was a handy skill he learned in his orphanage days.

Prefect Macarius office should be pitch black, but in Angel Mode, they saw everything plainly. Everything was hyper-neat and orderly and nothing seemed out of place. Even all the candies in different bowls appeared to have been arranged just so.

"We have to be very careful." David whispered. "Don't touch and move anything unless it looks important. He'll know someone touched his things. And make sure you return what you moved to its original position."

Lukas nodded at his words.

Their main target was the Prefect's desk, hoping he would have a guilty object stashed away in it. David and Lukas spent almost an hour carefully and meticulously sifting through the contents of the desk, only to come up empty handed. David kept glancing at the picture on the desk. It was Prefect Macarius and a woman who looked like his mother. They were holding huge candy bars in front of a candy factory. Both were smiling-sneering into the camera.

Now I know where he got his smile-sneer, David thought.

With the desk not yielding any relevant clue, they slowly made their way all over the office. They opened drawers, rifled through book pages, and even looked under furniture. Nothing.

All they got were Monastery papers on Monastery business, some tempting student records which they had no time to peruse, and the realization that this man led a most boring life!

"This is taking too long." Lukas hissed. He was pale and jittery again.

Yes, it was taking too long. Already, it was two in the

morning.

David positioned himself in the middle of the room and quieted down, staring at everything around him. Everything in the office was just as expected for a prefect. All the stuff and the papers, everything in the drawers – it was just too......*right*. And what David had learned throughout his life from having to make quick judgements and evaluation of other people for his survival, was that no one was perfect. Especially the perfect looking ones. Everybody had a skeleton in their closet and it was simply a matter of knowing where to look.

As he continued his assessment of the room, something caught David's eye. It was the rug he was standing on. There was a telltale fold in one corner. Just a tiny one, but it looked like someone flipped the rug and when they flipped it back, a corner of it had curled slightly on itself.

"I think there's something under this rug." David beckoned to Lukas.

They stepped out of its surface and holding opposite ends, they slowly flipped the rug to reveal the floor beneath it.

There was a trapdoor underneath!

"Yes!" David exclaimed under his breath. Finally, the proverbial closet. Now it was time to look for hidden skeletons.

The trapdoor wasn't large, more like a compartment that was carefully cut out just to stash some things in. There was a small hook that could be used to open the safe and it was clever because the purpose of the design was to ensure an unruffled and undisturbed rug on top of it.

"Let's see what he's got tucked away." said David, his eyes gleaming with anticipation. He sincerely hoped some Sator Square memorabilia was waiting for them just beyond the small door.

Lukas gulped at his words, shuddered and grew even more pale. But he held on.

What surprised David most was that there were no locks and no complicated codes to punch in a keypad. But he wasn't going to complain about their fortunate discovery.

Without further ceremony, David carefully pulled on the hook and lifted the small door open. Inside was a rectangular space filled with metal canisters.

David reached in for one and with the help of Lukas, they pulled it out of the safe. It was quite heavy and looked like a fat thermos. On its front were faded letters that on closer inspection spelled out *Waldenbach Brothers*.

What the-? David puzzled. He twisted the metal cap of the canister and he and Lukas peered inside.

It was candy. A fat thermosful of candy in clear, old fashioned wrappers.

David pulled one out and looked at it. Was it really just candy? He plunged his hand inside the thermos and sifted through the dark brown orbs until he reached the bottom. It was just plain metal underneath.

"Why would someone hide candy underneath the floor?" Lukas was wondering.

David meanwhile was venting his frustration on the candy and he tipped the canister over until all its contents poured out.

"There must be something more than just candy in here." he shook the canister determinedly, pawing at the metal bottom for further clues.

Lukas was suppressing a laugh. "I think it really is just candy."

"Still, let's check the whole compartment."

They spent the next few minutes removing every metal canister from the safe, peering inside each one, pouring all the candy out, and then David patted every inch of the compartment for any possible clues left behind.

Nothing but candy. Just jars of candy.

Frustrated and exhausted, David angrily hissed. "What weirdo lunatic would put candy in metal jars and hide them under the floor?"

"I would." a voice from the doorway said. "I'm the weirdo lunatic."

David and Lukas stared up into the cold, dark eyes of Prefect Macarius. In their busy rummaging, they hadn't heard the door open.

Beside David, whimpering in fright, was a quaking Lukas. His friend tried to put on a brave face but painfully failed as Lukas realized they had been caught in such a blatantly illegal act. With all his anxiety and fear bubbling up to the surface like popped champagne, Lukas violently vomited all over Prefect Macarius' precious candy.

David didn't know what was more excruciating. Their punishment or the howling shriek that came out of the Prefect when Lukas threw up on his candy.

David thought Prefect Macarius would rouse the entire Monastery and humiliate them in front of everyone, but instead, he locked the office door, turned on the lights, and in a clipped voice quivering with anger, told them to wipe the vomit off every candy. Every last one.

At first he was livid, pacing around the office, wringing his hands together in agitation.

"Who told you? How did you find out about my hidden safe?"

David and Lukas were still on the floor, Lukas covered in sickly vomit, staring up at Prefect Macarius in nervous dread. They had been caught! Were they about to be expelled? Would they really be sent to *Kalvarium*? It was breaking and entering and maybe what Prefect Macarius would label Intent to Commit Theft. They were in so much trouble.

"Answer me!" Prefect Macarius glared at them, spit foaming at the corner of his small mouth.

David could hardly tell him the truth: that they thought he was Arepo and they snooped in his office to look for evidence connecting him to the Sator Square Society. So he instead replied, "Uhh.....we heard a rumor sir,......just a rumor. That uhh, you probably had some rare candy stashed somewhere. So we....uhh....ummm......."

"Stop mumbling and finish your sentences boy!" Prefect Macarius barked.

David nervously fidgeted with his shirt. He hated lying, but he had to. "I dared Lukas that we could find it. It was my idea, sir."

Lukas shot him a startled glance but was unable to say anything in the midst of his hyperventilations. Lukas was the kind of honest person who could face off with demons tomorrow if need be and survive through the ordeal, knowing that he was in the right. But any petty misdemeanor would send him over the edge.

And so, while Prefect Macarius sat on his chair, snug in pajamas and a thick robe, watching over them like a vulture warden, David and Lukas cleaned each precious candy with a damp cloth.

They were not allowed to just dump the entire lot in a bucket of water to clean out the vomit, for fear of ruining the candy. Nope.

They had to thoroughly wipe off each one, getting vomit all over themselves in the process. Lukas had cleaned himself in the office lavatory, but his shirt was still sticky and his stench was sickly sweet and nauseating.

"I'm sorry. I'm so sorry." Lukas whispered miserably as they wiped and wiped each candy.

"Hey, don't worry about it." David tried to smile amidst the acrid stench of Lukas' regurgitation. It wasn't easy.

All the while, Prefect Macarius was muttering to himself as David and Lukas worked. "They just don't understand........rumors ....who else know.........rare.......*it is rare!* ....discontinued.......... ....never to be produced again!"

David had to bite his lip to keep from bursting out laughing, but the graveness of their situation kept him somber and more depressed by the minute.

Where would he go if he got expelled? Could he survive out there with demons constantly chasing him?

After they had cleaned the last clear-wrapped candy, put them gently back into their metal canisters, lowered them back to the floor safe, David and Lukas heaved a sigh of relief.

"Oh no." said Prefect Macarius with evil relish. "Your punishment is not over yet."

David and Lukas exchanged looks of utter dread. What was in store for them next?

"For humans it's usually salt and books, but since we're Nephilims........" Prefect Macarius trailed off.

In just a little bit, David and Lukas were kneeling down, their knees grinding into sharp pebbles especially placed there for their torturous benefit. Their arms were outstretched, and on each open palm was a heavy jar stuffed with candy.

David knew he would never look at candy the same away again.

"You will remain that way until I declare your punishment to be over." Prefect Macarius announced. "And each time a jar falls down, more time would be added to your punishment."

David didn't know how long they were in that position, having lost track of time. He had tried counting the seconds and minutes in his head at first, but gave up when he reached 8,743 seconds. He just knew that he had stopped feeling the sharp pebbles which used to stab shooting pains each time he adjusted his weight. Or maybe his knees were dead by now. His arms were probably dead too. They were still outstretched but he couldn't feel them anymore. They were so numb from lack of circulating blood that he was amazed they were still holding up.

Poor Lukas looked about to pass out. He was gritting his teeth from the pain and his arms would shake and twitch every so often from exhaustion. Lukas dropped a jar of candy twice. David once. Now they were pushing their hardest not to drop any candy jar again as it added more and more time to their painful predicament.

Finally, when David thought he couldn't hold up the vile candy jars any longer, or that his arms would fall off by themselves, Prefect Macarius said to them. "Very well. I think the punishment has been sufficient enough. Put the candy jars down very carefully and then you may leave."

It took some minutes to successfully lower the jars without causing damage – David wanted to hurl them to the walls – since each movement blasted shooting pains up and down their arms. And even more time to stand up from the gritty pebbles. Lukas and David had to sit on the floor, gasping, grimacing and holding on to their extremities as the blood burningly coursed back to their veins. That was the real torture.

Prefect Macarius only smiled-sneered at them. Then he warned them, "You will not speak of this to anyone. You will not speak about the candy hidden away and in return you will not be expelled. Do I make myself clear?"

Both boys nodded in relief.

"If another attempt is made to steal these rare sweets by you or anyone else, I will hold the two of you responsible. And next time, the consequences will be more severe."

Dismissed, David and Lukas hurried outside, incredulous that they had not been expelled or worse, incarcerated in Kalvarium.

The rising sun had lightened the sky to a pale pink signaling the arrival of dawn and while they were exhausted and sleepy from their ordeal, wishing for nothing more than their warm beds, David and Lukas had to soak under hot showers and prepare themselves for class. All-nighter or not, it was mandatory for them to attend classes.

As they trudged their way back to their rooms through (thankfully) deserted corridors, David asked Lukas. "About Prefect Macarius, I know we didn't find anything to implicate him with the Sator Square Society, but do you really think he's not connected to the group?"

Lukas snorted. "He's too much of an idiot to be Arepo."

Lukas had a point.

"Still, it could all be an act." David said. He remained even more convinced that Prefect Macarius was unlikable and untrustworthy.

29 Dark Gifts

Now that he was a supposed member of the *Society of the Sator Square*, David took to wearing their gold necklace with the Rotas pendant in case an officer inspected him on it. He knew Gertrude was being diligent about their espionage and it became their daily habit to check in with each other and compare notes about the Society's benefactorial generosity.

Over the succeeding days, the secret society asserted itself into David's life in many helpful and seductive ways.

When David had a difficult time grasping certain concepts in Angelology, they sent a creatively intelligent student to assist him in understanding the lesson in the person of Juliana Jacoby. She patiently tutored him through his rough patches and her unorthodox explanations and methodology somehow made everything click into place in David's brain.

The society also learned about his interest and enjoyment in weapon making and one late afternoon, Abraham, a third year and Satorian, handed him a treasure of a book on different kinds of weapons complete with designs and detailed instructions on how to create each one. David felt guilty about accepting the gift, but at the same time, he loved the book and challenged himself in creating his favorite selections during Carpentry and Metallurgy classes.

This appreciation of weapons also led to an invitation from

Samson, a senior and officer of the Society – also known as Opera (the worker) – who had a wickedly cool collection of rare weapons spanning several centuries, and David drooled over each one. He also had a terrific time discussing the weapons with Samson and arguing over the merits of each one versus the others.

Somehow, or perhaps it was their important duty, every officer and a barrage of members bore in mind that David and Gertrude were now part of their exclusive club and they went out of their way to make them feel most welcome. There was a constant stream of lunch or dinner invitations, frequent hellos and how are you's in corridors and everywhere else they met a member. David felt envious glances thrown his way from the other kids in the Monastery as cool, popular and accomplished students lavished him with attention and open friendliness. He earnestly tried to include Lukas in every conversation and event but being the puffed-up, narrow-minded elitist that they were, their attention was given only to David and Gertrude. Sometimes Lukas' mood would sour for a few days but fortunately, he bounced back from his bouts of bleakness.

Rafaella was more understanding of their secret agent situation, but she constantly warned David and Gertrude not to be lured into the Society's vortex of insanity.

Jerome Gallagher, David's immediate superior and known as Rotas (the Wheel), introduced him to Aerial Football and David had crazily wild afternoons playing football while flying. The players consisted of senior Satorians – because of the wings – and they had an exhilarating time playing the game several feet up in the air, wings flapping on offense, getting crushed in defense and experiencing the hilarity of getting tackled while flying. They had a wintry backdrop of endless snow and being out in the freezing cold only invigorated David even more. Amidst the sea of whiteness, his wings were a stark black.

It was only too easy to delude himself into thinking that he had found some sort of family, that he was special and that his new *brothers* and *sisters* truly cared for his well-being and happiness. The Society's proffered sense of family was very tempting and David looked constantly on Lukas and Rafaella to ground him to the reality and purpose of their mission.

David knew Gertrude was having a hard time resisting them as well.

They too were offering her gifts close to her heart and David could sense the corruption every time they accepted the gifts. It was as though they were letting go of themselves and selling their soul to the Society.

They knew of Gertrude's passion for music and they also discovered her proficiency in playing the harp. But some unnamed obstacle was blocking Gertrude's growth to absolute mastery in playing the instrument and so Antonia presented herself as mentor, displaying her formidable prowess with the harp. Some tutorials in, and Gertrude was playing the best that she ever did.

When David really thought about it, the most eerie part of the Society was how they just *knew* what he needed, what he craved for, what would make him happy. It was an unsettling feeling to realize that he was being observed and studied. To put it bluntly, he was being spied upon.

Every so often, Jerome would meet with him and Gertrude to inculcate them with the belief system of the Sator Square Society and how the roles of each individual complemented each other to comprise of a united and harmonious whole.

Caian as Sator the Sower took charge of recruiting new members to the Society. His openness and charm were his invaluable tools, but more importantly, he possessed the keen judgement of determining a student's potential and if that student had the ability to grow into that potential person. Each recruit invariably did, with the diligent and persevering molding of the Society.

Antonia as Tenet the Keeper acted as Purser and Historian. She managed the organization's finances (though David didn't know why they had money or where it was from) and was the primary person with access to their assets. Jerome disclosed that the Society had its own treasures in the Monastery – priceless artifacts, historical objects, rare books and documents – all of which were Antonia's responsibility for safeguarding. And as Historian, she also was records-keeper of anything and everything that involved or affected the Society.

Jerome as Rotas the Wheel was Peace Officer of the group. He and his subordinates such as David and Gertrude were tasked with defending the Sator Square Society. They were the military might and first line of defense against enemies. To this David questioned at the back of his mind, which enemies? Their eternal enemies, the demons? Or anyone getting in the way of the Society's goals? As David mulled over this, Jerome continued to outline their duties as Peace Officers and what was expected of them. There would be additional training from Satorians themselves on top of Warrior Training and Jerome promised David and Gertrude that they would learn fighting techniques not taught or known by their teacher-warriors at the Monastery, centuries-old stylized and secret fighting skills handed down from Satorian to Satorian and forbidden to be shared to 'outsiders'.

Jerome also expressed how pleased and honored the Society

was with Gertrude's presence and how excited they were to view Gertrude's lauded abilities as a Dream Invader. Gertrude reacted by quietly holding on to David's hand, her fingers trembling at the idea of her gift being used in such a manner, but her face remained as serene as ever. David promised himself to figure out a way to extricate themselves from the clutches of the Society and prevent the misuse of Gertrude's power for their questionable purposes and promotions. He would think of a way. He had to protect Gertrude!

Samson as Opera the Worker spearheaded every mission, goal or event of the Society. He worked in conjunction with and under the guidance of Caian James, who was also their official leader. Samson had the largest number of members under his command to carry-out orders. He mobilized the elite masses so that they could accomplish whatever mission presently being undertaken.

Jerome, as head of Defense had the second largest group under his command.

As Jerome segued into training schedules and future meetings at Uriel Lodge, David said, "Wait, there are five structures to the Sator Square. You only mentioned four. What about Arepo? Is there an Arepo?"

Jerome only smiled kindly and condescendingly at David. "All of that will be revealed to you when you have proven yourself worthy."

He and Gertrude were stunned.

It shouldn't have come as a surprise really. The Society had continuously proven itself to be layers upon layers of secrets and hidden heirarchies. Naturally, they would protect the identity of Arepo fiercely. But why? Why did his identity have to be secret? To what purpose?

And how would David find out who Arepo was?

Now that was definitely something to think about, David pondered. How would they prove themselves worthy? What would it take?

After that insightful but disturbing meeting with Jerome, Gertrude asked David to accompany her for a walk outdoors to clear their heads. It was late afternoon and the sun had begun its descent, the sky was a burst of deep oranges and pale yellows.

The snow crunched beneath their feet as they walked the grounds and breathed in the brisk air. David felt the frigid coldness blasting away the cobwebs in his brain and he felt suddenly lighthearted away from the deceptions and questionable agenda of the Sator Square Society.

He knew Gertrude was deeply troubled and it made him sad that she was and that her view of the world and her fellow Nephilims had been tainted. No longer were they the absolute good guys and the demons the bad guys. Their kind, despite being half-angels were very much capable of their own evil.

David and Gertrude walked in companionable silence, Gertrude leading them towards a glasshouse visible from the distance. David had seen the structure numerous times during Warrior Training but he had never been inside it. Soon enough they were at its entrance and with familiarity, Gertrude pushed open its double doors and led David inside.

It was warm and fragrant with the perfume of countless flowers.

"This is one of my most favorite places in the Monastery." Gertrude shared, shedding her thick winter coat as David did the same. She carefully hanged them in a nearby rack and invited David to look around the glasshouse.

David could feel the cold radiating from the glasspanes but

warded off by the warmth inside the hothouse. There were tiers of pots with a variety of flowers, some more commonplace, others unfamiliar and exotic looking. Tall bushes and miniature trees dotted the space and David could tell that Gertrude had a hand in pinpointing where each plant would go. There was a palpable harmony to the entire arrangement.

Gertrude pointed out the names of some plants, offering humorous trivia about each one, and David avidly listened. He still had a lot to learn especially in Botany class where as expected, Gertrude excelled.

Then she led them to a cushioned bench with an uninterrupted view of the setting sun beyond the glass panes.

They sat quietly together, just enjoying the magnificent view as the sun sank lower and lower into the horizon. They enjoyed the play of colors in the sky, the pinks and purples blending together.

David reached out and held Gertrude's hand. He felt suddenly awkward and shy but he knew instinctively that it was the right thing to do. Gertrude smiled at him and held his hand in return.

When the sun had set and only the crystal lamps overhead gave illumination, Gertrude spoke quietly, "I know that soon, the Society will make me Dream Invade someone. I do not want to give in to them, David."

David nodded, worry etched on his face too.

They were sitting closer now, their hands intertwined.

David leaned in, brushing away some wisps of hair from her forehead. He had wanted to do that for a long time – touch her hair, lightly brush his hand against her face. She was just so beautiful and kind and when David was with her, he felt all the anger from his past and the anxiety for his future simply draining away.

"We'll think of a way so you won't have to do it. I'll help you

Gertrude. We'll think of something." he meant every word but it sounded so lame that it was all he could offer her. Suddenly he wanted to be grown-up, to have more experience. To know what to do and say.

"I know you will David." she smiled again. "Thank you. You're such a very good friend."

David felt the balloons of boy and girl ideas in his mind popping in disappointment.

Was that all he was to her? *A very good friend*?

"Do you really think Prefect Macarius is Arepo?" she asked.

"I don't know anymore. He could be. Or Lukas could also be right about him, that he's too much of an idiot to be Arepo."

Gertrude gave a guilty giggle, then admonished him. "Do not say that. He is our Prefect." but her eyes were still laughing.

David suddenly stood up, a flash of idea energizing him. "That's it Gertrude! He's the key! The sooner we find who Arepo is then the sooner all this would be over."

She stood next to him. "And no one else would be hurt and the perpetrators would be brought to justice."

"Especially Arepo."

"Yes, especially Arepo." she agreed with surprising fierceness.

"And hopefully in time so you wouldn't have to Dream Invade someone." David added solemnly.

Gertrude looked up at him. He was a head taller than her but she easily brushed away the lines of worry on his face. "It is always better to hope."

David was instantly aware that there was a trickling fountain at the corner and hanging blossoms of jasmine nearby.

His heart was pounding so loudly that he was sure Gertrude could hear it.

David wanted to kiss her, but should he? Could he?

Just go for it David. A voice in his head urged.

Convinced, David leaned into Gertrude, barely acknowledging that she was moving towards him too.

They both closed their eyes and finally, finally, their lips met.

30  Curare

November slinked in like a student late for class, catching David unaware.

He was in limbo.

Try as he would, he just couldn't bring himself to be more worried or concerned about the Sator Square Society, about finding Arepo, about finding the person who set the hellhound on him and finding (or thanking) the person who poisoned Zachary.

He was in the throes of adolescent love. And when you're an adolescent – it meant everything. His every waking moment revolved around Gertrude, thinking about what she was doing and longing to spend every second with her.

When he had told Lukas that he and Gertrude were going steady, Lukas had swallowed his spit the wrong way, choked and coughed his congratulations at David then laughed like a little girl in disbelief and excitement.

Nowadays though, Lukas' thrill for David had faded and he would shake his head at his friend instead, saying things like, "You're pathetic." or "You were just with her a few minutes ago!" or "I swear I'm going to decapitate you myself if you don't pay attention to the training." and a smug, "Serves you right for being so out of it." when David doubled over in pain from deep gashes he received in their sword fight.

As for Rafaella, at first she was overly effusive about the news, punching David in the arm repeatedly as her way of congratulating him. Then she suddenly became distant and edgily evasive, her behavior towards David swinging from bewildering outbursts of anger to passive lukewarmness.

David noticed that she especially avoided him when he and Gertrude were together and David wondered whether Rafaella disliked Gertrude or if she disapproved of his choice for a girlfriend. But how could that be when they were all good friends and David was the unbelievably lucky guy going out with an incredible girl.

In time, whatever was bugging Rafaella went away and once again she was at ease with them and was back to her usual prickly, opinionated and annoying self.

In time also, David mellowed down and stopped running about as poster-boy of the lovesick teenager.

Lukas breathed a sigh of relief to have his friend back, archly inquiring, "Honeymoon stage over? That's great. Let's get back to work okay?"

Work meant delving deeper into the Society of the Sator Square while juggling his schoolwork, his precious time with Gertrude and Warrior Training.

In Angelology, Teacher Celestine led them into the study of Thrones or Ophanims who were the living symbols of justice and authority. These mighty angels were not human-like in shape, instead they were beryl-colored *wheels within a wheel*. And their rims were covered in hundreds of eyes. In the paintings and pictures that Teacher Celestine showed them, the Thrones appeared like burning suns in the sky.

David and his classmates had a blast in *Heavenly Art*. Teacher Verrochio arranged for an outdoor ice-sculpting class and each student was assigned a block of ice to work on for a life-size masterpiece. Even though David had no knowledge and training about sculpting, under Teacher Verrochio's enthusiastic guidance, plus their angelic inclination towards art, David was able to create a passable sculpture of his father. The class theme was to sculpt an image of their Angel Parent.

Teacher Verrochio even allowed David to use his wings and fly when working on the taller parts of the statue, but not wanting to draw unnecessary attention to himself, David used the ladder like everyone else. It would have been good fun to fly though.

In Botany, they worked in greenhouses scattered around the grounds of the Monastery under the unsettling instructions of a hyper Teacher Tellurium. Despite his nervous energy, he efficiently taught them the healing powers of herbs and then they were cutting, boiling, infusing, and bottling green syrupy liquids into glass vials for further studies. In another lesson, they donned protective smocks and glasses as they studied highly poisonous plants and how to extract their poison.

One plant in particular, the Curare from the *chondrodendron* family, looked innocent enough. Its leaves were heart shaped and it had clusters of greenish-white flowers. But when the roots and stems were crushed and cooked into a sticky paste, then it morphed into a deadly poison.

"Remember, do not allow the poison into your bloodstream. Take utmost caution when handling it." said Teacher Tellurium. He went on to elaborate on the horrible effects of curare.

"The victim will be awake and aware of what is happening to him. First his toes and ears will be paralyzed. Then the poison will render his arms and legs useless. Lastly, the victim, coupled with the realization of impending doom, will be unable to breath."

Everyone in the room gulped loudly at the Teacher's tale.

Teacher Tellurium broke out into a grin. "But curare is also medicinally effective and aids in calming muscular spasms and other neurologic maladies. So," he justified, "it's not *all* bad."

The class proceeded in transforming the plant into a paste, working with quiet concentration, until Dominic Karlinski – one of Zachary's disciples – accidentally cut himself with a curare laced knife, quickly paralyzing him from his extremities and inwards toward a rapidly failing respiration.

David could see Dominic's eyes looking wildly at them, panic-stricken but unable to speak.

Unfazed, Teacher Tellurium cheerfully darted him with an antidote and had him sent to the Infirmary. He gleefully reminded everyone the detriments and consequences of carelessness and exhorted all to be more intelligent and careful in their work.

When they had successfully presented their curare pastes to Teacher Tellurium, all of them were eager and relieved to put as much distance between themselves and the greenhouse of poisons.

It was only Gertrude who appeared unruffled by the exposure, saying, "Yes, plants can be aggressive creatures. But they are most helpful as long as you respect their properties and know how to handle them."

"Handle this." Rafaella muttered from behind David and Gertrude, executing a rude hand sign at Gertrude's back.

David didn't know whether to laugh or be outraged, but in defense of his girlfriend, he frowned and glared at an uncaring Rafaella, who quickly feigned innocence.

Carpentry and Metallurgy continued to be David's most

favorite subject, finding pure joy in creating objects. Teacher Coppersmith encouraged David to branch-out from his weapon making and try a hand at other things. David started with the basics – a chair – which he did well but wasn't as much fun compared to making a weapon. He also designed a necklace for Gertrude which he secretly and furtively worked on, embarrassed to be called on it and be mercilessly teased. Gertrude's happiness and glowing appreciation of the gift though, made all the sneaking around worthwhile.

Then they met up with Teacher Tellurium again for sessions in Chemistry where this time they had a more lighthearted laboratory lesson, conducting experiments from the absurd – hand held fireballs – to the solemn – achieving a controlled nuclear fission reaction.

In the middle of all this, Zachary Spencer returned to class, all jittery and paranoid, given that the person who poisoned him had not been found out. Towards that event, Zachary adamantly maintained that he remembered nothing, even his reason for being in that area during the tragic night and who he was supposed to be meeting.

Abbot Anderson saw to his safety by relegating bodyguards to be with Zachary at all times, in the form of five squealing Puttis. Although often overlooked and judged as mere babies, the cherubs were actually strong and quite capable of defending themselves and others from injury.

The downside of it was, the Puttis were incessant and annoying, too giggly and playful to remain still. They were forever being sent outside the classroom as they disrupted the class with unending fits of giggling, coupled with strings of baby farts from a lactose-intolerant cherub who stubbornly kept on drinking milk anyway.

Zachary looked about to murder his own guard detail, but until the poisoning perpetrator was found, he was stuck in a chattering, squeaky and flatulent purgatory.

Soon the Monastery was buzzing with preparations for Thanksgiving, the highlight of which would be a school show. Much to David's dismay, he realized that Nephilims loved performance and pageantry and in fact, each class was tasked in presenting a song or dance to be shown in front of the entire school.

Teacher Irayazel, their Angelic Chorale instructor, orchestrated and choreographed their would-be presentation, and to David's relief, he was designated to the props department alongside an equally relieved Rafaella and a grunting Giles. Needless to say, Gertrude, Lukas, Consortia, and even Joseph headlined the performance while Isaac enthusiastically waved at them from the chorus along with a sullen Zachary who always wanted to be the star in everything.

David observed that Lukas became starry-eyed, patchily flushed and dorkier whenever Consortia was around, but the haughty redhead remained oblivious to Lukas' feelings. His friend seemed content in admiring her from afar and machinated no advances in securing Consortia as his girlfriend. Not that anyone encouraged him to. Rafaella blasted Lukas every time she caught him staring at Consortia, going on and on about how shallow and vain and mean the girl was, until David had to kick her under the table to make her stop.

In Warrior Training, David continued mastering the Gothic sword, but he was also moving along nicely in his brazilian jujitsu lesson. He had a challenging but exhilarating afternoon with Isaac who deftly attacked him with rapidly thrown ninja stars while David did his hardest to evade them, using the Gothic sword as a shield to flick away the oncoming metal discs. They were painful little buggers, slicing deeply into his skin when some managed to get through.

He also had his first taste with a large, blunt weapon – a battle axe – wielded by Rusticus Reed, who turned out an okay person away from the toxic fumes of Zachary and Giles. Rusticus and David struck a tentative friendship so long as it remained unwitnessed by Zachary, whose mere presence turned Rusticus into an instant enemy.

With all the mental and physical activities, David was bruised and beat, but he was also having the most fun ever, now comfortable in the rhythms and schedules of the Monastery and unable to imagine his life otherwise.

Gertrude was his bright and quiet spot. Centering him and calming his spirit.

They spent hours whiled away in the glasshouse; Gertrude tried to teach him more about plants, David stole as much kisses as he could. He taught her to loosen up and be more silly, she helped him with his schoolwork and vastly improved his archery skills – despite the distractions.

David felt he could spend endless hours just looking at her, observing her, loving the way she smiled shyly, or smiled generously without artifice or guile. He loved her kindness and her quick wit. She delivered zingers so seriously that it took David time to process that she was actually joking or being sarcastic. He learned not to take her too seriously, that Gertrude was indeed fun and silly, only she did it without much fanfare.

But what David liked most about her was that she didn't have to use a thousand words and gestures to say what she meant, and she *meant* what she said. She was honest and sincere and expected the same from him. Gertrude brought out the best in him.

His paradise was not without its dark clouds and threatening thunder. The Sator Square Society remained as pervasive as ever, disrupting the lives of not only David and Gertrude, but also Lukas' and Rafaella's who pushed on perseveringly in solving the hellhound and poisoning crime.

The more the Society ingratiated itself with unsolicited *help* and unexpected *gifts,* the more David and Gertrude were repulsed by their offering. They knew the time would come when payment would be expected from them. Already Jerome was mentioning first missions and first demonstrations.

The four friends racked their brains and thought of ways to find more evidence in order to prevent Gertrude from being used to Dream Invade for the Society, but no clue or even a weak lead presented itself.

Each of them had taken turns trying to question Zachary about the night of the poisoning, using their best persuasive element – Rafaella – to no avail. Zachary still maintained that he didn't remember anything, but David could see the flashes of fear and panic in his eyes.

Zachary was lying.

He was hiding something and either he was hiding the truth to protect someone or, more believably, hiding the truth to protect himself.

Then the day they were dreading finally came.

Gertrude came to David in tears, so agitated that David was alarmed and panicked. Jerome had just spoken with her, going on and on about what an honor and service she would be doing, and had set a date for a Dream Invasion.

"Tomorrow night." Gertrude revealed, her voice quivering.

David hugged her tightly, patting her back to help calm her. "Did they say who you're supposed to Dream Invade?"

"Yes." she choked on the word, and shuddered with apprehension.

"Abbot Anderson."

As much as David wanted to spend the evening consoling Gertrude, he felt more productive and useful going about the Monastery ferreting out for clues. He went to the scene of the poisoning crime repeatedly – they had done so before when they learned where it was – but discovered no one and nothing to enlighten him.

He even chatted up Abraham, the third year Satorian who loved weapons and weapon making, and asked him how the Society felt about members who wanted to quit.

Abraham's mouth gaped open in unconcealed surprise and blustered that no one had ever asked to quit.

"When you become a member, you are a Satorian for life." said Abraham. "It is a privilege and an incredible honor that no one wishes to give up. Why do you ask it?"

"Oh, I don't want to quit." David swiftly reassured Abraham. The boy looked about to pass out from his *shocking* question. "I was just wondering about it, that's all."

Relieved, Abraham smiled. "Isn't it fantastic, David? Knowing that you have this family forever. We will always have each other as brothers and sisters, even when we go out into the world. We are Satorians. We always will be."

David wanted to punch him in the face, but thanked him instead.

They were in deep trouble.

But David wasn't about to give up. There must be a way. There had to be.

He had to talk to Zachary again. David just knew in his gut

that Zachary was withholding information. Maybe this time David could persuade him to talk, or beat the information out of him if that was possible. But he was desperate enough to try anything.

It was almost dinnertime at the Monastery, so many students were walking about, slowly making their way to the Cube. Some were just hanging out, laughing and jabbering in groups. Someone would fly every now and then, wings flapping wide and disregarding the danger of hitting someone, or doing it deliberately to smack someone in the head. Even the younger kids were about, running down corridors mischievously as harried cherubs fluttered after their charges. The young kids loved playing hide and seek with their sitter Puttis whether they wanted to or not, knowing they could get away with almost anything from their babysitters. Puttis were renowned push-overs and they easily forgave infractions committed against them.

As David walked towards Zachary Spencer's room, meeting fellow students along the way, overhearing conversations and their mundane concerns, he experienced pangs of envy for their relatively normal lives. They weren't worried sick that their girlfriend's skills would be used for nefarious purposes. They weren't draining their brain trying to figure out who poisoned Zachary. They weren't trying to seek justice for themselves because of a hellhound attack.

And where was Prefect Macarius in all this? What was his supposed investigation accomplishing?

David's thoughts were so rambling and knotted he almost bumped into a worried and concerned Lukas who was looking for him.

"How can I help?" his friend offered.

"I'm going to talk to Zachary again." David continued walking, almost jerky in frustration. "I don't know.......I just have to try again. You know, maybe this time........."

"Of course." Lukas said, catching up with David's fast pace. "I'll go with you."

They tried Zachary's room but there was no answer. Returning to the Cube where dinner was now being served, they still saw no sign of Zachary. At least Giles was there and though he stubbornly ignored them at first, when they continued to pester him for his friend's whereabouts, Giles finally garbled, "He's just in his room. We were on our way here when he went back to get something. He's there."

David and Lukas returned to Zachary's room, banging on the door insistently for Zachary to let them in. As they listened for a reply, they heard scuffling noises inside followed by a loud thud.

"Zachary! Open the door!" David yelled, banging on the heavy wood again.

Still the door remained closed and locked.

"I'm going to break the door down." David said to Lukas, pushed beyond the limits of his patience. He also wanted to investigate the sounds coming from inside the room.

Without further hesitation, he used his angel strength to crack the door open.

What greeted them was an incredible sight:

Five gasping but still cherubs were on the floor alongside an equally gasping and immobile Zachary.

"Hello David, hello Lukas." a girl greeted them courteously, smiling innocently at them. "I think you're both interrupting."

It was Liz, David's ten year old Healer.

In her hand was a sharp dagger, its tip sticky with black, tarry paste.

It explained the felled bodies. *Curare.*

309

31 A Fight for the Truth

David's first instinct was to rush at her and wrestle the weapon from her hand. Instead he clamped down the impulse and tried to reason with her. "Liz, maybe we can talk about all this first. Maybe you can explain things to us."

She remained where she was, eerily nonchalant as though they were simply catching-up with the latest school gossip, as if there weren't six gasping bodies strewn all over the room.

David kept his eyes on Liz, but he couldn't help glancing every now and then at the six victims. They needed to be brought to the Infirmary as quickly as possible – while they were still breathing – so an antidote could be administered and save their lives.

"What if we let Lukas bring Zachary and the Puttis to the Infirmary." David suggested to Liz, keeping his voice as gentle as he could. "How about that, huh? Can we do that?"

Liz smiled back at him, her baby blue eyes glinting coldly. "Do not even think about going near them, Lukas. And you too David." She continued to grasp the dagger tightly, her voice derisive. "You believe that by pretending to be all nice and patronizing, by being condescendingly gentle, I would throw down my weapon and quietly go with you so I can be imprisoned in Kalvarium?" her laugh was sharp and cruel. "Oh, David, you are deluding yourself."

David felt a tremor of worry in the pit of his stomach. This was going to be really tricky – Liz was obviously deranged.

"Oh I'm not insane." she grinned at him, her teeth a flash of pearly whites, her face amused.

"You *can* read minds!" David concluded with a sharp intake of breath. Was this how she had defeated Zachary and the Puttis?

Liz shrugged, looking very much like a gloating schoolgirl with a big secret to reveal. "Not really. Just a sense of things." her gaze focused and narrowed on him. "For instance, I can sense that you have a weapon under your clothes, a........dagger........hmmm, the same one used to kill the hellhound." Her smile widened with relish and looked absolutely creepy. "Very well then. Let's put it against this one, shall we?" she raised her own dagger, the tip still sticky with curare.

The time for verbal play was over.

"Let's do that." David replied, his voice hardening. He must stop seeing Liz as the kind little healer who helped him. She was not a regular kid, she never was. But now, she was David's enemy. And it helped that her face was cruel.

Beside him, Lukas was silently gauging the situation, looking for an opportunity to strike and rescue. David knew he could count on his friend and was glad he was there.

David removed his dagger from its sheath – *The Hand of God* – and pointed it at Liz. Then he motioned to Lukas. "Take Zachary and the Puttis. Bring them to the Infirmary. And then tell Abbot Anderson what's going on. Get help, Lukas."

"Tsk, tsk. Tsk." Liz shook her head. "Well, we cannot do that. I cannot allow it." her voice was soft. "That would get me in trouble."

"You're already in so much trouble, you psycho." said David harshly, quite sick of her games.

"They are not leaving this room." Liz warned David and

Lukas, her dagger now pointing at them.

"You have no choice." Lukas retorted back at her.

Then in a fast blur, Lukas went to Zachary and the five Puttis, dead set on rescuing them.

But not before Liz launched herself at him.

She really did have a sense of things.

She blocked Lukas' way, knowing exactly the direction he was taking and who he would rescue first. But before she could swipe him with the poison-tipped dagger, David was there, blocking the weapon with his own.

"Go!" David yelled, fighting a furious Liz as she wielded the dagger expertly. She screamed in rage as her attack on Lukas was thwarted, enabling him to lift Zachary on one shoulder then juggle the five cherubs in any position as long as he was holding on to an arm or leg. Then Lukas zoomed out of the room with the promise of help.

Liz was so furious by the rescue that her entire body seemed to burn with it. She concentrated on David, anticipating his moves and successfully blocking them.

She was fast and cunning, using her smallness to her advantage, darting in and out in a blur as she tried to slash David anywhere she could. She knew the location wouldn't matter. Any wound would count. So long as she cut him with her dagger then she would win.

"I know someone made you do this, Liz." David uttered amidst all the fighting. "Who made you? Who ordered you to?" David felt this was the closest he could get in discovering the true mastermind behind the crimes committed.

Liz only snarled in return. "I am not a traitor!"

It was a tight space to maneuver in but that didn't derail Liz and nor did David let it. He was fighting for his life! The little cutesy lunatic wouldn't hesitate to cut him and poison him and smile evilly as he gasped for his last breath.

Liz bounded for the bed, jumped on it then somersaulted rapidly to land behind David. He felt a powerful kick on his back, sending him straight to a solid block of wall, cracking his head sharply.

David saw lights pop in his head, but he just shook them off, refusing to black out, knowing that giving in meant certain death. There was hardly any time to recover. Liz was on him again like a pesky bee that wouldn't leave him alone, determined for an opportunity to sting.

Their daggers clashed, one hand weapon fighting, the other hitting and trying to get in as many punches as it could. Kicks, shoves, and body slams were thrown into the mix, anything that could cause the most pain and injure the opponent.

Liz was able to sneak in some low punches, hitting David hard in the gut. But David also knew that she was worried. Help was coming and she glanced now and then at the open doorway, apprehensive about approaching rescue. She also looked covetingly at the open window. They were only three stories high and as a Nephilim, she would probably survive the jump.

David took advantage of her distraction and in a flurry of attacks, changing his moves at the last second, he slashed hard and cut her on the arm. Her eyes glittered in disbelief, obviously insulted that David got past her defenses.

He grinned at Liz to infuriate her even more.

It worked.

Without warning, his legs buckled under him as she powerfully kicked them out. She could have stabbed him with the dagger when he went down, but instead she super-strengthed David, lifting him up then slamming him down on the bed.

The bed broke with a resounding crack and David thought his back broke with it too. They were making so much racket that David couldn't believe no other student had peeked in from the open doorway, either to help or run away.

Then he remembered.

It was dinnertime.

Liz was teaching him a lesson – painfully demonstrating that she could kick his butt even without the poisonous dagger – and she would win.

David was grateful for her need to show her superiority. If she had fought straightforwardly, the curare would be coursing through his system by now.

From his position on the broken bed, David delivered a strong and swift kick, directly at Liz's midsection. Her little body flew to the desk, slamming into it, splintering it to pieces.

David heard a satisfying clatter as her dagger fell to the floor.

In a second they were both on it. Fighting, struggling, grappling, each trying to get hold of the dagger. There were more kicks and punches, Liz even clawing at David's face.

She was huffing in effort now, her incongruently innocent face all red. Then, she smiled victoriously and David was horrified.

She had gotten hold of the dagger and was pointing it to his face.

David used all his super-strength, his body vibrating with it, all effort concentrated on preventing Liz from stabbing him and to turn the weapon towards her instead.

The dagger shook vigorously as they battled over the deadly piece. Then amazingly, David was dominating, changing the direction of the dagger's tip.

Liz's face was a mask of fear as she saw the weapon coming at her. Her jaw was locked, teeth gritting as she tried her hardest to stop David.

She lost.

With a loud and determined yell, David plunged the dagger at Liz. Its tip triumphantly cutting her cheek, deeply and aggressively. The curare entered her bloodstream and David saw the fighting light in her eyes diminish.

Then her arms and legs flopped beneath him. Unmoving.

She was now victim to her own signature crime.

David sat up, still near her, but making sure the dagger was beyond her reach. He was taking no chances for a last beyond human effort to grab it. He wasn't going to underestimate Liz.

But she had been truly poisoned.

Her extremities were now immobile and she was beginning to gasp for breath.

"Tell me, Liz." David urged her. "Please tell me. I know you wouldn't do all this on your own. Who made you?"

She only looked at him pityingly. "I would never betray him." she gasped. "I've loved him my entire life."

Then her eyes grew misty, tears coursing down at the corners. "He took care of me, you know." she revealed. "When I arrived here, I had been injured from a demon attack." she gasped again, her lungs seeking air. "He was my healer. He gave me all the time that he could. He read to me, he hugged and comforted me." Liz closed her eyes, looking more than ever like the ten year old little girl that she was. "I've loved him since." her breathing was more rapid now. "I....always......will."

"But he made you do all these things." David said. "He's evil

Liz. He made you poison Zachary, twice, and the Puttis too."

She would have shaken her head if she could. "No...no...." she murmured. "You have it.......all wrong......." Liz gasped loudly, fighting for more air. "He is......good.....He didn't order me......to do all these.......I did......by myself......." her face was proud of her achievement.

"Why?" David was aghast. "Why hurt so many?"

Liz looked at him clearly, as if the answer was so obvious that she couldn't believe David didn't know it. "To........protect him." Her last glance before her eyes closed in exhaustion was to look at the poisoned dagger longingly.

David picked it up, his entire self clenching in shock.

How could he have been so blind?

He had been so wrapped up in rescuing Zachary and fighting Liz that he didn't even recognize the weapon.

He had made it himself – The Stylet Dagger.

For Caian James.

Just then Lukas arrived in superspeed, breathless. "The Abbot is on his way. Zachary confessed. It was Caian James all along. He set the hellhound on you!"

"I know." David said, grim and betrayed. "Liz is still alive. You have to stay with her." He was rushing out the room.

"Where are you going?" Lukas yelled.

"I'm going after Caian."

Before Lukas could protest anymore, David switched to angel-mode and blurred his way through the Monastery. He was going after the senior Alpha Warrior.

32  Versus

David found Caian in their sprawling Warrior Training arena. He had looked for Caian at the Cube first but when he wasn't there, had demanded his whereabouts from a surprised Antonia Tremont – Caian's girlfriend. When she had revealed where he was, David zoomed out of the glass dining hall so fast that he didn't even answer Antonia as she asked, "Why? What is this about?"

Just before he exited the Monastery he heard Prefect Macarius announce over the speakers, "All students must proceed to the Cube immediately. Do this as calmly and as quickly as you can. Please proceed to the Cube."

David ignored the instructions and sped off towards the Training Arena. But he did feel a rush of satisfaction.

The school knew. It was locking down for safety measures.

Zachary and Liz were in Abbot Anderson's custody and now they were ensuring the safety of all students against Caian James.

David could have waited for help, he could have waited for the Abbot to take care of Caian. But he couldn't just wait around. His entire self rebelled against the idea of doing nothing. This was very personal.

Caian had singled him out to be ambushed by the hellhound. He had brought Tatiana and Innocent, Zachary and Liz, into it. David had to know why. And he had to make Caian pay.

There was also the Sator Square Society to consider and they still needed to find out who Arepo was. He had to find out if Arepo was behind all this.

David reached the large and heavy door that opened to the Training Arena. He pushed it wide open, his other hand gripping his faithful dagger, and stepped outside.

He was met with a blast of freezing winter wind and the sight of two Nephilims impressively training amidst the cold.

Caian wasn't alone.

With him was his friend and second-in-command, Jerome Gallagher.

Could David take them both?

David approached the two warriors. Their wings were spread wide, gleaming palely in the night, even more white than the snow surrounding them. Their swords clashed in powerful arcs and swings, rendering the air with metallic clangs – noises now so familiar to David that he could let himself believe that this was just another training session. But he pushed those thoughts away, they were dangerous and misleading.

Caian held a Persian War Sword while Jerome wielded a Viking Sword, weapons apparently favorites of theirs. These were the very same weapons they had used when David first witnessed their thrilling fight during Combat Circle. And tonight, here they were again, impressively skilled warriors battling each other. David sought reassurance from his trusted dagger, suddenly so afraid of what lay before him.

He could die tonight.

Refusing to succumb to his fears, David focused on his anger instead to energize him, and strode purposefully towards the two fighters. They looked so impossibly tall.

Caian saw him first.

"Hello David." greeted the senior. "What brings you out here? Have you come to observe our training? Jerome and I will head out for a mission tomorrow."

Jerome had speared the ground with his sword, casually leaning on it like a cane. He nodded his acknowledgment of David's presence.

When David drew closer, Caian and Jerome both frowned.

Anger was blazing from David's eyes and he had a dagger in hand.

"Why did you set the hellhound on me Caian?" David aggressively questioned the senior. "Why did you want to kill me?"

If Caian was shocked by the accusation, he didn't show it. He remained as cool as ever, his features untouched by David's verbal attack. Only a slight but sharp intake of breath hinted at his deeper reaction. "What are you speaking about, David?" Caian calmly countered. "From where did you get your information? Because I was never in any way involved regarding that hellhound incident." Caian looked at David straight in the eye. "Someone has been lying to you."

He looked and sounded so convincing that David almost believed him. But Caian's bold and dismissive attitude only served to make David angrier. "I bet a lot of people have been fooled by you." he spat out. "I just bet you looked them straight in the eye, like you're doing now, and you tell them whatever lie you want and they believe you." David's lip curled into a satisfied sneer. "Well, not this time Caian. Your lies have caught up with you. Nobody's protecting you or covering-up for you. In fact, there are witnesses against you this time."

There was a tiny glimmer of fear in Caian's eyes but he remained insouciant, acting unconcerned. "Alright, let me humor you and your delusions." Caian shot a laughing glance at Jerome, feigning amusement over David's accusations. "Who are these prized witnesses and what lies have they been spouting?"

David was more than eager to drop the bomb. "Let's start with Zachary Spencer." he revealed, wanting to wipe off the smug look on Caian's face. "Zachary just confessed to Abbot Anderson, that you ordered Innocent to Dream Invade Tatiana so that she would trap me in the catacombs." David blasted his fury at his supposed mentor. "You tried to kill me! And you let Innocent take the fall for you! He's in *Kalvarium* right now, doing hard labor because of what you ordered him to do. I don't know how you live with yourself." David finished with utmost contempt.

"Or so Zachary says." Caian drawled, with all the audacity of a person used to getting away with things. David knew he had unsettled Caian, but Caian managed to hold down his emotions, looking unperturbed. "From what I can deduce from your story David, Zachary Spencer has been telling lies about me. Tsk,tsk." Caian shook his head. "I always knew that boy would be trouble. He should have never been invited to the folds of our Society. I always thought him undeserving, and now he has proven himself unworthy and dishonest as well. Zachary Spencer is nothing but a bully with passable warrior skills."

"He happens to be telling the truth." David said, unable to believe that the day had come when he was defending Zachary. But this time, Zachary was telling the truth.

"Then it would be my word against his." offered Caian, his confidence restored. "I wonder who the Abbot will believe?"

"You're walking on dangerous ground David." Jerome contributed for the first time. "You have been hurling insults at my good friend and I will not stand for that."

Caian gestured for Jerome to calm down, now playing the generous patron. "It is quite understandable that David made such a mistake. I am certain that Zachary was persuasive in his confession. In fact, even Abbot Anderson may believe him."

They sounded so innocent that if David hadn't just battled Liz, he would have given in or second guessed himself. "Abbot Anderson will believe Zachary." David said. "You're forgetting that he was poisoned, and it was to shut him up about you and Innocent."

"Again," said Caian patiently, as though conversing with a toddler in tantrum, "it will be Zachary's word against mine."

David shook his head. Caian was so confident that he could get away with what he did, denying everything, still clinging to his upstanding image that it infuriated David even more. "I don't think you can talk your way out of this one Caian. The person who poisoned Zachary just got caught and *she pointed her finger at you.*"

"She would never do that -" Caian blurted out in defense before he could stop himself. When he realized his slip-up, his whole demeanor changed.

Gone was the affable and winning student. The Caian James who stood before David, sword at the ready, was a cold and calculating warrior.

"Well, clever, clever." Caian conceded courteously, ever polite in his arrogance. "I walked right into that one, didn't I?"

Beside him, Jerome was staring at his friend in horror. "The hellhound, you didn't really-?" he couldn't seem to finish his question.

Caian calmly turned to him and said. "Jerome, you have two

choices right now. Either stay here and support me, or go inside the Monastery and keep out of my business. This is between David and myself."

"I cannot let you do that." said Jerome, withdrawing his sword from the ground and pointing it at Caian. They both looked shocked that Jerome would go against him. "This time you have gone too far."

"Too far?" Caian seemed frozen by the accusation. The senior looked like a rigid statue in his stillness, but David could see fury flowing through him and little bursts of light emanated from his skin. Caian looked volatile and *dangerous*. "Is this more wrong than our missions for the Sator Square Society? Much worse than controlling world leadership at all cost?" he looked at Jerome contemptuously. "Do not pretend to be *righteous* with me Jerome. I know of the things you have done in the name of our cause." Caian spread his wings even more fully and directed his attention at David.

"They are coming for you Caian." David taunted, perversely wanting to push Caian over the edge, hoping for admissions of guilt. "And they will throw you inside *Kalvarium* just as you deserve."

"Then I might as well make it count." said Caian and quick as lightning he was upon David, his sword slashing furiously.

David was at a disadvantage. Caian held a long Persian War Sword and was dressed in training gear. At least the senior didn't have a metal chest plate on like he usually did during combat training. David's dagger looked pathetically small against the long sword and to top it off, he was dressed in school whites.

There was a reason why Caian was Alpha Warrior – he was prodigiously skilled and unmatched by any other student in battle. David knew he was an *infant* against Caian. In the Monastery, Caian was top seed, the demonfighter and rescuer to be remembered for years to come; and David – he was at the very bottom of the training ladder. Still, he parried Caian's attacks the best he could, mentally kicking himself for not going into the armory first and obtaining as many weapons as possible, starting with his Gothic Sword.

David slayed the useless thoughts away and concentrated instead in blocking Caian's swift and deadly attacks. David couldn't even see any opportunity to counter-attack Caian; he was fighting for his life! His mind was yelling *defense*! *defense*! And David did all he could to block and evade Caian. He was still standing, still alive, but in a matter of seconds David's hands and arms were covered in cuts and slashes, all from defending himself.

A triumphant smile was plastered on Caian's face. The warrior knew that David would be easy pickings.

David realized that he had to do something. Right now it was only his abnormally fast reflexes preventing him from being hacked to pieces. He needed more space, he needed to *think*.

David unfurled his wings and shot through the air, flying away from Caian to put some distance between them and strengthen himself.

Caian shot after him, with Jerome at his heels.

Jerome looked torn and confused. He clearly couldn't decide which side to choose. He didn't want David to get hurt but he didn't want to go against Caian either. So he hovered.

Wings beating strongly, David and Caian came at each other. Their weapons were glowing in the dark night, the winter wind ripping at them. It was freezing in negative temperature but David closed his mind to the cold and concentrated on the menacing sword that kept coming at him.

Caian lunged at David repeatedly, wielding his Persian war sword with amazing prowess. David couldn't help but admire his technique before snapping out of it as the sharp blade sliced him from shoulder to elbow. The long cut burned David's flesh, blood trickling down his hand from the deep wound. Somehow the pain made David's mind clearer, yanking him away from all fears and illusions, his brain absorbing the situation more fully. In a snap, he was behind Caian and pushing hard, they both flew with David's momentum and David shoved the warrior to the Monastery wall with as much strength as he could. He heard the satisfying crack of ancient stones breaking from the impact. Caian was momentarily dazed.

But he came out of it spitting mad. He had not expected that from David and he was furious.

David wasn't out to murder Caian or to fatally wound him – if he even could. What David wanted was this moment to confront Caian, to let him know that his evil deeds were now public knowledge. David wanted the triumph of making Caian realize that punishment was on its way, that his days of underhanded corruptness was over. And maybe, just maybe, he could make Caian pay for the hellhound attack.

Seeing Caian slam against that thick wall was hugely satisfying. David had to resist the absurd urge to stick his tongue out at Caian in childish taunting.

But Caian wasn't done yet.

David didn't even see it coming. The warrior streaked towards him in a heartbeat, swinging his sword with murderous intent. David's eyes widened as the silver flash of the blade plunged in the direction of his chest, horribly aware that this was the end of him. His eyes shut tightly, expecting white hot pain to lance through him.

But it didn't come.

Someone shoved him out of the way and with a loud clash of metal against metal, caught the arc of Caian's weapon.

It was Jerome, intervening with his Viking Sword and saving David's life.

David was grateful for Jerome's help, but obviously Caian wasn't.

"You traitor!" Caian yelled in absolute outrage, delivering a swift but punishing kick at Jerome's midsection, sending his friend spiraling down to the ground. Jerome recovered quickly from the injury even before he hit the snow-blanketed earth. Soon he was fighting with David and Caian again, a confused combatant whose sword interrupted frequently to block Caian's slashes at David and to block David's attacks on Caian. They were flying every which way as they battled, and whenever they came close to a Monastery border, a hissing demon would pop up at the other side, eager to get hold of any Nephilim who overstepped the boundary.

David, Caian and Jerome were locked in a triangular sword fight, until Caian, who had now lost his patience with his friend, punched Jerome hard in the face to render him unconscious. It was a well delivered blow. Jerome was knocked out cold and spiraled to the ground once more, this time landing with a loud thud.

"Why Caian?" David yelled over the howling wind. "Why do you want to kill me? Is it Arepo? Did he make you do this?"

Caian's wings flapped angrily in reply, as though David had committed a blasphemy by uttering Arepo. "Arepo had nothing to do with it." Caian said. "It was my decision to entrap you with the hellhound. Mine alone." he finished in a boast.

"But why? Why kill me?" David wanted to know, needed to know, and this time he saw the hint of truth in Caian's furious eyes.

"The moment he laid eyes on you, Arepo knew instantly that you were the son of an Archangel. Even before you discovered the truth for yourself, Arepo knew, and he wanted you." there was fury and pain in his voice. "Already he coveted your still absent skills and he dreamed of grooming you to be the best warrior the Society had ever seen."

David shuddered at the revelation, at the plans that had been laid out for him without his knowledge or consent. Caian's next words stopped him cold.

"I could not have that David. I could not allow you to step in and take away what is mine!" Caian's voice was harsh and he was lost in his desire of complete possession of the Sator Square Society and of being Arepo's favorite. "I am second in command. Not you! I am the best Satorian warrior! Not some untrained and untutored upstart from nowhere." Caian was shouting now too, frighteningly furious for what he believed David was going to steal from him. "I have worked too hard to be where I am and to have the trust and favor of Arepo. I refuse to be bested by lineage! By blood!"

"You're insane!" David shouted back. "You wanted me dead because of your Satorian status? All this to be a favorite? What about Liz and Innocent? What about Tatiana and Zachary?"

"Pawns! Nothing but foot soldiers!" Caian said with derision. "They can all rot in *Kalvarium* for all eternity." Caian looked ugly now. His handsome face twisted in expressions of cruelty and bitterness.

"You'll be joining Liz and Innocent there and you can rot with them." David said.

But Caian only laughed. "I will not be punished." he confidently announced. "Arepo will defend me."

David's mind was working furiously, wanting to finally get to the bottom of everything. "Who is Arepo, Caian? Who are you protecting?"

Caian only sneered at David. "As if I would reveal him to you.

As if you are worthy of the knowledge of him. You will die first before knowing who he is!" Caian brought down his sword, aiming for David's wings.

David was horrified by the gesture, that Caian wanted to cut his wings off. He evaded the attack and threw his dagger at Caian, cutting the warrior on his sword hand, making Caian drop his sword.

Caian retaliated by grabbing onto David's wings and with his super-strength, he hurled David towards the ground.

David fell through the air in a rush, struggling to get hold of his falling dagger, chasing after the much needed weapon. He was still falling fast when Caian dived and torpedoed his way towards David, hellbent on causing injury – his Persian War Sword back in his hand. At last, David felt in control of his wings again, and with determined flaps to stop his fall, he rushed at Caian head on, clutching the *Hand of God* tightly.

Caian swung his sword powerfully and David twisted his body away from the attack. He didn't escape in time, the sharp sword slicing his back, cutting through his clothes and piercing flesh.

Caian gave David no room to recover and he was at David again, willing his sword to wound David, his complex fighting skills both mesmerizing and frightening. By some miracle, David blocked Caian's moves and then it was his turn to aggressively attack Caian, successfully embedding his dagger on Caian's shoulder.

Caian roared in fury. Dagger still in his shoulder, he gripped David and threw him to the glasshouse now beneath them. David smashed into the roof, panes of glass and wood structures collapsing with him. He crashed to the ground in a mess of broken glass, really lucky that no large piece had imbedded in him. The nicks and cuts he could live with.

It was Gertrude's glasshouse.

David felt boiling hot anger erupt within him as he saw the now destroyed glasshouse. Gertrude would be devastated! And to think of the many hours they had invested in their special place! He was like a livid victim of a home invasion.

David flew through the clear opening in the roof, eager to punish Caian for the added offense. He charged at the senior who was hovering above the glasshouse before David realized that he had no weapon. He wanted to end the fight as quickly as he could, but he didn't know how.

The moment that David cleared the roof, Caian came at him, flying and spinning fast, sword out. David had no dagger with him and he rapidly searched the roof of the glasshouse for any weapon he could use. Broken glass? Broken wood? Nothing looked satisfactory, but he was desperate.

Then David remembered. He did have a weapon! They all did!

Calculating Caian's trajectory, David grabbed atop his head to the now existing halo which he conjured with his thoughts. He spun his halo towards Caian, but skilled as ever, Caian escaped the halo whirring towards him. Caian didn't miss his aim at David though, and his sword swiped David's midsection, leaving a long gash at its wake. David was lucky the cut wasn't that deep or else the fight would have been over.

David's halo completed its arc and boomeranged back towards them. Caian heard the returning halo in time and ducked, but not before the halo singed the top of his head, burning off some of Caian's beautiful golden hair.

Caian threaded his fingers through his hair, his entire self just thrumming with rage and fury and undisguised vanity. If a Nephilim could burn and catch on fire from anger, Caian would have.

Caian landed on the ground, flung his sword away and pulled

out David's dagger from his shoulder with a grunt, then threw the weapon away as well. Facing David, he readied his fists and said, "Come here Son of an Archangel. Show me what you've got."

It seemed that stabbing at David would no longer be enough. Now he wanted to beat David senseless.

David squared himself for a fight, wanting to swipe good punches in and cause Caian some pain.

Caian moved in on David, his body shifting continually for fast evasion of oncoming punches. David made several attempts to hit Caian, his arms landing to exactly where Caian was a second ago, but he was always too late, too slow.

And then Caian was throwing punches, getting David every time. Angel mode only made it worse because for a blinding minute it seemed Caian was everywhere. David was putting his hands up in defense, his body hunching and clenching, his wings beginning to close in protectively. Pain exploded in his gut, on his head, on the sides of his body. He was just getting clobbered.

Do *something*! His mind screamed and David moved his body as fast as he could. Still he got pounded, bashed in repeatedly by Caian's battering-ram fists. Then Caian came at him from an angle, kicking him hard on his left leg.

Snap!

David felt the bone break in his leg and he went down, collapsing from the pain of it. It was excruciating! But gritting through the pain, David tried to get up. Cain delivered a powerful roundhouse kick and sent David sprawling to the ground in a heap.

David had to get up! To use his wings instead and fly.

His dark wings began to flap, pulling him up, but again Caian was there, blocking his way. This time he had his sword in hand.

"You will never be the warrior I am." Caian said, so wrapped up in his alpha status, obsessed with pitting himself against David and proving that he was the best warrior.

"I don't want to be." David bit back at him, still trying to get up. "You're sick and evil and you've hurt many people to get what you want. I will *never* be like you."

David could swear Caian's eyes turned red with rage and with a nasty bellow, Caian swung his persian sword and cruelly aimed it at David's heart. David was paralyzed by shock, unable to believe that Caian would kill him.

Just before the tip of the persian sword plunged into his chest, someone shoved him out of the way again, screaming "No, Caian! No!"

And then it was Jerome Gallagher under the sword, and Caian had no time to stop his action. The sword plunged into Jerome's chest, straight into his heart, impaling him.

"Noooo!" Caian howled, instantly beside his friend, trying to save him. But Jerome was fading quickly, twitching in spasms and coughing up blood.

David was beside him too, not even noticing the tears streaming down his face. He was choked up and incoherent, unable to speak as Jerome's fatal injury tried to imprint in David's brain. He held on to Jerome Gallagher, the incredible hero who defied his bestfriend in order to save David and do what was right. Jerome looked at David, his face stunned at what was happening to him and yet at peace at the same time.

"I'm so sorry. I'm so sorry." David was mumbling now, cradling the brave warrior. Caian's sword was still plunged into his chest, but Caian had left their side, pacing madly on the now reddened snow, crazed with grief.

"*I'm sorry.*" Jerome muttered weakly. "For what......I've done.

For all.....we've done." his voice was thready, so weak now it was almost impossible to hear. "Arepo must be stopped.....the Society.......stopped........"

"Who is Arepo?" David asked Jerome as quietly as he could without alerting Caian. "Please tell me Jerome, please help me stop him."

Jerome tried to nod but winced instead. He was gasping for breath now, gurgling and coughing with the overflowing blood. David could feel the light burning out from Jerome, the life leaving this person he didn't really know, but who nevertheless gave up his own life to save David. Even now, Jerome was fighting and struggling for his last heroic act, grimacing in pain, barely able to speak.

"Arepo is...........Victorinus." Jerome whispered. "Teacher Victorinus........stop them David............" his words were followed by a coughing fit, blood spluttering everywhere. David held on to him, willing his own strength to transfer to Jerome. He gripped Jerome's hand tightly in his, letting him know that in his last moments he was not alone, that in his last moments, he was a hero.

Then Jerome slumped against David, eyes closing forever.

Gently, ever so slowly, Jerome's wings covered his body, enveloping him, cocooning him in a funeral of feathers. Then his body glowed from within, burning bright in the night like a celebration of light. Then just as rapidly, the light dimmed, faded, until there was nothing.

Jerome was truly gone. Only the cruel reality of his cold corpse remained.

In the darkness and desolation of the night, it was only David and Caian again.

Caian was hunched on the ground, trembling and shivering,

spasms wracking his body. "What is happening to me?" Caian screamed. "What's happening to me?"

David raised his head to look at the fallen warrior.

He was changing.

33 † Beyond the Wall

Caian was on all fours, clutching his midsection. His face was a reflection of agony, his body clenching and wrenching with spasms.

What was happening to him? David wondered, confused but wary. He didn't know whether to approach and help or to simply watch and wait.

Then Caian's head snapped up with a loud crack and he was looking straight at David.

His eyes were a burning yellow.

There was panic and terror in them and both he and David were unable to grasp what was happening before them.

Caian was coughing up sulfurous vapors even as he moaned and whimpered in pain. His arms were changing, lengthening......his skin mottled and pulsed, erupting into strands of rubbery grey microdermis that creeped all over his body, covering him.

Caian was screaming now, scared witless but absolutely powerless to stop the brutal transformation.

His spine arched and twisted, and he convulsed in unnatural angles, choking in excruciation but unable to yell out under the weight of so much pain. There were ripping sounds as his clothes gave way to the bony protuberances now thrusting from his spine.

Caian was helpless as his mouth pulled into cruel lines, his teeth sharpening into repulsive fangs that dripped bright, acidic sulfur. His nose flattened into slits and then he was gasping and clutching for air, his body now a battleground between sulfur and oxygen, his lungs fighting for its natural need but soon overpowered by the mutation. In no time, Caian was breathing out sulfur, his entire body drenched in a nauseating cloud.

Caian's body convulsed again, this time accompanied by a gruesome splitting, of skin tearing......lacerating. David heard the shuddering crunch of bones, and he whitened as he heard each bone snapping, fracturing, molding, melding, aligning in ways so hideous........and Caian was feeling every bit of it, gritting his sharp teeth, muted by waves of pain, tears streaming down his rubbery cheeks.

There was a rumbling, an unrolling.......and with a sharp snap two enormous black wings unfurled at Caian's back – thick, oily smooth, skeletal and obscene. His wings flapped and pulled Caian upright.

And then he was standing on monstrous legs, the punishing mutation over.

His body was frightening – a malignant mass of contradictions – muscular but cadaverous, smooth but repugnant.

And then Caian roared, interrupting the night with a hair-raising and carnivorous bellow.

Still on the ground, David gaped at the creature before him.

There was no more Caian James.

Gone was the student warrior, the handsome and charming boy who everyone looked up to. He had morphed, mutated. He had become the embodiment of his crime – Demon.

The demon looked at David.

With such hatred. With such evil.

David backed up as fast as he could, scrabbling his way to where his dagger was and dragging his broken left leg while panting from the pain. He was a Nephilim, he could withstand much pain and survive through it, but that didn't mean that he didn't feel every bit of it.

David's hand clasped around his dagger with relief but not for long, the Caian demon had flown over him, pulling David up by the front of his shirt and before David could slash him with the dagger, the demon hit him hard in the face. David crumbled to the ground from the impact, his head ringing from the blow. It was like getting hit by a train.

"This is all your fault." the demon growled, and when he looked at himself again, David saw Caian's fear reflected in the now yellow eyes. "Look at me! Look at what's happened to me!" He gestured to hit David again but suddenly his legs were burning up, his feet smoking....

"Protected ground." the demon realized, grimacing in agony, his large bony feet blistering on contact. He was also having a hard time breathing and the space where he stood seemed to contract and ripple, crushing him.

David attacked, hoping to catch Caian unaware, but even in his distracted demonic state, his reflexes remained fast. Caian blocked David's maneuver, then flapping his enormous wings, he shot through the air and took David with him, clutching onto David's wings again.

David struggled, bucking his body every which way, but Caian had gripped him in a lock. David's wings were beating hard, trying to escape the firm hold, but he failed to get away from Caian's sharp talons. David slashed his dagger as he twisted in midair, hoping to slice Caian with it. His angelic substance would cause the demon considerable damage or would vanquish him for good.

By now they were over the Monastery wall. David felt the stirrings of panic, struggling again in an effort to break loose. What was Caian's plan? Was he going to bring David to demons outside the walls? He had to break free from the grip! They were about to cross the border!

Caian stubbornly and determinedly held on, clutching the bones of David's wings, his razor-like nails digging in.

Suddenly, the doors of the Monastery burst open and he could see people rushing their way. David could make out the shapes of Lukas, Gertrude and Rafaella at the front.

David only had time to yell, "Arepo is Victorinus! It's Victorinus!" then Caian viciously yanked him through the protective dome and then David was outside Monastery walls.

Somehow the temperature beyond the invisible barrier seemed even colder, the land more desolate. David's heart was beating fast. He had never ventured outside the Monastery but he knew what awaited him here.

The Caian demon laughed in cruel triumph, relishing his revenge on David. "I will make you pay for what you did to me, David Cross! I will make you pay!" Caian's voice was a hideous shriek with screeching undertones of a thousand chalks scratching the surface of a blackboard.

When Caian heard himself, he screamed in anguish, howling into the night as he mourned the loss of his angelic self. Even in his state of heightened fear, David felt sorry for him, but he knew it wasn't his fault. Caian had caused his own transformation. His altered being was the result and consequence of Jerome's death.

Abruptly, Caian threw David to the ground and flew off into the dark night.

He had left David behind.

David was just puzzling over Caian's decision as he struggled to get up on his one good leg, his wings slowly and achingly aligning.....trying to gain strength, when sinister rushing sounds erupted all around him. Caian's intentions became very clear.

He had left David for other demons to finish off. And now he was surrounded.

David made a quick assessment.

Thankfully, he had his dagger with him and it reassured him a lot to see his weapon glowing with the infusion of his angelic substance. His left leg was useless, he would have to rely on just his right one if forced to fight on land. His best chance was to face the demons while flying – he was now regaining control of his wings although they still ached from the damage Caian had caused. There were several bones still aligning and Caian also cut some feathers off as his talons dug into them.

David was already weakened from his fight with Caian and right now the only strategy he could think of was to get away as quickly as he could from the demon pack and zoom back to the protective walls of the Monastery. He was some distance away, Caian had made sure of that.

In a flash, David was enveloped in a cloud of noxious sulfur and with absolute dread he knew the demons had arrived.

He stared around him in surprise and repulsion.

Thirteen eerily beautiful cheerleaders surrounded him.........their eyes a sick yellow.

"Well hello Nephilim." their leader cheerfully greeted, nauseating vapors flowing from her dainty mouth. "Beautiful night for a walk, isn't it?"

The other cheerleaders cackled at the greeting, then grinned winsomely at David like sinister cheshire cats with malevolent plans. David refused to gulp in fear or demonstrate fear in any way even though he was quietly shaking in his shoes. He felt like the tiny mouse they wanted to pounce on and devour, after playing with their food first of course.

David raised his dagger higher and determinedly said, "Just get on with it." keeping the quaver out of his voice. He was at the end of his rope and had no patience for games any longer. Fight! was all he could think of.

The cheerleader pouted, "But where's the fun in that?" there was a teenage whine to her voice. "Besides, we've been practicing cheers and now here you are – the perfect audience." her yellow eyes gleamed more......*yellow*. She nodded to her fellow demons and to David's increased dread and amazement, they formed two lines with their leader front and center.

"Ready, let's go!" she yelled.

They executed a series of moves, arms moving in perfect alignment, synchronized to the second like a single entity but performing as a group.

"Ah – Ah – Abhorrent." the cheerleaders chanted. "Angel Mutations!"

The first seven chorused, "We want to be your friends."

"- But not!" the second line countered.

"We wanna play with you."

"- Not really!"

"We wanna kiss you."

"- slap you."

"Hug you."

"- slash you."

"Squeeze you."

"- kill you. Kill you! KILL YOU!" they all cheered together.

All the while their cheer actions had been malicious. There were acted out stabbing, maiming, punching and kicking, choking and decapitating. The performance was very good though and if they weren't murdering demons out to get him, David would have clapped.

"Pathetic." he said to their expectant faces, perversely enjoying their insulted looks and outrage at his comment.

The head cheerleader glowered at him, her hair bursting into flames at her fury. She signaled to the other cheerleaders. "Get him."

"Jeez, how sensitive can you get!" David commented, bracing himself. The real show was about to begin.

The cheerleaders reached for something behind their backs and just like that they were holding wickedly curved scythes, all directed at him.

Time to fly.

David propelled himself up, his wings powerfully flapping as he flew to the direction of the Monastery. Behind him, the cheerleaders also sprouted their bat-like wings and chased after him. When he felt one coming very close, David did a quick dive and brake in mid-air so that she would pass over him and when she did, David slashed quickly with his dagger, the blade slicing into her wing.

The demon cheerleader exploded into a fume of sulfur, his weapon and angelic substance combined vanquishing her. David was bolstered by the win, strengthening him. One down, twelve to go.

Meanwhile her demon sisters shrieked deliriously at losing one of their own. If they had been perversely playful and arrogant before, now they were incensed and out to get him.

The demon cheerleaders swarmed at him, scythes somehow imbued by a certain darkness, looking more sinister, sucking the light from all around. And they descended on David in buzzing ferocity.

David did his best to wield his dagger, slashing at any oncoming cheerleader, but the advantage of their experience prevailed and they writhed out of David's attacks and happily countered with their weapons. David was just glad their scythes weren't reeking in poison because he was cut repeatedly and soon it became apparent that they were toying with him. There were cruel cackles and wheezing laughter around him.

A more determined demon cheerleader came at him and David saw the evil and purpose of her face – and he knew that she wanted to end it, end him.

Well, not without a fight. David thought.

Her scythe came up and aimed at him, determined to cleave him in half. David raised his dagger as well, ready to cut his enemy to bits. But then his hands were suddenly behind him, painfully wrenched at his back as two cheerleaders grabbed his arms and secured them.

David struggled hard, doing his best to dislodge the cheerleaders holding down his arms. In front of him, the attacking cheerleader was grinning widely, proudly revealing her filthy, drippy fangs. Then she swung her scythe downwards, going for his head.

Before she could break skin, David heard a sharp thwacking sound and saw a gleam of silver pass before his eyes – *Hope*. The arrow rushed past David, hitting its target accurately. The cheerleader screamed in the most awful voice as she saw the arrow hit her smack between the eyes.

"Oh crap!" the demon cheerleader whined and before she could say or do anything else, she exploded into sulfurous dust.

David felt his heart leap as he saw his friends running towards him. They were zooming as fast as they could – Lukas, Gertrude and Rafaella – ever faithful, coming to his aid. He was so happy to see them but he also wanted to yell, *Go back! Get back in the Monastery*! He didn't want any of his friends to get hurt, especially Gertrude.

"Oh, isn't that adorable!" cooed a demon. *"Le enfantes*! They can't even fly yet."

There were titters and manic giggling all around.

"I've always wanted to play with a little duckling." purred another.

"Come babies......" the head cheerleader called out to David's friends, "Mommy has something for you." Her singsong taunting was accompanied by a friendly wave from her scythe. "You." she pointed at her eight minions, "go play with the toddlers. We'll handle this little Nephilim." she finished with disdain, referring to David.

Two cheerleaders were still clamping down on David's arms, pinning them behind his back. He was struggling against their grip, doing his best to shake them off. David saw the eight demons fly towards his oncoming friends and his heart almost stopped as he saw them bear down on Gertrude, Lukas and Rafaella.

Facing him, the head cheerleader happily showed David her scythe, brandishing it about to make him suffer. "It's going to hurt a little bit." she smiled, exposing her long fangs and blowing sulfur on David's face. David gagged from the disgusting smell.

"Oh," she pouted. "You don't like how I smell? I know!" she shook back her long mane of thick blond hair. "I have been bathing in perfume!" her face drew close to his in a conspiratorial manner. "You cannot believe the amount of designer perfume I have been pouring on myself, but, nothing seems to work." she shrugged forlornly.

"Stop talking and start fighting." David whipped at her. He wanted to vanquish these three demons who were *handling* him so that he could help his friends. "Nothing you do will improve you." said David cruelly. "You literally smell like hell."

Her eyes welled up with yellow goo. Ugh! Was that what demon tears looked like? "You hurt my feelings." her lips trembled. "Now I'll just have to kill you."

She swung her scythe at David and as she did so, David retracted his wings as fast as he could, then he unfurled them again with a hard snap, hitting the two demons behind him. They were caught off guard and released David as they staggered backwards.

David dropped towards the ground before the head cheerleader's scythe could cut him and her weapon sliced another demon instead, the one who had been restraining David's left arm.

"Ooops!" said the head cheerleader while her demon victim shrieked.

"Sorry! I'm sorry!" she yelled as she watched her sister demon go up in smoke. She turned towards David who was readying to battle the two remaining cheerleaders. "That wasn't funny! Look what you made me do!" she wailed. She and her other minion zoomed purposefully at David while he hovered steadily, waiting for their attack, dagger ready.

He struck out his dagger in rapid succession at the minion, keeping his back protected, circling so the head cheerleader couldn't get to him. He felt his dagger slice into demon flesh and he yelled in triumph as the demon vaporized before him.

Now it was him and the head cheerleader.

David was also keeping an eye out for his friends. Lukas had brilliantly shot down three more demons with his masterful archery, Gertrude was battling two demons with her blade-tipped whip while Rafaella clashed her butterfly swords towards two demons as well. They just might have a fighting chance to survive!

The head cheerleader came at David, her scythe gleaming with promise. "You know Nephilim, I like you. Wanna turn demon and come with me?" she invited, striking a sultry pose, her eyes burning bright.

"No way!" David shuddered at her. "Just shut up and fight will you!"

"Was worth a try." she grinned evilly at him. She advanced on him, her scythe rotating rapidly like a twirler's baton. The blade gleamed this way and that and David kept his full attention on it and on her, his dagger looking for the moment to strike.

First cut – head cheerleader. She giggled with malice as David's shoulder dripped blood. She struck again and again, cackling and laughing hysterically each time she wounded David. Although he was doing his best to evade the attacks, her weapon had the advantage of length while David had to be near her to strike her with his dagger.

She lunged at him again. This time David twisted away in time, his elbow connecting sharply with her face. Her head snapped up as she fell backwards, her clawish hands releasing her scythe. David instantly grabbed her weapon and threw it away with as much strength as he could. Then he advanced on her with *The Hand of God*, his dagger thirsty for demon blood.

"Time out! Time out!" the head cheerleader squealed at him.

"Nope." David shook his head. "Game over." And with deliberate thoroughness, he plunged his dagger into her, even as she attempted to fly away, his angelic substance overpowering her demon core. She exploded in a cloud of billowy sulfur, engulfing David. He didn't wait for the dust to dissipate as he flew off. Now he could help his friends.

They were doing great.

Rafaella was so sickeningly happy to be in a real fight that she was actually grinning. Her pale green eyes blazed as she wielded her butterfly swords expertly. The demon cheerleaders were flying and swooping in on her, their own scythes unforgiving, but Rafaella was countering their attacks.

Lukas had set his bow aside as he entered into closer combat with two demons. He was now brandishing a longsword and successfully battling his demon opponents. His face was a mask of concentration while he agilely tried to outmaneuver and outsmart them.

It was towards Gertrude that David zoomed. He knew that she was a skilled warrior, maybe even better than him, but he couldn't live with himself if anything happened to her. His heart was pounding fast as it was, seeing Gertrude in true combat, warding off demons with her whip and dagger. When the demons saw David approaching, they realized that their head cheerleader was dead and the five remaining shrieked in unison. It was a horrifying cacophony of anguish and wrath.

As if on a predetermined signal, three of the demons changed form and David heard horrified gasps from his friends. Lukas was facing a tall, thin and studious looking woman with the warmest smile, her arms outstretched towards him. Rafaella nearly fell to the ground in shock. Standing before her was a rugged looking man with a kind face and Rafaella was whispering, "Daddy? Is that really you?"

Nearby, Gertrude had also stopped her fight as she gazed in awe at her father, a man with twinkling and joyful eyes, exuberant with an infectious chortle. "Papa?" Gertrude asked tentatively.

It seemed his friends were enthralled by the apparitions before them, but David knew the truth. These people were not real. They were demons in disguise.

"They're demons!" David yelled. "Look closer! They're not real. They're not your parents."

Rafaella was reaching up to touch her father's face, tears coursing down her cheeks as she gazed at the parent she loved deeply. Behind her, the other demon was raising its scythe, ready to hurt her.

"No!" David yelled, swooping in between Rafaella and the demon, his hand gripping the demon's weapon arm and his other hand cutting the demon with his dagger. As soon as his burning dagger connected, the demon burst into yellow vapor.

Lukas and Gertrude now realized the trick, the horror of the mutations evident on their faces. They were ready with their weapons but unable to hurt their pretend parents even though they knew these were just demons in disguise.

"Switch!" David yelled again. "Gertrude, Lukas, switch places." that seemed to snap them out of their tranced states and with angel speed they switched places, Lukas battling with Gertrude's demon-dad while Gertrude took on Lukas' demon-mom. Soon the two demons were nothing more but sulfurous dust.

As for Rafaella, she had chosen to fight her disguised demon-dad, anger vibrating through her as she attacked the demon ferociously with her swords. "You SICK. DECEIVING. OPPORTUNISTIC. BAT DROPPING!" she punctuated with each slash of her swords. The demon was staggering backwards, unable to attack under the weight of Rafaella's vehemence and brutal blows. Rafaella was really incensed, her skin burning and glowing with her righteous rage. With double swings from her butterfly swords, she broke the demon's scythe and her swords continued their fatal arc at the demon's chest. With a loud and satisfying whoosh, the disguised demon exploded into smelly vapor. There was the scent of a million burnt toasts in the air.

David was nearly at Gertrude's side; he was significantly slower and weaker from his injuries, otherwise he would have covered the distance in half the time.

The demon Lukas was fighting craftily realized that Gertrude was precious to David and in retaliation for David's vanquishing of their head cheerleader, she flew away from Lukas and sneaked up behind Gertrude.

And then the demon wasn't a cheerleader anymore, but Mrs. Kathleen Littlefield, David's foster mom. She was hugely pregnant as always, her face achingly familiar but deviously corrupt. She smiled in the most twistedly sweet manner while her eyes burned blood red.

Shooting David a triumphant smirk, she swung her scythe down at Gertrude's back. The night was broken with Gertrude's piercing scream as the scythe cleaved into her.

David reached her in a murderous frenzy, slicing his dagger at Mrs. Littlefield who had dared attack Gertrude, punishing his foster mom repeatedly without pity or mercy. It was retribution. It was justice! It was revenge for the slow but deliberate torture they put him through.

David struck again and again without stopping even though there was nothing more but sulfurous smoke in front of him.

And then Rafaella was beside a fallen Gertrude after she and Lukas vanquished the last demon. And Lukas was beside David, trying to calm him down as he continued his rampage towards the now vaporized Kathleen Littlefield. David snapped out of his blind fury and instantly crouched down beside Gertrude, wanting to rip out the malevolent scythe still imbedded in her back but knowing he mustn't, that it was the worse idea ever, that the weapon was in fact preventing the fatal waterfall of blood.

Gertrude's eyes fluttered open and she gazed at David with such love and relief. "You are alright." Her voice was weak but her smile was deeply contented. Even when mortally wounded her thoughts were of his well-being.

"She's still alive." Rafaella said briskly. "Hurry! We have to bring her back to the Monastery. We can still save her!"

David cradled Gertrude gently in his arms, his wings powering into the sky, his only thoughts were *Fly! Fly as fast as you can!*

"Hang in there Gertrude." David whispered. "Please, please don't die, don't die, you can't.........please....please........don't die..........."

Lukas and Rafaella also ran towards the Monastery, on the look-out for anymore attacking demons.

Determined to save her life, David flew with all his remaining strength and power pushed beyond limits, and soon they were crossing the Monastery border, into its sprawling grounds, inside its glass edifice, straight to the Infirmary.

Gertrude had lost a lot of blood and she was now unconscious in David's arms, her face frighteningly pale.

Thankfully Doctor Vitalis was there and David didn't even have to say anything as he efficiently administered to Gertrude and then several healers and nurses were at her side, doing their best to save the gentle girl while David looked on helplessly, pacing with disbelief and anger at himself for not rushing to her aid sooner. For not being by her side when she was fighting. That she was fighting in the first place because of him!

And then Lukas and Rafaella were beside him, stopping his destructive spiral of self-blame and loathing.

"She'll be fine." Rafaella soothed him. "They're the best medical crew in the world. Gertrude will be fine. She'll be fine."

David didn't know whether her words were meant to comfort him or convince him.

34 Angelical Law

David woke up slightly disoriented as he looked about the room wondering where he was and what had happened to him. His head was a little fuzzy and his mouth dry and cottony, but otherwise, he felt okay. Yes, bruised and sore, but he'd been in worse before.

He glanced at the bed beside him and saw Gertrude smiling back at him. She was still pale and fragile-looking but she was awake! And smiling!

"Hi warrior." she whispered, wincing when she tried to shift her position to face him more.

"Don't move." David said, trying to get up and help her. He was obviously in the Infirmary and as evidenced by his left leg in a cast, he remembered the reason why. David smiled ruefully. "I'd completely forgotten about my leg."

He *had* completely forgotten about his leg. When he had brought Gertrude to the Infirmary last night all his attention had been on her and he was so filled with worry that he hadn't felt any pain from any wounds or injuries. His whole system was pumping adrenaline and pain had been pushed away from his thoughts. Until Lukas pointed it out.

"Dude, your leg.......it's angled wrong. And is that....*bone*....sticking out?"

When David looked down on his leg his brain flooded with memories of the injury and how Caian broke it and just like that, all the pain came rushing back. Especially since he was standing on it.

David had to quickly hold on to Lukas before he collapsed on the floor, the pain now coming in throbbing and sickening waves. "Did you have to remind me?" he gasped.

A nurse directed David to an empty bed and then some bone alignment was done. Then several cooling and numbing herbs were lathered on his leg and finally a cast was molded in place for rapid healing. David was counting on his supernatural healing powers for his leg to mend immediately. He wanted to be up and about and aware of the ripple effects from last night's revelations.

Although staying at the Infirmary with Gertrude was not a bad idea too.

"How are you feeling?" he asked Gertrude.

"Oh you know," she tried to shrug it off. "Somewhat sore and achy but it is not a big deal." She had suffered from a punctured lung and God knows what other internal organs had been sliced by the scythe. Her chest was a thick wrapping of bandages. But as usual, she was a picture of serenity and it was clear that she didn't want to be fussed over or coddled. "What happened last night? What about Teacher Victorinus? Is he really Arepo?"

David nodded. "I have no doubts about that. Jerome........." he inhaled, feeling acute pain with the memory of Jerome's death. "Jerome.....told me himself."

"He was very brave, wasn't he?" said Gertrude quietly.

"He saved my life." admitted David. "I wouldn't be here if it weren't for him."

They both fell silent, taking time to process that thought and how their lives were now forever changed.

"Victorinus is Arepo. And as we have suspected, the Sator Square Society had many underhanded and secret goals that were only known to a few." David said.

"Particularly its Officers." Gertrude agreed.

"Also, from what Caian was saying last night, they had done some pretty nasty stuff – all in the name of their society."

"I wonder what all those things were." Gertrude shivered. "I want to know, but at the same time, I dread the knowledge of it." She looked at David with concern and trepidation. "We became part of this society -"

"As spies!" David protested.

"-and we know these people, we know the Officers. How terrible it is to imagine them perpetrating these unnamed acts because of their loyalty and their duty to the Society."

"I still can't believe last night happened." David said. "And Caian........" he trailed off.

It was in this somber mood that Lukas and Rafaella walked in on them. They both looked grim.

"I guess we're attending the same funeral." said Rafaella tactlessly, forgetting that there was a funeral to attend to eventually. Jerome Gallagher's.

"We know why we're depressed." David said. "Why are you?"

"Victorinus escaped." Lukas revealed, his face furious.

"What!" David yelped, sitting up immediately, again forgetting about his leg – it was probably healed anyway.

Rafaella was nodding. "Abbot Anderson, Prefect Macarius and loads of other teachers searched the Monastery for that scum last night. He was nowhere to be found. No trace of him whatsoever."

Lukas added, "Word is, Victorinus must have realized that the secret was out when the Abbot began looking for Caian James-"

"-plus that announcement over the speakers for all students to gather in the Cube-" David interjected.

"-so Victorinus upped and left. If he took anything with him, it wasn't much. According to Froggy, most of his stuff is still in his quarters."

"I wonder where he went?" Gertrude pondered. "It's terrible out there unless you are on protected ground. Would someone harbor him, you think? Or is he simply running every day?"

"Even though I hate to admit it, but that traitor is a great warrior, so he'll survive out there." David concluded. "As for anyone harboring him, that's a giant possibility. This is Arepo we're talking about. He must have loyal Satorians out there. How long has the guy been teaching here?"

"Almost fifty years." Rafaella replied, realization dawning on all of them at how immense the Sator Square Society really was. "Each year different Officers. Each year new recruits! That's one heck of a human resource."

"It is an army." Gertrude said, rightfully horrified.

"Abbot Anderson and the other teachers have been rounding up the officers and members of the Society last night. They've been pretty thorough. I think he's going to talk to you two." Rafaella said. Then she stood up in frustration. "I wish we could find out what really happened! Did the Officers talk? I wonder what Abbot Anderson knows by now."

"Don't forget," Gertrude reminded all of them. "There will be documents. Did not Antonia Tremont mention that she was keeper of it all? There will be evidence."

Lukas rubbed his hands in gleeful anticipation. "A paper trail. If only Froggy could get a hold of those."

Rafaella sat down again as a new thought occurred to her. "Can you imagine........Caian James........"

"Tell us what happened." Lukas urged David. They had wanted to talk last night, but it had not been possible with Gertrude's injuries and David's bad leg.

So David filled them in on what happened at the Training Arena, telling them about Caian's confessions, about his arrogance and disregard for Tatiana, Innocent, Liz and Zachary, about Arepo and how he had known that David was the son of an Archangel, and about Arepo's twisted plans for David. Most of all, he told them about Jerome's courage and bravery and selfless act of heroism.

His friends quieted down even more when he described Jerome's last moments and Caian's brutal and shocking transformation.

"I can't believe it. I can't believe." Rafaella was muttering. "Caian James......the Alpha Warrior, Class Valedictorian. I can't believe it!"

David was suddenly angry. Rafaella always had a soft spot for Caian and even now, she seemed to be defending him. "Well Rafaella, believe it and get over it." he snapped at her.

As usual, Rafaella only glared back and snapped back at him. "Excuse me if I'm having a hard time *getting over* it. I looked up to the guy! He was Caian James! Everyone looked up to him!"

"Everyone wanted to be him." Lukas said, the words getting out with difficulty. He was having a hard time too. "I think that's the worst of it. He was this certain person for all of us, but really, he wasn't that person at all."

"Idols are usually disappointing in real life." Rafaella said, still looking quite crushed.

"Yes. Especially if they're really murdering, scheming, overly ambitious lunatics who kill off people who threaten their reign of glory." David added harshly. He understood his friends, he really did, because he felt the same way too – betrayed. But Rafaella could really get under his skin. He was just mad that after all that happened to him last night because of Caian, she was still swooning over him.

Gertrude spoke up again, her calm and compassionate manner bringing a dash of peace to the conversation. "It truly is a lot to take in and process, but let us not forget our important experience last night. We were out there. Beyond these walls. *Fighting demons!*"

And just like that Rafaella was grinning ear to ear again at the memory, Lukas brightened up, but David could only say, through gritted teeth, "And you almost died."

Gertrude waved his worry away. "Just a nick. Minor injury. I have forgotten about it already."

"You're still in the Infirmary wrapped up because of it." David pointed out, but he was smiling now.

"Did you see me fighting those demon cheerleaders?" Rafaella was saying. Sheesh! She could really be insensitive and tunnel visioned. "I was attacking with my swords like this, and I caught the little rat right at the chest -"

"When I shot those demons down with my arrows," Lukas closed his eyes in complete bliss, "and it hit right on target and then boom! Sulfur dust!"

David tried to reach out to his friend. "Hey Lukas, thanks for saving my life. If you hadn't shot that demon with your arrow, her scythe would've cleaved me in half."

"David!" Gertrude gasped. "Do not even say that!" then she looked at Lukas, tears welling up her eyes, "Thank you Lukas for saving David's life. How can I ever repay you or thank you enough?" tears were running down her cheeks now.

Lukas looked panicked by the tears and he half bent by her bedside, patting Gertrude's back awkwardly. "It was nothing.....I only did what I could." he reassured her. "You don't have to repay me. *Really*, I mean it." he added fervently, so freaked out by a crying girl.

David turned serious. "But really Lukas," he said. "You saved my life. Thank you."

They were all beaming up at him and Rafaella hugged him saying, "You were great."

Lukas flushed and blotched and mumbled his thanks and sat down becoming so quiet – aside from the loud gulps – that it was obvious he was trying to hold back tears himself.

"Getting back to Caian -" Rafaella interrupted the moment.

"For the love of -" David bit out.

"No. Not what you're thinking." she shot David an icy, impatient stare. "I want to piece things together. So, Caian found out Arepo's plans for you,"

David nodded.

"and he ordered Innocent Reichenberg to Dream Invade Tatiana -"

"to lure me into the catacombs." David verified.

"but somehow Zachary found out what Innocent did,"

"I think Innocent told him." Lukas said. "They're buddies. Innocent must have confided in Zachary."

"And surprisingly, Zachary turned out having a conscience." David wryly said. "I'm guessing he must have said something to Caian about exposing the truth."

"And Liz?" Rafaella asked.

"Liz loved Caian, to the point of insanity, from the looks of it." said David. "She poisoned Zachary to keep him quiet, which was a huge mistake because it only led to an investigation -"

"And threw the suspicion off Zachary." said Rafaella. "We were so convinced it was him."

"I think it's sad though." said Gertrude. "Liz is an incredibly intelligent girl, an amazing and dedicated Healer. She thought she was doing the right thing for the person she loved."

"She was unhinged, Gertrude." Lukas bluntly put it.

"Are we not all slightly unhinged?" Gertrude asked. "On the eve of coming here, her family was attacked by demons. Her mother died, but Liz was rescued and brought here to the Monastery. And who was the person who showed her kindness here? Who took care of her and spent time with her above and beyond his duty as Healer?"

"Caian James." they mumbled.

"We're all seriously flawed." admitted Rafaella. "We carry around so much emotional baggage I'm surprised this Monastery hasn't collapsed into the mountain yet from sheer excess weight."

"Well, the Abbot did tell me this wasn't heaven." said David.

"Far from it." agreed Gertrude. "But we can be more compassionate, especially to those who need it most."

That same afternoon, Abbot Anderson came to visit David and Gertrude. The man looked thinner than usual and a deep groove of a worry line was between his brows. He pulled up a chair between David and Gertrude's beds.

"I wanted to speak with you both, Miss Greer, Mr. Cross. It appears we have much to discuss and I'm sure that you have questions to ask me. Ask what you wish to, do not hesitate. Everything must come out in the open now." the Abbot firmly said.

David went first. "Where's Victorinus, sir? Do you have any

idea?"

The Abbot gave a sad smile. "Ah, how I wish I could correct you, David, and say *Teacher* Victorinus, which would have been the proper way to call him. But he has indeed broken faith with all of us. I say this in laid-bare honesty, his betrayal is felt acutely in the entire Monastery, especially with us, his co-educators. We have known him for so many years. At least, we thought we knew him." the Abbot sighed. "As for your question, yes, I have some ideas as to where he may be hiding, but nothing concrete or confirmed for now."

He looked at them both very seriously, as though wishing to talk more in his silence and to offer some sort of reassurance. "All teachers and instructors here in the Monastery have communicated globally and to other Protected Grounds, warning others of what occurred here and the grave misdeeds that Victorinus have done."

"Sir," said Gertrude. "Would it not be more prudent to speak with Pure Angels and to ask for assistance from heaven? I'm quite certain that they know Teach....Victorinus' whereabouts."

"I'm sure they do." Abbot Anderson acquiesced. "But you see, Gertrude, we as Nephilims have our own laws too. I have spoken with the Nephilim Angelical Council and they have decided that we must resolve this matter before bringing it to a higher assembly. We must take responsibility for our own problems since Pure Angels have the entire world to look after."

"But this Council, and other Nephilims, they're looking for Victorinus, right?" asked David.

"Yes. Victorinus has been declared wanted by the law and is now a fugitive. We think someone may be sheltering him. A loyal student perhaps-"

"Or a fellow Saturian." David said in disgust.

"Quite so." nodded the Abbot. "If you could please tell me,

how did you come to suspect that the student fellowship at Uriel Lodge was something else entirely and was in fact this sinister Society of the Sator Square?"

David proceeded to tell the Abbot about the card that Zachary Spencer dropped the night that he was poisoned and the curious palindrome printed on it. "And when Caian James invited me and Gertrude to join his exclusive club, we just followed a hunch and went after it."

"It was during the first Official meeting when the Officers and Members welcomed us, and the name of the organization was revealed at last, that we knew for certain that there was a connection." Gertrude revealed.

"Sir, what have you found out about the Society? Were you able to get any evidence about what their real goals are?" David asked. Then he added, "When Caian was arguing with Jerome, he had mentioned some underhanded stuff about the Society, about occupying world leadership at all cost." David sat up straighter. How he wished he wasn't confined to this bed and was out there instead looking for clues against the Society.

"The Sator Square Society has been formally abolished." announced the Abbot. "We have acquired their roster of Officers and Members, and Antonia Tremont – albeit with great reluctance – has turned over to me all their documents and important papers. Last night, we gathered all students connected to the Society and we spent the entire night interrogating each of them." Abbot Anderson looked more weary than ever. "I have said this before, David, and I say it again, I apologize, to both of you, that your lives were put in peril."

"Sir -" David and Gertrude protested, aghast that the Abbot would apologize to them.

"Please, I insist." Abbot Anderson said. "I truly am sorry. I should have been more knowledgeable about the goings on in the Monastery. I should have questioned the exclusivity and secrecy of the Uriel Lodge. Most of all, I should have suspected something of Victorinus." Abbot Anderson looked ready to crumple in his seat, to pour his face into his hands and signal defeat. Instead, he inhaled, sat upright and gazed at them with determination. "I am sifting through every document we now possess and further investigations will be conducted. We will also pursue Victorinus most decidedly, that I can promise you."

David remembered. "What about Liz, sir? What happens to her?"

The Abbot sighed again, the weight of his decision upon him. "Liz will be sent to Kalvarium and she will serve time there as befitting her crime. She will also undergo intensive counseling and therapy to assist in her mental recovery." the Abbot shook his head sadly. "I feel deeply for Liz. She is such a loving and caring person, a devoted Healer who has lamentably been led astray. I sincerely hope that in time, and with much therapy, she will be healed."

"And Zachary Spencer, sir?"

"Mr. Spencer will receive detention and suspension of some privileges for withholding the truth, but since he eventually confessed, and we must take into consideration that he was under constant threat if he ever revealed the truth, then such is his punishment and he will not be sent to Kalvarium."

David thought about the Abbot's decision. He had mixed feelings about Zachary. He did withhold the truth and had allowed his friend, Innocent, to take the fall. But he could also understand Zachary's fear of going against Caian James. Still, to have allowed the lie to continue for a long time, to have been poisoned and remained silent until fate and Liz had forced him to finally confess. Zachary

Spencer was no hero. He was a coward through and through. But did David really want him in Kalvarium? Was detention and suspension enough? Well, it had to be enough for now.

"Do you still have any questions to ask of me before I let you rest?" asked the Abbot.

"Sir, what happened to Caian.....is it our law when murder is committed? That we turn into a demon?" David had to ask.

"When the gravity of the sin is so great. When it involves taking a life, then we become like fallen angels. Whether the life taken is Human, Nephilim, or Pure Angel, the end result is the same." Abbot Anderson looked at them most solemnly. "Taking a life is the greatest offense and whoever does so is immediately cast out from Protected Ground and is stripped of his angelic substance. Hence he becomes a demon."

"What will happen to Caian, sir?" David asked, hesitant to know but compelled to find out.

"He will now join the world of demons. It will be up to him whether he will take orders from their generals or if he decides to become a rogue demon and wander the earth on his own. Rogue demons rarely survive, attacked by both sides, they eventually choose to become soldiers of the underworld." Abbot Anderson stood up, bluish circles under his eyes, his posture suddenly fragile. "Now, I must really let you two rest. Thank you to both of you for exposing the Society of the Sator Square, for putting to light the crimes of Caian and Liz. You will each receive commendations for Acts of Bravery, alongside Mr. Lukas Hackett and Miss Rafaella Pierce. Well done." with brief nods but a warm smile, Abbot Anderson left.

And then it was David and Gertrude again with a lot of time to rehash the previous night's events, to ask question after question just to make sure they hadn't missed anything. And when Gertrude became tired, they settled down to rest.

David scooted to the edge of the bed so he could reach Gertrude's hand. He wanted to touch her, to reassure himself that she was really there, that she survived.

"Thank God you're here, Gertrude. Thank God." David whispered.

She opened her eyes again and smiled at him. "And not just me, but the four of us. We all made it back, David." after relishing those words, she then added mischievously, "I heard that the demon head cheerleader was very sweet with you."

David groaned.

"That she invited you to *join her*." Gertrude teased.

"Stop it."

"Awww, she thought you were cute."

"That's not funny, stop it." David tried to look mad.

"Oh well, if only she didn't disintegrate......."

35. Honoring a Hero

That weekend, a Memorial Service was held for Jerome Gallagher. The church overflowed with mourners as everyone in the Monastery attended to offer their respects and give tribute to the courageous young man. White roses were in profusion; so were ivory columns of candles, its flames flickering and impermanent – so easily snuffed out, just like the person whose life they were remembering.

David had personally asked Abbot Anderson if he could be one of Jerome's pallbearers. He wanted to do something, he wanted to honor Jerome the best he could, knowing that he could never repay Jerome's sacrifice. It was a strange feeling, to be walking around, functioning, doing the most basic things each day but pressed with the blunt truth that his life had been paid for in blood. David caught himself at times staring raptly at the clock, counting seconds and realizing that each beat of the clock was a drop of Jerome's blood. He was alive but only because someone died for him. It was both a gift and a burden.

David had asked his friends to help him prepare the church for the Memorial. No doubt the Nephilim staff didn't need their assistance and could decorate everything perfectly by themselves, but David wanted, *needed* to do as much as he could for Jerome. His friends were more than willing to support him and tender their gratitude to Jerome as well.

Physically, David was completely healed now, his cast had come off the day after that tragic event. As for Gertrude, she had maneuvered for a while in a wheelchair, but today, she was walking on her own, sporadically wincing when she overreached or forgot to take it slow, but otherwise, she was okay.

David, Lukas and Rafaella had thrown themselves to the frenzy of making Jerome's memorial as beautiful as possible and looking around the church now, David felt a measure of satisfaction. *This is all for you Jerome*, he thought.

Then it hit David.

If Jerome hadn't saved his life, this would have been *his* Memorial. It was a powerfully humbling realization. David reached out to grasp Gertrude's hand in his, so immensely grateful that they had both survived their ordeals.

The funeral service began with a very solemn Mass, followed by a touching tribute given by Abbot Anderson. Gertrude sang a sad and soulful *Amazing Grace*, her voice soaring to the heavens, and then David was on his feet along with five of Jerome's closest friends. They positioned themselves around the sealed white coffin, three pallbearers on each side, and as David grasped a portion to lift, he remembered Jerome's final moments – his body cocooned by his wings, a light burning so bright inside of him and then dimming to nothingness as his soul departed. He hadn't really known Jerome except for those moments when he mentored David and Gertrude. It was a testimony to how good a person he was that despite the corruption of the Sator Square Society and the dark influence of Caian James, Jerome had chosen what was right and had saved David's life.

They slowly marched towards the cemetery, all teachers and students following them in somber procession. And then they were lowering Jerome's coffin to the ground, lowering him deeper into the earth in his final resting place. Friends and admirers walked up to the open grave in order to say their farewell with a carefully placed white rose, and overhead, against the backdrop of clear blue skies, student warriors flew magnificently in perfect formation as a salute to Jerome's bravery. A choir of cherubs sang a melancholy hymn.

Gertrude was silently crying and David knew how she felt. They both were a mess of confusing emotions – guilt, gratitude, sadness – all rolled into one. To one side, Satorians clustered, perhaps they couldn't help themselves or maybe it was out of habit that they gravitated towards each other, but there was an outpouring of grief from them. David was surprised to see Antonia Tremont openly crying, and even Samson, also known as Opera, was blinking his eyes rapidly, his expression mute as he stared blindly at Jerome's coffin. They were the only Officers left. Rotas was dead, Sator was now a demon, and Arepo had fled.

David felt his chest tighten and his throat clench as the memory of Jerome's death overpowered him. This courageous person had died in his arms. He had pushed away his longtime friend when Caian had crossed a line that Jerome couldn't follow. David thought that this too was one of Jerome's bravest acts, to stand up for what was right even though it meant losing his bestfriend. If it had been David in that situation, would he have chosen to do the right thing?

When every last mourner had placed a rose on Jerome's coffin – Puttis included – David grabbed a shovel, and with the other five pallbearers, he slowly shoveled mounds of snow on the open grave. This was honoring Jerome, this was thanking him for a life spared, and each scoop of snow that covered his coffin was laced with regret that his life had been cut so shortly.

After the funeral, David walked up to his friends, all of them silent and sad over Jerome's fate. Even Wolverine was subdued and not his expectedly playful self. Some distance from them they saw Antonia, walking around with the vacant and shell-shocked expression of a widow whose husband had gone off to war and never returned. David heard that she had conducted a private memorial for Caian James and anyone who had loved him or looked up to him was welcome.

To be honest, David was still angry at Caian, and he had every reason to be. Everyone had looked up to him and he had duped them all. He had basked in the admiration of others when he didn't deserve any of it. Caian had saved his life too. Caian had rescued him from demons out in the world and had brought David to this place. Of course he was angry. His 'Ideal' had turned out to be false.

"Poor Antonia." Gertrude murmured, her hand slipping into David's. "I don't know what I'd do if you were........" she shook her head, all choked up.

"Uh, since I have no plans of turning into a murdering psycho anytime soon, you don't have to worry about that." David said flippantly, trying to lighten the situation although his heart fluttered when he saw how much Gertrude cared.

"You are an idiot." she gave him a watery smile, trying to fight back tears.

David looked at Antonia again. She really did seem absolutely lost. "Do you think she knew? Do you think Caian told her about his plans?"

"I don't know." Gertrude frowned, "But I am willing to give her the benefit of the doubt."

Of course Gertrude would. She hoped and looked for the best in people. It was one of the reasons that David liked her in the first place.

"I think Caian trusted her enough to confide in her." said Rafaella. "I'm assuming that they shared many secrets from the Society and they had a kind of duplicitous bond together. Maybe they even got a rush from fooling so many."

"Rafaella!" Gertrude admonished.

"That's what I think." Rafaella shrugged. "Look, I'm not one to pity Antonia Tremont. Even if Caian James hadn't plotted that hellhound attack on David, they are still guilty of whatever crimes they committed for the Sator Square Society. Is she not being punished for that?"

"I think the Abbot is still going through all the evidence they've gathered." said Lukas. "He can't just throw everyone connected to the Society in *Kalvarium*. One's too many already."

"It must be breaking Abbot Anderson's heart." murmured Gertrude. "Can you imagine? We are barely in the middle of the school year and two students are in *Kalvarium*, Jerome is dead and Caian has become a demon."

"I just hope that's it for the year." David said. "It's not the usual trend here, is it?"

His friends shook their heads.

"Know what?" said Rafaella. "I think it's you, David."

"Me, what?"

"I think you jinxed the Monastery." she announced.

"Shut up, Rafaella."

"Yup, you jinxed the place. All hell's breaking loose from now on."

"That is not even funny." Gertrude came to his defense.

"Yeah, shut it, Rafaella." David frowned. He knew she was just teasing, but it stung all the same. What if he really had jinxed the place?

Over the next few days, life reverted to a rhythm of normalcy. As in any reality, despite whatever tragedy that happened, life must go on, everyone must push forward.

David once again became immersed in all his lessons and got caught up in the fervor of excelling in school. He welcomed the routine of his classes, paying closer attention in Essential Angelology as Angelic hierarchies and laws were discussed. He continued to have an awesome time in Chemistry as they explored the birth of the universe with Matter and Anti-matter. Of course, he still did poorly in Angelic Chorale, extremely relieved that he would forever be a Mouther and just content to let Gertrude and Lukas and even Joseph, shine. Preparations for the Thanksgiving Concert continued frenetically and David and Rafaella happily doubled as stagehands, working on props and helping out with any number of chores while Gertrude and Lukas practiced earnestly center stage.

Elementary Guardianship continued to be mayhem. By this time their newborn cherubs had sprouted wings and they had moved the class outdoors, setting up mock rescue situations and training their newborns to fly. The Puttlings loved jumping off of anything whether they knew how to fly or not and the guardians had to be on high alert, ready to catch the hyper cherubs whenever they fall. It was exhausting!

Carpentry and Metallurgy remained one of David's favorites and he returned to his passion for weapon-making, on an agreement with Teacher Coppersmith that for every two weapons he made, he would craft a project that was on the curriculum. Not that those works weren't interesting as well, David just loved making weapons more. In Heavenly Art they continued painting, reeking of oils and turpentine after class, their white clothes dotted and streaked with paint.

Warrior Training became more vital than ever. The recent events had been a cruel lesson on just how much of a beginner he was. Caian had toyed with him, the demon cheerleaders had captured him and would have slain him had it not been for Lukas' timely arrow. Jerome had died. All these thoughts became the catalyst to David's training harder than ever, challenging himself constantly beyond his known limitations. Teacher Peregrine replaced Victorinus as Head of Warrior Training but he continued to oversee David's training regimen.

David, Gertrude, Lukas and Rafaella experienced an embarrassing amount of adulation and attention over the next two weeks as their sophomore peers and even students older than them went out of their way to congratulate them on their win over the demon cheerleaders. Juniors, Freshmen and even some Seniors chatted them up for a blow-by-blow account of the fight, and young graders ambushed them with squealing bouts of hero-worship. For those who had never battled with an actual demon, they persistently asked what the demons were really like and how it felt to fight them.

Lukas was floating on a cloud from the rockstar treatment, Rafaella tried to shrug it off but it was obvious that she was really proud of their victory over the demon cheerleaders and that she liked talking about it. Gertrude retreated to her shell and became even more shy when the subject was brought up while David really took the time to answer questions and give his observations about the demons in the hope of preparing his fellow students for future combat with the foul creatures. The sooner they realized the seriousness of going up against demons, the harder they would train, then the more prepared they would be for the fight.

There was an undeclared truce between them and Zachary's camp. Of course they hadn't become best buds overnight, but the petty bullying had stopped. Zachary showed his gratitude to Lukas and David for saving his life by being civil to them and leaving them alone. Somehow, because of what transpired with Innocent, Liz, Caian and Jerome, petty bullying became just clearly ridiculous when much bigger things were going on around them. But then, David didn't know how long this 'turning over a new leaf' of Zachary's would last, but he was somewhat willing to follow his girlfriend's example and give Zachary the benefit of the doubt. To this, Gertrude looked on with approval.

As they continued picking up the pieces of their lives, so too did they pick up the pieces of their beloved glasshouse. Every after dinner, David and Gertrude made a pilgrimage to the glasshouse which had been repaired by Monastery carpenters, but it was up to Gertrude and David to restore their hideaway to its previous state and to clear it of debris and glass fragments.

Gertrude's pet plants needed extra care from all the winter wind exposure and they spent countless wonderful hours enjoying each other's company inside their hideaway. At times Rafaella and Lukas joined them, sipping coffee or tea for Lukas, paired with mouthwatering cakes and warm pies. These were moments forever encapsulated in David's memory, these pockets of time just hanging out with his friends. Sometimes, in the middle of it he would be jolted in remembering that less than two months ago he was alone and homeless and running away from unnamed monsters. It was an opportunity to send up a prayer of thanks especially to his mom who he knew for sure to be in heaven, and to think of Michael, his dad, who was probably off on some epic battle with demons to save mankind.

He was quite surprised when in the middle of November, announced by flickering lights and abrupt power failure, his dad came for a visit. David wasn't hostile anymore, he wasn't jumping for joy either – well, maybe his heart was, secretly. He was happy that Michael came to visit although he still had conflicting feelings towards his father. He pushed his anger aside and cautiously enjoyed the presence of his dad. Michael congratulated him on his victory over the demon cheerleaders, patiently listening as David unburdened himself about the terrible night with Caian and the resulting death of Jerome. Eventually they reverted to the mundane topic of David's classes and his progress in the Monastery.

"I've been meaning to ask you something," said David. "about my dagger."

"*The Hand of God*?" Michael confirmed, eyes intent on David. He seemed to have an idea about what David was going to ask.

"My dagger is only a copy. Yours is the original. But how come it was able to vanquish the hellhound?" David puzzled.

"I imbued it when you were asleep, before Tatiana came for you." his dad confessed.

"You did?"

Michael nodded. "Otherwise, your dagger would have remained a copy, without the needed power to defeat the hellhound." his voice became more serious. "You must be armed as I am, in order to destroy our enemies."

David breathed deeply, trying to draw the courage to say the words. It was hard. "Th-thank you." he never thought he'd say those words to this man so soon.

"You're welcome." his dad replied quietly. They both fell silent, overcome by the exchange and feeling awkward.

"I have a present for you." his dad said, fumbling in his

pocket. It was quite something to see – The Great Michael – fumbling and nervous. He extricated a gleaming package from his pocket. Did all objects from heaven glow?

David accepted the gift, not knowing what to say so he chose to remain silent. The wrapping felt different, *otherworldy* in his hands. He was reluctant to tear it open but Michael just laughed and said, "Go ahead, tear it up. That is the purpose of the wrapping."

David grinned at his father's words and slowly tore into the package, revealing the gift inside. David felt his breath stop, his heart stop.

Cradled in his hand was a framed picture of his mom, in heaven.

Much to his horror and embarrassment, David felt hot tears spilling out his eyes and onto his cheeks. He lowered his head to hide the fact that he was crying.

Michael sat beside him and gave him a hug. David had to bite hard on his lip to stop himself from bawling like a baby.

"I know you miss her very much. And she misses you terribly too, every day." his dad said. "She watches over you constantly, you know. You are always in her thoughts."

David gazed at the picture of his mom, wiping his blurry eyes and drippy nose on the sleeve of his pajamas.

She was smiling her joyful, lit-up smile. A smile that seemed to say, *I love you David*. She was sitting in the middle of a tropical paradise with a magnificent waterfall behind her. The sky was a perfect blue, the grass greener and the flowers blooming to perfection. Everything seemed to glitter with millions of diamonds but they all faded in comparison to the brilliance of his mom's smile.

"Thank you." David choked up. "I........" he wanted to say more, but couldn't. Instead he just held on to the picture for the duration of Michael's visit and when his dad left, he lay in bed just looking into his mom's smiling face. He searched every detail of the photo, wondering where in heaven she had been photographed, looked at it until the image was burned to his brain. It was an incredible gift. David continued to hold on to it until he drifted off to sleep.

During Thanksgiving week, another wondrous surprise was in store for David and his friends. Before dinner started, all students were summoned to Saraquel Hall – the opulent theater where Gertrude and company had the concert before – and much to David's shock and amazement, the four of them were called to the stage and presented with medals of honor for their Acts of Bravery. Abbot Anderson also announced that plaques commemorating their accomplishment would be displayed in the Hall of Trophies as the school's gesture of gratitude for their courage on that fateful night.

Their faces were varying shades of red. David was grateful but embarrassed, Gertrude was tongue-tied and blushing, Rafaella was actually crying while Lukas beamed like a lighthouse, his back pole-straight, his lanky frame rigid in a military stance. He also kept glancing at Consortia who returned his looks contemplatively, as though sizing up his current worth and status.

The recognition certainly elevated their year and from then on Lukas pinned his medal of honor to his clothes daily, as did Rafaella and Gertrude. Only David declined to do so, too uncomfortable and embarrassed to wear an announcement of bravery every day. This perhaps showed the big difference in their upbringing. It was expected of them in the Monastery to value and carry their award. Out in the real world, it would have been considered arrogant and showy and maybe just a little pathetic.

Thanksgiving Day arrived, chilly and bright. It was David's first holiday at the Monastery and he didn't know what to expect, but certainly not this.

He stared at the sprawling, snow covered grounds of the Monastery with his mouth agape. "Wow. I heard all the cranking and hammering last night but I didn't expect it to be like *this*. This is insane." he was shaking his head in wonder.

The entire front lawn of the Monastery had been transformed into a Fair. There was the trademark Ferriswheel, only this one was gigantic. And scattered all over the grounds were promising rides with amped up thrill factor and David wanted to try them all.

The four of them were dragging each other every which way, fighting over which rides to try first, then they raided the concession stands, hungry and thirsty from all the rampaging they had done.

The rides were free, the games were free and the food was free. It was David's idea of heaven. It was an afternoon of soda-coming-out-of-your-nose laughter, vomit-inducing rides and the absolute pleasure of lugging around cool prizes won at the Fair.

When darkness crept in, everyone went inside the Monastery to bathe and change for the Thanksgiving Feast. They were all dressed formally since the Concert at Saraquel Hall would commence after dinner. David kept shifting in his seat, finding the tuxedo confining, and the requisite bow-tie constricting. How he wished for the favorite pair of pajamas he had in his room.

Gertrude smiled at him, noticing his discomfort. "You look very handsome." she whispered. "And this will all be over soon."

Lukas looked neater than ever – a crease wouldn't dare appear on his clothes, nor would a hair even think of sticking out of place. His nostrils kept flaring every now and then as he tried to stop himself from grinning ear to ear like an idiot. Consortia had finally agreed to go on a date with him, much to all their silent chagrin. Rafaella continued her eye-rolling, done behind Lukas' back to prevent from ruining his big night, while Gertrude kept biting her lip to stop herself from blurting out an honest opinion. She directed tiny, barely discernible frowns at Consortia which was her version of a display of disapproval. As for David, sure he didn't like Consortia, but if Lukas was this happy with the girl beside him, then he was going to keep his mouth shut and tolerate the snobbish, disdainful redhead who kept raising her eyebrow at them in nonverbal judgment.

If David had thought that every day dining at the Monastery was a feast, then this Thanksgiving Dinner blew all those previous meals away. He couldn't even begin to categorize the grandness of the preparations. Every goodie he could think of was being served. And he sampled all of them. Well, the most that he could without bursting out of his fitted tux.

Gertrude, Lukas and Consortia excused themselves before the feast ended, their early presence required at Saraquel Hall in preparation for the show. So it was David and Rafaella who once again walked through the glass halls leading to the theater and he was reminded of how that previous concert night had ended. Zachary Spencer must have been thinking the same thing, his face glum and morose, but he did give David a brief nod of acknowledgement as he caught David looking at him.

Then the Thanksgiving Concert started and David was swept away again by the performance. Gertrude was her bright, shining self, so incredibly talented and soulfully beautiful that David sat on his seat, his mouth dry, unable to believe that she was his girlfriend. Lukas came out a more powerful baritone than in his last performance, perhaps buoyed by a coquettish Consortia whom he sang duets with. David and Rafaella shot up from their seats when the show ended, joining the entire theater in standing ovation for the brilliant performers. The Pure Angel, Teacher Irayazel, also came out to take his bows to resounding applause.

"And so we go on." Gertrude murmured to David, later on in the early hours of the morning, after the celebration ended, and they were standing outside her room.

"Huh?' David asked.

Gertrude lightly followed the lines of his eyebrows, gently smoothing them. "You've been.....contemplative most of the evening."

"Just thinking about losses........"

"And gains too, I hope." she smiled up at him, concern clearly written on her face.

David hugged her to him. "Especially gains."

"All we can do is live to the fullest, you know." she gently advised. "To be prepared, to keep on fighting."

David hugged her tighter. "What if I lost you......or Lukas, or Rafaella?"

Gertrude pulled back and held his face in her hands. "We can never live in fear. If we did that, then we are defeated already."

David pondered her words and he continued to ponder her words after he had kissed her goodnight and while he was lying in bed getting ready to sleep. Gertrude was right. He couldn't live his life in fear – fear of losing loved ones, fear of losing friends.

The future was frightening. They were at war. As half-angels they would always be at war with demons. David realized that he had indeed stopped running and that he didn't want to run anymore. It was now time to face and fight enemies.

But at least for now, they were on Protected Ground.

Still, he patted his trusty dagger to make sure he had it with him.

As he was drifting off to sleep, a knock sounded on his door. When David opened to see who it was, he was startled to be face to face with the person who started it all – Tatiana.

"Would you believe me if I told you that your girlfriend Gertrude is trapped in the catacombs?" she squeaked at him.

"Tatiana!" David admonished.

"Kidding!" the cherub trilled. *"Please let me come in. I brought hot chocolate and freshly baked cookies for you."* she showed him a cup and a platter of cookies. *"I've been promising forever but haven't gotten around to it. Please."* her lashes fluttered.

"You're not here to poison me, are you?" he asked suspiciously.

"Of course not!" Tatiana scoffed. *"Besides, would I tell you if I really were?"*

"Goodnight, Tatiana." David said, closing the door on her.

She tried to push her way in, high-pitched and insistent. *"I was kidding! Really! At least take the hot chocolate and cookies!"* she shoved the cup and platter through the narrow opening.

"Oh, okay." David gave in. He had no intention of eating or drinking any of the stuff but he didn't want to hurt her feelings too, so he accepted her offering.

"Need a cuddle tonight, David?" she asked through the almost closed door, her baby blue eyes wide.

"No!" David yelped in horror.

"Are you sure?" she singsonged.

"I'm sure!" he pushed the door firmly closed, locking it for good measure.

"Goodnight David." he heard from the other side.

"Goodnight Tatiana." He replied wearily, wishing she would go away. Girlish giggles erupted from outside his door, and then there was silence.

Finally!

He dumped the cookies in the trash bin, placed the cup of hot chocolate next to it, and then climbed into bed.

"Goodnight mom." he said to the photo by his bedside, then he turned off the light, and went to sleep.

He was home.

Acknowledgments

This book is a family project. It really is. My origin as a writer can be traced back to my parents who had shelves packed with books; fiction novels that made my weekends and summers go by so fast. My love for reading morphed into a love for writing because as I read those novels, my own stories popped into my head.

Thank you to my dearest Mama for reading every nonsensical story I wrote as a little girl AND for keeping every story written in her precious filing cabinet. Thank you to Papa for buying me books, from beautifully illustrated picture books, to the mysteries of Nancy Drew, to teen romances and then bestselling adult fiction.

To my sister, Arlene, the kindest and most generous in the world, thank you for reading my stories, for listening to my stories, and for supporting this story. You are one of my very first readers and critic. For every time you tell me to write, thank you. To her husband, Nitoy, thank you for all the printing and paper. Those early drafts came to be because you share what you have.

Thank you to my brother, Nolan, who is such a fan. This book got published because of your persistence and your constant question of: When is your book coming out?

To Philip, my clever little bro, all your detailed questions made me even more vigilant with specifics. Thank you for each observation and for paying attention to the minutiae. You're an awesome brat.

To the rest of my family, my brothers, Norman and Nelson, in-laws, nephews and nieces (yes, my family is that big), my gratitude to you all for the encouragement and support.

Thank you to Nicole Solis, my artist, who put David on the cover and converted my imagination into a tangible work of art. You're such a joy to work with over pizza and coke. To Mark Ceasar B Gariando, my lay-out artist, thank you for swooping in and saving me from all the technical nightmare, and for executing such impressive work with incredible patience. To Tessa Dare, successful author and my go-to person for all publishing questions, thank you for your generous and patient spirit and for replying to my emails. To Cynthia Borgueta-Pease, another fellow author and my mentor in all things Amazon, I'm grateful for every advice you have shared. You are a Godsend. To Sally Faelnar and Claudette Estrella, thank you for your inputs and feedback.

To my Six Brats, thank you for bravely acting every grade school play I wrote and to my college girlfriends, my thanks for reading early stories and poems. And to my GIFT family – my second family – thank you for two saturdays a month of prayer and worship, and for Growing In Faith Together through the years.

To my eternal source of joy: Matt, Joshua and Mariana, my anchor, my collaborators. Matt, my husband, my love, thank you for reading each chapter I handed to you, for being honest about my work, for talking plot and fight choreography, for believing in me and my stories, and for wanting more. Joshua and Mariana, thank you for getting out of my way when Mommy needed quiet time and for cheering me on and cheering me up during days when my brain was slow. Thank you for acting out fight scenes with me and inspiring David's choice of weapons to use. But I'm most grateful for your presence, love, laughter, hugs and kisses, when I was done playing inside my head. I love you three so very much.

And above all, thank you Jesus, from whom all good things come. I write only because you will it so. To God be the glory.

Made in the USA
San Bernardino, CA
23 April 2014